Late afternoon ray  sputtering fire. Her s̶l̶ ̶q̶u̶i̶e̶t̶e̶d̶, and feeling returned to her face. "Thank you for taking care of me."

Kip grinned as he fed scattered wet kindling into the laboring fire. "Didn't have a choice. Del would skin me if I didn't."

"You like him, don't you?"

A nod. "There's somethin' about him. I don't make friends easy and Del don't seem to either, but we took to each other right off. He's about as levelheaded as they come."

"Yes, he is, and so are you."

"Don't know about that, but I never had a good friend. Don't know if it was me or them. Del strikes me the same way." Kip gathered some larger pieces, and the fire popped as it went to work on damp wood. "And I know how much he cottons to you. Hard to miss the glint in his eye when he's with you."

Her heart jumped. "Does he say that?"

"Doesn't have to. Easy to see."

"Tell me about him, Kip. Tell me about Del. You're like two peas in a pod. I don't know much of anything, except for the misery he's carrying."

A Score to Settle

by

Mike Torreano

A Score to Settle

Cover Art by *Abigail Owen*

The Wild Rose Press, Inc.
PO Box 708
Adams Basin, NY 14410-0708
Visit us at www.thewildrosepress.com

Publishing History
First Vintage Rose Edition, 2020
Trade Paperback ISBN 978-1-5092-3281-9
Digital ISBN 978-1-5092-3282-6

Published in the United States of America

Dedication

To my grandchildren,
who I hope will grow to embody the timeless values
of The Code of the West

Acknowledgments

My wife, Anne, is always a tremendous sounding board, helping make my stories more authentic and believable.

My daughter, Lisa, is unmatched as my chief researcher and storyline brainstormer.

My critique group does a wonderful job of holding my literary feet to the fire with their commentary. They provide excellent feedback on aspects like character development, dialogue, description, tension, and pace. I cannot thank John Andrews, Marilee Aufdenkamp, Rex Griffin, Scott Hibbard, and Margaret Rodenberg enough.

I'd also like to thank my three primary beta readers, Gary Scheimer, Rich Hogen, and Allison Byers for their invaluable comments. Gary helps keep my cowboying straight, Rich offers spot-on insights throughout, and I rely on Allison's keen editing eyes.

Finally, the inspiration for my westerns has been, and always will be, Zane Grey.

Thank you all so much!

Chapter One

Eastern New Mexico Territory, Spring 1871

The lonely howls of a wolf woke Del Lawson. He shifted in bed to the sound. The gray wolf. The one with the penetrating light eyes, the one that trotted the low hills surrounding his small ranch. Never bothered his dog or the chickens that pecked invisible specks from the dirt yard. In turn, Del would fire a shot in the air when he came across carrion for the wolf. He'd found the animal as a pup. Mother must have been killed. He left carcasses for it when he could.

The animal sounded different tonight. Several short yowls instead of the usual long ones. The strange calls set Del on edge. Was it anything? He glanced over at his sleeping wife. No sense waking her. He got up and checked on his son and Rodrigo sleeping nearby in the two-room cabin. Both boys sound asleep. He eased toward the front door and pushed aside a thin curtain covering the dusty front window. A full moon cast eerie light on darkened horsemen stealing silently toward the house. He couldn't tell how many as murky forms advanced like backlit ghosts. His stomach knotted. Whoever they were, they weren't up to any good. He reached over the fireplace and wrapped his fingers around his rifle stock. He hurried to the bedroom. "Demi, get up! Night riders!" He woke the boys and shooed them out the rickety back door into the black night. "Head for the tack room. Don't stop for nothin'!"

As he rushed back and brushed the curtain aside again, the front door burst open. Rifle barrels filled the dim opening. Del fired once, twice. Two intruders fell, but a third got off a shot that struck him above the ear and put him down.

A voice in the dark said, "Don't kill him! Wilkins don't want him dead."

Del's rifle lay at a distance on the floor. Pain shot through his head. He pressed a hand over the wound, a sticky stream running between his fingers. He got a fleeting glimpse of the intruders as they rushed past him.

The big one said, "I tol' you to shoot the boy, not Ansel's son. Find the kid."

Del's sight faded to nothing.

****

Ansel Lawson rode for his life. Even in the dark, he knew the rough land his horse was flying over better than his pursuers. He hoped to trade on that now. He raced down a long rocky drop skirting a large granite formation that loomed toward him in the dim moonlight. A yank on the reins to the left at the dry wash. He stopped and listened. Horseshoes clicked faintly off rock in the distance. He jabbed his spurs into the horse's flanks, searching for the small trail that hid in the darkness somewhere ahead. Damn! Where was it? There. After a short burst, he pulled his horse left again, up into a field of low granite where the sign disappeared. A little rock shelter he knew of there would give him a chance to live.

The dark was doing its job. By the time he'd

circled a few times and found the recess, the horsemen were closing in. He jerked the horse down next to him, panting. Fought the urge to stick his head up to locate his trackers—they had to be near by now. Besides, he knew who they were. The loud clattering of hooves told him just how close. He'd never heard such a deafening noise in his life. In the shadowy dark they'd just keep on riding past, wouldn't they? They couldn't know he was up here. Even he had a hard time finding the place, and he knew where it was. When the clip-clop of their hooves faded, he'd lead his horse out and double back the way he came. The heaved-up ground they'd trampled riding here would surely hide his sign. He'd slip away while they combed the hills for him. A good plan.

As horses thundered by, his heart jumped in his throat. He stroked his mount's neck. Stay calm. Quiet. He waited until the clicking sounded distant and breathed again. He eased the horse up by the reins, led her onto the packed dirt next to the rounded granite slope, and started to steal away on foot. A click of a hammer brought him up short.

"Not so fast, Lawson. Freeze—unless you want my voice to be the last thing you ever hear."

Lucas Skinner's drawl. Damn!

The outlaw fired two shots into the dark sky. The reports disappeared along with his hope.

Soon, Ansel heard riders coming. The clattering of horseshoes sounded like the seconds he had left to live. He hung his head. No way Skinner could have known he was hidden there. He'd had it all figured out, too, but he'd stayed one day too long, trying to mend fences with his wife.

3

"Over here, Pete. Lawson's here. Got him covered. He ain't so smart now! I always said that—don't know why we ever let him ride with us in the first place."

Pete Tyson eased off his horse. "There's lots of things you don't know, Lucas. That's why I do the thinkin' around here." He turned to Lawson. "Did you really think you could get away?" He pulled a bullwhip off his saddle. "That we wouldn't figure out where you were?" He uncoiled a length until the tip touched the ground. He snapped it and drew blood as it flicked Ansel's cheek. "I'da thought you knew me better than that by now. You know what we did to your boy and his family. Name was Del, wasn't it?" He chuckled. Moonlight cast a faint shadow behind him. Tyson's voice dropped to a whisper. His mouth broke into a thin smile. "Ansel, you tell me where the gold coins are. We got your son, his wife, and boy but couldn't find the coins or the kid. You know the one I'm talkin' about." The whip danced in front of him. "You gonna do this the easy way or the hard way?"

"You stay away from that young'un!" Ansel pursed his lips. He'd feel the bullet any time now.

Tyson considered Ansel's reaction. "Think hard now. Come across, and I might let you live."

That was a lie. No way was Pete going to let him live. He'd never let anyone live who got in his way. The only thing Ansel still had going for him was the gold coins' whereabouts. If he was going to die, he'd take that secret with him, out of spite, if nothing else. He'd stolen them to build a new life for his wife and son. But since Del was dead, and his wife didn't ever want to see him again, he was just ornery enough not to let Tyson have his way. "Guess it's gonna be the hard way, but it don't matter none. Not no more." He drew in a deep breath.

"Hold him, boys. Take his shirt off and tie him to that scraggly pine tree there. The scratchin' from rough bark'll add nicely to the hurtin'." His men knifed off enough low branches to shove Ansel against the coarse trunk. Tyson reared back. The lash sliced into Ansel's back, and the trunk raked his chest as he lurched against the tree. He swallowed a scream. His insides shuddered, and he saw white for a moment. If that was the worst he was going to get, good—it was already behind him. Two more lashes and his knees deserted him. His stomach scraped raw against the sharp bark as he dropped, chest held tight by ropes.

"You gonna talk?"

Ansel kept his eyes shut, forced saliva into his mouth, and spit on the ground. "You kill me…and you ain't never gonna find…that gold." The coins gave Ansel the upper hand on Del's killer, if only for a little while.

"Don't know how we didn't find the kid that night, but the boy's luck is about to run out, for sure. We did find your son's wife—yes, we did. Pretty little thing, she was."

Ansel's heart hammered in his ears. Another lash tore into his back. This time he felt the impact more than the pain—his upper body one pulsing throb.

"Last chance, Lawson. I *will* kill you."

He didn't doubt it for a minute. Tyson always had been a mean one. He'd seen enough of his cruelty over the years. His head pounded, and his throat tightened. "Like I told you…don't matter if you do." He gasped for breath. Gritted his teeth.

5

Tyson shook where he stood. "Damn you! I'm givin' you a chance to live. Take it!"

Ansel tried to spit on the ground. "Go on...get it over with."

"I hear you got a pretty woman, too."

The thought stung. She had been his beautiful bride at one time. So pretty, but he'd worn out the light in her eyes with his lies over the years. "You stay away...from her." He slumped.

Tyson's narrow smile widened until his rotten breath poisoned the moonlight air. Time to end this. Lash after lash tore Ansel apart. His body jerked at each stroke as blood streamed down his legs and pooled in the pine needles below. He sagged until he couldn't sag anymore. His eyesight narrowed. With his last breath, he managed a feeble grin.

"Dammit! Damn him!" Tyson's red face almost boiled over as he eyed the small grin on the dead man's face. "Stupid sodbuster. Gotta hand it to him, though. Took it like a man." Tyson turned toward his men, whip still in hand. They edged away, eyes never leaving the leather snake. He flicked the tip toward them. They stayed just out of range. "Cut him down easy. Man deserves some respect for holdin' out."

"We gonna bury him?"

"He don't deserve that much respect."

Lucas Skinner said, "How we gonna find the coins now, Pete? And what about the boy?"

"Don't you no nevermind about that. You let me do the figgerin'. Right now, we're ridin' to Ansel's spread, so mount up!" The men backed toward their horses, eyes still on the whip. "Get a move on."

Tyson wiped the blood off the whip and coiled it

on his saddle horn. He swung up and wheeled the stallion in the direction of Ansel Lawson's ranch. A couple of hours of hard riding and they neared the small farmhouse. Stark black night held the place captive. Faint light in a front window disappeared. Darkness was complete. Tyson squinted as he walked his horse forward. He yelled in the direction of the shadowy, ramshackle building. "Hello in there!"

The front door creaked on the darkened porch. A female voice rang out. "Better stay sittin' your saddles less'n you all want to die right here, right now. Ride on out!" The unmistakable click of a hammer echoed sharply in the still night.

Was the woman holding a rifle or a six gun? Tyson motioned to one of his men. The bandit quietly reined his horse left and stole away in the darkness to circle behind the house. Tyson kept up a conversation to buy time. "Don't want no trouble, ma'am, just came lookin' for your husband is all. We're friends of his. It's Maybelle, isn't it? I mean your name. Maybelle, right?"

"Don't be botherin' with my name. And Ansel don't got no friends. No real ones. If you're ridin' with him, you're as worthless as he is, so be on your way or you'll wish you were."

"Well now…since you put it that way, we'll leave, but can we water our horses before we go?"

"No. I told you to git, so do it." She fired a round in the air to make her point. "Y'all wheel your horses, or you'll be spittin' lead."

That shot was the unmistakable whine of a Winchester. "Hold on, ma'am, if you would. I'd like to ask a question before we head out. You see, Ansel has something of mine, and I'd like it back. Maybe he told

7

you of its whereabouts?"

"That makes us even. He took something from me, too. My youth and my dreams. Would I be living in this hovel if I had anything valuable?"

Just then, Tyson's man yelled out in the distance behind the woman. "Drop the rifle, lady. Don't turn around. Just lay it on the ground and back away. I got you dead to rights."

The woman wheeled and fired into the darkness. Her shot was met by one from Tyson's wrangler which put her down. A dog's growl was followed by a second shot and a yelp. As the woman lay moaning, she cried out. "Damn you! You had no cause, no cause at all."

Tyson stepped his horse to where she lay with a hand to her side, the rifle a few feet away in the dirt. "Just wanted to find somethin' out, ma'am. Didn't mean you no harm. Why don't you tell me what I want to know now?"

"'Cause I don't know anything. Haven't had nothin' to do with Ansel for years. You've likely seen him more recent than me." She looked at them with hate in her eyes, then spat Tyson's direction. "You're the cowards that shot my son and his family, ain't you?" She groaned, then reached an arm out. "Ohh…help me!" Her head dropped slowly to the ground.

"Just got your husband, too." Tyson called out to the shooter. "Blane. Over here." The outlaw rode slowly from behind the house. Tyson leaned forward in his saddle. "Why'd you shoot her? I was talkin' to her—needed some information."

"She fired first, Pete. It were her or me, and I didn't want it to be me, so it weren't." He said it with some hesitation but also with what sounded like a touch of pride.

Tyson drew his Colt and put a bullet through Blane's forehead. The man dropped from the horse like a rag doll. The acrid smell of gunpowder hung in the still night air. He turned to his men and waved his gun. "That's for shootin' the dog. Nobody shoots any animals less'n I say. Fire the house."

Skinner said, "Ain't we gonna bury him, Pete?"

Tyson squinted the man's direction. "That's the second time you asked that tonight. You don't catch on quick, do you? I reckon I'm doin' the wolves around here a good turn by leavin' bodies right where they are, but I always did have a big heart." He chuckled, then eyed Skinner. "Did you hear what I just said? Get over there. Burn the place. And the barn."

Soon, a blaze danced in the darkness while flames played over the woman's face. She moaned. "Oh please. Don't leave me here to die!"

Tyson wheeled his horse away, followed by the rest of his men. The crackling whoosh of a red-hot fire drowned out the woman's whimpers as the gunmen stole away in the night.

Chapter Two

A year later, Spring 1872

Del Lawson scanned the gray afternoon New Mexico sky. Storm clouds hung in the air looking for a place to strike. He snugged his hat and winced as it tightened above his ear, then cinched his collar. He stroked his horse's neck and surveyed the two-thousand-head herd. The wind was up. It wouldn't take much to scatter these cattle to the hills. He only hoped there wouldn't be hail. He motioned to the other rider at the rear of the herd, Kip Holloway. They joined and rode toward the front of the longhorns. Other drovers rode the flanks.

Del pulled up next to Stoney Goodwin, the trail drive's foreman. He shouted, "I figure there's lightnin' hidin' in those clouds, Boss. Maybe we oughta shift more men to the front before it gets dark. Me and Kip can head up there if you want."

Kip was about his same age, early twenties, with about the same regard for the foreman as he had. Del met Kip when he joined the drive two weeks ago. First time he'd ever seen a black man in his life.

He thought back to how he came to be here and shook his head. Waking up with a hangover and finding he'd signed onto a cattle drive wasn't exactly what he had in mind when he started drinking in the Roswell saloon. But now, with a clear head, being here was starting to grow on him. He had nothing better to do, anyway. There wasn't anyone to send money home to, so ten dollars a month would keep him in whiskey, if nothing else. He'd buried his hurt so deep it'd never find its way out. If he could just get Goodwin off his back, the drive would be almost tolerable. He glanced toward the chuck wagon for the boy. There he was.

The foreman pointed a finger at Del. "Don't ever tell me what to do, Lawson. You go where I tell you." He squinted. "When the cows start to boltin', you're gonna be ridin' point. Got it?" Stoney Goodwin was not a man to cross.

Del nodded. That's what he'd just said he wanted, anyway. Couldn't figure the man. He leaned toward Kip and cupped a hand around his mouth. "Let's go rein the lead doggies in before the cracklers hit." The two riders kicked their mounts and dug toward the arrow point of the herd. Del leaned forward in the saddle as he neared the front. These cows were the fastest and most willful ones, which made the job more dangerous. All the better. A torrent of rain spilled from the sky.

Kip ran a hand over his short black beard and glanced at Del. "Keep your eyes peeled. No tellin' what these fool cattle will do once they start to fussin'. Don't let 'em run up our backsides. And stay away from those horns."

Del nodded and tugged at his hat.

Kip said, "What'd Goodwin say, anyway? Didn't look like neither one of you was too happy. Speakin' of happy, I ain't too excited to be ridin' point right before this storm hits."

"Happy don't much matter right now." Del pulled his gloves on. "Looks like we're gonna have our hands full in a minute." Just then, a muffled rumble rolled over the low piney hills that flanked them. A chill blast hit. Del spurred his mount. "Here we go!"

He kept his head low as the quartering wind struck full force from the west. A gust danced his hat high in the darkening air. Didn't matter. A jagged bolt of white splintered the dark sky and raised the hair on his neck. He raised a ruckus in the rain and the mud, yelling at the longhorns. They bellowed back, eyes wide with alarm. Fine with him. He could let loose on the trail, shout his anguish, and no one would notice. No one here cared what he did, anyway. He fired his Colt into the wild sky with abandon, as alive as he'd felt in a long time. Maybe the wind would carry some of his grief away with it. Let the heavens open up, he'd ride right into the heart of the storm. Welcomed it.

Off to his right, Kip's horse matched his, stride for stride, as they neared the front. The sky pulsed again. A solid sheet of gray backdropped by fleeting silver flashes pummeled the open range. A downpour that chilled to the bone. He'd never find his hat now. A biting cold knifed through his jacket and seized his soul. Del tried to tie his raggedy bandana around his head one-handed as he galloped, but he gave up and let the tempest have its way with him.

Before the cloudburst, the lead cows had already been milling uneasily. Now, lightning sent them hell-bent in an unreasoning rush ahead. Del grinned. Go ahead and run. Stampede your fool selves ragged. He was set on harassing them until they got tired of being harassed. He fired a couple more rounds into the clouds, the reports swallowed up in the bedlam. He kicked his horse into a sprint on a looping turn that would put him ahead of the point. All he had to do was screw up the courage to stay in front of the reckless mass and turn them. Not a problem—he didn't much care if he came out of this in one piece or not. Kip met him partway and they joined ranks, sideways to the front of the herd now. The roar of two thousand Kay-J cattle hooves pounding the basin floor matched the crash of the roiling sky. The land became furious slop. Windmilling an arm, Del held his ground against the thunder and the trampling hooves. The cows began a wide curving turn while lightning crashed. The raging wind began to whip the storm eastward.

Del needed to impose his will on the unruly beasts. He veered toward the herd and kicked his horse directly at the lead cows, which angled away at the last minute. The turning was complete. He pulled up as the rest of the longhorns slanted away. They milled aimlessly, jostling against each other, hot breath steaming in the frigid air. He wiped the rain from his eyes and shook a fist to the skies. "Damnation! Is that the best you got?"

Kip trotted up as the cattle halted, still unsettled. "Why on the Good Lord's earth do you go 'round riskin' your life like that? That was awful close, Del." He whacked his gloves against his saddle. "Chargin' those cows the way you did weren't the smartest thing you've done today."

Del nodded. "Seemed to work out." He stood in the stirrups and hollered at the retreating storm clouds. "If we're lucky, that storm'll head back our way and we can whup it again!" They ambled back to camp at a walk, horses snorting and panting. Del turned to his friend. "Don't expect Goodwin will be pattin' us on the back or nothin'—just don't let on how much we like bein' point."

Kip shook his head. "Not me—you. You like it. I don't wake up in the mornin' lookin' forward to gettin' trampled by a bunch of bad-tempered beeves."

"Come on. You can't tell me that wasn't the best part of your day!"

Kip smiled. "I don't know where that comes from in you. I swear I don't. Stoney's not gonna like you runnin' his herd. You got Rodrigo, that young boy traipsin' after you, to think about, too."

Del's neck warmed. Deep down, Kip was right, but charging that cow pushed away the ache he carried for just a moment. A vision of his wife and child haunted him. Burying bodies he would never see again. He drove the memory back as he and Kip closed on the hundred-horse remuda.

Kip said, "What's that mangled bullet hangin' off your neck for?"

Del started to wrap his hand around it but stopped. He didn't need to feel it to be reminded. He kicked his horse into a gallop, yanking to a stop just shy of the corral.

At the campfire, Goodwin sipped a steaming cup of coffee near orange embers. "'Bout time you boys got back. Didn't know if you'd stopped to pick wildflowers for each other or what." He flung the dregs away, tossed his metal cup back to the cook, and glanced sideways at Del. "From what I could tell, almost looked like you enjoyed yourself out there, Lawson."

Del shrugged. "Was better'n gettin' a tooth yanked, that's about it." He wasn't going to let Goodwin know he'd be up for anything like that he needed doing. Del still held the man a grudge for taking him on drunk. He walked toward the chuck wagon when someone called his name.

"Lawson! How come you got a slug around your neck? You even know how to fire a gun?" The words ended in a mocking laugh.

The cowhand's name was Jake. Del didn't know his last name, didn't care to.

The man turned to the drovers around him. "Let's see if he can handle that gun. Right fine-looking weapon. Bet it's just for show." He strode over, thumbs stuck in his waistband. Del turned to walk away. "How about a shooting contest, Lawson? You and me. I'll even let you pick out the targets. Give you a little advantage."

Del kept going.

"Bet that gun's never even been fired." The bigmouth followed right behind Del. "You and me sometime. You and me. I'll look forward to it."

Rodrigo stood next to Buck, the cook, helping him stir a large pot of steaming stew. Buck was talking the youth through holding the coffee pot, so it didn't burn his hands. Del knew it wasn't fair, but every time he looked at the boy, a vision of his murdered wife and son came to mind. Rodrigo was who the killer had been looking for. The boy had cost him his family. And for whatever reason, it seemed like the kid never took his eyes off Del.

Buck spoke up. "Son, you keep takin' chances like I seen you doin' the last few days, and you'll have just about used up whatever time you got left on God's green earth." The cook's voice rose at the end of every sentence, which made everything he said sound like a question. "And your boy here is a natural-born cook."

Del wanted to say he wasn't his boy but held his tongue. Del couldn't tell how old the cook was. His bushy gray beard added years as did his round frame. Either the man had a hard life and was younger than he looked, or he had the misfortune to look his age. Del bet on the former.

The cook slopped runny potato stew on Del's plate and leaned toward him the way a friend would to tell a secret. "Don't look like you made a buddy out of Goodwin yet, neither. I'd back off from him some if I was you. Stay away, I would."

"Ain't nothin' about him I can't tear myself away from, Buck, so don't you be frettin' about me." He scanned the plate. "You usin' carrots now, or are those potatoes so old they're orange? But gimme some extra, huh? A second helping might wash away the bad taste from the first."

A hint of a smile appeared around the corners of the cook's eyes. He shook his head. "Nothin' doin', cowpoke. Try polishin' off what you got on your plate first, then we'll see." He turned to the next drover with a slight shake of his head and splattered more stew.

There weren't a lot of things Del liked about being here, but he *was* partial to Buck's cooking. Better than anything he'd had in a long time. But that wasn't saying much. He'd make sure he stayed on the man's good side. Drovers liked to say only a fool argues with a skunk, mule, or cook.

Del held his steaming tin plate by the edge, a hot cup of coffee in the other hand. He heard Rodrigo trailing after him as he walked. He angled to the outskirts of the roaring-again campfire. Hunched-over drovers slurped as they ate. Smoke from wet wood made his eyes water as the fire fanned his way. He grabbed a wet seat on a slight rocky rise nearby and dipped his stale bread into brown sauce of some sort. He glanced at Rodrigo. "You already eat, boy?"

A nod.

The boy ate more than he did. "You ever gonna talk to me?"

A nod.

Del shook his head. He hadn't gotten anything out of him since that night. "Wish I could tell what's in that head of yours. It's a muddle, for sure." A vision of his wife floated before him. He pursed his lips and wiped at his nose. Must be the smoke. He took a sip of Buck's tolerable coffee. Burned his tongue. A twig snapped behind him. He looked to see Kip ambling his way.

"Mind some company?"

"Nope. Have a seat."

"Any reason you always eat by yourself?"

"I ain't by myself. You're here. And Rodrigo. 'Sides, I figure the campfire would be a more agreeable place without me intrudin' on it."

Kip glanced at him sideways. "What's that supposed to mean?"

Del took his time chewing a mouthful. "Don't mean nothin' by it, I reckon. Just me sayin' somethin' stupid to pass the time with. Don't mind me." He gazed in the distance toward where he thought his ranch had been. His eyes misted. He tipped a whiskey bottle to his mouth, then quickly stuffed it back in his shirt. The trail wasn't doing its job.

Neither was time.

Chapter Three

Tyson eased off his horse in front of the noisy saloon. The town of Lost Creek, Texas, wasn't much to look at from what he could make out in the dark, but that wasn't keeping the bar's patrons from enjoying a rowdy night. He eyed his men as they dismounted. He rested a hand on his nickel-plated Colt and twisted one of the ends of his bushy, brown mustache. Adjusted his eye patch. "Gimme a few minutes before you barge in. Don't want to scare nobody—right off." He straightened as he entered, his medium frame as tall as he could stretch it. No one looked up as he made his way to the bar. A little place like Lost Creek likely didn't have a lawman. Shouldn't be too hard to persuade someone to give him the answers he wanted.

Five ragged-looking men lounged against the bar. Bushy beards, dirty clothes. Loud voices drifted from a poker table. A whiskey glass flew through the air. Men held women on their laps at scattered tables. All heeled. The bartender poured a whiskey.

Tyson squinted at him. "Mind if I ask you a question?"

The man gave him a quick glance, then continued to pour while talking to a cowboy.

Tyson reached over the bar and grabbed the bartender's arm. "I'm speakin' to you."

Quick as a wink, the barkeep pulled a shotgun from

beneath the bar and aimed it at Tyson's chest. "Here's my answer." Four customers drew in quick fashion.

Tyson put his hands up. "Whoa! I ain't lookin' for a fight, just came in to drown the dust in my throat. Little touchy, ain't you, boys?" There'd be time enough for gunplay if need be. Right now, he just wanted some information.

The bartender kept the shotgun squared up on Tyson. "Why don't you start over, mister?"

"Best idea I've heard lately. I'm lookin' for a young fella, brown hair, short dark beard, not from around here, taller'n me. Heard he was probably by this way in the last couple of weeks. A loner. Rides a dun horse."

The bartender placed the gun back under the counter. The cowboys holstered theirs and resumed drinking. "Lots of men fit that description."

"Nobody new in town recently?"

"Not that I recall." He turned away and started wiping down shot glasses then holding them up to the light one by one. "What can I get you?"

Tyson rubbed his chin, then eyed the bottles behind the bar. "Whiskey." Lost Creek wasn't very friendly, but he'd be on his way soon enough. He grabbed his shot glass off the bar and glanced around as he walked to a table next to the card game. Some of the men there were dressed well—must be the town's leading citizens. Others were scruffy, likely making the most of a night off. Dance hall women worked their way among the crowd. A curvy, young redhead maneuvered by with a tray of drinks, caught his eye, then quickly looked away. Did she mean anything by that? She stole a glance at him again and started back to the bar where she loaded up another tray.

Tyson downed his glass, gazed her way, and lifted his empty just off the table.

She eased toward him through the throng of men. "What'll you have, mister?" While she leaned down and cleaned crumbs off the table, she whispered, "Meet me out back in half an hour."

"Another whiskey." He watched her stroll away, his glass balanced delicately on her tray. As he appreciated the sway of her hips, a ruckus came from the swinging front doors. Five of his men strolled in like they owned the place. Dusty, rowdy, ready. They sauntered over.

Lucas Skinner said, "Got your business all done, Pete? We couldn't wait no longer. Thought we was gonna die of thirst, listenin' to all the pretty women talkin' things up in here."

Thirty minutes and more drinks than they needed later, the cowboys were still occupying the ladies. Tyson slipped out the front door, to no one's attention. He walked around the side of the building and glanced left and right, his hand tight to his holster. When he reached the back of the low building, the woman stood backlit by lamplight streaming out the door to the alley. He scanned their surroundings again, his hand still covering his pistol. "Who are you?"

"No one, just someone who heard you askin' about a fella. Sounds like the hombre I spent some time with recently."

"That right? Tell me about him. What was his name?"

"Not sure I remember. What's it worth?"

The woman looked better here in dim light than she

had inside. "Not much. Don't really care if I find him or not." He thought that sounded pretty convincing.

"Heard that one before, mister. Twenty dollars." She glanced around quickly.

Tyson considered. "Ten. His name."

She held a hand out.

Tyson fisted a bill out of a pocket. He let it fall to the ground.

She started to bend down.

"Not yet. Leave it. Name."

"Dale something."

"Del?"

"Yeah, Del."

So what the bartender back in New Mexico Territory said was true. Ansel's son had survived after all. A couple of bullets was all it took to put his wife and kid down, but Lawson had dispatched two of his men and whizzed a shot past his ear. Four Lawsons dead and Tyson still didn't have the kid or Del Lawson. Killing was better when you had something to show for it.

"What'd he tell you?" It was a question with an answer that could lead anywhere.

"He said lots of things when he was drunk, which was most of the time. Wasn't makin' a lot of sense, maybe because of that head wound. Scarred over but looked like a fairly recent one. Was fuzzy-soundin' more often than not."

So one of their bullets *had* hit Lawson in the head. Either that or Lawson hit his head on the way down. "When'd he leave? And which way?"

"This is soundin' like it's worth more than ten bucks. Five more to keep me talkin'." She glanced around and rubbed her fingers together. "Now."

Tyson threw five more to the ground. He wanted to smack the answers out of her but took a deep breath and held off. Couldn't afford to cause a ruckus in an unfriendly town. Already had several guns pointed his way tonight. "Talk."

She stuffed the money in the cleavage of her tawdry dress. "Left a few weeks ago, said he was headin' to New Mexico Territory. Seemed to have a particular place in mind, but I'm not...sure...I remember where."

Tyson fumed. "Reckon five more might help your memory?" He held out a five-dollar bill. She stared at him like the money wasn't even there. A flush ran up his neck. He wanted to strangle her but couldn't afford to. She was the only lead he had. He lifted the gun out of his holster. Aimed it at her stomach. "Take it." He flung the money at her. It floated to the ground between them. She didn't move. "That's all you're gettin', so you better pick it up."

She stood stock-still and didn't take her eyes off him.

Infuriating woman. Just take the money and tell him where Lawson went. Bend over and pick it up. Damn her. Finally, he reached down and handed it to her. He drew his gun and pressed it against her chest so she wouldn't mistake his intent. "Now, where?"

"Ten—not until. I got nothin' to lose, mister. Go ahead and shoot me."

"Damn you, woman! If you was a man, I'd skin your hide right here." He holstered the pistol.

She held a hand out. "If I was a man, I wouldn't be in this shithole bar."

Tyson reached into his pocket and peeled another five from a wad of bills. He hesitated. She reached for it, but he held on as if it was a thousand dollars. Finally, he eased his grip, and she pulled the money away.

"Said he was goin' to some town with a 'well', as far as I recollect."

Roswell. So Lawson was headed back toward his ranch. But why? There was no reason to. He had already taken everything from Lawson that he could. His blood boiled. He slapped the woman on the cheek. She stumbled backward against the coarse wood of the building. "You stay here 'til me and my boys are shut of this place, hear?" He drew his pistol again. Cocked it.

She held a hand to her reddened cheek.

Tyson walked back inside the saloon and shouted to his men. "You're done drinkin'. Saddle up and ride. Now." He walked out and mounted up. He'd give them a long count of ten. Anyone still inside after that was liable to meet a painful death somewhere along the trail, like Blane did. His men knew it. They scrambled out the swinging doors, grasping shot glasses and handfuls of females. As they swung up in the saddles, they loosed the women, heaved empties into the air and fired, trying to make them dance in the night sky. Some of the locals scrambled out of the saloon, guns drawn, but Tyson and his gang had already disappeared toward the badlands of New Mexico Territory.

Chapter Four

Del wasn't making many friends on the drive. He'd taken Kip's advice to try to mingle with the drovers more, but he didn't much feel like having company. Even during the best of times that wasn't his way, and these weren't the best of times. Nights, he watched Kip work his way into the group around the campfire. Part of him wished he could do the same. But being alone as evening drifted in was fine, too. Time to think, reflect. Drink his worries away. Try to make sense of his torn-apart world. Goodwin must have been real hard up to take him and the boy on.

Where'd he hide that last bottle? Ought to be a town soon. He'd stock up on the one thing he could count on to push his heartache back, even for a little while. He shook his head as he sat on a riverbank near camp. Stars twinkled to faint life overhead. What was he doing on a cattle drive with his family and ranch just...memories? And a mute boy following him.

They camped by the Pecos River that streamed out of rough New Mexican country to the north. Rodrigo sat nearby, imitating Del as he whittled an oak branch to nothing. He'd given the boy an old knife he found lying on a barroom floor back in Texas. Didn't remember the town's name. Could have been any one of a number. They all seemed to blend together in a haze in his head. The dried stain on the blade was likely blood, but he wouldn't share that with the boy. Kip's voice startled him out of his reflections.

"You're starin' at nothin' like you're percolatin' on something, Del Lawson. Looks like you could use some company."

Del looked up to see Kip eyeing him with a smile on his face. Seems like he always had one, warranted or not. Just as well. Time he roused himself to stand watch, anyway. He drew his coat collar tighter, stood, and stretched. "No need. I'm done thinkin' about things. You just comin' off watch?"

"No, dummy. I'm gettin' ready to go stand watch with you. Let's set out."

Del caught Rodrigo's eye. He nodded toward Buck, and the boy hurried over to the cook. Del took a last swig. As he and Kip strolled to the remuda, Stoney Goodwin blocked his way. The foreman poked a finger just short of Del's chest. "So, still with the rotgut whiskey? You stand four hours again tonight. Left flank. You'll pull doubles 'til I say so. And I ain't said so yet. Understand? Don't ever let me see you drinking out here again."

Del tried to go around the man, but Goodwin sidestepped in front of him. "Like I said, understand?"

"No problem, Boss." He wanted to square the bigger man up and was sure he could, but he took a path around the foreman instead, Kip in trail. The farther away from Goodwin right now the better. The two friends saddled a couple of mounts and trotted toward the ever-present sound of cattle lowing in the gathering dusk. An early evening wind sighed a faint tune through the waving sage sprouts and early spring grasses.

Kip glanced sideways at Del. "What was that all about?"

"Wants me to stop drinkin', but that only makes one of us. We ain't had a civil word 'tween us since we met." He cracked a small smile. "I'm startin' to get the impression he don't like me."

Kip grinned. "You catch on quick for a dirt farmer."

Del had shared some of his background with Kip—about his ranch—but not his family. He wasn't that close to the black man yet. He sat up in the saddle and pointed in the distance. "Looks like a bulge of longhorns off to the left. They'll need ridin' back in." He spurred his mount. On the way to the breakout, he scanned the huge expanse of nearly two thousand Kay-J cattle, still restless as they settled in for the evening. He'd been riding long nights since he came. Days, he usually worked drag with Kip at the wedge-shaped end of the herd, which meant the most riding. Also the most dust, dirt, and crap.

"Let's go rein in those outliers." A wolf howled somewhere nearby and set Del on edge. His mind spun to thoughts of his family, his ranch. He wished the wolf that night had howled a little sooner.

Kip said, "I ain't so sure that's a wolf. Comanches can sound like almost anything they got a mind to. They like raidin' early drives every year, then they sit back and pick and choose after that. Usually hit on moonlit nights toward dawn. More often than not they're just after horses. Not sure about Apaches, though."

Del was clear. "That's a wolf."

Kip drew his rifle out of the scabbard. "Cussed

animals pick off newborns and stragglers, so keep an eye out. There'll be more than one. And right about now it's dinnertime."

Del knew about wolves, he'd almost raised the one that hunted around his ranch. He gripped his rifle stock. As he neared the straying cows, a commotion off to the left caught his attention. Wolves had taken down a calf and growled 'stay-away' warnings for all to hear. Their snarling split the night's peace. Del drew his Colt but stayed his hand. Confusion reined in the pack, then the big one grasped the still-bawling youngster and lugged it away by the neck, leaving a dark trail in the dim light. The rest trotted behind as the alpha made off toward a shallow draw and disappeared. The calf's wails faded, and its momma protested all alone.

Kip rode up. "I was waitin' for you to drop the wolf. Why didn't you?"

Del couldn't put his finger on it. Something had stopped him. "Wolves have to eat, too."

It took the herd some time to settle down. Del had his hands full minding the rear of the restless mass. The night wind whipped stronger from the west now, which always made the animals dodgy. As clouds shrouded the moon, Del scanned the overcast night sky. It looked like it had a storm in mind, which might set off another stampede. But the wind soon died, night sounds reclaimed the land, and the herd quieted.

Not long after, Kip bid Del farewell. "Goin' back in. Wish you were, too. Keep your eyes peeled, huh? You got reason to."

Del tapped a finger to his hat brim and watched his friend disappear in the dark. He patted his horse's neck. Another couple of hours. Not that he minded being out on the prairie by himself. Out here he didn't have to listen to barbs around the campfire. He was getting tired of Goodwin singling him out. And there was no doubt he was. He'd overheard other drovers laughing about it. One of them in particular. Jake. Kip said the man's last name was Potter. The hand kept calling him greenhorn, making fun of everything about him, including his town clothes. Del did allow as how he could use some boots. And a hat with a tie string.

All he wanted was to be left alone to settle into the bottom of a bottle. Just let him roam, like he and the boy had been doing the past year. He didn't know anyone on the drive, and no one knew him. Should have been a good change of scene, but he hadn't counted on running afoul of the foreman. And Potter.

And he still didn't know what to make of Rodrigo.

The trail boss was someone Del hadn't figured out, either. He pretty much let Goodwin run things. Nighttime, Old Tom Sammons often sat by himself near, but not at, the campfire. Why did the white-bearded man keep riding these hard trails? By reputation, he was a trapper times ago. Surely, he'd led enough drives to know better than to keep doing it. Old Tom didn't seem like someone Del would go to for much of anything.

He checked the western sky. Dark from more than the night. He opened his coat a little to let the air cool him. The evening wind had its own way of swirling. Del looked forward to when it picked up, more so than when the new grasses stood still. Breezes wound around and over him as he sat his horse. A sudden chill ran up his back. Nothing much was right these days. He was growing tired of wandering—looking for something that wasn't there anymore, yet already knowing it wasn't. Drifting with that same night wind wherever it pushed him. He fingered the crushed bullet hanging from his neck.

He was roused from his reverie by the crack of a gun somewhere off to the east. Was it one of the other drovers on watch—or something worse? Two more shots split the air, then faint shouting carried on the wind. Goodwin made it clear Del's job was to guard the herd's left flank, right where he was. He considered staying for a moment, then kicked his horse into a gallop on a looping route toward the gunshots that vanished in the evening air. His wide swing took him south of the herd, trying to pick up any sounds the wind lifted his way. It was hard to hear anything over the protests of nervous cattle as they bellowed to one another. Gunfire wasn't on the short list of things they liked.

He hurried along and soon picked up muffled voices. Couldn't tell who they belonged to as the wind played its night tricks. He flicked the loop off his hammer and loosened his rifle in its scabbard. Just ahead now. He pulled his horse back a notch and searched the dark ink to his front. The cattle protested louder here. Several large knots of animals would have to be driven back in as well.

He recognized the two drovers in the saddle dead ahead. One of them was Carl something. They turned his way. He slowed, one hand in the air, the other on his holster. They'd be nervous, no doubt. There was already trouble—riders don't didn't go firing in the night for nothing. "It's Del Lawson—don't shoot me. What's goin' on, boys?" Del brought his mount to a halt and drew his gun as he eyed his surroundings.

"Jumpers," said Carl. "They put Ed here down and got away with some head. How many, don't know."

Del hadn't seen the cowhand on the ground at first. He recognized him but hadn't had much to do with him or any of the drovers. "Rustlers gone?"

The third drover whirled with his sidearm and peered into the darkness, swinging the barrel left and right at nothing.

Carl said, "Yeah, they were already hightailin' it by the time we got our shots off. Long gone now."

Del knelt by the unconscious man and put a hand to Ed's neck. "Still got a pulse, but..." He felt around the man's chest until he found the bloody wound. He pressed his bandana on it and surveyed the surroundings. "His horse still here?"

"Yeah, spooked, just over there." Carl pointed to a shadow.

Del said, "He'll die if we don't get him back to camp soon. Help me lift him up on his horse."

Between the three of them, they slumped Ed crosswise on his saddle. Carl said, "I'll take him back. You two stay and shape the herd up again. Run those stragglers in."

As the horses galloped away into the night, Del turned to the other wrangler. "My name's Del, tell me yours again, willya?"

"I know who you are—you're Jake's favorite drunk." A short laugh. "Easy to figure how you got on the wrong side of Goodwin so quick. He don't drink. Usually takes new hands longer than that to annoy Stoney, though. You done it the fastest I ever seen."

Del ignored the insult. "We got some head to ride

back in." He trotted toward the yawning bulge, yelling in their direction. He looked back, but the other wrangler sat still, watching. Del waved for him to come help, but if the drover saw, he didn't let on.

Damn! Another herder hanging him out to dry. So be it. He turned back to the runaways and kicked his mount harder. Sooner or later, he'd need to return to the flank. Goodwin would have his hide for leaving, just for the hell of it. Where were the other wranglers? There should be at least another two out tonight, posted on swing, toward the front of the herd. At least he hoped they were still out there.

Whooping and hollering, he managed to box the wayward animals in as he rode side to side. Soon, the cattle had no place to go but to rejoin the herd. For a tenderfoot, he was getting good at this. He was handling cows better than some of the regular crew. He started back to his post.

"Hey, Lawson!"

Another drover rode up. Jake. Damn.

"You're supposed to be over there, ain't ya?" The wrangler pointed in the direction Del came from when he heard the shots.

Del started to tell what happened but decided it wouldn't do any good. "Yeah…was just heading back there now. You my relief?"

"You don't listen so good, boy. I oughta let you stay out here all night. You ain't real smart, sodbuster." That was about as low a name as a cowboy could be called. "Foreman's not gonna like this."

"Didn't think he would." Goodwin didn't like him whether he was doing right or doing wrong. No sense in trying to please a man who can't be pleased.

"If it wasn't so late, I'd give you a good whippin' myself."

Del's adrenaline surged. He was ready to mix it up with this two-bit wrangler. He pursed his lips. Trading insults with a weasel wasn't going to help things. He took a deep breath. "Be on the lookout for rustlers and wolves." Del yanked his horse away before his mouth failed him. He drifted along the outskirts of the herd, letting the evening air cool the burn in his cheeks. The clouds were gone with the wind in the night sky. Satin starlight lay softly over the land.

He nodded to two more of Goodwin's outriders on his way back to camp. They didn't bother to look his way. No matter. He took his time as he scanned the dim land—gently rolling hills that vanished in the distance. He patted the horse's neck. He'd always taken potluck from the remuda, but he kind of liked this one. Blackest animal he'd ever seen, had a certain spirit about him. A good gait Del took to right away. He leaned forward in the saddle. Might as well get back to camp and get it over with. No doubt Goodwin would notice he wasn't back. The drive wasn't turning out to be the salve he'd hoped it would be. A long shot that wasn't working out, but he was just stubborn enough to see it through. For once, he'd used his head and left a bully—Jake—alone. No sense getting in a fracas with him. There was likely a bigger one waiting for him back at camp.

Chapter Five

Del rode to the remuda where the horse wrangler stood like a sentry. Almost looked like he was waiting for him. The cowhand was a lean one. He went by the name of Laramie and had the enthusiasm of an unbusted mustang. Wasn't any older than Del. Maybe younger. Said he was from Kansas somewhere.

Laramie smiled as he took the reins. "I was lookin' for this one, then remembered you was the one took him."

Del dismounted and smoothed his hand over the horse's neck. Black that went so deep it doubled back on itself. Neat white blaze on his forehead. He turned to Laramie. "I'd like this horse from now on. That okay with you?"

"That's a fine-lookin' animal, that is. I was thinkin' of cuttin' him out for myself." Laramie wore a wide grin. "But I'd be happy to share him with you whenever you want. What's your name again? I know I heard it; I just don't remember so good. Never have."

"Del, Del Lawson." He thanked Laramie and walked toward the dim campsite and Goodwin—just the person he didn't want to see. The foreman and bigmouth Jake huddled over a tired campfire. Damn! He prepared to get braced.

Goodwin turned his way. "Lawson, over here. Been lookin' for you."

Del's insides hiccupped. He wasn't scared of the man; he just didn't like getting rousted. Especially lately. Why couldn't people just leave him alone? He gave fleeting thought again to riding out and disappearing, but quitting had never been his way. He wasn't about to let Goodwin or anyone else buffalo him.

"Yes, Boss?" He forced a frown from his face.

Goodwin drew himself up to his full height. He wiped the remains of dinner bits from his beard, grimaced and pointed a crooked trigger finger at him. "Why'd you leave your post out there, the one I told you to stay at?"

Del's frown won out. How'd he find that out already?

"Wonderin' how I know? Your friend Jake here told me."

Del tried to hold his tongue, but the words spilled out. "You tellin' me he left his post to come here and tell you I left my post?" He fairly spat the words.

That stopped Goodwin, but only for a second. "Jake ain't your concern right now—I am—and I won't have any of my men disobeyin' me, hear?"

Del didn't trust his mouth, so he stood silently. No use telling Goodwin about helping the wounded wrangler, it wouldn't change the foreman's mind about anything. Just keep quiet and let the man bluster. All Del wanted was to turn around, find his bedroll, and lay it out. Take a last swig. At least he could get a good night's sleep. He looked toward the chuck wagon for Rodrigo. There. Watching him.

Goodwin turned back to Tom Sammons. "Jake here says there's riders out there rustlin' and rilin' the herd, Boss. Figger we can't just let them make off with head whenever they want."

Sammons squinted into the campfire. "What do you want to do about it, Stoney?"

"Need to find 'em first." He pointed at Del. "That's your job. Track 'em and let me know where and how many there are. Be quick about it."

Kip crowded closer to the campfire. "Say, Boss, you ain't gonna send Del ridin' off by himself, are you? Why, he don't even know what he don't know about this land. His first drive. Let me go after 'em." When Stoney didn't answer, Kip said, "At least let me go with him."

Del stared at Goodwin. "I don't need nobody else stickin' up for me. Can handle myself." He wanted to punch the foreman, knew a fight with him was probably coming sometime. Another scrap he'd welcome when it came. A warm flush ran up his neck.

"Shut up, Holloway. This ain't your worry." Goodwin pointed Del's way. "Understand, Lawson? If I was you, I'd get goin' before daylight steals your cover."

Del pushed his anger back, turned on his heel, and strode toward the remuda. Swallowing his feelings was getting harder to do. Cool night breezes swirled around and calmed him. He looked forward to seeing the black again.

Goodwin called after him. "Don't you want me to tell you where I think they probably are?"

Del kept walking without looking back. Didn't want Goodwin's help. Didn't want anything from him. Or that damn Jake. At least this would put distance between him and those two. He needed to fork a saddle right now more than he ever had in his life. When he got to the makeshift corral, he whistled in the dark but figured the big black wouldn't respond. He'd only ridden him a couple of times. He tried another whistle.

Laramie interrupted Del's search. "Guess I know who you're lookin' for." The overgrown kid wore a big smile, straw hair askew just like his scruffy, sparse beard. "Didn't want nobody else ridin' him 'cept me or you, so I hid him. Don't tell nobody." He spoke in a whisper and glanced around. "Over here." He smiled broadly as he led Del to a little stand of trees, some of the few on this windswept prairie.

Laramie loosed the black, and the horse ambled Del's way, like a stately apparition in the dim light. Ears pitched forward. Del smoothed a hand along the horse's silky neck. The stallion needed a name, but Silky wasn't it. The horse had too strong a gallop for 'silky'. Shade popped into his head as he gazed at the prettiest horse he'd ever seen, much less ridden. Shade. It fit. He dropped a hand into his pocket. After Stoney chewed him out, Del had gone to check on Rodrigo and snagged a carrot from Buck. He palmed it now as he patted the big animal. Shade bobbed his head, though, as if he knew. Del couldn't hide a smile, something that had been scarce lately. He opened his hand, and Shade plucked the carrot out of it. This was the horse for him.

Up in the saddle, he trotted away from camp. He hadn't tracked horses for a while but had done some on his ranch in the past. Another chance to forget, if only for a little while.

He soon put the herd behind him. From here, he'd head east and try to locate the killers' track. What he'd do if he found them, he didn't quite know.

He'd figure something out.
Always did.

Chapter Six

Pete Tyson scanned the broad eastern New Mexico plain. It had its own stark beauty, which even a killer like him had come to appreciate from a lifetime here. Tawny antelope strolled wide open stretches on taut legs, toying with coyotes foolish enough to try to run them down. Come late spring, the sun had a way of making this land downright inhospitable during the day. He eased his horse to a halt on a slight rise. "Damn animal is lame!" He slid off. "Check him out, Skinner."

The outlaw knelt by the horse and ran a hand up and down one of the forelegs. "It's the tendon sure enough. Bowed it is." A death sentence for a horse out on the endless prairie. He looked up at Tyson. "Want me to take care of it?"

Tyson shook his head. "Nah, my horse. Unsaddle him." He drew his Colt .44 and put a bullet in the horse's brain. The animal dropped like a stone. Tyson turned to Skinner. "Put my gear on your horse and gimme your reins."

Skinner started to protest, then shook his head. "What'll I do for ridin', Pete?"

"Find another mount. Do I have to do all your thinkin'?"

Skinner turned to the youngest member of the gang. Just a kid. He rested his hand on his pistol. "Looks like this ain't your day, Billy. Saddle Pete's gear on your horse." The youth held onto his reins for a moment until Skinner's backhand sent him sprawling. The other toughs laughed.

The boy lay on the ground with a hand to his cheek. He struggled up and started saddling Tyson's new mount. "Don't leave me with no horse, Lucas. Please!"

"You'll get another soon as we catch up to Lawson."

"When's that gonna be?"

"When we find him."

"Why we after him in the first place?"

"Ain't no concern of yours, boy. Just keep doin' what I tell you to do, and you'll see more sunrises."

Skinner glanced toward Tyson. "This here has to be New Mexico Territory, Pete. Looks like we're already west of that chopped off mountain to the north. Think young Lawson's here? I mean...that saloon gal...what if she weren't—"

"She wouldn't have known there was a Roswell if Lawson hadn't said that name. He's out here somewhere, sure as shootin'." He gazed over the barren, wide expanse to his front, as if he could see his quarry. "I can feel it."

"But how we gonna find him?"

"I'll find him. That gold's as good as mine—was meant for me. Ansel wouldn't have taken that secret to his grave. Musta told somebody in his family about it. Didn't tell his wife, her livin' in that shack and all. I figure Ansel told his son 'cause of the way he snarled when I said I was comin' for his family. The boy's probably with Lawson, too, and Lawson's likely not stayin' put, so let's get a move on."

They rode for another day before they pulled into the little settlement of Roswell. Tyson scanned the low brown bluffs to the east that rose from the basin floor. The area was as close to a home as he'd ever had. He gazed north in the direction he grew up. A sudden picture of his mother beating him ran through his head. A pile of blackened rubbish lay where the house had been.

Roswell's small saloon was one he knew from robbing travelers and stagecoaches along here for years. All that thievery and he had nothing to show for it.

The bartender eyed Tyson as he walked in. He didn't look happy to see him. Tyson strode to the scuffed wooden bar. "Whiskey, Herman."

"Don't want no trouble here, Pete. This is a nice, quiet place since you left."

"Well, now, you can keep it that way by tellin' me where young Lawson is."

"Lawson? You mean Del? The kid you almost killed last year? Came mighty close, too." He resumed wiping down the counter.

"Where is he?" He eased a hand back to his Colt.

The bartender put a hand up. "Hold on there—he ain't worth me dyin' for. Ain't seen him for some time. Was in a bad way after you shot him. Wandered around here and there drunk mostly, then one day he disappeared and ain't been around since."

"You oughta try to be more helpful, Herman. My patience's runnin' thin, and my finger's itchy. Used to be there weren't anything around here you didn't know about. My guess is that's still the case. Let's have it."

The bartender glanced at the customers in the small room. "Won't do, havin' you spark trouble, Pete. Don't think nobody knows where he is, includin' his ma."

Tyson's head jerked backward. "His ma? Whaddya mean his ma? I shot and killed her a while back. Self-defense it was. Same time as I…uh…" He left the part about killing Ansel dangling.

"You near did. She was in a bad way when one of her neighbors brought her in. Guess he saw the fire. She'd lost a lot of blood. Tiny at the stable saw to her 'til she was some better. Said Maybelle was as strong as his best horse."

"Where'd the woman get to?"

"Don't know that, neither. Up and left when she was able. Guess she thought you might come back some day. Like you just done."

"Damnation!" Now he had two people to look for, but he didn't have a solid lead on either. "I'll say it once more. Where is she, Herman? You tell me true, or this place burns to the ground tonight. With you in it."

"You know I would if I knew, Pete. I ain't brave enough to hold out on you."

"Did he have a boy with him?"

The bartender nodded.

Tyson reached across the bar, grabbed the man by the collar, and bounced him off the back of the bar.

Tyson waved his pistol around the room as cowboys edged away. "I'm takin' my leave now. Anybody follows me out this door has made his last mistake." He shot the mirror behind the bar and watched a thousand glass shards dance in the air. As he backed out of the saloon, a man came in. Tyson whirled at the sound and pistol-whipped him across the face. He looked down at the writhing cowboy. "Wrong place, wrong time, pardner." He stepped over the moaning man and walked toward the stables, searching the early evening streets. His men joined on him as he strode down what passed for main street, spurs jingling, gun still handy.

His thugs gathered around. He said, "You two go fetch the stabler out. Skinner, get the rope off my horse. Prepare for a hangin'."

The blacksmith came out of the shanty stable with a Tyson cowhand to either side, pistols drawn. He was a large man who dwarfed the two outlaws covering him. "What can I do you for, mister?" He wiped meaty hands on a dirty apron, but he couldn't wipe away the surprise on his face.

Tyson grinned. "So they call you Tiny?"

The man nodded, never taking his eyes off Tyson. "Guess I outgrew it." He flexed his fingers. "Need a horse stabled?"

"No, we're here about what I can do for you. This is your lucky day—you get to live if you tell me what I want to know."

The blacksmith stood impassively.

"Where's the Lawson woman, the one was married to Ansel. You tended her. Maybelle."

"Don't know, ain't seen her for nigh on a year."

"Now, that's not what I want to hear…Tiny."

"I speak truth—take it or leave it."

"Well now, you'd do well to come up with better than that."

"Like I said, don't know no more."

Tyson lifted his Colt free.

Tiny grabbed each of the outlaws by the collar and spun them together, head-knocking them silly. They fell limp to the street. He lumbered Tyson's way until a .44

caliber slug in the chest stopped him. He sank to the ground at Tyson's feet. The shooter shook his head. "Don't know when these folks are gonna learn, I just ask once." He leaned over the dying man. "Where is she?"

Tiny gasped for breath. "If I didn't tell you...standin' up...I sure as hell...ain't gonna tell you...lyin' down, dyin'.."

Tyson jammed the gun under Tiny's nose, but the stabler had drawn his final breath. "Stupid smithy, coulda lived. Protectin' a woman who didn't mean nothin' to him. Didn't have the brains he was born with!" He kicked a bootful of dirt on Tiny's large body and turned away.

One of his men wobbled to a stand. "Where you goin', Pete?"

"Saloon." He busted into the place and drew on the barkeep. "Tiny's dead. Big men always fall hardest. Now, you got one chance to live." He cocked the hammer. There was no mistaking where the gun was aimed. A man's privates take on particular importance when he's faced with losing them.

Herman threw his hands in the air. "I told you I don't know nothin' about her, Pete."

"...And I reckon I believe you. You're too yella to lie to me. Tell me what you know about Del Lawson."

"He's messed up. Plumb loco, what with that head shot."

"So you seen him?"

"Yeah, I seen him."

"How recent?"

"Near a month now. Was talkin' about startin' over, but that's when it happened."

"Go on."

"Some trail drover took him on one night when Del was drunk. He staggered out with a bunch of 'em. Ain't seen him since."

"Where was they headin', Herman?"

"Don't know for sure, but they had to be ridin' north, toward Colorado Territory. That's the only direction cattle drives go this time of year."

"What makes you think they was on the trail?"

"His boys. They was shootin' their mouths off about how dry they were gettin' eatin' cow dust for days on end. Started out in Texas. Skirted Comanche territory. Goodnight-Loving trail."

Tyson rubbed his chin. "More like it. You get to live another day, tendin' bar for these drunks." His gaze swept the room. He leaned over the bar. "That your dog?"

The bartender's eyes grew wide. "What do you want with—"

Two shots rang out, followed by a yelp and a scurry of toenails scraping the wooden floor. Tyson belly-laughed. "Don't worry, just jolted him some." He blew barrel smoke away. "That's for not tellin' me the first time." He turned from his handiwork back to the room. "Pretend you're statues, boys." He strolled to the door, his men covering his exit. At the swinging doors, he paused and turned. Doffed his cowboy hat. "Always get a warm feelin' comin' back here. Almost like the home I never had. Appreciate your hospitality. I'll be sure to come back." He eyed the shattered mirror behind the bar. Already shot out. He quick-drew and blew apart an oil lamp at the end of the bar. Started a small fire. The saloon doors swung several times, and

Tyson was gone into the night.
Closing in on his quarry.

Chapter Seven

Scant moonlight cast uneven light over the plains as Del rode, searching for sign. Ragged clouds matched his spirits. They seemed to tease him as he trotted from shadow to shadow on the still prairie. He oriented himself on a low rise ahead littered with dark scrub oak, a backdrop to where the drover was shot. Riding the south edge of the herd, he crisscrossed level ground spotted with clumps of new grasses. The cattle hadn't gotten them all yet. Even a greenhorn like him knew it was best to be lead drive when spring came. He stroked Shade's neck and leaned forward in the saddle.

He'd seen many a darker-than-dark night, times when the moon shirked its duty. This was one of those, even with faint moonlight overhead. When Del reached the spot the wrangler was cut down, he gave Shade a quick nudge with his thighs. The horse angled away from the herd at an easy trot. Track should be easy to follow from here on. Trampled ground on both sides spoke to him. Del held Shade's reins lightly, the horse never veering off line, as if he'd followed night sign on the prairie all his life.

Del gave fleeting thought to angling back west and heading for home. Would be the easy way out. But where was home now? He sure didn't owe Goodwin anything, and no one else had given him the time of day. Except Kip...and Laramie...and Buck. And then there was Rodrigo. Okay...he'd stay. But not for them—for himself, mostly. Time he got back in the saddle of life. Drinking his days away hadn't done any good, and the headaches from his wound didn't batter him as bad anymore. Besides, he was never one to cut and run. He'd seen his daddy do that too many times.

A storm was long gone, and Del had the stark landscape to himself. The muffled sounds of the herd died out behind him as he made his way over slightly-rolling land by dappled light. It wasn't hard to follow the track, he'd done it on his own range. Hard to hide sign made by that many cattle and horses, even in a land so big it disappeared into the daylight horizon. He pushed his troubles back and gazed at the beauty of the clearing night sky. Glittering stars seemed to reach out to him from the blackness. His mother taught him about the heavens as a child. He patted Shade's neck and pointed. "That one there is the Big Dipper. See how it looks like a ladle? Don't see its little cousin right now." He rode free and sober, for the first time in—he couldn't remember when. The soft night wind seemed to want to hurry him along so he let it. It could help itself to some of his grief, too, if it had a notion.

Shade kept a steady gait that gobbled distance. Jumbled sign encouraged Del on. He came to a slight rise, sparsely wooded in low, dark shrubs. He slowed. Shade climbed the back side of the knoll. From the top, Del had a clear view of the dim landscape that surrounded him. A deep black blanketed the land. A coyote raised a howl in the distance, more like a holler, soon joined by another. Stillness reclaimed the land. As Del drew Shade's reins back to leave, the horse nickered and pawed at the earth. Del stopped for one last glimpse. That's when he saw it.

A faint light in the distance.

He hadn't seen it at first because he'd been scanning too quickly. Del blinked rapidly. Must be a fire—a lantern wouldn't carry this far. The wind swirled at his back and hadn't lofted any sound his direction, but it had to be them. The rustlers and the stolen Kay-J cattle. He laid the reins left on the stallion's neck and eased Shade down the rise, headed straight for the small glow.

What was he going to do when he got there? No way he could steal the cattle back by himself. The only thing to do would be to pull up somewhere short of their camp. As he neared, the light disappeared and re-appeared. Must be low hills between him and them. He slowed Shade and entered a broken land of shadowy, round-granite formations. He dismounted and tied the horse to a scrawny juniper struggling to survive dry, high plains. Circling behind a large rock outcropping, he gazed down at a grudging campfire. Sparks flew and disappeared into the night as piñon wood popped in the flames. The fresh, smoky pine aroma reminded him of fires back home growing up. Four wranglers warmed their hands around the campfire. Del rubbed his as he watched. Late spring nights here were cool. At least two more drovers were likely out on night guard so there were probably six all told.

One man looked to be in charge. He wasn't big, but his manner was. His deep voice carried on the night air. Del crept closer. He couldn't make out the man's features as flames flared in the night. Dark shadows danced across his face. Had he seen him before? Dim images flashed through his mind. Cobwebs filled his head, too thick to shake away. His heart almost pounded through his chest.

A rider came in and dismounted. He made his way to the campfire and another hand rose to leave. Time to back away, trail the outlaw, and locate the cattle. They couldn't be too far away. Shade nickered softly. Del put a finger to his lips and took a moment to stroke the stallion's neck. The horse was about the only good thing in his life right now. After leading him quietly away, Del was up in the saddle and trotting. He kept an ear out for the rider in the distance ahead. Even if the man looked his way, he stood little chance of seeing Del in the ink-black night. But he might hear him. Sound carried for miles on the high plains.

He let a larger gap develop between him and the rustler. Not long after, the *whuffs* of cattle and their sour smell carried his way. A light tug on the reins. He'd need to stay a ghost to size things up. When the thief pulled up near the animals, Del urged Shade in a circular walk around the small herd. The horse took to stealth as if he'd been born to it. Looked to be about thirty-some head. His heartbeat slowed. Now what?

A shot rang out from somewhere in the blackness ahead. Del ducked—the bullet whistled by his ear, far too close. He spun Shade away, but the shot set the cattle off. They bolted his way, blocking Shade's path. The horse reared. He felt the animal stagger for a moment as the longhorns rumbled past. Del fell off Shade backwards and hit the ground with a thud. The air thundered as the startled cows stampeded by. He curled into a ball and absorbed punishment from glancing hooves. No direct hits but enough to stun him. By the time the cattle started to settle again, Shade had nudged Del several times. He groaned as he pushed himself to a lopsided stand, a hand to his side where several ribs were no doubt broken. His scalp was sliced, too. Warm blood trickled down his neck. At least this head wound wasn't the same side as last year's.

He crouched, searching for the gunman. Whoever it was must have been caught up by the stampeding cattle, just like him. Del willed himself up on Shade. It wasn't until he started back for camp that he noticed the horse's gait was off. Definitely limping. Clear of the rustlers now, Del dismounted. He ran his hand over Shade's legs, then his flank. In the dark, a wet, sticky feel told him Shade was wounded. How bad he couldn't tell. He was having more than enough trouble staying upright. His head throbbed. Much as he would have liked to walk Shade back to camp, Del struggled back up on the horse. Who shot at him? And where was he now? He bent low in the saddle and scanned his surroundings as he rode. Between his and Shade's wounds, the roundabout return took twice as long as it should have. The land was lightening by the time Laramie met them at the remuda.

"Where you been, Del? 'Bout time you brought Shade back. Lordy, you're a surefire mess. You all right? Let me help you down." Laramie settled him on the sparsely-grassed ground. The next thing Del heard was, "Gol' dang it! What'd you do to my horse? He's plenty cut up, maybe a goner. He's taken a beatin', for sure."

Del wanted to see to Shade, but a loud commotion at the campfire caught his attention. "What's goin' on over there?"

Laramie shrugged. "Dunno, but sounds like a real

scrap for sure."

Del limped that direction.

"Damn thieves is what you is! Nothin' but crooks."

That voice! The same one Del heard at the rustlers' camp not more than a couple hours ago.

"You're harborin' a cattle thief, and I want him. Trailed him right to here. Just busted in on us and roiled my herd somethin' fierce." His partner stayed silent behind him.

Stoney Goodwin stood with his feet slightly apart, drovers circled behind him. His deep drawl carried on the night air. "Don't know who you are, mister, but it'd be best if you rode on back to whatever hole you climbed out of." Goodwin reached toward his pistol.

The intruder pointed at Stoney. "Name's Tyson, Pete Tyson, a name you best remember."

Del's heart skipped a beat. Tyson? He remembered that name only too well. This was the bastard that Tiny, the stable owner, said shot his ma. Del staggered over to the foreman. Rage rose in his throat. "That there rider is the head cattle thief, boss." Del pointed to the grimy man on the big chestnut horse. "I tracked the beeves to their camp. He was sittin' at the rustler's fire, braggin'. Raid must have been his idea from the start. They stole about thirty head. Someone shot at me but missed."

"Looks like somethin' messed you up pretty good, though. How many was they, Lawson?"

"Must be about six hands, Mr. Goodwin." He moved toward the raider, fists clenched.

Tyson squinted. He looked the young man up and down. Blood dripped from under the cowhand's hat. When Lawson looked his way, Tyson saw it by the light of the campfire. There. Just under the hat brim, running front to back above one ear. A light scar. He'd found what he came looking for. Lawson! Tyson's eyes widened when Del's eyes met his. Click of a hammer as the foreman raised his gun. The killer yanked his horse away and hightailed it away into the night.

Del got off several shots at the fleeing duo. The thunder of hooves on the evening air seemed to mock him. He'd been so close to his family's ruthless murderer.

Stoney shook his head. "Don't that beat all. Rustlers tellin' us they're lookin' for thieves here. Our own cows, too. I swear, I never—"

Del's heart raced as he stared at Tyson's disappearing back. He glanced at Rodrigo. The boy stood with Buck, pointing at Tyson wide-eyed. So Rodrigo knew him, too. Del made for the remuda in a limping run. No time to lose. He struggled up on a horse and rode out slumped in the saddle, headed east on track he'd already been over twice tonight. Only adrenaline kept him upright.

****

Goodwin turned to the trail boss. "We need to up and chase 'em down, Mr. Sammons. Can't afford to let 'em get away with it, or we'll lose lots more 'tween here and Denver. Likely those two will lead us right back to our cows."

Sammons nodded and took a sip of coffee.

Goodwin yelled. "Need six men for a nighttime raid. Who's with me?" He hurried to the remuda, several men in tow.

"Laramie, fetch me that black stallion."

"Can't do it, Mr. Goodwin. He's all stove up, just like Del is."

Goodwin whacked his pants with his stained hat. "Damn! Say, where'd Lawson get to, anyway? I need him to lead us to those cattle."

"Already rode out, Boss."

"Rode out? Where?"

"Looked like he was goin' after those riders just left."

"He better not get killed until we locate them cows."

Kip said, "Like as not, they'll be easy to find. Just stick to the most trampled ground."

Goodwin yelled to Sammons. "Keep a good watch 'til we're back, Boss. Those two could have just been a ruse to split us in half."

Sammons stood with arms folded.

Goodwin grabbed his horse's reins. "Riders up! Let's go. They got too much time on us already."

****

Darkness hid the agony on Del's face. Pain jolted him with every thudding hoof. He didn't know which hurt worse, his head or his ribs. Sharp stabs in his side told him some were busted. Focusing on his wife and son's killer helped push the pain back. That had to have been Tyson that deadly night. The first murderer through the ranch house door. Tyson's face was the last sight he saw. Next he knew, Rodrigo was shaking him awake on the floor. The killers were gone. Nothing but dead silence. Didn't know where the boy had hidden, but Rodrigo must have seen Tyson slaughter his son and wife. Del buried them in a daze...

He shook the memory away. He was groggy, but nothing was going to keep him from running Tyson down. Besides, riding hurt was a new experience, something he was always up for. The assassin was somewhere dead ahead in the night. Fury drove Del on. Anger had been his closest friend for the past year. He'd used it to push the worst pain back, to mask the ache in his heart. Now, there was no hiding it. Pain surged from deep inside. He listed to the left in the saddle, trying to protect his aching ribs. Should have brought a bottle of whiskey. He was good at stuffing his pain in those.

Kicked-up dirt pinpointed the rustler's track. Del perked his ears to catch sounds, but the pounding of his horse's hooves drowned out any chance of that. The rustled beeves lay about an hour ahead, unless they were already on the move. No doubt Tyson and his renegades would up and drive them away as soon as he got back. Maybe not, though. Maybe Tyson would set a trap for anyone who followed. That made more sense. Tyson couldn't outrun Goodwin with thirty stolen cattle.

A shot rang out in the dark. The bullet ricocheted off the butt of Del's rifle. It drove his horse sideways and knocked Del off onto hard ground. The next thing he knew, he felt a slap to his cheek. Kip. Rodrigo had a hand on his arm. Morning light stole through a canvas wagon cover.

Kip had a wry smile. "You're a hard man to wake up."

"I ain't…awake. What happened?"

"Well, when we rode out after you last night, we heard shots ahead. Found you layin' there on the ground. Whoever was shootin' had you just about zeroed in. Musta took off when he heard us comin' 'cause we couldn't find anyone."

"What about Tyson? And the rustlers?"

"Gone. Left the cattle just standin' there dumb like cattle will do. We drove 'em back here last night. Propped you up in your saddle and trotted you back, too."

"How long have I been out?"

"Long enough to get a good night's sleep. Considering how many times you've knocked your noggin lately though, wasn't sure you were ever gonna come back. Give that head of yours a break, willya?"

Del slowly turned. "Ow!" His neck protested. Rodrigo sat by his side. Del's heart pounded at the thought of Tyson. He'd been so close...Come to think on it, though, Del hadn't considered what he'd do when he *did* catch up to the murderer. The boy's wide eyes were the last thing he saw before he drifted off again.

Chapter Eight

Pete Tyson slowed as he neared the low, sprawling ranch house. More like a whitewashed Mexican palace. Thick adobe style, the richest kind. Everything in its place. Even the dirt around the house looked groomed. He'd ridden here after abandoning the rustled cattle. He wasn't bringing good news for his boss, ranch owner Elijah Wilkins. His men peeled off behind him for the stable. Tyson pulled up out front and handed the reins to a small man in a wide sombrero.

"Will you be long, señor?"

He ignored the man. This could be a short visit. He'd stopped in at the Roswell saloon after losing the beeves. The bartender said el jefe wanted to see him. A quick stab of fear had run through him at the news. Just like the one that coursed through him now as he dismounted. What was he going to tell Wilkins? He gazed at the imposing house. Sun-baked brown tiled roof that went all the way from here to there. White stucco walls kept the house cool. He knew that much from the couple of times he'd been inside. Ceramic-tiled porches boasted fancy wrought iron railings. A massive oak door stood open, ready to swallow him. An old man dressed in spotless white stood inside the entrance, impassive. Stock-still, like he was part of the house.

Tyson walked in. "How are you, Purk?" At least

there was one friendly face. But he took that back when he noticed the servant's blank expression.

The white-haired man said, "The library, please." He disappeared.

Tyson stepped down the hallway, imagining the kind of welcome he was going to get.

Wilkins didn't get up from his massive leather chair. "Sit, Mr. Tyson. I can tell from the uneven thump of your boots that you didn't bring the news I want."

For a blind man, Wilkins could tell a lot. Tyson cleared his throat. "No sir, Mr. Wilkins, but I know where Lawson is." He said it quickly so the land baron couldn't interrupt before he got his excuse out.

Wilkins shifted the cat curled in his lap and signaled the butler standing behind him. The man poured something from a crystal decanter beside Wilkins' chair. Tyson wondered if he was going to offer him one. Guess not.

The rancher took a long sip. "Do you think Lawson knows where the gold is?"

"Yup. Ansel must have told him. Likely he ain't dug it up yet, though, or he wouldn't be eatin' trail dust on a long drive. Good news for us, bad for him."

"The only thing that's going to be good for you is if you corral Lawson. Having a good idea where he is, and knowing where aren't the same thing—are they, Mr. Tyson?"

"No sir, they ain't, but I got a bead on him now. I was closin' in on him when I got word you wanted to see me. Just need a few more days."

Wilkins drummed fingers on the fine inlaid marble end table next to him. "Good thing your man didn't kill Lawson that night. No doubt the boy's with him. I'm giving you one last chance to round them both up. You should have made sure of the young'un when you killed the rest of the boy's family."

Tyson smiled. "Yeah, accidents happen."

"Frequently, at your hands."

"But he's only a kid, what—"

"He's more than that, he's the last remaining heir to the Abriendo Grant, which I'll file on when he's dead. That spread's three times the size of mine. And I'll buy it with the gold coins I stole from them." Wilkins paced the room with the slightest grin, the calico nestled in the crook of his arm. "So find those coins! And kill the boy, or you'll be the hunted one…" He picked up his brandy and swirled it under his nose. "That will be all."

Tyson leaned forward slightly, then caught himself. What the hell was he bowing for? Wilkins couldn't see him. Wasted respect. He considered giving him the middle finger but didn't. What the blind man could 'see' was legendary. "Yes sir." He picked his hat up and headed out the yawning door.

He rousted his men at the stable. "Mount up you no-accounts. We're headin' back north." He'd end this and deal with Wilkins later.

Chapter Nine

Del forced his eyelids open. His head was on fire. He lay flat on his back, getting bounced around in a wagon. He glanced left and right, trying to get his bearings. There was Rodrigo, squatting on the wagon bed, back pressed into a corner. Who was driving? Kip? Another man lay next to him, unconscious. Where were they? And why was he in a wagon? He croaked Kip's name. "What's...goin' on? Where are we?"

Kip leaned back from the bouncy seat up front. "So you decided to quit your slackin' off and join us again? About time, I'd say. You do pick the oddest times to black out. Almost like you know when things are gonna be hardest." He laughed and snapped the reins.

Del saw the grin on Kip's face through the open flap. "Where—"

"We're just out for a little drive. Thought we'd head up to Fort Sumner. Nicest place for miles around."

"Sumner? Why?"

"To get your head taken care of, you dope. You ain't been right for several days now, but then you ain't right most of the time anyway. You got busted ribs, too. I told Goodwin you weren't no use to us right now. He agreed, but for a second there, he almost looked a little worried about you. But he put up a fuss when I said I was gonna take the supply wagon to haul your busted-up body in." Kip smiled back at his friend. "So I knew he wasn't goin' soft on you, after all."

Del pondered that. Why'd Goodwin sign him on in the first place? Likely would have been better for both if he hadn't.

"Who's this?" Del eyed the unconscious man.

"That's Ed, the one got shot off his horse by the rustlers. In a bad way. Hasn't come around since."

Del looked at Rodrigo. The boy stared at him with wide eyes, but then his eyes were always big, brown saucers. "Come here...son." Rodrigo inched toward Del. "You all right?"

The boy nodded.

Del wished he knew what was going on in that young head. Must still be a terrifying place. "Kip, you bring any grub on this picnic?"

"Sure did. Check that burlap bag under your head. Lots of good stuff in there, if you ain't already squished it."

Del turned toward the bag. "Ahhgh!"

Kip laughed again. "I swear. Didn't I just tell you you had busted ribs? Have Rod get it."

Rodrigo motioned to Del to lift his head. The boy pulled the bag out and loosened the drawstring. Corn pone, pemmican, and coffee beans spilled forth. Del looked the contents over. "You sure do know how to pack, Kip." He reached for the pemmican and started chewing. He handed several pieces to Rodrigo. "Even my teeth hurt." He spit the rest of the fatty jumble out. "Got any coffee?"

"Nah, that'd just keep you awake, and I like you better asleep. Water's behind Rod."

"His name's Rodrigo, amigo." He nodded toward the canteen which the boy handed him. He took a bigger swig than he should have and coughed himself sick, all the while with a hand to his aching head and the other on his cracked ribs. Rodrigo patted him lightly on the arm. When the pain subsided, Del's eyes drooped, then closed.

He was startled awake when the wagon hit something large in the road. Soon, the ride smoothed out and his heartbeat returned to normal. He started to stretch, but sharp rib pain stopped him. "What time of day is it?" He tried to sit up but sagged back to the wagon bed.

"It's gettin' on to the afternoon. Wind always picks up this time of day."

"How long 'til we get there?"

"No tellin'. We just might get lucky and sneak on into Ft. Sumner before that storm to the west hits us. Or before the Mescaleros do. Then again, we might not. I'd say keep an eye out for both, but the only thing you're seein' is a canvas sky right now anyway. Dirty one at that. Don't smell so good, neither. Wind's to my front, though, so I'm fine, thanks."

Del drifted off to Kip's laughter. He woke to the sound of wind slapping canvas against the iron hoops that supported the cover. The wagon wasn't moving.

Kip bustled in from up front. "Damn, that wind's cold. We're stoppin' here for the night. Couldn't do more'n scatter some feed and set out a bucket of water for the horses—too blustery." He shook his head and drew his coat tighter. "Let's break out that feast I brought for dinner. Just the three of us so we ought to have a high old time eatin' our fill." He reached for the burlap bag and drew the pemmican out.

Del slowly rolled to one side and pushed himself to

a semi-seat. His insides were on fire. He took several short breaths. "You shouldn't have gone to all the trouble, Kip." He picked out a hard biscuit and tried to chew it. A swig of water helped. "This here's a right nice dinner. Only thing missin' is a waiter and the silver."

Kip smiled. "The silver? I thought you brought it. We probably ought to circle back for that."

A small grin creased Del's face. "Don't bother on my account. Rodrigo, you need to eat somethin', boy. Kip, help him with some vittles, willya?"

Fffffft! Fffffft!

Arrows buried themselves in the side of the wagon. "Get down! Stay below the wooden sides." Kip scurried to the front and peeked out under the bouncy seat. "There's three of 'em flankin' us. They look like Comanche from here. Too dark to tell. Oughta be about as cold as we are, too."

"What'll we do?" Del's heart was in his throat. His first thought was about the boy. He worked himself up to a crouch, holding his side. He dragged a blanket over to Rodrigo. "Get under it and don't move!"

Two more arrows found the wagon. Another twanged into the front seat. Kip jiggled it free and brought it back inside. "Thought they might be Comanch, but markings on this shaft say they're Apache all right. Mescalero. There's likely more where they came from, too. We've crossed into their territory now. No tellin' what they intend to do, they're just sittin' out there flingin' arrows at us. Could be they're waitin' to see if we'll fire back. Only thing we got goin' for us is they don't know how many's in here. Or how we're fixed."

Del's thoughts raced. The Indians hadn't shot the pull horse or their horses tied on back. That would have been easy to do. "If they were gonna kill us, they could have already killed the horses. Why don't we cut our two trail ponies loose? See if that's what they want."

"That's better thinkin' than I've come up with." Kip drew a knife from his boot and knee-walked to the rear of the wagon bed. He slid a hand out of the canvas, blade extended.

Whhhit. Whhhit. Two more arrows slammed into the back.

One slice of Kip's knife and the rear horses' reins dropped free. They drifted away.

Del drew his pistol and peeked out under the canvas. The pain almost paralyzed him. He rested the gun on top of the wooden side rail and tried to breathe. He said, "Kip, get the wagon horse to hurryin'. I'll keep an eye on things back here."

Kip reached out and snapped the reins laying under the front seat.

Del kept his Colt trained on the three Indians as they side-stepped their mounts toward the two pack horses.

Kip managed to draw the wagon away at a distance. "Hope those arrows were just to get our attention."

The Indians held rifles at the ready. One grabbed the trail horses' reins and pulled away, while the other two eyed the wagon. They turned and disappeared into the night.

Del exhaled and dropped back to the wagon bed. He lay still for several minutes while his body dealt with the pain. When the worst eased, he arm-crawled back to his spot in the middle. They should have been dead. He lowered his head on the burlap bag and let his hurt subside again. His breathing slowed. He forced his eyes open again. Rodrigo lay still under the blanket. Del pulled it off. "You okay?"

The wide-eyed boy nodded. He crept closer to Del.

Kip dropped back inside. "It's all right; they're gone now."

Del stared upward. "Not happy we lost those horses, but glad that's all they wanted. Should we stay here tonight or keep on?"

"My guess is this's the safest place to be. When those braves lead our horses into their camp, the rest of 'em likely won't come out and bother us. Tomorrow may be a different story."

Del wiped his bandana across his forehead. "That was awful close, even if they were only after horses." His eyes drooped. "I gotta get some shuteye. Wake me and I'll spell you," although the idea of him keeping watch was probably crazy. "Daylight can't come quick enough to suit me." Del got as comfortable as he could laying on the unyielding wooden bed. As much as he needed it, sleep would come hard tonight.

Chapter Ten

Maybelle Lawson regarded herself in the wavy hotel room mirror. Green satin dress that set off her attractive face. Fine bustle, matching pale green parasol. Light brown hair up, slightly mussed, but it would do. She put a hand to her side and winced. Still tender, a year later. She didn't know if she had the courage to pull this off, but she'd spent months preparing. Her eastern upbringing—speech, clothing, manners—had come back surprisingly well after being out here so long. On the coach trip here to Sinola, she'd considered turning around and returning to Santa Rosa. Fooling her would-be killer and coming out of this alive was going to take all the luck she had. It needed to be done, though—not just for her, but for her son's family. And Ansel, she supposed.

She took another look in the mirror. Was that firmness or uncertainty staring back?

When she first arrived at the Sinola hotel, the desk clerk said they were full. She'd glanced at her new banker, who had accompanied her to the small lobby.

Graham Bunch stepped forward. In a syrupy voice, he'd said, "Mr. Lawrence, I'm sure you have a room, perhaps a suite, for Mrs. Perkins? This is such a nice establishment—that the bank owns." He said it so smoothly Maybelle wished she had the same composure. Bunch arched an eyebrow at the clerk.

Lawrence reddened. He looked down at the registration book. Pages flew as if he was searching for a vacancy. He turned back to the banker, a smile pasted on his face. "Why, yes...here's a room I must have overlooked. Just happens to be our best in the house." He wiped at his upper lip. "It also appears to be ready, ma'am. Shall I have your things brought up?"

"No need, thank you. Mr. Bunch's men and I will see to that."

The clerk smiled the most excruciating smile Maybelle had ever seen.

With her valise safeguarded in her room, her heartbeat finally slowed. Back downstairs, she grasped the banker's arm.

He said, "Shall we continue our discussion in more comfortable surroundings?" At the bank, he settled Maybelle into the large stuffed chair in his office. "Now, madam, I trust your journey here was uneventful?"

"Why yes, your two men provided ample security. The wind was near-dreadful, though. I got blown by so much dust in the coach I must look a mess." She waited.

Bunch held a hand up. "Not at all, why I couldn't even tell you'd just traveled here. You look wonderful...uh, fine."

"You're too kind, I'm sure." She fanned herself.

"No incidents, nothing unexpected?"

"Thankfully not. This Territory is not what I imagined when I got off the coach in Denver, though. But then, I have so looked forward to experiencing the American West. My imagination just gets the best of me sometimes. What I've seen of New Mexico is so different from Ohio. Dear me. Will I ever get used to it, Mr. Bunch?" She drew his name out as she said it.

Bunch's smile looked somehow forced. "Yes, of course. Just wait until the desert greens up in the coming months. Quite pretty, actually." His face reddened.

This was going to be easier than she thought. At least with Bunch.

"Madam, it is most important that we provide a safe repository for your valuables. Gold and the like, did you say? I'm proud to state we have never been breached." He glanced around quickly. "As long as I'm here, you can be assured your money is safe with me—us. Might I ask, madam, how you came to choose our fine bank?"

"Why, Mr. Bunch, you are modest to a fault. I inquired of others of my station, of course. Which bank in this part of New Mexico Territory has the most sterling reputation? The name of your establishment kept coming up. Surely, you're aware of the esteem in which you are held." Maybe she was pouring it on a bit thick. She'd back off. "A simple choice, really." Coy smile.

"That is always gratifying to hear, Mrs. Perkins. You don't know the half of trying to maintain the bank's image in this...this wonderful example of the wild west."

"Then your repute is well-founded." She curled a hand around her parasol. "I suppose you have other large depositors? I wouldn't want my wealth to feel lonely in your safe. I also wouldn't want to be the only target of robbers. If there were any, of course." She forced a smile.

Bunch's chair squeaked as he straightened up. "Most certainly not, madam. Several notables keep their money here, all of the highest character I assure you. Why, the biggest rancher hereabouts trusts his money with us. Has for years. Sizeable holdings he has, too."

"That is indeed reassuring. If I fancied to meet him, perhaps you would introduce me?" Maybelle put on her best demure half-smile. What would Bunch have to say about the rancher, her real target?

"Why certainly. That can be arranged, and I'm just the one to do it." He leaned forward. "Now then, not to be crass, but how much money are we talking about, madam?"

Maybelle leaned back in her chair and waved a hand in the air. "I don't rightly know, it's all so confusing. Some is in cash, some in gold coin." She'd exchanged some of the coin for currency in Denver before coming here. "Perhaps you could give me an idea." She knew exactly how much was there. "I'm sure you've dealt with this kind of thing before." She gave him what she hoped was a demure look, calmer than she thought she'd be.

Bunch grinned. "Why, yes, I'd be happy to appraise whatever you've brought."

Maybelle nodded. "It's all in that valise in my room…Perhaps you'd like to come up?"

The invitation hung in the air. A pause. He flushed. "Well…it might be better to assess it here, ma'am. Better light and all. Security." He wiped at his brow. "Can you have my men bring it to the bank?"

"Why yes, it is a bit heavy for me. I have a pain in my side, you see. Must be from the ride here." That and the gunshot from Tyson's sidekick last year. "Why don't I have them bring it down?"

"Fine. I'll have my clerk escort you."

"Lovely, thank you." The pleased look on Bunch's face told her she'd pulled off this first part of her deception.

Maybelle returned from the hotel, Bunch's gents lugging her brocade bag. They hefted it onto Bunch's desk where it made a distinct *klink*.

The bank clerk said, "That sure is heavy, ma'am."

Bunch hurried in. "That'll be all, Navin. Thank you." The young man stepped back, eyes glued on the maroon prize. Bunch dismissed him again, and he backed out the door. "Shut it, please." A nod, a thunk, and they were alone. Bunch took center stage as Maybelle feigned disinterest. "Now then, um…may I open it?"

"Why, of course."

The banker undid the leather latches atop the satchel. His eyes grew wide as he stared inside. "My, my, Mrs. Perkins. This is quite a…tidy sum. Quite. Wherever did—" Bunch stopped. "No one followed you here, did they? I mean, from the hotel to here? Did you notice anyone watching my men carry this?" His glance darted around the windows.

"I don't believe so, Mr. Bunch. You make it sound perfectly dangerous, though." Her heart had been in her throat the whole time as they crossed to the bank.

The banker's eyes were already fixed back on the contents. "I don't know quite how to do this, Mrs. Perkins. Count it, I mean. Can't very well just tally the coins here on my desk. Out in the open." He looked out the office window toward the town's only saloon. "Yes, well, why don't we retire back to the safe. More room. Nice locking mechanism there." He started to reach for the bag then stopped. "Uh, may I take this there?"

"Certainly." She was enjoying his unease.

The banker called out. "Navin, unlock the cage and put two chairs in there, then come help me." The two men hefted the bag and placed it on a wooden table in the middle of the secure enclosure. Bunch stared at his clerk. "Go get something to eat." He swung the cage bars closed. A smallish bank safe stood like a sentry against the far wall.

The lad loitered outside the cage. "But sir, it's only ten o'clock."

"Better to eat early than late I always say. And lock the door on your way out. Turn the sign to closed. Goodbye." When the clerk disappeared, Bunch wiped his brow with a hanky. "Now then, madam." He turned the bag over. Currency and coin littered the table with a steady tinkling sound. The coins formed a golden pile a good foot high. "My goodness. There must be five hundred double eagles here. How did you—"

Maybelle raised her index finger. "Perhaps five hundred fifty-eight…or thereabouts. My late husband was a land speculator back east. He was good at his business, apparently." She brushed at her hair, allowed herself a small smile, and folded her hands back in her lap. Bless Ansel for stealing all this. One of two good things he'd ever done. Del was the other. Still, she'd never have found the gold if the barn hadn't burned to the ground. A fortune glittered among the ruins.

"At twenty dollars each, that would be…" Bunch unlocked the cage and grabbed an ink pen and paper from the teller's window. He clanked himself back in the barred room. "That would be…" He whipped the pencil over the paper and stared at Maybelle. "Eleven thousand, one hundred and sixty dollars!"

"If you say so, Mr. Bunch. I've never been good with figures."

Small beads dotted his upper lip.

She patted her hair. "Plus the cash, I think. How much is that?"

Bunch hunched over the bag counting hundred dollar bills. Moisture beaded his forehead. "One hundred thirty, one hundred thirty-one." He glanced up. So that's…let's see…thirteen thousand one hundred dollars. A total of…with the eleven thousand… uh… twenty-four thousand one hundred dollars. Goodness gracious—"

Maybelle cleared her throat. "I'm sorry, plus what did you say before, another one hundred and sixty dollars?"

"Why yes…that would be…twenty-four thousand two hundred and sixty dollars." He wiped his brow again.

"Oh, my. That sounds like a lot of money." She was enjoying his reaction.

Bunch stared at the fortune spread before him. "Is there any more? I mean…I don't mean…"

Maybelle chuckled to herself. "Let me just say this is all I'm prepared to deposit at this time." A nice response if she did say so herself.

Bunch nodded. "Of course. Yes, well, I'll have to double check this and all. You understand."

"Certainly. Should we do it now?" Another demure smile. The banker was hers.

Chapter Eleven

The jarring wagon ride was taking its toll as afternoon turned to early evening. Del didn't even have a bottle to beat back the pain. He shook slightly and licked his lips. Every time he winced, Rodrigo did the same. Del was sure the wagon bed came from the hardest wood to be found anywhere. The wounded drover lay unconscious nearby. Del yelled through the canvas opening up front. "How much farther to the fort, Kip?"

"We ain't gettin' there any faster 'cause of your askin'. Just lay back and enjoy the ride."

Del grabbed at his side as they bounced out of a large dip. More a dirt trail than a road. Dusk must be making it hard to see. "You tryin' to hit all the ruts this road has? 'Cause it feels like you're doin' a pretty good job of it."

"I keep aimin' for 'em, but some slip by. Want me to go back for a couple I missed?"

Del shook his head. "Why don't we stop and break out something to eat? My stomach hurts as bad as my head. Plus, Ed here smells pretty ripe."

"Your call, cowboy."

"You know I ain't a cowboy. Don't know their ways. Don't hardly fit in. Guess Goodwin can see that." Here he was, a small-time dirt farmer on a cattle drive. In over his head.

Kip shouted back. "There's a little grove just ahead. I figure we're shut of the Indians, too, so we can likely breathe easy. They got what they wanted last night." He pulled the wagon to a stop and peeked into the wagon bed. "So what's on the menu, Rodrigo? Anything left?"

The youth grasped the burlap bag and dumped the contents. He pointed to the greasy, last pemmican bar, sandwiched between a couple of small biscuits. Coffee beans lay scattered. What Kip would give for a hot cup right now.

Del said, "You eat something, boy. You too, Kip. Guess I ain't as hungry as I thought." He lay back on the wagon bed and waited for his heart to slow. Every movement pulled at fading strength.

Kip raised Del's head and held a canteen out. "You're first, Lawson. Don't argue, just drink some."

Del sipped from the hand-held water jug. And coughed. "That's enough, Now, you two."

Kip split the pemmican bar into thirds. He handed one piece to Rodrigo and gave another bit by bit to Del. Worry framed his face. "I'm gonna sit here 'til you finish that."

Del tried to chew the fatty mixture. No saliva.

He reached for the canteen, but Rodrigo already held it near. What was he going to do with the boy? He couldn't keep wandering the country with him. His son's best friend, but he hadn't uttered a word since that night. Del had all but ignored him this past year, but still the youth tagged along. What was going on in his head?

Del took another small sip, then rested the canteen back on the wagon bed. He couldn't tell how he felt, other than awful. His head pounded harder now than yesterday. One eye seemed out of focus, like his mind. Was Kip saying something?

"Don't you go dyin' on me, Del Lawson. I ain't here to cart your big carcass around. Like Goodnight did with Loving. Finish up and let's get out of here. I don't cotton to spendin' another night on the trail. Figure we oughta just ride through the night and get to the fort. Ed here don't look like he's gonna make it much farther." Kip laid a hand on the drover's chest, then his neck. Burning up. "Can't tell, but if he's got a pulse, it's hidin' pretty good."

Del fought to form a thought. "Whatever you think best, Kip. We're just along"—shallow breath—"to keep you company." Even that sapped his energy. He needed rest—lots of it.

"Don't think the Mescaleros will hit us again tonight. They like early morning, just before dawn. We need to be a lot closer to the fort by then. Think you can handle me hurryin' faster down this bumpy trail?"

Del groaned as he lay back. "Guess I'll have to. If we're gonna go, let's get a move on. Slow bouncin' ain't any better'n fast bouncin'."

Kip disappeared out the front and soon the wagon jolted to a start. "Hyyyah! Hyyahh! Get up!"

Del pursed his lips hard. Night sounds crept into the wagon bed behind the hustling of the horse. Sounded like a coyote—no, it was a wolf. The howl settled him a bit, somehow. Wolves always seemed to calm him; he didn't know why. Smartest animals he knew. The canvas cover flapped steadily in the brisk wind. Rodrigo crept close, and the boy's eyes drooped. He soon lay next to Del fast asleep. Warm where he nestled. Del glanced at Ed. Still, pale.

Kip shouted from somewhere.

Del willed himself to a slight rise. Deep night. How long had he been out? Lightheaded. He said, "What's wrong?" in more of a croak than anything.

"Got a feelin' somethin' or someone is out there. Closing in on us, too. Don't think it's Indians again. If it was, we wouldn't even know they was anywhere near. I hear faint hoofprints pounding behind us, drawing nearer."

Del rolled over on his stomach and muffled a cry as he eased up off the wagon bed. He steadied himself against the wooden wagon side. His heart raced. "Rodrigo, fetch me that rifle." Del chambered a round. "Get down! And stay down!" He struggled to the back and snuck a look. Looked like five riders—no, six, seven—galloping their way out of the darkness. Not Goodwin's wranglers. Whoever they were, they weren't friendlies. Del targeted the lead horseman and blew him out of the saddle. He paused to catch his breath and glanced back again. Sweat beaded his forehead and ran down his cheeks. His hands shook. The riders drew back some. They split, coming on both sides of the wagon.

Del tried to think. Focus. "Kip, take the ones on your right." How far was the fort now? He felt a lurch. Must be Kip laying a whip to the horse. Bullets split the air as he hunkered behind the flimsy sideboard. Wooden shards flew as the assault continued. He had to return fire. He leveled the barrel on the top board and inched the canvas up. A rider closed in on his side with a flaming torch. Del struggled to hold the rifle steady. *Pow!* He missed. The night rider flung the flame and broke off. The wagon filled with the sounds of Del's panic. "Rodrigo! Down! Kip, on your right!" Wagon wheels protested, swerving left, now right. The wagon shuddered as if it was coming apart. Del expected to see the cover's curved iron ribs spring away in the night.

The torch struck the canvas but bounced off into the darkness. The horseshoe-shaped rear opening was likely their next target. That's where he would aim. He arm-crawled there and positioned his rifle on the wooden lip of the drop gate. No time for careful aim. A galloping rider filled his vision. Another torch. Del fired. The man tumbled from his horse but not before winging his flame skyward. This time it hit its mark. The oily missile struck the canvas opening, and a blaze spread in a golden semi-circle above Del's head.

The wagon careened down the dark road, tipping crazily on the right two wheels first, then swerving back up on the left. "Kip, hold it steady, or this thing's a goner!" The wagon made one last stagger, teetered on the right wheels again, then crashed on its side, spilling everyone and everything. The horse struggled to a halt, then broke free of its harness. Del struck the ground hard. He lay groaning as dust and confusion filled the air. He looked up to see Rodrigo crouching near, holding his shoulder. A rider closed in, leveling a rifle at him with a barrel as big as a cannon.

"Watch out!"

A shot from behind him and the man dropped. Del tried for his gun but couldn't get his arm to cooperate. Rodrigo pulled the pistol out, but Del couldn't wrap his fingers around the stock. The boy brought it up against his own shoulder and fired at the riders rushing their way. A bullet whizzed by Del's ear. Good thing it missed. He couldn't move if he tried. They were closing in, no more holding them off.

A different sound arose from somewhere. Was that a bugle? He couldn't turn to see, but small arms fire from a new direction tore through the night sky. The nightriders broke off, firing back over their shoulders as they bolted. Rodrigo huddled behind him. Kip slid to a stop by his side. Six mounted troopers streamed around the wagon, two bracketing it, the other four already after the retreating bandits.

A voice called out. "You all right?"

Kip said, "No! We ain't all right, and it's a good thing you showed. You from the fort?"

"Yeah, sentries heard gunshots and saw a faint fire out this way. Didn't think it'd be Indians, not this time of night, but knew it likely weren't nothin' good. Captain said to see to it. Our boys'll run 'em down, sure as shootin'."

Kip walked to where Ed lay sprawled in the dirt. He rested a hand on his neck then shook his head. "Don't know if he gave up the ghost in the wagon or if the wreck done him in, but he's gone."

Del said a little prayer for the man. That could have been him—still could be. He put a hand to his pounding head, then lay back, still. He wanted to look around for Rodrigo, but couldn't. He shook his head slightly. Who said, 'Watch Out' during the attack? Wasn't Kip.

Rodrigo?

His vision faded.

Chapter Twelve

Del tried to blink, but his crusty eyes wouldn't cooperate. He forced a hand to his face and pried them open. The modest log room seemed dim and blurry. A small oil lamp in the corner of the tidy room gave off a faint glow. No light through the little window. Must be night. Everything hurt. He shook slightly. A rope hugged him to the bed. Where was he? A voice interrupted his scattered thoughts.

"Mr. Lawson. Welcome back. My name is Rose Lyle."

Del turned toward the sound. A pretty young woman sat in a nearby chair, knitting. Hair a tan blonde. Pleasing face, serious look. A large brown dog lay nearby, ears perked toward him. He tried to speak, but nothing came out. His mouth was parched and his tongue a foreign object. He worked a bit of saliva up. In a croak, he said, "Where…am I?"

"Fort Sumner. And this is as close as we have to a doctor's office."

"How long—"

"You didn't miss much. Just a couple of days away from that cattle drive you've been on."

Two days? He'd been out that long? Who was this woman? And why was she here? He shifted his legs on the bed. They still worked, sort of. He tried to push up off the cot but the pain in his left arm got the best of him. Where was Rodrigo? And Kip? He knew his head was a mess, but what about the bandaged arm? His whole body ached. He strained against the rope.

"Your arm may be broken. Maybe not. Elsewhere, you're more bruised than anything. How long since your last drink?"

How'd she know? "A while."

"You're not shaking as much today. If I take the ropes off, will you stay in bed?"

Del nodded. She struck him as the kind of woman you listened to. She leaned over him, undid the knots then drew the cords off. He was alert enough to be stirred by her closeness.

The woman took a sip of what Del guessed was coffee. An aura of someone who knew something you didn't surrounded her. And yet she looked about the same age as him.

"Here, take a drink of water."

He sipped from the tin cup and forced his mouth to work again. "Who...are you?"

She dipped a small piece of cloth in a water bowl and placed it on his forehead.

The cool sensation cleared his head.

"I told you already."

"But why...are you here? Where's...the doctor?"

"My father was the camp doctor. He died recently...suddenly." She turned away, ending the conversation.

Del stared at the rough lumber ceiling. He wasn't sure what that meant. He wasn't sure of much of anything. His pounding head made him wish he was still out. "Where's Rodrigo, the little boy?"

"He's with your friend, doing fine. He spent most

of the last two days watching over you. Doesn't talk much, does he?"

But Rodrigo *had* said something out on the trail, during the attack. He was sure of it. Or was he imagining it? The way his head was working, he couldn't be sure. "Where are they?"

"Post adjutant's got them bedded down with the enlisted. You can see them in the morning."

Del nodded. "If it's all the same, I think I'll leave now. Thank you for tending me. Obliged." She was prettier now that things weren't so blurry. Hair up in a bun. Proper dress. Starched? Eyes that looked light green in the dim light.

"You're welcome, and when you can walk out of here without falling down, you can leave. Try sitting first."

Del forced himself up, then slowly swung his legs over the side of the bed. He righted himself with legs dangling, a hand to his head. A knock at the door and Rodrigo and Kip were ushered in by…what was her name?

Rodrigo swiped his hat off, eyes wide.

Kip removed his as well and strolled Del's way. "*Buenos días, amigo!* Good news. You don't look any worse than usual. Same sour face, too. You must be feelin' okay."

"I'm doin' all right. Time to be gettin' back on the trail."

"No hurry. Goodwin and the boys pulled in this afternoon. They're all bedded down, nice and cozy. Herd's grazing a stone's throw away. We'll be here a few days, dickerin' over cattle for the fort."

Del started to get up. The room spun. He put both

hands on the edge of the bed and sat back. Sweat beaded his forehead. "Need a second, and I'll head out with you."

Rose stood to the side, arms folded. "You aren't going anywhere, Mr. Lawson. Another bump from falling off that bed and your head will likely be as useless as…"

She didn't finish the sentence, but Del got the gist. He lay down and glanced at his visitors. "I'll just stay here tonight and see you boys at breakfast. Go with you then, okay?"

Rodrigo nodded.

Kip shook his head. "You ain't the smartest drover we got. Here you are, a pretty woman tendin' to you and you want to leave for some bad-smellin', foul-mouthed wranglers? Your head must be still messed up." Big smile.

Del ignored that and eyed Rodrigo. "I thought you were talkin' now, boy. Didn't you say somethin' to me on the trail? When we were bein' attacked?"

Rodrigo looked away.

Del frowned. "By the way, Kip, who were those varmints? Did the soldiers catch 'em?"

"There was at least four of 'em left after two got shot, and I guess they split up in the night. Troopers brought back a couple but looks like the rest got away." Kip smiled. "Soldiers are politely questioning the ones they caught right now."

Del beckoned his friend over. He pulled Kip close. "Bring me a bottle when you come back, hear?" His eyelids fluttered. "I just need a little shut-eye…" He tried to block out the pounding in his head. His thoughts drifted as sleep stole over him. What was her name again? Time enough to ask when he woke up.

A pleading voice roused him. He glanced toward the anguished sound. Dim moonlight streamed through the small front window. He could just make out a dark form on a small pallet to the side. The woman talked in her sleep. Surely that wasn't what she usually slept on. No. She must have given him her bed. What was she saying? Mumbling.

"I don't want…don't you dare…go!" She tossed and turned on the little raised platform. A hand flew up. "No, no nearer…Oh!"

A last gasp and the woman lay quietly, as if dead.

Del struggled up and steadied himself on the edge of the bed. A few deep breaths and he pushed off the cot. He shuffled to her and bent down. The dog stood stiff-legged watching him. His head throbbed. Should he touch her? He reached a hand out, then drew it back. A little dizzy. Not his business, ought to go back to bed. He stood for another moment, then put a hand lightly on her shoulder.

"What…?" Her eyes opened and she shifted his way. "What?"

"It's just me, ma'am. You were having a bad dream, sorry to startle you." Del dropped his hands to his sides. The pained look on her face seared him. Whatever she was dealing with was tormenting her. Like the raid on his family did to him. He stepped back.

She brushed a hand over her eyes. "Thank you for waking me. I'm sorry for disturbing you. I don't know…things get blurry when the dream hits. Sometimes I can't tell if I'm asleep or awake."

Del nodded. Her thin army blanket had slid mostly off in her thrashing. Pale moonlight couldn't hide her attractive features. She grasped the blanket and drew it back over her high-collared long gown. Brushed a hand through her hair.

Del cleared his throat. "You need to sleep in your own bed. I can make do here on this."

She started to protest, but Del held a hand up. "Won't hear of anything else. Please change places with me now."

"But you need a comfortable place to recover. I'm fine here."

"You already got me through the worst of it. I can get the rest of the way on that pallet just as well as that bed." He motioned that direction and stood aside while she made her way there, blanket drawn tight. He eased down on the raised wooden platform. As he worked his aching body flat, rough slats pressed on his tender ribs. Maybe this wasn't the best idea he'd had today. But he was here, and that's where he was going to stay.

Morning found him with his eyes still open as golden sunlight stole through the small window. He'd been careful not to shift much. It hurt, and he didn't want to disturb her. What was her name? Del reached his good arm to the floor and unbent himself from the curl he'd lain in for hours. Stiff. Painful. The dog raised its head off the blanket on the bed. Good looking hound. Big enough to give an intruder pause. Dark brown with white socks. The look of a watchdog.

His ribs let him know they weren't ready to get up. As he pushed to a seat, his head sent only a muted protest. At least that was getting better. He took the splint off his arm and flexed it. Wasn't broken. Working to a stand, he hobbled to the door. Squeaky hinges betrayed him, and the woman stirred. He looked back. Her longish hair spread casually on the white pillow. In the morning light, it was as if he was seeing her for the first time. Dark green blanket drawn up to her waist. Stop it. She's your nurse. You can't even remember her name, and you'll be on your way soon. Never see her again…

His thoughts were interrupted by a knock on the door. He creaked it open farther to see Rodrigo staring up at him, Kip standing tall behind. He put a finger to his lips. "Shh, nurse is still asleep."

From behind him, "No, I'm not. I'm just waking, it's past time to get up. You all turn around for a minute while I get dressed." The dog stood guard.

Del felt his face flush. He wondered if she'd seen him staring at her a few minutes ago. He turned back to his friends. "Everyone out for a minute." He closed the door behind them and whispered to Kip. "Where's my bottle?"

"Musta forgot."

Del scowled. Rodrigo held a cup of coffee up to him with a grin. Wasn't hot, but still warm enough. "Why, thank you, son."

The door opened, and she called out, "All right gentlemen, I'm decent."

Del walked in with a hand to his ribs. She was so beautiful. He fumbled with his coffee. "Uh…you remember my nurse. Best I ever had." She wore a different dress today. Drawn tight around her waist. Soft morning light danced off her hair. She'd let it down this morning, and it framed her face.

"I'm sorry, I must look a fright."

Del wiped at his moustache. She looked anything but.

Kip broke Del's spell. "My name's Kip, ma'am. Yours?"

"Rose Lyle."

Del cursed himself for not remembering. "Pardon my bad manners…Miss Lyle."

Her eyes smiled back at him. "Rose. The patient is doing better, as you can see."

Kip shook his head. "Don't rightly know about that. From what I see, he may need lookin' after a while longer. He's standin' there like a downright dope."

Warmth rose from Del's neck upward. He usually had a good comeback for Kip's digs but didn't have one for that. He glanced down at Rodrigo for safety. "…Uh, you doin' okay, kid?" An enthusiastic nod. The boy walked over to the dog.

Rose said, "Best you not touch her. She doesn't know you and doesn't take kindly to strangers."

Rodrigo didn't seem to hear her. He put a hand on the dog's strong head, then ran it along the animal's back.

"Why, doesn't that beat all. Haven't seen her take to anyone like that before. Seems Daisy's already your friend." Rodrigo settled down next to the dog, who lay with the boy's hand resting on her back.

Del cleared his throat. He snuck a glance at Rose. "I can walk without fallin' over, which is what you said I needed to do before leavin'." All of a sudden, his mouth was failing him. He didn't want to go yet but couldn't seem to stop his tongue.

She put her hands on her hips and rescued him. "That and when you can ride. You're not going to walk to where your herd is grazing, are you?"

He hadn't thought about that. Good excuse for

staying. Not that he supposed he could ride yet, anyway. "No, guess not." He glanced at Kip. "Maybe tomorrow."

Kip nodded. "Even old Stoney asked about you last night. I told him you were a goner from what I could tell. Those red cheeks of yours say I'm right. Don't think those are from gettin' hurt, though." He chuckled and gave Rodrigo a nudge. "Let's go, little *muchacho*."

Before he knew it, Del said, "Why don't you leave the boy with me? Haven't seen him for a while."

Kip's eyebrows arched. "Didn't know you were gettin' so attached. You know how to handle a nine-year-old by yourself?"

"A sight better'n you." He grinned and motioned to Rodrigo to stay put. The boy's face lit up.

Kip swept his hat in a low bow to Rose and closed the door behind him.

"Let me check your head wound." She made him sit in the room's small chair and unwound Del's bandage. Her faint smell went to his head. Wasn't perfume, it was her. His heart beat so loudly he was sure she could hear it pounding. Rose Lyle. Breathe. Again. Slow down. Fix on something else.

She finished cleaning the gash and wrapped a clean cloth around his head. "There. Healing nicely."

"I am in your debt, Miss Lyle. Again." He beckoned to Rodrigo. Daisy came with him. "You okay? Didn't get hurt when they attacked?"

The boy shook his head.

"Thanks for lettin' me know to duck out there."

Rodrigo shrugged.

"Followin' me around for a year has been hard, hasn't it?"

Another shake of the head, but the boy's bottom lip quivered.

Rose cleared her throat. "Uh, excuse me, but I need some things in the post supply. I'll be back directly. Daisy can stay here." She smiled at Rodrigo.

Before she reached the door, Del called after her. "I could sure use a drink, ma'am. Throat's still mighty parched." If she heard, she didn't say anything. When she closed the door behind her, Del drew Rodrigo close. "I been doin' some pretty stupid things. Puking in saloons, gettin' whipped in fights, sleeping in stables, scroungin' food for you and me. You've seen all the bad, haven't you?" He kept his voice low. Wasn't anything to be proud of or said loud. "Want you to know I'm sorry for not takin' better care of you. Haven't been takin' care of myself." He put a hand on the boy's shoulder. "Not hard to see it's been hard on you. Losin' your family…" He thought of his son and choked up. "Bein' near-killed when the outlaws hit my ranch, not havin' a home anymore, no schoolin', no friends, always on the move, livin' day to day. You seen more than your share of misery for a boy your age. No wonder you don't say nothing. Not sure I would either."

Tears welled in Rodrigo's eyes. He wrapped his small arms around Del's neck and laid his head on his shoulder.

Del's throat seized. He didn't deserve the boy's affection, didn't deserve to be cared for. By anyone. Why had Rodrigo stayed with him? He'd been wallowing so long it was like he didn't know anything else anymore. He wiped at his eyes. "Let's forget the past year, okay?"

Rose bustled in. Del glanced at her sideways. No bottle. He reached for his glass of water.

She laid out a small stack of cloth on her little table, which she began to cut into pieces. Bandages?

"I know what you're thinking—that I didn't bring you a bottle. Never considered it. I don't want you falling down drunk here, ruining all my care. Back on that cattle drive you can drink to your heart's content. Get stupid drunk. Not here." Had she heard what he and Rodrigo were talking about? Their eyes met for a moment. Her gaze penetrated into his soul. He felt naked and searched for something to say. "So maybe I can leave tomorrow? And Rodrigo."

"If you feel up to it. Of course." She stared at him for a moment. "I had an interesting conversation with the provost marshal just now. He asked if I knew anything about you. Said he'd spent some time with the two outlaws they dragged in here. The ones that shot you all up." She continued fiddling with the cloths. "Any idea why those men would attack your wagon? They weren't Indians, just bandits. He said that after a little encouragement, they let slip they were after someone in particular—a man—likely injured. Sounds like they were looking for you." She looked away and started folding cloths.

Del paused. He hadn't been prepared for this. "No...don't know why they would have been after me, maybe they thought we had some valuables." That sounded thin, even to him. The shooters must have been Tyson and his underlings. But Del still didn't know why the murderous cur was after him. "Are those bandages you're making?"

"You know they are. I see you're trying to change

the subject." She unwrapped a cloth bundle of beef and put it in the wooden icebox.

That night, Rodrigo slept on the floor next to him covered with an army blanket. Daisy curled up by Rose on the bed. The next morning, Del whispered the boy awake, but Rose was already up, a respectable wood fire radiating faint warmth. Most of the smoke had the decency to escape via the ceiling pipe, but some lingered toward the top of the small room. Sizzling beef filled the air with a mouthwatering aroma. A coffee pot steamed on the stove.

Rose had them sit at the room's small table. "Rodrigo, would you like to feed Daisy?" The boy jumped up and took the pieces she handed him. "Fill her water bowl, too—from that pitcher, please." She handed Del a cup of hot coffee, his hand steadier. "Are you leaving today?" She turned back to the stove, eyes fixed on a spitting black pan.

Del took a sip. Best he'd had in a long while. He hesitated. "Yes, I believe I will. I'm fine to ride. I'll take Rodrigo with me. Do you know if there's a horse available? Maybe a couple?"

She spoke without glancing back. "…I'm sure you could find one or two in the post corral."

She wore a different dress today. Looked ironed, with a faint floral pattern in white and light yellow. A figure even a loose dress couldn't entirely hide. She started to say something when his mouth took on a mind of its own.

"I won't leave if you don't think I should. I mean, if I'm not healed enough. I could stay…"

She turned toward him with a spatula in one hand, a crumpled, dirty white hanky peeking out of the other.

A frilly lace collar framed her face, her hair done up. "I only have three dresses and you've seen them all now, so you best be on your way."

Regret swept over him. He fumbled for something to say. "Uh...I...how much do I owe you? For fixin' me up and all."

"Did I ask you for any money?"

"No, but I thought—"

"You thought wrong."

Del's cheeks burned. Just then came a knock on the door. A large officer filled the entry. He smiled at Rose. Didn't take off his hat. "Haven't seen you for several days. Been busy nursing these two?"

"Captain Jacobs! What are you doing here?"

The captain didn't look Del's way. Kept his gaze focused on her. "They look right healed. How about you and me going for a picnic?"

Del sized the situation up. Fear flashed in Rose's eyes when she first saw the man. Boyfriend? Her face said no.

She shook her head. Blinked rapidly. "I...can't today. I have to put this place back together. Have to put my father's affairs in order, too." She looked away.

The man's eyes darted slightly at Rose's remark. A long silence.

"Guess that's a 'no', Captain." Del felt adrenaline starting to flow. For the past year, that was usually followed by a fight. He motioned for Rodrigo to move back and rose from the table. Steadier, but not steady.

The intruder laughed. "You got a white knight now, after three days? You always did like taking in strays. This one looks like he can barely stand."

Del clenched a fist, paused, and took a deep breath.

He relaxed his hand and wiped the other across his bearded chin. A flush still warmed his neck. Nothing good would come of tangling with this man. For now, he'd keep his powder dry. Didn't want Rodrigo seeing him fight anymore, anyway. His guess was Rose probably wouldn't like it either. He turned his back on the officer.

The man leered. "What's the matter, dust-eater? And what's that smell? Stinks like cattle crap in here. Cat got your tongue?"

Del glanced back over his shoulder and squinted. "Yup."

Daisy stood with a low growl. Rodrigo grabbed Del's pant leg with his little hand. Silence screamed throughout the room. The man's face reddened. He threw the wildflowers he'd brought at her feet and stormed out. When the door slammed, she slumped into the small chair, shaking. She covered her face with her hands, head bowed.

Del wanted to put a hand on her shoulder, tell her everything was okay, but he knew it wasn't. Jacobs had triggered something deep within her. He didn't know what, but he'd felt her kind of anguish before, wallowed in its emptiness, struggled against its power. He sat on the wooden pallet and drew an arm around Rodrigo. It was some time before she stirred. When she did it was like nothing had just happened. She drew herself up to full height. "I *was* going to say, come back and see me in a couple of days." Her eyes widened. "I mean, not me...but, so I could see how you're doing." She smoothed a quick hand at her hair. "But I've changed my mind. I'm done with all this now. I'm going to pack up and leave." She paused. "Will you take me with you?"

Del couldn't believe what she'd just said. "You're going to leave the post? But…"

"Yes. Been thinking on it ever since my father…died…just haven't had the courage to do it until now. I'm going—with or without you." Her eyes locked on his.

Del tried to gather his wits. He was returning to the drive—no place for a lady.

It was as if she read his thoughts. "A cattle drive would suit me fine until I get to Denver. I'll be no bother. Then I'll head east. Back home to Ohio."

Del rubbed his stubbled face. He didn't know what to say. "I don't…I…"

"If you're wondering who will care for the men here, another army doctor is due to arrive any day. I wouldn't leave with no one to tend them. Besides, I'm not under contract to the Army. They're not even paying me, just feeding me. Housing me in this rundown room."

Del wondered. All this seemed to come from Jacobs' visit. Fear clouded her eyes when she looked at the captain. What was the connection? Del had no right to ask. He'd leave any telling up to her.

She interrupted his thoughts. "I'll be back soon. We'll leave in an hour. All right?" She hurried out the door.

He walked to the window and watched her purposeful stride down the dusty street. She disappeared into the civilian sutler's small tent. It struck Del that he didn't have anything to pack up. Not much to show for twenty-nine years. He turned back to Rodrigo. "We're leaving soon. That okay with you?"

A vigorous nod backed up by a smile. He pointed to the dog with a question in his eyes.

Del nodded.

Rodrigo hugged Daisy around the neck.

Del was as confused, yet intrigued, as he'd ever been. The unexpected feelings came from starting to care about something, someone again, for the first time in a long while.

Chapter Thirteen

Tyson lit out from el jefe's ranch for Santa Rosa. He and his men re-provisioned, then rode south to Fort Sumner. Last he knew, that's where Lawson was laid up. Whenever he found him again, he'd end it. Shoot the boy, grab Lawson, and force the secret of the gold from him. When he found it, maybe he'd steal it all and take off for California.

Tyson sat his horse on a low rise on the New Mexican plain. He held a field glass to his good eye. In the distance, Fort Sumner spread over a middling-sized site that held the only trees for miles around, hard against the Pecos River. He wasn't sure if soldiers were looking for him anymore, or even knew he and his men were near. He *was* sure Lawson was down there in the compound. Lawson was hurt, but he didn't know how bad. The boy was likely with him, too.

He gazed over the broad expanse. Land colored a light brown spread to the horizon. Patience had to be the long suit for vultures that scavenged this harsh country. He thought about his mother's deadly handiwork that put end-dates on his father's and his brother's headstones long ago. He'd put the same date on hers afterward. Thinking of her still made his throat tighten. He missed the eye she'd taken from him but didn't miss her.

Small details of soldiers rode in and out of the

distant fort. Scouting for him or something else? He glanced sideways at one of his men. "Get on down there and search for Lawson. And the boy. Lawson's likely in the post dispensary, hurt. Pretend you're passin' through and need a place to bunk for the night."

"Sure, boss. What's Lawson look like?"

Tyson shook his head. "He's the one that ain't in uniform, dummy. After you find him, go find a Captain Jacobs. Quartermaster staff. Tell him I'm up in the bluffs and I want Lawson. He'll know what to do. Get back here pronto." He watched the horseman shrink in the distance. He pointed to another of his bandits. "You're standin' first watch. The rest of you get some shut-eye, you'll be spellin' him soon." He flipped a saddlebag open and drew out a burlap bag. He let the horse's reins fall to the ground and scattered oats around. While the animal ate, Tyson smoothed a hand over the horse's muzzle then down along the neck. Should give him a name. Closest thing to a friend he'd ever had.

By the time the rider returned, the sun had slipped below the western heights. The outlaw tied his horse off on a scraggly bush. "Was just like you said, Pete. Found Lawson about as soon as I rode inside. They give me a hard time at first, me ridin' in all alone, but I fooled 'em right quick with a story about huntin' buffalo. Saw a captain comin' out of the doctor's office so I walked by the open door. Pretty lady inside with Lawson and a kid." He warmed his hands over the small fire on the back side of the hill. "Asked around about Jacobs. Turns out he's the one what come out of the doc's office. Trooper asked if I was part of the cattle drive bedded down to the east. I said 'yeah.' Went and saw the captain. Told him you was up here and wanted Lawson. Funny look on his face, then I took off on back here."

"'Tweren't smart, that. You don't look like no drover, and if the trooper was quick, I'll bet he kept an eye on you leavin'. You didn't ride off toward the herd, but came direct here, didn't you?"

The man's hesitation told Tyson all he needed to know. He wanted to shoot the idiot but forced the impulse back. He'd likely need every one of these jackals unless he missed his guess about what was ahead. The cattle were bedded down on a large grassy area east of the fort. No doubt the trail boss was dickering with the quartermaster about how many head the army needed and at what price. Damn! He wished he still had those rustled cows. He could have herded them to the fort before these cattle got there and sold them to Jacobs. The man didn't care where he got beef, rustled or not. Time to change his plans. He'd figured to spend the spring carving off head from herds as they drove up the Pecos. Jacobs would buy them and take a cut. To Tyson, it was all profit one way or the other. All the drives came along here, the Goodnight-Loving trail, which skirted west of Comanche territory. Selling rustled cattle was small pickings though, compared to getting the gold coins back. And Lawson—or maybe the kid—were the only ones who knew their whereabouts. Surely Ansel hadn't been ornery enough to take that secret to the grave.

Pretty good plan he'd had to steal the gold. His boss had him wipe out the Spanish don and family. The kid's family. Destroyed the ranch house. Big Spanish land grant from decades ago. He'd heard a hundred twenty thousand acres or more. Rich spread. Cattle, crops, feed.

His gang had surrounded the large bunkhouse that night. Blew it and the vaqueros away with dynamite, then stormed the big hacienda. Caught el jefe and family wide-eyed. The señor held his hands out as if he could stop the bullets. Tyson still saw the disbelief on the old man's face as the rounds tore through his heart. When the screams died away and silence reclaimed the ranch, there was one less body than Tyson figured on. A child was missing, but there was no way to search the mayhem in the dark.

He'd turned his attention to the large safe hidden in a small paneled alcove at the rear of the ruined bedroom. Solid and thick, it boasted elaborate enamel engravings that disappeared when four sticks blew. He'd never heard a more deafening sound. The thick adobe wall he hid behind shook to its foundation. He peered into the hazy room after the blast. Debris littered everything and the sharp stink of gunpowder burnt his nose. He pried the skeleton of the rugged safe open. Thick smoke almost hid the glittering gold coins scattered inside. Had his men scoop them up in burlap bags. Took two to carry them out. Thought about torching the house, but quicker to just ride out. Besides, this spread might be his one day.

They'd hidden the gold deep in a small cave on a rocky ridgeline between the Spanish ranch and Santa Rosa. A large sandstone formation that resembled a stooped old man rose near the entrance. Tyson shook his head at the memory. He'd been careless enough to let Ansel Lawson guard the coins one night. Ansel and another outlaw lugged the bags out of the cave, then stole away. He'd found the accomplice dead miles away. No Ansel. Where had the turncoat stashed the coins?

With Ansel dead, his son was the only hope of finding the hiding place. Seeing him sprawled on the floor in the dark that night, Lawson looked dead. Still, Tyson shouldn't have left him there. He was furious enough to skin his man for near-killing young Lawson but stopped short. If he murdered everyone he wanted to, there'd be no one left. Maybe that wasn't so bad. He'd have the gold all to himself.

An echo of a shot from the fort shook him out of his musings. Maybe they were executing a deserter. In this desert, he could understand how a soldier would be tempted to do that.

Tyson mounted up and stared down at the post. Soldiers would find him soon enough if he didn't move. He'd keep shy of army patrols but needed to stay near. From what the rider said, sounded like Lawson would be well enough to leave the fort soon. He'd circle toward the drive's campsite. Find a way to cut Lawson out from the rest of the drovers. Finish the boy this time, too. He was closing in. He could feel it.

****

Maybelle Lawson started down Sinola's hotel staircase. She fluffed her blue layered skirt as she floated over the steps. The lady in the Denver dress shop said the color made her eyes look less brown. Her banker was waiting at the bottom. "My, but you look beautiful, Mrs. Perkins."

Maybelle curtsied slightly. "Why Mr. Bunch, you do know how to flatter a woman."

"Please...call me Graham."

She knew he was waiting for her to say 'call me Maybelle', but it was too delicious not to. He stood with his mouth slightly open, leaning forward a bit. She extended her hand. He gave it a quick kiss, a shade of disappointment framing his face. "Do you have a dinner reservation for us…Graham?"

"I most certainly do, the best table in town. Right over there in that corner. Makes for nice, private conversation."

"Why, Graham, are we going to need some privacy?" She batted black eyelashes at him.

A blush reddened his neck. "Well no, but I just thought, um…this way, ma'am."

She had wriggled him at the end of her fishing pole long enough for now. "Thank you." A pause. "And do call me Maybelle, won't you?" He brightened. Dangling the man was going to be fun. She let him pull the chair out to seat her. This was one of the nicest rooms she'd seen since she was a child back east. Before she came to this hard, barren landscape. Burgundy velvet wallpaper and dark wood wainscot. A patterned tin ceiling and a small chandelier radiated a thin veneer of gentility. A stocky waiter brought a menu. Bunch reached for it. "Shall I order for both of us?"

Ire rose in Maybelle's throat. The arrogance. "Why that would be lovely, I'm sure, but I do always like to look over new menus." Pasted-on smile. "May I?" She saw him blanch slightly. Serves him right. Give me that.

"Certainly." He handed it to her.

Maybelle considered. She wasn't used to eating in fancy restaurants, although she had done just that recently in Denver, where she'd changed some of the gold coin for currency. The banker didn't need to know that, though. She stalled for time, fancy names obscuring what the dishes actually were. She'd seen a well-dressed woman in that Denver restaurant sweep a fashionable arm in the air while talking, so she did the same. "This hotel is very nice, the dining room in particular."

Bunch looked pleased. "Yes, finest around. We're lucky to have Elijah Wilkins nearby. He holds papers on the place. I mean the bank owns it—through Elijah. He's the one with the big spread I mentioned earlier. About five miles out of town. Richer than Midas. Right good fellow."

"So this Mr. Wilkins is one of your depositors?" She smiled broadly, hoping her question had come off casually.

Bunch leaned in with a conspiratorial little smirk. He whispered, "Can you keep a secret?" He glanced around the room. "So happens he's my biggest depositor. He has company now, though." He beamed her way, eyebrows arching.

She reflected on that. Bunch just revealed something she had hoped was true before she came here. Wilkins *did* have his money in this bank. She'd use Bunch to get close to him. Figure how to meet the bastard who'd dispatched killers to murder her family. Her husband, Ansel, wasn't much, but he didn't deserve to be run down like a dog. And Del. He'd disappeared after being nearly killed. Where was he? And oh, her sweet grandson. Shot dead. Her heart hurt when she thought of how terrified he must have been that night. She forced back tears. Wouldn't do to start crying for no apparent reason in front of Bunch. She'd use him to ruin Wilkins. All in good time, though. Meanwhile, she'd draw the banker in more.

He said, "Are you all right? You look flushed."

She gathered herself with a clearing of her throat. In a thick voice, she said, "Yes, fine…I feel even more comfortable hearing that." A hanky to her warm neck. "He obviously puts great trust in you. As I do." Her false smile hid a broken heart.

"That is so nice of you to say, Mrs. Perkins. I…we…pride ourselves on providing worry-free banking." He almost giggled, as if he'd just said something worth remembering.

"Again, please, call me Maybelle. I'm sure we'll be seeing a lot of each other."

Chapter Fourteen

Del went over the last few days in his mind. Rustled cattle, sudden stampede, Indian and outlaw attack on the way here. First time he'd been on an army post in his life. Then there was Rose. He stared out the small room's window onto the post plaza. How did she figure to leave the fort? He glanced at Rodrigo. "Come sit by me. I want to show you something." He pulled a small knife out of his pocket. "Watch what I do with this piece of wood." He'd retrieved a stick of firewood from the stove's small woodpile. He shaved the rough outline of a steer, forcing his bad arm to work. "Want to finish it?"

A quick nod. The boy reached for the wood.

"Just see the animal in your mind, then you can make it come alive." He handed the knife to him. Rodrigo set to it as if whittling the steer was the most important thing he'd ever done. His little hands worked the knife over. He pursed his lips when he came to a rounding part.

The boy had seen too much for someone his age. Del wiped at his cheek. Rodrigo was his last connection to his son. A son he might be whittling with now on their front porch. When the boy finished, he held the carving at arm's length in triumph.

"Now, that is a nice job, Rodrigo. I can see this steer at the head of the herd, bawling for the rest to

102

come on."

Rodrigo's smile was sunshine in the small room.

The door opened, and Rose strode in. She carried a medium-sized bag. "All my worldly goods are in this valise. Including my medical equipment. Sad, isn't it?"

Del knew better than to say anything.

Rose glanced sideways at him. "So, everything's ready. You?"

"Yes, we're ready to go, but...I thought you might want to wait until it's dark...darker."

"Daylight suits me just fine. Come on, Daisy." She grabbed her satchel and was out the door without looking back. The drive's supply wagon waited outside, repaired, horse hitched, some provisions in the bed. As Del boosted Rodrigo up, he heard a booming voice behind him.

"You aren't leaving are you, Rose? Trying to slip away?" Del turned to see Captain Jacobs walking toward them. "Sergeant, take this wagon back to the stable. Bring the cowhand and the boy to my office. They're wanted fugitives."

Rose yelled. "Stop! Don't you so much as touch those two. You are a killer and a traitor, Jacobs. You murdered my father after losing to him that night at poker. You said he shot himself in that alley? Ha! The man never held a gun in his life, much less fired one. You wanted him dead so you could court me, because my father knew what kind of a butchering skunk you are!" Troopers gathered behind the captain in a loose semi-circle on the fort's main square.

She pulled a small gun from a side pocket of her bag. Aimed it at his face with both hands. "I'm gonna shoot you exactly where you shot my father. Right in the middle of the forehead where what passes for your vile brain is." She cocked the hammer, aimed, and fired. The bullet whizzed over his head. "The next one goes through your skull."

Jacobs extended his hands toward her. Fear filled his face. "Sergeant Major, disarm that crazed woman. Must still be overcome with grief. Talking nonsense." The sergeant major didn't move. The post commander came out of his office and stood on his porch. Jacobs turned to his men. "Soldiers, take her down!" They stood motionless. "She's gonna shoot me, Sergeant Major, I order you to kill her."

"Belay that order, Sergeant Major." Lt. Col. Mangess strode forward. "I've heard Miss Lyle's accusations and will not allow her to come to any harm. I've also heard idle rumors about you being involved, Jacobs. We'll conduct a proper investigation and find out if those are true. Stand down, Captain."

Jacobs turned to the colonel. "But there weren't any witnesses…" He stopped.

A corporal spoke up. "That ain't exactly true, Colonel. I was a little drunk that night and saw him shoot the good doctor in the alley. Stumbled away, I did. Should've said somethin' before but him bein' a captain and all…"

Colonel Mangess approached her. "I am truly sorry for your loss and the trouble you've had here. You've given my men excellent care even after you no longer had to."

The pistol shook in Rose's outstretched hands.

Mangess said, "Put the gun down, please."

Del approached her, hands in the air. "Please lower it, Rose. You don't need it anymore; you've already done the bastard in. The army will see to justice for your father."

Her bottom lip trembled, her face red as the unit's colors. "This is your lucky day, Jacobs. My guess is the army won't like a killer in their midst." She turned to Mangess, eyes locked on the man who would decide the assassin's fate. He nodded. She dropped the pistol to her side, chest heaving.

Mangess said, "Rest assured, I will see to him, Rose. Sergeant Major, form a detail and escort Captain Jacobs to the stockade." He turned back to her. "Is there anything I can do for you?"

"Yes. Do right by my father. And me. Be the commander your men already think you are. I'm leaving. Jacobs is your problem now."

He turned to the sentries. "Open the gates!" He bowed low. "I wish you well, madam. We all do."

Del took her by the arm. He didn't know what to expect from her, but he hadn't expected that. He helped her onto the wagon.

She grabbed the reins. "I'll drive. Your arm may not be broken, but it's still not right. Just get me headed the right direction."

"But you're still shaking, maybe I should—"

In a quavering voice, she waved him off. "I could drive this blindfolded if I had to. Anything to get away from here, so please sit and keep me company. Daisy, come on, girl." The dog jumped into the wagon bed with Rodrigo.

Del wasn't sure what to think. Maybe she didn't believe he could handle the wagon yet. Maybe he couldn't. Worse, Del hadn't been out to where the herd was grazing, but Rodrigo had. "Rodrigo, show Miss

Rose where camp is." The boy beamed and pointed east as Rose drove through the gate and onto the seemingly endless prairie. She brushed the fort's dust from her dress.

As they rumbled along, Del pondered. He'd never met a woman so straightforward. So matter of fact. Not even his wife. He rubbed his hand over the mangled bullet around his neck. Rose was stirring up feelings he'd just as soon were left asleep. He'd been more or less happy on the drive, or at least what passed for happiness these days. The track they took bounced the wagon. His head was better, but the ribs still protested at the thumps. He peered over his shoulder to see if anyone was coming after them. He glanced sideways at her. Her bottom lip trembled. She stared straight ahead, white-knuckling the reins. He laid a hand on her arm. "Stop the wagon, please."

She didn't look at him. "Why?"

"Would you mind stopping for a moment?"

"Are you all right? Head hurting? Ribs?"

"No, I'm fine, but I'd appreciate it if you'd stop."

She pulled the work horse to a halt. They were still in sight of the fort, a dwindling dark blotch on an otherwise empty light green plain. "We need to find the camp before it gets dark."

"We still have time." He wasn't sure how to say what he wanted. "I'm sorry for what happened back there. Sorry about your father. And you. I didn't know how terrible the place had become for you." He waited.

Stony silence, then the dam burst. "My father was a wonderful man. A good doctor, he cared for the men in that fort. Looked after them." She paused. "But he wasn't a saint. He drank, he gambled, but he didn't deserve to be killed. Jacobs is a murdering..." She left it unfinished. "I only stayed this long because I—I don't really know why I stayed." She wiped at a cheek. "We'd better get moving." She fixed her eyes on the horse. "Thank you...for stopping...and listening..." She snapped the reins. The old horse strained against the horse collar around his neck, and the wagon rolled again.

Del looked back at Rodrigo. He sat in the wagon bed near the front seat, petting Daisy. The boy smiled. Del was likely the nearest thing to family the boy had left. He wasn't sure he wanted that responsibility, but he had it anyway. Even if he didn't care about himself much, he felt a need to keep track of his son's friend. Was he ever going to say anything? Maybe Del could find a way to bring him out of his shell, get him talking. Then again, he hadn't wanted anyone intruding on his grief this past year. Maybe Rodrigo didn't want any help either. He hoped time would find a way of softening the edges of both their pain.

The rest of the ride was spent in near-silence, other than Rodrigo pointing and Rose asking the occasional, 'this way'? Del had pushed her enough. He didn't want her—or anyone else—digging up his past, so he'd let the rest of his questions about her simmer. There'd be time on the drive north, if Sammons even agreed to take her.

But he wondered if that was true. Once the drive got going again, there wasn't much time for talking about—things. He'd stash his feelings back in their dark hole, like he'd done a lot recently. His thoughts turned to the drives' wranglers. No doubt Rose would be a hit. He had no special claim to her...nor she to him. Figuring Rodrigo out was enough to handle for now.

The camp soon came into view in the distance. Cattle covered a large area this side of the Pecos. A thin column of light gray smoke rose from a lazy campfire as if a beacon. Del's heartbeat quickened. He hadn't thought about the reception he'd get from Goodwin until now. The foreman would probably accuse Del of slacking off in the fort dispensary. And what about when the trail boss saw Rose? Would he let her stay? He could handle the foreman's barbs, but what if Stoney slighted Rose? Could he control his reaction?

Soon, they were within hailing distance of camp. Del tried to let out a shout, but it came out as a high squeak that disappeared in the thin air.

Rose said, "Don't strain like that. Your body doesn't like it, and they can't hear you."

"Yes ma'am."

She pulled the wagon up at a distance from camp and turned to him. "You worried about something?" Without waiting, she said, "I saw that look on your face. If I had to guess, I'd say you were wondering what the trail boss was going to say. What the drovers were going to think. Whether I'd be safe."

A blush warmed Del's face. "Just about right. I reckon these cowboys haven't ever had a drive with a woman on it. Don't know how they'll feel. Let me do the talkin' to start, okay?"

Rodrigo clambered up on the bouncy seat between them. Del scooted to one side. He didn't know if he'd ever seen a bigger smile on the boy's face.

Rodrigo pointed toward the chuck wagon, where Buck must be.

Del hoped Goodwin wouldn't wipe the smile off the boy's face.

Or his.

Chapter Fifteen

It was nearly dark when Tyson and his men pulled into Santa Rosa. He figured Lawson's cattle drive was still camped south near Fort Sumner. There was plenty of time to catch up to them—they'd be coming his way. In the meantime, he'd bide his time in more pleasant surroundings. After paying for a room at the boarding house, he headed to the saloon, trailed by his men. There were five now, six with him. He'd lost some during the night attack but picked others up on the way here. Bad hombres seemed as plentiful as snakes.

He ran the conversation with the boss through his head. He wasn't sure why he did Wilkins' bidding anymore. El jefe couldn't even see. Time to stop taking orders from him. He hit the swinging doors and burst into the saloon.

The bartender looked up and his mouth turned down.

Tyson said, "Hey, you—yeah, you. Never can remember your name." He'd seen the man a number of times over the years. "Pour me a couple whiskeys. Better yet, give me the bottle." He surveyed the room. No empty tables. He picked one out and stalked toward it, bottle in hand. He said to the three lounging men, "Find another spot to drink your lemonade."

One of them squinted his way. "We ain't drinkin' lemonade, and I ain't partial to leavin'. And you ain't big enough to make me."

"Didn't say you wanted to leave, said you was goin' to." He placed the bottle on the table and dropped his hand casually to his holster. Spread his legs slightly. One man rose to the challenge. Tyson pointed at him with his other hand. "Why don't you start walkin', mister? Right out that door. You'll live longer. Tonight's not the night you want to die, is it? I can tell from your miserable face it ain't." He said to the other two, "Y'all get gone, too. I'm tired and grouchy—but that's when I do my best killing. One, two—"

Wooden chair legs scraped backwards on the bare floor. The three slunk away while several other tables cleared out. Tyson yelled at the bartender. "Fetch me something hot to eat and be quick about it."

The bartender hurried out the open front door as Tyson's men strolled in.

Tyson yelled after him. "Get us *all* some food." He wasn't in the mood for chatter.

"What's the matter, Pete?"

Tyson planted his elbows on the table and rubbed his forehead with both hands. "I keep killin' people, but it don't seem to get me nowhere. I'm tired of it."

Skinner said, "Tired of the killin'?"

"No, dummy. Tired of the not gettin' anywhere. Drink your drink. I ain't talkin' to none of you anymore tonight. When you've got yourselves good and drunk, get back to the stable. Be ready to ride out in the morning."

"What about the food, Pete? We're awful hungry."

"Tell the bartender, not me. And tell him to bring my dinner to my room." He threw back two more drinks and gazed around the place. It was the first time

111

in—he couldn't remember when—he hadn't shot up a saloon. Relief showed on scattered faces as he left.

By morning, Tyson's mood hadn't improved. Darkness still dogged him as daylight broke. He swung up and growled at his men. "Y'all better be ready to ride long and hard today. Anybody falls out we leave 'em. Or worse." He dug his spurs into his horse's flanks. The animal leaped away. He knew the horse couldn't gallop all day, but he was ornery enough right now to put him to the test. Why was he always so angry? The men straggled behind, struggling to keep pace. He mulled over why they stayed with him. He wouldn't stay if he were them. But then, gold was a powerful draw. Seemed like he could do anything he wanted to them, and they'd shake it off. Worthless no-accounts, all. He prodded the horse south toward Fort Sumner. Stark brown landscape flew by. As morning clouds cleared, his foul temper lifted, and he eased up on his mount.

Several miles of tamer trotting passed before the horse's breathing returned to normal. Foam trickled off the animal's sweat-soaked neck onto Tyson's pants, threatening to plunge him into a fury again. He took a deep breath and wiped at his trousers. The fort wasn't far now. Jacobs would know if Lawson was still there. Likely the boy, too. He didn't really care about killing the boy anymore—despite Wilkins—what he wanted was to whip the gold's whereabouts out of Lawson, like he'd tried with Ansel. The greening-up plain gave way to darker, low hills in the distance. Tyson had been over this land so many times he didn't need daylight to orient himself. The fort sat just this side of that notch in the hills ahead. His men caught up to him. "Keep an eye out for Indians, boys. They don't much attack during daylight, but you can't never trust what they'll do."

Skinner said, "Say, Pete, why you been drivin' so hard? Lawson'll still be wherever he is whether we get there today or tomorrow."

Tyson pushed back his irritation at the remark. Time to ease up. Give these crooks something new to hold onto. He'd been riding them hard long enough. He faked a smile. "I'm feelin' generous. First one finds Lawson and the boy gets an extra helping of gold coin." He was surprised at his own thoughtfulness. "...And drinks tonight is on me. Less'n we find Lawson first." Maybe he shouldn't have said that. He'd just given them a reason to get drunk instead of hunt.

A small dust cloud rose in the distance. An army patrol approached from the west. As far as he knew, he wasn't wanted for anything that they knew about. Besides, they weren't the law around here. Not that there was much of that anyway. A circuit marshal was all. "Keep your mouths shut, hear? I do all the talkin'."

"But we can outrun 'em with the head start we got, Pete."

"Now why'd we want to do that?" He wanted to thrash Skinner but took a deep breath. "They ain't lookin' for us, but they'd be after us lickety-split if we was to skedaddle. Just sit tight, like I said." Tyson scoped the troop with his eyeglass. Led by a lieutenant by the look of things. Regular Indian patrol probably. They closed on his small band. When they were within hailing distance, he called out, "Howdy, Lieutenant, glad we ran into you."

The officer held a hand up to halt his detail. Ten

uniforms, all outfitted with good-looking Winchesters and Colt 44s. "Identify yourself."

Tyson feigned a friendly smile. "Name's Pete Tyson, from Texas, and these are my men. Off my ranch. We're lookin' to join up with a cattle drive headin' north. You seen any around here lately?"

The lieutenant squinted at Tyson. "If you're lookin' for a drive, you must have passed one or two already on your way up here."

"Why, we shore did, Lieutenant. Shorely did. What I meant to say was we're lookin' for the lead drive. I always did like frontin' everybody else." He turned to his men. "Ain't that right, boys?" They nodded in unison. "What brings you out this way, Lieutenant?"

"Searching for Mescaleros who been raiding ranches around here." He dropped a hand to his pant leg. "Also heard about some bandits attacking a wagon on its way to Sumner."

Tyson thought fast. Change the subject. He'd mention Jacobs, that ought to give the lieutenant pause. "Fort Sumner? Why, we're headed the same direction. Know a fella there, a Captain Jacobs. You must be familiar with him."

"Jacobs, eh?" The lieutenant's face darkened. "What's your business with him?"

The officer's curt response surprised Tyson. "No business, just thought I'd pay him a visit, long as we're this near."

The lieutenant squinted. Talk died away. His men shifted in their saddles. "Don't know as you'd be able to see him in the stockade."

"Huh? What'd he do?"

"Ain't no business of yours, but he's been

skimming money. In league with someone he's buying rustled cattle from. Also facing a murder charge. Not someone I'd be bragging about being friends with." The lieutenant unsnapped the leather flap over his holster.

Tyson ran his tongue over dry lips. Damn! "Didn't say we was friends. Always thought he was a little shady." He shouldn't have mentioned Jacobs, but it was out there now. "Thanks for savin' us a trip. Guess we'll head back over toward Goodnight-Loving. Try to hook up with a drive there." He noticed the troopers behind the lieutenant moving hands toward their holsters. He heard his men rustling behind him. Don't anyone do anything stupid. Last thing he wanted was to get in a shootout with soldiers.

The lieutenant leaned forward in the saddle. "Maybe you ought to accompany me back to the fort. Throw down your guns. We'll escort you there."

Tyson considered his options. If he rode to the fort with the detail, Jacobs would surely finger him as the rustler. So it was either face a deadly future there, or vamoose. Not that he'd get far trying to outrun the patrol. Or he could…he fast-drew his Colt and aimed at the officer. "Anybody moves and I plug the lieutenant. You may kill me, but I'll get him and my men will get most of the rest of you, too. Y'all throw your hands high." He motioned with the barrel for his gang to spread out behind the soldiers. "Ready to die today, Lieutenant?" No response. "No?" He didn't dare look, but no doubt his men had guns at the ready.

"Now, one by one, throw your pistols and rifles on the ground. Start with the last man. You there. Slow and easy. Good. Now, you next. That's right." When he'd disarmed them, he said, "I'm willin' to let you live, Lieutenant. Feeling charitable today. But I'm movin' off. I'd be most upset if you followed, so Skinner here is gonna mind you and your men while we take our leave." In a loud voice, Tyson said, "Anyone so much as moves, you take the lieutenant's head off, hear?" Skinner pointed his pistol at the officer. Tyson leaned close and whispered. "When we're over that ridge to the east, shoot one of 'em. They'll be busy tending him, so ride for us fast as you can."

"Won't they light out after me, Pete?"

"Not if you scatter their horses and keep firing behind as you gallop. There's extra gold in it for you, so hurry on back." Tyson spurred his mount east toward the low hills in the distance, trailed by all but Skinner. When he reached the top of the rise, he heard a single shot. He didn't turn or break stride. A minute later, several more shots. He smiled. One less share to divvy up. He wouldn't have thought it at the time but running into that patrol had been a fine thing.

It was shaping up to be a pretty good day.

Chapter Sixteen

Del had Rose pull the wagon up at the chuck. Buck
stood by, spatula in hand, grinning ear to ear. Mr.
Sammons looked toward him from a low campfire,
coffee cup resting on a knee. Del turned toward Rose.
"Let me help you down."

Rose shook her head. "No helping needed, or
wanted, cowboy. If I'm going to be on this drive, I'll
need to stand on my own two feet." She smiled.
"Maybe I should help you down."

"Don't you dare," Del said in a low voice. "Can't
let these roustabouts see you doin' that." He eased to
the ground. "Let me introduce you." He walked her
toward the trail boss. "Mr. Sammons, this is Miss Rose
Lyle, from the fort. Rose, this is our head man, Mr.
Sammons."

Sammons touched a hand to his hat brim with a
slight nod. "Tom Sammons, ma'am. Nice to meet you.
Good to have you back, Del."

Del nodded, then glanced around.

Sammons must have seen him searching. "Stoney's
not here. Out on the range, tendin' to bad-tempered
beasts and rowdy drovers. Be back soon enough." He
turned to Rose. "How can we help you, ma'am?"

Del cleared his throat. "I invited her, Boss. Rose is
the one healed me up at the fort. She'd like to join the
drive, here on up to Denver. Long story, but she did

117

such a good job, I'm a sight better than I used to be." For one thing, his shakes were gone. He forced a slight laugh and waited for a response.

Sammons ran a hand back and forth across his stubbled chin. "Don't know. Never in all my born days have I had a woman on a cattle drive. Need to percolate on that some…meanwhile, why don't you show Miss Lyle around camp?"

"Thanks, she'd probably like eyeballin' what passes for our medical wares. Likely she's got better'n we have. She's pretty good at doctorin'."

Kip strolled up. "Did I hear you just say she's pretty?" He bumped Del out of the way and doffed his hat with a low bow. "Kip Holloway at your service, ma'am. Nice to see you again." He grinned sideways at his friend.

Del stammered. "I said she's pretty…I mean she's good at…you know what I meant!" A flush warmed his face. He didn't dare look at Rose. He slowed his breathing and recovered. "Kip here used to be my friend."

Rose grinned. "Nice to see you again, Kip Holloway. I hope you'll take better care of this cowboy next time he's in a scrape."

"I don't know, Miss Rose. Looks like he hit the jackpot getting busted up and havin' you tend him. Wouldn't be surprised if he don't find a way to get hurt again soon."

Del shook his head and motioned to Rodrigo. "Let's go introduce Miss Rose to your friend Buck." Daisy trotted next to them as the three walked toward the chuck wagon. Rodrigo's little hand grasped Del's. He snuck a look at the boy, who was gazing up at Rose.

The start of a smile creased his mouth.

Rodrigo ran and hugged Buck, who lifted him in the air. "Where'd you get to, son? I been lookin' all over camp the last few days and couldn't find hide nor hair of you."

Rodrigo looked like he wanted to say something but just pointed in the direction of the fort. He smiled broadly at the little circle of people surrounding him. A tug on Buck's sleeve and he petted Daisy.

Del pursed his lips. His throat seized. He couldn't have spoken if he wanted to. He was the closest thing to family Rodrigo had left in this world. The boy should have latched on to someone else. Like Rose. Caring for others wasn't his strong suit anymore. And a cattle drive was no place for a boy with no family, no roots. But then *he* didn't have any roots either these days. Even spring grasses had something to hold onto. And what was he going to do if Mr. Sammons said Rose couldn't stay?

He looked back at the trail boss. Sammons stood by the middling campfire talking with Stoney. That didn't look good. Anything Del suggested, like Rose joining the drive, was sure to rile the foreman. Del walked their way. Sammons shooed everyone else away. He said, "Son, why don't you join me by the fire?"

"Thanks. Have you decided if Miss Lyle can stay, Mr. Sammons?"

"Come and sit a spell…that's good. What I am about to say is not about Miss Lyle, it's about you." He held a handful of small twigs. Del was used to seeing him toss them into the campfire at night. "You seem lost, Del Lawson. Ever since you joined the drive.

119

Don't know what's eating at you, but it's there. I recognize the look. Been there myself." He tossed a twig into the flames. "My guess is now you think you can find your way back through Miss Lyle. Is that pretty much it?"

"I don't feel lost."

"A man does not always see what he is. And you and Goodwin have been toe to toe every single day. Why do you think that is?" Another twig went up in flames.

"Don't know, sir. Seems like he set against me almost before he even laid eyes on me."

"You hold him a grudge—want to square him up, right?"

Del pursed his lips. Fighting the foreman probably wasn't a good idea, but it appealed to him, nonetheless.

"No need to answer, I can see it in your eyes. They blaze at the mention of his name. I could fix that for you...but I won't. A man settles his own troubles. But you have worse worries than Stoney Goodwin. Something else is gnawing at you, deep in your gut. Until you deal with that, you will drift with the wind. Your anger at Goodwin isn't about him, and your new hope about Miss Lyle isn't about her. The turmoil you're feeling comes from inside you. And things won't change until you deal with those troubles." Another twig disappeared in the flames.

Del couldn't believe what he was hearing. Where was all this coming from? Sammons hadn't uttered more than a few sentences during the whole drive. All Del wanted to know was if Rose could stay, nothing more. Just answer that. He didn't need any talk about being lost, whatever that meant. He was doing fine.

Him and Rodrigo. All right, maybe not fine. Him with a hole in his heart and a boy with no words. Quite the pair. A blush warmed his face, but it wasn't from the roaring fire.

"You disagree?" The boss waited. "And that boy. You can't help him until you help yourself. Until you set things right inside here." He pointed to his chest and flicked another twig. Stared Del down without looking at him. "End of the day, though, I believe you will. I have seen enough to know something about your character, even though you hide it under false bravado. About all you have going for you right now is Rodrigo."

Del's eyes misted. He resisted wiping them—he just wanted to be gone. He didn't need any of this. It was like the man was peering into his soul, uninvited. But his body wouldn't move. He fingered the bullet around his neck and forced his mind back to what he came to find out. "I…don't know what…" He bowed his head in silence…His thick voice came out in a whisper. "Can Miss Lyle…stay?"

"Yes. She can. And she is welcome to tend to us as she sees fit. We will escort her to Denver. From there, she can find her own way to a new life." The last of the twigs disappeared. "You ought to be ready, though, for the dangers you will face from here on out. Not because of her, nor Stoney. How you handle yourself the rest of this drive is how you will handle the rest of your life." He rose. "Goodnight, Del Lawson."

Del watched the man disappear into the gathering dusk. The trail boss had scrambled his mind, just when he thought he was starting to figure things out again. No one had ever talked to him like that. Deep down, on some level, he knew the boss was right. His thoughts turned to Rose. He glanced around for her. Goodwin stared at him from a distance, arms folded.

Kip hailed him as Del walked back to the chuck wagon. "What was all that yammerin' about? You tryin' to get in good with the boss? Get Goodwin off your back? Get off night ridin'? Get extra rations?" He punched Del on the shoulder.

Del didn't even know how to answer that. "No, it weren't any of the sort. I'm not sure what it was, exactly. But I *can* tell you, there's more to Old Tom Sammons than first appears." At the wagon, Rodrigo ran to him, Daisy loping along. Del gathered himself. "How you been, son?" The boy pointed toward the working end of the chuck wagon. "What's up?" Rodrigo grabbed him by the hand and pulled him there.

Rose stood next to Buck, who was fast at work in his chuck box. Her eyes were fixed on something he was whipping up in a cast iron skillet. She looked fascinated by what he was doing so quickly and so well. Del couldn't tell what the mixture was, but it had a faint cinnamon smell to it. Buck ladled some for Rodrigo to sample, which the boy slurped enthusiastically.

Buck grinned. "Guess it's okay if Rodrigo takes to it. But then he likes 'most everything." Buck dribbled a little into Daisy's wooden bowl. "Spell me for a bit won't you, Miss Rose? This particular dish takes a lot of stirring."

She said, "What is this, Buck? It looks like cheese mostly."

"Yup. Savored it first in San Antone. Mighty tasty on bread. Liked it so well I set my sights on getting the recipe. Had to whip a woman at poker, though, to get it.

Took me near all night. Then I collected on the…second part of the bet…when she lost the last hand. A good memory." His ears reddened a bit, and he didn't lift his eyes from the pan.

Del glanced at Rose to gauge her reaction. She didn't look up either, but the corners of her mouth turned up slightly. He said, "Reckon you've found a new hand to go along with Rodrigo, Buck. A whole lot better lookin' than you, too. With Rose helpin', you got no excuses for your bad cookin' anymore."

Rose turned to him. "Does that mean the trail boss is going to let me stay?"

"Yup. He said you can practice fixin' us up on the way north, too." To Del's mind, she looked very pleased at that. "Speakin' of fixin' up, we need to do something about your clothes." She wasn't outfitted for a cattle drive. Her dresses would set her even further apart from the cowhands than her sex already did. Buck looked about her size. Maybe. Probably not. Close enough, though. "Come dinnertime, I'll introduce you around. Tell you who to stay away from, mostly." Stoney and Jake Potter came to mind. He gazed at the campfire which Buck and Rodrigo stoked higher for dinner. Good way to ward off the cool evening air, too. A couple of the drovers sat in the fire ring, idly glancing Rose's way from time to time.

****

Rose watched Rodrigo throw another piece of firewood into the flames. He beckoned to her. His little hand flew, as if to say, 'hurry!' She hesitated. What was she doing, leaving the fort in the middle of this wilderness with nowhere to go? The few happy times there were—from another lifetime it seemed—

overwhelmed by the sad ones. She didn't belong in this heartless desert anymore, wasn't sure she ever did. Rodrigo grabbed her hand and pulled her to the fire, pointing to the towering flames.

Del came over and offered her a cup of coffee. "You're lookin' a mite sad. What's on your mind?"

"Nothing, I'm fine; there's just been a lot lately." Rodrigo gave her hand a slight squeeze. She looked down into his downcast eyes. Now, she really wanted to flee.

Del said, "Thank you again for mending me up." He threw a twig into the fire and cleared his throat. "I've never been an easy man to help, never wanted anything from anyone…so thank you."

She glanced sideways at him. "You're welcome." She leaned toward Del and whispered. "Guess I better not pout; I don't like seeing that face on Rodrigo."

Del put a hand on the boy's shoulder. "Why don't you help Buck get dinner ready, son? Looks like he could use it."

Rose watched him scamper back to the wagon. "What's he like to do? Hard to figure what he's thinking when he doesn't talk. Did he ever?"

"Yes. He used to." Del looked away. He didn't know much about what Rodrigo liked to do. Realized he didn't know much about the boy at all. "Just about time to eat."

"So that's it?" She stared into his eyes, not allowing him to escape. "That's all you're going to say?" Before she could corner him further, a voice rang out.

****

"Hey, you two. Don't want to interrupt your cooing

at each other, but there's work to be done." Kip flashed his broad smile as he came their way. "I told Goodwin you wanted his job, Del. He said fine, take it. Well, that's not exactly how he put it. Something about shoving…"

Del shook his head. "Enough of this dancin' around. I don't even know what we're talkin' about." He headed toward the wagon, when someone called his name.

"Del Lawson. Come here, please." Tom Sammons motioned to him from the campfire.

"Be right there, Boss." Buck handed him a cup of coffee, and he walked back to Rose. "Sounds like it's time for you to meet the boys."

The drovers gathered, some with thumbs hooked in pants pockets, others with arms crossed. All dusty, most smoking hand-rolled cigarettes. A faint stink of old sweat drifted on a light breeze. Stoney Goodwin stood like a statue, working a chaw in his mouth. He spat. "Ready to go back to work, Lawson? You look like crap. Restin' up hasn't helped your looks none."

Del squinted. Don't say anything. Not the return he'd hoped for, but not a surprise either.

Rose leaned close and whispered, "You two don't sound like best friends."

So she'd noticed it, too. There wasn't much Del could say to that.

Tom Sammons surveyed the circle of men. "Boys, this is Miss Rose Lyle. She's going to be joining us for the rest of the drive up to Denver. She's a nurse, but hopefully none of you will need her services."

One of the drovers piped up. "All of a sudden I don't feel so good, Boss. Got chills and sweats at the same time. May bear some lookin' into."

Sammons chuckled. "Sounds like something night duty would cure. Doubles in fact."

"Uh, startin' to feel better already. Think we oughta keep her, though, never can tell."

The drover Del tangled with that night out by the herd—Jake Potter—spoke up. "Never been on a drive with no woman." His tone was hard.

Sammons squinted at the man. A ring of cigar smoke rose around him. "I shouldn't have to say this, but I will. You all treat her right, or you can draw your pay. Anybody has a problem let me know. Now." He scanned the group. No one moved. "Anything you want to say, Stoney?" Goodwin stood silently. Potter stood behind the foreman. "That's all then. Dinner's getting cold. Regular shifts tonight. Get to it."

Chapter Seventeen

The small buggy seat almost wasn't big enough for the two of them. Maybelle felt banker Bunch press against her as they rode out of Sinola. He hadn't looked that big until they sat side by side. Maybe she shouldn't be out with him. After all, she'd only recently met him. When he counted her money back at the bank, he seemed somewhat fawning, but out here, a bit commanding. Different. She took a quick look back at the small town receding in the distance. Was he on to her charade? She'd played enough poker to know her bluff might be in trouble. She figured she had two choices—come clean about why she was here, or—

She took a deep breath. "Mr. Bunch! I do not appreciate you pressing up against me like I'm a saloon girl. Please move to your side of the seat. I cannot for the life of me think what would have given you the impression you could be so familiar. In fact, turn this buggy around this instant. Take me back to Sinola, and drop me at my hotel." Her heart pounded in her throat.

Bunch's eyes widened. He moved away. "Dear me, Mrs. Perkins, I did not mean to offend you. I didn't realize I was that close. Must be this thick coat. Please excuse my manners; I am terribly sorry."

She sensed control again—she'd bury him deeper, stay on the attack. "I declare. Did you take me for one of those hussies?"

"No ma'am, never. Not at all. I'll escort you back to town, if you will let me. Again, my sincerest apologies." He started to turn the buggy around.

She fanned herself, then extended a hand out by way of stopping him. "Well…your remorse sounds sincere…and I'm sure it won't happen again, will it?"

He shook his head.

"In that case…why don't we continue on to that picnic spot you have been bragging about? Seems a shame to waste this fine day on what turns out to be a simple misunderstanding."

"Yes ma'am, certainly will, right away."

Her rapid heartbeat slowed. Even though Bunch held the reins, she was still in charge.

The passing landscape offered little of interest. They rode on an almost treeless plain that struggled to regain some color. Low bushes dotted the undulating, dry surroundings. Waterless washes told of now-dead streams. A cloudless early spring sky warmed the black buggy. Maybelle wore the expensive flower hat she bought in Denver, hoping it would make her seem more sophisticated.

Bunch broke the silence. "It may not look like much here, but wait until we get to the river."

"What river is that, Graham?" She drew his name out.

"Why, the Rio Verde. I know you aren't real familiar with the land hereabouts, being from back east and all. It's real pretty when it greens up. Of course, not like Ohio, I'm sure."

"I would enjoy seeing it in full glory. The desert seems to have its own beauty."

"Just like you, if I may be so bold, ma'am."

Maybelle pretended to blush. "Again, call me Maybelle, please."

Bunch smiled. He pointed into the distance. "See that run of trees? Over there? The river cuts through this valley right there. Makes for a real pleasant retreat."

Bunch slowed the buggy as they neared. Maybelle had always loved this land, stark as it was. There was a solitude to it that soothed her soul. A good place...*was* a good place...to raise a family. She sniffed and brought a hanky to her nose.

Bunch said, "Why Maybelle, are you crying?"

She shook her head but wiped at an eye. "Just a runny nose, always acts up this time of year around here." As soon as she said that, she wanted to snatch the words out of the air. Bunch furrowed his brow, but she broke in before he could say anything. "It's certainly lovely, Graham. Do you bring all your customers here?"

"Why no, I—"

"I can see why you're partial to it. Splendid trees give it a pleasant shade. Will you help me down?" Had she distracted him enough? "I'll lay out that wool blanket you brought." Bunch held his arms out toward her hips, and she slid into them, resting her hands on his shoulders as he lowered her to the ground. "Do you have a favorite spot, Graham? I'll bet you do."

They spread out near spring-fed gurgling waters. Maybelle flounced her dress as she sat and drew her tan gloves off. "This is beautiful, just so pretty. I wouldn't have thought it so from the drive here." She started fishing. "Do you bring your wife here?" She opened a small basket she'd filled with ham, apple pie, and a bottle of red wine he'd given her.

"Well now, never been married. Just haven't taken the time. Get so busy at the bank. I suppose it could still happen, though."

She noticed he avoided eye contact with her. "I didn't mean to pry, Graham." She wondered if he believed her. "So, no children?"

"No, none."

"No matter, let's just enjoy the day. Why don't you tell me more about Sinola? I'd love to hear about the town and its people." She'd never been here before, although her devastated ranch wasn't much farther than a day's ride away.

"Sinola started out as a way station because of the river. Wasn't more than a dirt street with a couple of buildings when I arrived. The place has grown steadily since, mostly from nearby ranching." His eyebrows arched. "We're well known for having excellent grazing early spring through the fall. Town's nestled down a bit, protected from the worst of the wind by the summits surrounding this valley. The place has been good to me, but recently I've considered—" He left the words hanging.

His unfinished thought piqued Maybelle's interest. "It's very appealing. The land does seem to have been favored. I noticed lots of head—cattle, I mean—on the way here." She wanted to kick herself. "Is this, how do you say, 'open range,' as I've heard it called?" She told herself to speak more simply, as if she'd never been out west before. She reached for the bottle of wine.

"Yes, it's open range, but most of the cattle belong to one rancher, Elijah Wilkins, the bank's biggest depositor, the one I mentioned before."

"So how big would a large herd like Mr. Wilkins' be?"

"Currently twenty-six hundred, all told. I keep close track of most everything Elijah does. Always good to stay on top of things, I say." He looked rather proud about that.

"My, that does sound like a lot. Dear me, how much land would it take to support all those—do you refer to them all as cattle?"

"Yes, cows and steers. Bulls, too. The steers he sells off during the year, mostly to the army at Fort Sumner or to cattle drives heading north. Calves get sold in the fall."

"Cattle drives. That sounds so romantic. Have you ever been on one?"

"No, no place for a soft, beat-up banker."

"Why Graham, you don't look soft to me. Not at all." She batted her eyes. The man blushed. All in all, she was doing a good job recovering. She handed the wine to Bunch. "Would you mind opening this? A glass would be so nice about now."

"Don't mind if I do." He swept his arm in a big arc to the west. "Elijah has more than ten thousand acres." He leaned close. "Can you keep a secret? Just between us?" His eyes gleamed. Without waiting, he said, "Word is he's got his eye on an even bigger piece of land next to his. An old Spanish grant whose ownership recently came into question. Doesn't appear to be any of that family left."

She forced herself not to react. "So they all died off?"

"Yes, after a fashion." He pulled the wine cork out. "Rather suddenly."

"Oh, my. Does he have anyone to purchase the land from?"

"Rumors are there's a young heir, but it sounds far from certain. If none can be found, Elijah will have a clear path to buying it from Territorial land officials. Will end up owning a large parcel of southeast New Mexico."

"That sounds quite ambitious, very impressive." Her thoughts flew as she cut up the cooked meat. Confirmation that Wilkins had Rodrigo's family killed, too. Was she in over her head? "I hope you like ham, Graham?"

"I do have certain sensitivities, but I could possibly eat a small bite without too much trouble."

Such a feeble thing to say. "Good. They brought it to me right from the oven at the hotel, so I hope it's still warm."

Bunch opened the wine and poured two glasses. He filled hers less than his. Maybelle wanted more, but she'd wait. Wine was one of the few things that gave her solace these days. She knew she drank too much, but didn't care. But she'd be careful out here with the banker.

"Such a big cattle ranch. Exciting, indeed. I might be interested in a buggy ride out to visit Mr. Wilkins sometime." She made herself take a small sip. "I would normally receive him in town, but I would enjoy seeing a real ranch, especially one you've spoken of so highly. Would a visit be possible, Graham?"

The banker seemed to puff his chest out. "I would be most happy to arrange that, madam. When would you like to go?"

"Oh...I don't know, I suppose in the next few days.

Of course, if that's not something you could set up…"

"By all means, Maybelle. Consider it done."

She smiled her pasty smile. "I would want you to accompany me, of course." She tilted the glass to her mouth and took another, larger sip. "So with all that land, Mr. Wilkins must have a large family."

Bunch drained his glass. "No, not at all. His wife died a ways back, so now he only has a young son. The boy's back east somewhere in school."

Maybelle drew a deep breath. Wilkins has a son. Her mind raced. So much the better. "This is a delightful wine, what kind is it?" She wanted to down hers and a second as well, but couldn't do that in front of him. Not ladylike.

"Not sure, no label, but Elijah gave it to me sometime back. He's got quite a large assortment. I think he has these brought in by coach from Denver."

"All very fascinating, I'm sure, but tell me more about yourself." She'd learned enough about Wilkins for the moment.

"Don't mind if I do. I must say I take some pride in being successful in a land where most just scratch by. I have given some thought to running for mayor. This town needs a firm hand, and I could provide that."

Maybelle crooned, "I can see that." Egging him on was the easiest thing she'd done in a long while. "Sinola is lucky to have you." She took another quick sip to wash the foul taste of those words away.

"Truth be told, my biggest regret is that I've never found the right woman to settle down with." He glanced at her sideways.

"I still find that hard to believe, Graham. Any woman would be lucky to land you." She wasn't sure she could stand this bantering. "I would look forward to spending more time with you."

He smiled and leaned toward her. "And I you."

"Oh dear, it's getting late. The sun seems to want to vanish behind those hills. As much as I hate to, I suppose we should head back."

"Yes, quite. Let me help you up."

They engaged in small talk on the return, Bunch pointing out the beauty of the land, as if trying to convince not just Maybelle, but himself. At the hotel, he took her hand and kissed it. She wanted to draw it away, but instead said, "A delightful afternoon, Graham. Thank you for taking so much time from your busy schedule."

"My pleasure, Maybelle." Her name seemed to trip easily off his tongue now. "I look forward to our next outing."

She curtsied. "I as well," and was gone inside. She wiped the back of her hand on her dress and climbed the stairs to her room. The picnic had been worth it, though. Wilkins had a son.

An only child.

Chapter Eighteen

Del made sure Rose had what passed for a suitable bed in the chuck wagon. Kip said Charles Goodnight, the trail's namesake, invented the wheeled contraption a few years back. It was getting crowded in there with Rodrigo, and now Rose, but was still better than her bedding down on the cold ground. Buck moved outside, sleeping near the fire with Daisy on guard. The dog let Del ruffle her ears from time to time, pressing against him and looking up for more. Rose helped Buck cook, with Rodrigo at her side. The boy had taken to her. Del felt a tinge of jealousy as he watched Rodrigo follow her around. At least he wasn't always Del's shadow anymore—but part of him wished he still was.

Buck clanged the dinner bell hanging off the back of the wagon. He put Rose to work helping serve. Boiled potatoes, with a runny brown sauce and beans, kept salt pork company on the wranglers' plates. Dried apples for dessert were always a treat. Del wasn't quite up to riding yet and felt a little awkward lining up with the rest of the men at meals.

"Hey Lawson, why'd you come back? You ain't no cowboy. Thought you woudda figgered that out by now. Had a lot of time off at the fort, didn't you, while we been bustin' hump out here."

Del recognized the voice behind him without turning around. Jake Potter. He forced himself to stare straight ahead. Rose's uncertain expression caught his eye as she spooned up gravy. Wouldn't do to tangle with the blowhard the first day back. Goodwin probably wouldn't put up with any more trouble from him. Three weeks on the drive and he still hadn't settled in.

"Lawson must be hard of hearing, boys. He brings a woman into our camp and acts like we ain't even here."

Kip moved right in front of him. "Shut up, Potter."

Jake's voice rose. "This ain't no business of yours, black man."

"I just made it mine, you waste of a cowboy hat."

Del faced the drover. "You seem awful interested in me, Potter. Why *is* that? Got a crush on me?"

The men guffawed. Potter hurled his plate to the ground at Del's feet. Kip stopped the bully's rush with a well-placed hand to the man's chest, then held him tight by the collar.

Del's heart raced, and his ears burned. Push it back down. Breathe. "How about we leave each other alone?" He turned away.

"Don't turn your back on me, sodbuster." Potter came and stood an inch from his face. "I don't like the name you just called me, and I don't like your whore either."

White fury stole Del's sight. He punched Potter in the face, but Potter reared back and hit him in the mouth. A scream from somewhere. Del stumbled backwards to the ground, and Potter flew on top of him. The cowhand raised a fist, but a voice sounded before he could strike.

"Don't move, Jake." Click of a hammer. Goodwin stood over the two of them. "Ease up off of him. Now.

Stand up." Rage showed on the bully's face. "Undo your gun belt and leave it on the ground." The foreman released the hammer and holstered his gun. He drew a roll of money from his vest pocket and threw a twenty dollar bill on the ground. "There's your wages, now draw your gear and get gone. Your six shooter stays here."

"You can't be stickin' up for this farmer, Stoney. Why he ain't even—"

"I said, grab your gear. Kip, you make sure of him."

Del watched Kip escort the rogue away. As he started to get up, Goodwin reached a hand out.

Del worked himself to a stoop with Goodwin's help. "Won't stand for no bullies, nor those who disrespect women. You stood your ground, Lawson. There may be more to you than meets the eye. Clean up and get something to eat."

Del nodded. Why had Goodwin sided with him? He'd had a few surprises in his life, but this had to be one of the biggest. He was almost afraid to look Rose's way. She'd warned him about getting knocked in the head again, and he'd gone and done it anyway. He guessed he felt okay, if a little wobbly. He wiped blood from his mouth. Wiggled a tooth he hoped wouldn't fall out. He glanced her way, but she looked down as she slopped pork on plates. Soon, he stood in front of her holding his tin plate out. She didn't even glance at him. Damn! Why was she mad? It wasn't his fault he tussled with that jackass. He didn't start it. He was defending her honor, too. Dammit! He should've turned away. She splatted something on his plate hard, and he almost dropped it. He mumbled, "Sorry," but she had already turned away to the cowboy behind him in line. He grabbed a hot cup of coffee and walked to the campfire.

He didn't know how to feel. He hadn't been back more than a few hours and Rose was mad at him and Goodwin had stuck up for him. He wouldn't have thought either. He shook his head as Kip took a seat next to him. "Can't figure it, Kip. I'm still doin' stuff I tell myself not to do. Keep gettin' in trouble without half trying."

Kip went to work on his plate. "Time you simmered down, Del, but you did the right thing. Can't let the good-for-nothing get away with that, even if it did get you in trouble with Rose."

"So you saw that, too."

"Even a dusty old cow hand like me has eyes. Give her some time to cool down before you go tryin' to make up." Rodrigo came and sat by his side. Del glanced sideways at him. "I didn't put up much of a fight, did I?" Rodrigo shook his head. Del smiled, then grinned, and the grin grew into a chuckle. Kip joined in, then Rodrigo broke into a laugh. Soon, the three of them were guffawing like the kids they still were.

Cool evening breezes picked up as the drovers gathered around the roaring fire. One of them, Carl, the rider Del met when Ed was shot, lifted his voice in song.

"Oh give me a home, where the buffalo roam,
Where the deer and the antelope play,
Where seldom is heard
A discouraging word,
And the sky is not cloudy all day."

The cowboy could carry a tune. Other voices joined in.

"Home, home on the range,
Where the deer and the antelope play,
Where seldom is heard…"

Del was beginning to feel the tug of the trail. He gazed at the darkening landscape. Faint stars drifted to life overhead. They had the evening sky to themselves as the wind chased clouds away. A rare sense of peace came over him. He lifted a silent prayer to the heavens, asking the Lord to protect Rodrigo and see Rose safely to Denver. He finished with words of thanks for his blessings.

Rose interrupted his thoughts. She stood in front of him. "Please stand up. Let me see your face." She leaned toward him and brushed a wet cloth over his open mouth. It came away bloody. He wanted to press her close to him. Those eyes stole his heart. "You have a loose tooth. How is your head?"

"Uh…okay."

She stood back, hands on her hips, a mild frown framing her face. "Del Lawson! You are the most…the most maddening man. Can't you stay out of trouble?"

"I guess you got a right to be mad. You told me not to go 'round gettin' hit upside the head. But I'll let no one call you what he did."

Her eyes crinkled at the edges. "Aggravating cowpoke! Please sit."

"Won't you join me, ma'am?"

She shook her head. "I'll sit next to Rodrigo, thank you." She wrapped both arms around her shoulders.

"Cold?"

"No."

He draped his coat around her shoulders.

"Thank you…I'm sorry…to have been upset with

139

you. I worry…about you…about Rodrigo." Her voice drifted off.

Rodrigo shifted close to her. She put an arm around him with Daisy sprawled at her feet.

Talk died to nothing as flames danced in the cool night air.

****

After breakfast, Del hurried to the remuda.

Laramie greeted him with his ever-present smile. "You on herd this morning?"

"Yup."

"Guess I know who you're lookin' for, then. The big black is doin' good but ain't quite ready to ride yet. You best take another one you can be sure of. Don't want Shade gettin' crippled up." Laramie chuckled. "You, neither."

Del patted the stallion while Shade nuzzled his jacket. The horse had a good memory. Del drew several carrots out of his pocket. Shade had them gone in a wink. He rubbed the big black's white blaze. "Can't take you with me today, fella, but once you're healed up, it's you and me."

Del drew a sturdy-looking roan and rode out with Kip to ride flank. At least Goodwin didn't always put him on drag anymore. Since leaving Fort Sumner a couple days ago, it seemed like everything was going along without a hitch. Rose had become one of the crew, if not one of the boys. Rodrigo spent his time with her and Buck, a perpetual smile lighting his face. Potter was a bad memory. Del finally felt better, too. Ribs, arm, and head all seemed to be in working order now.

He hadn't been able to spend much time with Rose

these last few days, but maybe that was a good thing. For both of them. Buck lent her some clothes that suited the dust and dirt of the trail. Loose-fitting boots, tough jeans, a tan cotton shirt along with a faded green bandana to pull up over her mouth. The duds didn't do much to hide her figure, though.

Bathing was always a problem. Or rather, not bathing. That was another reason Del didn't spend much time around her. Whenever they crossed a stream, he took a few extra minutes to wash up. Kept a small bar of soap handy in his shirt pocket. Once, Kip asked him what the bulge was but he just mumbled something. Del trimmed his beard shorter, neater, too. Buck was an expert with a razor and scissors.

Nights, he'd sit close to the campfire with Rodrigo and Rose. Kip would be in the middle of things, entertaining the boys, sometimes singing a passable Clementine, other times strumming a small fiddle. Del didn't have any such skills. In fact, he didn't have much of anything to offer such a good-looking woman.

Rose didn't seem to mind his company, though. Daisy was her constant companion, so Del didn't worry about her safety. The dog had the run of the camp, scarfing up bits of food from the drovers as they ate. She stayed away, though, until invited to have a scrap. The men ruffled her ears and patted her as if she were their own. The only time Del had seen her upset was when that jackass Jake beat him up. Furious barking then, but Rose kept a grip on her.

The more he was around Rose, the more he thought he didn't measure up. She was educated, pretty, mannerly, smart. He was a dirt farmer from nowhere. His father was a robber, and his mother most likely dead. He'd started drifting with Rodrigo after that night—some son. Still, the drive was passing well enough. Maybe the last of the dangers was behind them.

Kip interrupted his thoughts. "I know you're thinkin' about the chuck gettin' across that river." He glanced sideways at Del. "Shouldn't be a problem, long as the quicksand ain't deep yet. There's only fifty yards or so they won't be on solid ground, and usually wagons can float for a bit."

Somehow that didn't ease Del's mind. This one was extra loaded.

Stoney Goodwin gathered the drovers as morning sun split the eastern horizon. Del knew why the foreman called everyone together. The river ahead had been all the talk the last few days.

"Men, we're headed into the most dangerous part of the drive. We have to cross the Pecos, and at one of its angriest spots. No choice. It's about as high as it ever gets right now with spring runoff. I've sent two men forward to scout the best passage. I'd tell you what to expect if I knew myself. Every crossing's different, and a swollen river is an unforgiving place. See Laramie to make sure you got a good swimming horse. Stay alert. That's all."

Del figured most of the cattle would likely get over all right, one way or the other. Even if some ended up downstream. He wasn't sure how the wagon was going to fare. Daisy would be okay, even if she spilled, but Rodrigo, Rose, and Buck...well that was something different. Goodwin pulled him aside. "Sometimes there's rustlers along the river or hiding in the bottoms. You keep an eye on those in the wagon, we'll deal with any varmints." He rode off.

Goodwin halted the herd a few miles this side of the Pecos for the night. He sent Del and Kip to patrol the strip between the cattle and the river and guard against a nighttime surprise. Moonlight cast faint light on the low surroundings. The sound of rushing spring waters made for a soothing background. Spring sage lent a musky aroma to the night air. Del and Kip walked their horses back and forth along the river for several hours. The two friends took to talking the time away. Del had been curious about Kip ever since they met. "You know how I came to be here, drunk and all, how'd you join up with this outfit?"

Kip was silent for a moment. "It's a long time now since I been anywhere I could call home. Been ridin' these ranges the past few years, ever since the war. Back home in Tennessee, I had my freedom but still didn't feel free. People out here don't seem to mind ridin' with a black man; they're kinda nice, in fact. Don't think you'd agree, but Stoney's got a good reputation. Has always cut me a fair deal. Guess I feel about at home here on the trail as anywhere I've been."

That was good enough for Del. Kip's friendship had made the drive tolerable. The night wind picked up, and clouds rolled in. Del glanced back in the herd's direction. "Hope it doesn't blow too hard, the cattle get restless."

Kip nodded. "They smell water. Think Stoney must have kept them dry today so they'd be all the more ready to hit the river."

Del knew all about restless. And wayward. Like the wind. Even growing up, he'd always thought it seemed to have a purpose. But now, wind had driven him any direction it wanted for too long. Time to make a stand—make things right. Let it blow on by and be gone—find another lost soul to fool with.

Chapter Nineteen

Morning broke low and gray as Del stirred on his bedroll. Billowing dark storm clouds hung overhead like predators searching for prey. Rain pattered throughout the night, leaving cattle and cowhands a soggy mess by daybreak. Worst were the big fat drops that smacked Del in the face. He'd grabbed the Stetson Kip lent him and laid it over his head as he lay sleepless, but it made a bad sponge. His canvas slicker didn't do much to deter the rain, either. He'd been pulling doubles as the stock wouldn't bed down this close to the river. Especially during a storm. When daylight came, he lay soaked under a drenched blanket.

Who was patting him? Del rolled over to see Rodrigo crouching near. At least someone made it through the night dry. A faint smell of coffee drifted Del's way. He needed lots of that, and Buck's was some of the best he'd ever had. He looked around for Rose. There. The only other one who didn't look bedraggled. She bent over the low campfire, stirring something in an open pot. Their eyes met, and she glanced away. He guessed he wasn't much to look at in the morning, sodden hair plastered to his bruised face. He wiggled a front tooth with his tongue. Not too bad, he'd likely keep it. A few hands trailed to the chow line. Time to get up. Today's weather would be another test he could do without.

Del unlimbered from his thin bedroll. Best get some hot food while he could. Dragging to the chuck, he grabbed a plate. He always brought his own dented coffee cup. He smiled at Rose, who gave him a quick one back. Hurt to grin, but didn't hurt to look at her.

He said, "Good morning."

"Yes, it is. Sorry you had to sleep in the rain, you must be freezing."

"Feels like freezing, but hopefully the sun will wake up soon. How did you sleep?"

"Best I've had in a long while. Brisk air helps. That and being cozy warm under cover during rainstorms."

Del didn't begrudge her that. Cotton shirt and pants never looked better on anyone. She made anything she wore look special. He pointed to her skillet. "What's that?"

"Just something Buck and I cooked up. Eggs and cheese all together. Let me know how you like it."

Del sat near the embering fire pit. The sound of rushing water filled the air. He'd never been in a sizeable river crossing. Streams, yes, but this was a full-grown waterway.

There was no hurry in the men this morning as they prepared for the crossing. Kip told him cattle do better in warmer water. They wouldn't be fording until the sun heated everything up some. If it ever did. The gloomy sky didn't look promising. After breakfast, Mr. Sammons stood to the side of the fire, head bowed and eyes closed. Was he asleep?

Goodwin called the drovers together. "Listen up. Dunno if we're gonna be able to cross today, river's still high. I'll let you know as the day goes. We'll break into six swimmers and six herders when we do cross.

Post, Holloway, Anderson, Jingles, Lawson and me are swimmers. The rest of you keep the cattle bunched together and separate them into groups of around five hundred. I'll tell you when to bring your herd forward. Swimmers over here."

Del and Kip warmed their hands around the fire. Springtime still gave way to cool mornings hereabouts. Stoney shook his head as he glanced around. "This is as high as I've seen the Pecos. When we go, the remuda leads, then the chuck. Once they're across, y'all head the cattle forward. Swimmers cross in relays of two. Start a couple hundred yards upstream from where you want to land 'em to handle the drift. When you get to the other side, drive the beeves up and over the bank onto the prairie. Let 'em eat to their hearts' content. They'll be tuckered out so they won't go anywhere. Get 'em settled, then get on back here and grab another group."

He stared at them from under his hat brim. "Wagon's another story. Can't be replaced, nor can the folks in it. We'll tie a tree trunk on each side and attach guy ropes to keep it lined up. Cut a couple cottonwoods down and drag 'em to the crossing point." He waved everyone off and strode toward the herders.

Del shook his head. He hoped they couldn't cross today with the river so high.

Kip said, "No sense mullin' it over. Let's grab axes and get to it."

Del studied him. His friend didn't look worried, which gave him some confidence. "What are you thinkin'?"

Kip finished a last bite of biscuit and wiped at his mouth. "I'm thinkin' we got one chance at this, so we better get it right. River will swallow us if we don't."

They picked up axes from the supply wagon and were soon in the saddle headed toward the cottonwoods that framed this side of the river. Del was drying out by the minute in the breezy air. As he neared the water, he leaned forward. His heart thumped when he caught sight of rushing whitecaps spilling crazily past. A low roar had a threatening edge to it. The riverbed was no doubt being scoured. No way they could ford today— even Del knew that. Surely Stoney did, too. Still, the trees needed to be dropped, so might as well get to chopping.

At dinner, Goodwin called the outfit together. He took his hat off and whacked it against his pants. "Don't look too promising for tomorrow, either. We'll stay here until the water drops, which should be a few more days if we don't get more rain. Grazing is good, so the cattle will have a chance to rest and fatten up. When you're on herd, let 'em get a drink, but don't let 'em cross. Keep an eye out for strays and rustlers, we're easy prey right about now." He walked off, huddled with Mr. Sammons.

Del looked forward to the break. The cattle would still need tending, but the riding would be easy. Dig a few wanderers from river eddies and washes, but that was a good diversion. He wondered about Indian attacks now that they were waterbound.

Kip must have read his mind. "Doubt Indians will hit us, but watch your topknot out there. Keep an eye peeled, we're still trailin' through Mescalero territory. Don't know which is worse, stampedin' cattle or Indians on the warpath."

When he wasn't riding watch, Del spent time with

Rodrigo. Somehow, the boy always saw him coming before he saw Rodrigo. They mostly sat together, Del talking while they both whittled. His eyes always seemed to drift to Rose, though. It was timid not to say anything more to her than 'hello' or 'good morning' or 'thank you.' Several days later, he screwed his courage up one night. Cowhands were telling tall tales, no one really paying attention to what anyone was saying.

He met her on the way to the chuck wagon. "Rose, I got somethin' to say to you. Will you walk with me?" They strolled away from camp.

"I'd like to talk to you, too." She turned to him. "Why do you avoid me? You haven't said more than a few words to me in the last couple of days. Can't you tell I need a friend?"

"I'm sorry...but I don't talk so good when my tongue's twisted in knots. Stomach, too."

"What in the world are you talking about, Del Lawson?"

The words spilled forth like the raging river nearby. "I haven't felt much of anything since my wife and son...died...a year ago. I been more like an empty bucket with a hole in it."

Rose drew in a sharp breath. "Oh, my Lord."

"Didn't want to go on living—tried my best not to, but God cheated me of the easy way out. I figure He must have sent Rodrigo to help me from the depths of Hell. The boy says more than most without talking."

"I've noticed that, too."

"No way you could know any of this, and I didn't feel like talkin' about it 'til now." Del's throat tightened. "It's taken some time, but I'm givin' the sorrow free rein, lettin' it have its way with me. Got an anger buildin' in the pit of my stomach that's replacin' it. Kept it bottled away 'til recent. Went through the last year drunk and numb. Right now, the memories still hurt pretty good. But the pain is mixin' it up with another feelin', and that's caring about you. And I don't know what to do about that."

"I'm so sorry, Del. Thank you for sharing that with me. I could tell something's been weighing heavily on you." She searched the dark sky. "I'm struggling, too. One minute I feel fine, the next I'm furious about what Jacobs did to my father. I don't know what I feel, but I care about you, too. I would look forward to talking with you more sometime. For now, let's be friends and enjoy this beautiful evening."

Del nodded. That was enough for him right now, too. A breeze picked up and scampered along the ground, setting the new grasses to waving in the dim light. It was a swift wind, the kind that danced around but still pressed lightly against him. Her words rang in his head. He relaxed. Maybe he didn't need to have answers for everything—maybe he could just enjoy her company.

****

Foul weather greeted the outfit again the next morning. Seemed to be their constant companion lately. It wasn't raining, but a gray threat hid the sun and hung over camp. Del glanced at the ominous sky. It had the look of hail, something he knew about. His ranch had weathered many such storms—squalls that battered small corn crops that struggled in his nearby field. Scattered the few head he had. He pitied the trees and plants budding out here in the spring. His wife cried every time the white destruction shredded her little

150

flower garden. But she always replanted. Never gave in. He pursed his lips. What he'd give to see her again. Comfort her. Hold her. And his son. How terrified they must have been that night. His throat seized. He couldn't even help them when they needed him most. Their faces were already fading from memory.

Del and Kip rode out to herd. That afternoon a cloudburst let loose not long after. It swept in with a savage wind that sent the cattle pointing away from it. Del knew what was coming. He cinched his collar tighter. A slanting blizzard of white diagonaled out of raucous storm clouds. The cattle shrugged off the pea-sized hail as if they were flicking flies off their back. He loosened his tight grip on the reins. If it didn't get any worse than this—okay. The skies were already lightening and the rain slackening. He'd seen enough of these storms play across his ranch to know they usually brought an early round of hail, if they brought any at all. But it didn't bode well that the wind was still up. The herd was mostly still intact except for drifters. Del nudged his horse after the outliers. He and Kip started riding some of them back in, but with more difficulty than he thought it would take. The animals' constant lowing indicated their displeasure. Suddenly, the skies split as if God himself had opened a faucet. This time the hail drove into him like a hammer. How would the cattle react to being pummeled by dime-sized hail? He didn't like it and was sure they didn't, either. They jumped as much as cattle can jump as pellets belted them.

It wasn't a stampede—more like a full-scale rout. The herd scattered, not knowing which way to go to escape the pounding. The few piñon trees dotted about offered scant shelter but acted as magnets with animals crowding each other out. The surrounding brown plain became a winding blanket of white which promised to spill into the river and raise it even higher.

Kip cupped a hand to his mouth. "Del! Don't worry about roundin' anything up right now, just keep your hat snugged." At least Del had a slicker to take some of the punch out of the hard, white chunks that hit him. Head low, he faced away from the storm as the cattle bolted. How long would this one last? Most hail blew in and out in minutes, but this tempest looked like it found a favorite spot. Wasn't any sense to hail—its only purpose seemed to be to leave things in shambles. What good was destruction? He'd given up trying to understand why his family had been killed. Some things there wasn't any figuring to. The rage he'd felt when he first joined the drive had started to flow away, like the waters of the nearby river. He'd weather this storm no matter how long it took. A vision of Rose appeared, and a sudden calm took hold. He looked in the direction of camp. The hail eased off as quickly as it had begun and the skies lifted. He windmilled an arm. The bruising wouldn't last. He'd be all right.

The cattle were spread out for miles. Most stood dazed where they were, protesting softly. Some moved stiffly about, complaining with every step. He nudged his mount and started after them.

Kip rode up alongside. "You okay?"

"Yeah, but the herd looks the worse for wear."

Kip squinted. "Don't know as we're gonna be able to ride all the stragglers in right now. Think we oughta leave 'em. They're not goin' anywhere, sore as they are. Let 'em recover some, and we'll start after 'em tomorrow."

"Sounds like a good idea, hope Stoney agrees. My horse ain't in shape to do much more than walk back to camp anyway. Let's go."

****

Morning dawned fair. As a blinding sun baked the ground, Kip sidled up to Stoney. "Seen some dust blowin' up behind us, Boss—and not a little. Could only be another herd on our heels."

"You and Lawson, ride with me." They swung up in the saddle and hurried south along the edges of the low, scrubby mesas, keeping to what scant trail they could find. Kip pointed in the distance. "That there herd stretches all the way to the horizon. Must be near twice our size. More crew, too."

The foreman angled out onto the basin. "Let's find their boss." They rode for several miles, swinging around the front of the big herd to the other side. Several drovers pointed the way to camp. The three dismounted. Stoney approached the campfire. He said to no one in particular, "I'm here to see your trail boss."

An older man stood. "That'd be me, pardner. They call me Big Jim Wilson." He said it like it meant something. "Who're you?"

"Foreman for the Kay-J herd just to your front, Mr. Wilson. We're hard against the river. Once the water falls, we'll be on our way across."

Wilson said, "Waaal…that's fine for you, but I cain't keep these beeves here forever, they's already chewin' grass down to the nub."

Stoney ignored that. "So I reckon a couple days from now, we'll be able to head on over."

Del figured this for what it was—a courtesy call.

Lead drives always had the right of way. An unwritten code, but even he knew the first drive of the spring got the best prices.

Wilson smiled. "Knew you was there. Already sent scouts ahead and they tell me the river ain't that bad. So just move your herd off, and we'll be on our way across." He twirled one end of a huge gray mustache, then dug his thumbs under his belt and spread his legs slightly. He was a tall man with a phony smile that revealed missing teeth.

Stoney rubbed at his stubble. "If you been ramroddin' drives, you know that ain't the way. We'll cross when it's time, and we'll do it from right where we are."

"Mebbe we'll just have to go 'round you then." Some of his men gathered around in a loose semi-circle.

Stoney pointed his finger in the big man's face. "Stay back from my herd." He dropped a hand near his holster.

Wilson laughed. "What, you gonna shoot me?" He turned to his drovers. "Better stand back, boys, don't know if he knows how to handle that thing." His face was mean when he looked back at Stoney. "Anything else, little man?"

Stoney's face went hard, and his hands became fists. Kip grabbed one of his arms. "Boss, let's go, ain't no reasonin' with people dumber than their stock."

Wilson pointed. "Awful big talk for a black man."

Kip hesitated, then used both hands to turn Stoney around.

Del led the way back to their horses. He wanted to look back and see if guns were aimed at their backs, but held off.

As they trotted back to camp, Kip asked, "What do we do now, Stoney?"

"Nothin' that we wasn't already plannin' on doin'. He wants to kill a bunch of his cattle and some of his men, I won't stop him from bein' a damn fool." Gray skies matched their moods.

The next day the sun broke through another stubborn cloud cover. It burned the gray shroud into submission as it rose and clear skies reclaimed the land. Thunderous noise surprised Del as he rolled off a damp, early morning bedroll.

Rose rushed to him from the wagon. "What in the world is that, Del?"

He ran a hand through his hair. Something that loud could only be one thing. The herd in the rear was moving past them to the west.

Stoney's voice rang clear in the morning air. "You swimmers, fork a saddle. Form a line between us and the other herd. Don't let them beeves mix. I don't want to have to cut any of theirs out after we cross. Wouldn't trust myself meetin' that bastard again. Get a move on! Herders, mount up and steady the cattle. They'll be restless with another big group movin' so close. Don't let 'em get to runnin'."

Sammons mounted up and motioned to Del. Together, they quickly covered the several miles between Wilson's herd and the roaring river. Del didn't know how Sammons was able to find Wilson in all the chaos, but find him he did. What did the boss have in mind? Sammons hailed Wilson and trotted his horse next to his. He drew his Colt. "Stop. Get down."

Wilson pretended not to hear him. Sammons fired a round past his ear. "Down. One, two—"

155

Wilson's eyes widened.

Del glanced around. None of Wilson's drovers had drawn their guns. Yet.

"Three." He fired another shot under his chin.

The man scowled, pulled up, and dismounted.

Sammons shouted above the fray. "Del, keep him covered. Kill him if any of his men interfere."

Del eyed the wranglers, and drew his Colt. This wasn't exactly how he thought his life would end, but here he was. Would have been nice to at least kiss Rose. Just once. Say goodbye to Rodrigo. Was that too much to ask, Lord? He squinted at Wilson's men, their hands resting on top of their saddle horns. Maybe they didn't like the oaf, either.

Sammons stood with the easy look of someone who'd backed men down before.

Wilson squinted. "What, you gonna shoot me for runnin' your herd?"

"You are breaking the Code, something I take seriously. I will kill you if you do not stop." He reached for a handful of dirt and rubbed his hands with it. "See, there is nothing about you that scares me. In fact, I would like very much for you to draw down on me." He holstered his gun and stood with arms crossed. "Last time I will say it. Move back. Now."

The intruder licked his lips and glanced around.

"Your men cannot help you in this, Mr. Wilson. It is just you, me, and your God if you have one, and my guess is your God is sitting this one out. Stop or draw. Any time."

Beads of sweat formed on the big man's face even in the swirling dust.

"I cain't stop 'em now, even if I wanted to."

"Any time."

Wilson fidgeted, then drew.

Before Wilson could get a shot off, Sammons nicked his ear, then hit him in the foot.

The man dropped like a sack of flour, screaming his head off.

"Watch my back, Del." Sammons threw the man's gun to Del and stood over the writhing blowhard, who didn't seem to know which wound to grab for first. "Do you want to tell your men, or do you want me to do it?"

Wilson whimpered.

"That your foreman sitting his horse right there?"

A piteous nod.

Sammons holstered his sidearm and strode over to the man. "I do not care how you do it, but you stop your herd right now, then draw them back behind us again. You are in charge now, understood?" Sammons stared at the other drovers.

"Yessir." The man jerked his horse away and signaled his men to follow.

Sammons returned to Wilson. "You have just run your last herd over this trail. If I ever see you again, I will kill you." He mounted up.

Adrenaline pulsed through Del's body. As they rode, he heaved Wilson's pistol into a small creek. Miles later, the two were back with their own herd.

Del said, "My heart got a pretty good rest back there, Boss. I believe it even stopped for a while!"

Sammons grinned. "Bullies are always the easiest hombres to handle. Watch out for the quiet ones, though."

Del dropped his horse at the remuda and dusted himself off.

Laramie wore his big toothy grin. "Have a good ride?"

Del nodded. "The most surprising one I've had in a while."

Back at camp, Kip strolled over. "Where you been? You were supposed to be flankin' with me. Time to head back out. Keep the herds separate."

Del said, "Be with you in a minute—no hurry anymore." He walked to the chuck and stood stock still, watching Rose help make lunch. He rested an arm on Rodrigo's shoulder. The boy wrapped an arm around his leg. Del's bottom lip trembled, and his eyes watered.

Rose glanced at him and put her wooden spoon down. "What are you doing, Del? It's not time to eat yet."

He moved closer to her. "I wanted to see you, hear your voice. See Rodrigo." Her sandy brown hair hung in loose curls around her neck. The image burned itself into his mind.

Rose looked at him with a question on her face. "What's wrong? Did something happen?"

Del reached for her hand, still covered in flour. This time his heart pounded for another reason. He stared into her searching light green eyes before sharing a lingering kiss with her.

Rose put a hand to her cheek. "Oh, my."

He held her in his embrace. "I needed to spend a few minutes with you and Rodrigo." He gently squeezed her hand for a moment before letting go. He hugged Rodrigo then walked back to the campfire. A calm came over him that he hadn't felt in a long time. Kip gave him a look as they sat. He wondered if his face reflected the awe at what he'd just seen. And felt.

The trail boss had more than surprised him, but the surge of tender feelings fueled by a long-awaited kiss topped that.

Chapter Twenty

Pete Tyson scanned his men as they gathered around. Scruffy-looking bunch. He wouldn't turn his back on any of them. Only four left—two new—after that army patrol dealt Skinner a losing hand. But they were all he had, and he'd use them to get what he wanted. He still hadn't made up his mind if he was going to haul the gold to Wilkins when he found it. Maybe he'd take a couple of his gang into his confidence and waylay the other two. Then, he'd shoot the last ones in their sleep and be on his way. Never did like sharing. He lit his cigar with a satisfied smile.

"We'll hole up here tonight." 'Here' was north of Fort Sumner on the open plains, alongside the Pecos. Low bluffs to the west provided scant protection from the ever-present wind. Dust rising to the south in the afternoon sky told him a herd was heading their way. Had to be the lead drive.

Lawson.

Tyson fiddled with his eye patch. Damn thing was always coming loose. "Got ourselves a stretch tomorrow to ride Lawson's drive down. Suppose they're up against the Pecos right about now. Likely near where it bends west. May already have forded it but I'm guessing not, with water this high." He squinted. "Cold camp tonight. 'Tween Indians, patrols, and cowhands, we best keep out of sight."

A small copse of piñon pines showed just ahead at the base of a tawny-colored bluff. The sloping ridge rose from an uneven basin floor. Tumbled rocks at the bottom formed a rough blind. They pulled in, hobbled and fed the horses. After a cold meal of jerky and biscuits, Tyson lay under his thin blanket while stars peeked around retreating storm clouds. His saddle made for a rough pillow. Maybe he wouldn't wait. Maybe he'd see if he couldn't rid himself of one of his ne'er-do-wells now. Might as well have some fun. He whispered to the lowlife on the bedroll nearest him. "Collins, lean this way." He glanced at the other three, settled a distance away, lying down, smoking. "Donovan said we oughta get rid of you before we find the gold. I told him we'd do no such thing. Said he'd deny he ever said it. Just thought you oughta know."

Collins' eyes blazed. He stared at Donovan, resting on his back. "Get up you whelp of a whore! We'll see who's got rid of."

Donovan's eyes grew wide. "What're you talkin' about, Tom?"

"Get up I said!"

"You hearin' voices again?"

"Mine's gonna be the last you hear, I'll gol' damn guarantee it. Fill your hand."

Donovan pushed himself to a stand.

Collins stood with bent fingers on his pistol grip.

"I ain't drawin' on you, Collins—don't know what you're so flummoxed about." He held a hand up, palm outward. Quick as a wink, he fast-drew with the other.

"Pow!"

Collins fell, a hand to his stomach.

"Help me, Bill. You went off and killed me."

Collins rolled back and forth on the rocky ground, bleeding out. "Oh, Lordy. Why'd you do that?"

Donovan looked over at Tyson. "What just happened, Pete? Collins must be crazy."

Tyson said, "Dunno. Better put him out of his misery, though. He's gut shot, not gonna make it. Will be a slow, painful way to go if you don't finish him."

Collins reached a hand out and pointed a finger at Tyson. "He said—"

Tyson yelled. "Do it!"

Donovan put a bullet through the dying man's heart. He shook his head as he stood over his dead friend. "What was that all about? He never should've braced me. Knew I was faster'n him."

Tyson shrugged his shoulders. "Don't rightly know, he just said he was gonna square things with you. Before I could stop him, he was on you."

"Don't make no sense, we ain't had a foul word 'tween us the whole way." He holstered his gun, smoke still trailing from the barrel. "Don't make no sense. Reckon we ought to bury him."

Tyson shook his head. "He stays where he made his last play." He stared the others down. He rolled a cigarette and lit it, smoke curling from his smiling mouth.

Morning brought a louder rumble of cattle coming their way. The thunder of hooves echoed off the bluffs behind Tyson. Rising dust said they were still miles distant, but the size of their dust cloud had to be from at least a couple thousand head. He wondered how he was going to cut Lawson and the boy out from their drive. He needed to lay eyes on Lawson's herd first, then he'd figure the rest. After a cold breakfast, they broke camp and pushed south.

The land shimmered in the early morning sun. Long grasses gently swayed as if to say 'this way.' Wary tan-brown antelope stayed maddeningly just out of rifle range. Tyson knew the low surroundings well. Whenever he ran away as a child, he'd ride along these high plains, letting the wind carry his burden away. If he'd had another place to land, he wouldn't have come back, but he always did. This was home, for better or worse. Mostly worse. Maybe if things had been different...

He shook his head. Find the gold and leave. Start a new life. Maybe he'd take some of the coins to Wilkins after all—it wasn't as if the man knew how many there were. The hours passed quickly. Faint sounds drifted his way on a fickle wind. Lawson's herd lay just ahead. Need to stay clear of the point drovers, find a spot to lay up until night. He scanned the stark surroundings. He couldn't see the cottonwoods lining the Pecos from this distance, but they were there. The herd would be lounging somewhere this side of the roaring water.

He glanced sideways at his men. "Pull off here. We'll disappear into this arroyo for now." When night fell, he'd...what? He thought about stampeding the cattle, but there was little chance he could pick Lawson out in the middle of that chaos. And that wouldn't help get the boy either. He needed both. He eased his horse to the bottom of the sandy draw and dismounted. Then it hit him. He'd send Donovan into their camp to locate the kid. That's what he'd do. Like he was a rider just passing through, asking for provisions. Nice and friendly. "Donovan!"

The man turned his way.

"Got you a job." When he'd outlined the plan, he sent the rustler on his way. "Get back before dark so I don't shoot you by mistake." Tyson leaned against the warm sandy bank, and the day soon turned drowsy.

Donovan galloped up in the fading dusk.

Tyson rose. "Tell me good news."

The man smiled. "Found him, Pete. Right there in the middle of camp, like you thought. Stays by the chuck with the cook. There's a lady there, too. Good lookin'. Can't figure that. Mighta been the one I saw in the fort that day I rode in. Didn't get the best reception from their cook, but you can't turn a hungry man away. Good vittles. I can corral the kid tonight while you're out runnin' Lawson down. Can I have the woman, too?"

Tyson considered. He wouldn't mind having a pretty woman to keep him company. He'd dress her in San Francisco's finest fashions. Someone on his arm to show off. He wondered if she'd like a one-eyed man.

"Pete! Pete."

He snapped back.

"What about the woman?"

"No. Leave her be, dammit." He heaved a rock in the air. There'd be plenty of women looking to spend time with a rich man. Eye or no eye. He rubbed a dirty, rough hand over his craggy face. "Gather 'round. When it's dark, we'll give the beeves a wide berth and circle 'round, watchin' for drovers. First thing we do is locate Lawson. If we don't find him first shift, we hunker down and wait for the relief. He's got to be on first or second shift.

"Once we find him, Donovan you ride on back to their camp." He smiled. This next part was pure genius.

164

He pointed at the new men. "You two ride north toward the river and start shootin' holes in the night sky. Keep up a good, steady fire. That'll likely set the cattle to runnin'. All the drovers—the ones in camp too—will be up and gallopin' toward the ruckus. I'll grab Lawson. Donovan, you grab the boy. Shoot anybody gets in your way. We'll meet back here at the draw. If we get separated, ride for the highest hill to the east and wait."

One of the men said, "Uh, Pete, won't our shootin' give us away? They'll know right where we are."

Tyson smiled inwardly. They'd both likely get killed in a running shootout. That'd be two more down. He wasn't going back to the wash either—he'd light out due south when he had Lawson and the boy. He squinted at the soon-to-be-dead men. "Nah, no way they could run you down at night in all the commotion." If the drovers didn't get those two, the Apaches would. That only left Donovan to get rid of. He grinned.

"Let's ride."

Chapter Twenty-One

Maybelle picked at her dinner in Sinola's faded dining room. She signaled the waiter. "May I have another glass of white wine, please?"

"The same again, ma'am?"

"Yes, thank you." Refined women drank whites, but she'd always preferred a full red. Not that she'd tasted wine for a long time. She used to...back east...but that was another lifetime ago. She finished the meal with a small, stout port. She wanted a large glass of red, but that wouldn't look good. Other diners were already glancing her way often enough.

Ever since she learned Wilkins was behind the killer's devilry, she'd been planning her revenge. Get Wilkins, then the murderer. To do that, she'd study his ranch house, get a feel for the lay of the land. She wanted to have her first glimpse of Wilkins without banker Bunch, but a buggy ride there wouldn't do. People would wonder what a single woman was doing traveling on the plains by herself. She'd wonder too, if she were them. Night would be the best time to go. She'd draw a horse from the town stable. Should she buy the stable hand's silence about her trip?

She'd go tonight...but no, she'd had a fair amount to drink. Then again, why not? Back in her room, she changed into her ranch clothes—cotton blouse, men's baggy pants, sturdy boots, and a cowboy hat to finish the ensemble. She gazed at Ansel's old gunbelt. Wasn't sure why she brought it, wasn't even sure the pistol still worked, hadn't been fired in years. She strapped it on. Too loose, but if anyone saw her, she'd look like a man from a distance, which was her aim. Darkness would help, too.

She quick-stepped to the stables. "Good evening. My name's uh…Samantha, Samantha Brooks. I would like to borrow a horse."

The young hand looked her up and down. "Yes, ma'am, when do you need her?"

"Tonight. Now."

"Uh, tonight?"

"Yes, tonight. Is that a problem?"

"Nope. Pick the one you want." He tipped his hat.

"By the way, you didn't see me this evening." She handed him a dollar bill.

He smiled. "You're right about that. Didn't see nothin' all night. Been real quiet of late."

"I'll have her back by morning."

"No hurry."

Maybelle headed out of town on the only dirt road that travelled west. She had a general idea which direction to go. At the hotel, she had discreetly inquired about the ranch's whereabouts. To disguise her interest in Wilkins, she'd asked about other nearby ranches as well. The farther she rode tonight though, the more her resolve dwindled. She didn't know the land, didn't know the man, and most of all wasn't sure she could pull this off.

The flat, open basin rose slightly ahead. Early moonlight shone on pine-covered heights that mirrored each other on either side of the rutted road. The dirt trail faded as she climbed. This didn't seem like her best idea right about now. She pulled up on the reins, looked back toward town, then kicked the horse's flanks and set out again. As she moved over the crest of the rise, she searched for any light in the valley below. Nothing. If she couldn't see anything from this height, she wasn't sure how she'd see anything from the basin floor. She let the horse dictate the way into the shadowy land ahead. Surely there'd be a light still on in Wilkins' ranch house or bunkhouse—it wasn't that late.

The horse picked its way through a jumbled field of small granite rocks and trotted out onto the broad plain. Maybelle glanced at the starry skies. There was the Big Dipper. She'd keep it just off her left shoulder. She had more time than courage and continued what she thought was due west. An easy lope brought her to a second low rise of sparsely-treed hills. Maybe that's why she couldn't see anything, maybe his spread was over this knoll. A pause at the top and she caught a faint glimmer in the distance. Soft ground muffled her horse's hooves as she eased toward the light. At a short distance away, she began a slow circle around the ranch. An imposing main house with a long roofline, a large wooden bunkhouse, a sizeable corral, a two-story barn with a pitched-roof stable to the side. She tied her horse off on a low bush and approached the house in a crouch. A quick peek in a window. An older man she assumed was Wilkins leaned back, smoking in a big, overstuffed chair. He was holding court with several men who looked to be his cowhands. Cigar smoke hung thick, and a calico cat lay curled in his lap, tail twitching idly over its nose.

The large room looked grand, befitting a land

baron. Dark wood wainscot climbed halfway up the walls, and ample leather chairs filled the polished wooden floor. Maybelle had never seen such luxury. As she scanned the men, Wilkins glanced her way—looking directly at her through the window. She drew back into the shadows and flattened against the white stucco wall. Had he seen her? Her heart raced, and she struggled to catch her breath. What was she doing out here? What did she think she'd find out? She slunk away and grabbed her horse from the bush. Up and into the saddle, she fixed the Big Dipper again and hoped she was galloping for Sinola. She glanced back at the fading ranch light until she topped the nearest ridge, then relaxed. Enough for one night.

She slowed the mare to a walk as it navigated the rocky hilltop. Moonlight did little to reveal the way. The horse stumbled in the dark and went down. In a flash, Maybelle found herself facedown on the hard ground, her cheek creased by a sharp rock. She lay motionless for a while, then struggled to a stand. Her right hip ached, her left arm felt broken, and blood ran down her cheek. Her face stung where she touched it. The wound was long. She ran a hand over the horse's foreleg. Didn't feel like the tendon was bowed. She strained up into the saddle and walked the horse back to town. By the time she got there, her bleeding had stopped, but her clothes were splattered in red.

As she stabled the animal, she kept a hand over the wound on her face.

The stable hand stretched and peeked out from a straw bed. "Everything go okay, ma'am?"

She didn't turn around in the dim light. "Yes. Fine. Goodnight." At the hotel, she snuck in the front door.

The clerk lounged asleep in his chair behind the counter, head lolling as he snored. She tiptoed up the stairs until she stepped on one that creaked loudly. She stopped and looked back, heart pounding. The clerk hadn't stirred. She saw his hidden bottle now. In her room, she poured water from the pitcher into her bowl—and hesitated to look. Faint light from an oil lamp didn't make her feel any more ready. As she squinted into the wavy mirror, she saw a horror story. That couldn't be her. She brought a trembling hand to her crusted cheek and cried. Her legs gave way. She slumped to the floor, fat tears winding through clotted blood. She leaned against the wash basin, arms hanging listlessly to her sides.

The room still held a faint glow from the oil lamp when she woke. How long...what time was it? She struggled to a wobbly stand, her left arm and right hip protesting. At least the arm wasn't broken. Still dark outside. This time she turned away from the mirror, wet a towel, and dabbed at her face. She winced with each wipe but swallowed the pain. The towel came away crimson every time. By the time she finished, the wash bowl water was as red as the velvet wallpaper in her room. With the towel pressed to her throbbing face, she extinguished the lamp and sagged into bed, staring at the dark ceiling. How foolish!

Maybe revenge was out of reach.

Chapter Twenty-Two

Del eyed the restless cattle. He rode flank tonight, working to keep the unruly beasts from breaking out sideways at the slightest sound. Drovers said every little noise can set them off, and now he was witnessing it firsthand. Could be the howl of a wolf, crack of a gun, or whirling dust devils roiling the land. Laramie, enthusiastic as ever, had picked the best available saddle horse for him to stand watch with. He'd checked on Shade. The horse didn't shy away anymore when Del ran a hand over his side. Shade was probably ready, but no need to take him yet. Looked like a quiet night. He'd ride him again soon, though.

Kip rode up, a worried look on his face. "Back of my neck's crawlin' and that don't usually happen without somethin' bad followin'."

"What's got you spooked up? It's a pretty night"— Del swept an arm at the sky—"though the beeves do seem twitchy."

"Dunno, just a feelin' I get sometimes and I got it now."

"Ride along with me. We'll make an up and back trip this side of the herd."

The cattle's uneasy lowing made it hard to hear anything else. Del stood in the stirrups, scanning the dim surroundings as his horse jogged slowly. Kip's edgy feeling was catching. Del noticed his friend tug his hat tighter and did likewise.

Kip cupped a hand to his mouth. "Now's the most chancy part of a drive, right here, when you got cattle backed against a river and held off from drinkin'. There's not a lot of good and lots of bad that can happen."

A stab of worry ran through Del. He'd change the subject. "I think Rodrigo's doin' better, don't you? I mean, he's made a friend out of both Buck and Rose. And her dog. Learnin' to cook some, too. Always smiling these days." He glanced at Kip, hoping he agreed.

"I guess he's doin' fine. Seems like he don't have to talk though, everybody does for him without him sayin' a thing."

A flush ran up Del's cheeks. It was true. Was he helping the boy by not prodding him? Not encouraging him? Rodrigo could talk. He'd been a chatterbox, playing with his son before that night. When Del got back to camp, maybe he'd—

Gunshots split the night air. Kip reined up. "Don't know who the hell's doin' that, but he ain't likely none of ours. Let's split up. You try to front the herd. If they start to stompin', do everything you can to turn 'em away from the river. Ride back and forth shootin'. They get in that current and we'll lose the lot of 'em in this dark."

Del already knew how difficult a swift-running river crossing was in daylight, much less at night. Half the herd would drown if they stampeded that way. More firing and the cattle's loud bellowing drowned out everything else. The animals were on the move, as if they were a river themselves.

Kip yelled. "I'll go run those shots down." He disappeared into the darkness.

Del wondered if he'd ever see his friend again. Surely he would, but then again, there was little either of them could control. He kicked his horse into a sprint and drew his Colt, firing into the black air until the hammer clicked hollow. The lead cows were still rumbling directly toward him—and the river behind. The ground thundered. Damn! Del had less than half a mile to stop them. A couple of other drovers joined him in full sprint as well.

Del shouted. "Get to shootin', I'm ridin' nearer the water!" He dropped the reins and loaded bullets from his gun belt as his horse flew. Cows raced alongside him almost as fast as his horse ran. Gradually, he gained their front and crisscrossed back and forth a quarter mile this side of the roiling current. He reached for his rifle. Made more noise. His rapid firing made its deafening presence known, and the others joined in. The lead cows reacted. They slowed but didn't know which way to go. Del angled them off to the west, away from the river. The other cowhands kept the push up and soon the whole herd made a wide, winding turn on dry soil back to their grassy basin.

The foreman rode up. "Good job turning them. Grab a couple wranglers and search the arroyos for strays. I'd guess fifty or so probably drifted off during the rampage. Any range cattle you find, herd them in, too." He spun his horse away.

Del stared at Goodwin's retreating frame. First time the foreman said anything halfway nice to him. He shook his head. The herd was settling again, but his heart rate was still up. He'd get to searching, but first he'd find Kip. Del spurred his horse in the direction of the first shots. He swung wide around the river side of the herd, pushing some here, running a stray in there. Straining to see in the distance, he whacked the horse's rump with the reins. Soon a large bluff loomed out of the darkness ahead. Kip wouldn't be farther than this, would he? A yank on the horse's mane brought the animal to a walk again. Where was Kip?

A voice sounded off to his left. "Help me up, will you, cowpoke?"

Kip! "What're you doin' down there?"

"Just takin' my ease. Stupid question. Whaddya think I'm doin'? Got knocked off my mount, but not before I drilled one of them raiders."

Del reached a hand down, and Kip swung up behind him.

"Any idea who they were?"

"Nah, just a couple hombres, more skittish than the beeves. Hightailed it into the night when I braced 'em. The one I hit's probably lyin' out there right now, dyin'. Senseless way to go."

"Where's your horse?"

"Shouldn't be far. Likely we'll run across him on the ride back." He rubbed his shoulder. Red stained his shirt sleeve.

"Rustler hit you in the arm?"

"Just a scratch—I'll live. He ought to have plugged me in the chest, I weren't no more than a few feet away when I ran across them. After he hit me, he panicked and almost shot himself." Kip guffawed.

"Good thing he didn't hit you in the talk box, 'cause I wouldn't have seen you down there. You scared me for a second."

"'Course you didn't see me—dark's my advantage. Saw you and your pasty white face comin' a mile away."

"No, you didn't. No way."

"Smelled you, too. Smell worse than the cattle. When's the last time water landed anywhere on your body?"

"Uh…" Del raised an arm and sniffed as they rode. Right ripe. He thought about Rose. "Maybe I'll take a quick dunk on the way back. No, make that a leisurely soak. That'll give your arm time to fester up some. You'll get more sympathy that way." He grinned. "No need to thank me, I'm always thinkin' of you."

"Sympathy? From this bunch of ne'er-do-wells? 'Tain't likely. Take your time, the cattle ain't goin' nowhere. They're tuckered out, and my arm'll feel better when you smell better."

Del chuckled. "Want me to bind that up?" It was deeper than a scratch, but Kip seemed to be holding up well.

"What would you do that with? One of your dirty bandanas? No thanks. The river'll do it just fine."

They chuckled as they came across Kip's horse.

At the river, Del doffed his clothes, held them by the hand, and waded in. The swift current wanted to knock his legs from under him. Kip followed, cleaning his wound. Del grabbed handfuls of wet sand and rubbed it through his hair and beard. Wiped it across his armpits. Sank to his neck in the cold, fast-running river. Leaned into the rushing waters. Let the Pecos have its way. Rubbed his clothes together in the water then threw them to the river bank. A sudden wave of sadness swept over him like the current he was caught up in. A year ago, he was ranching a small place with a beautiful wife and a son. How did the sun still come up, the rivers run, how did people still laugh, as if nothing happened? A chill coursed through him. On the bank, he hurried his wet pants, shirt, and boots back on and swung up into the saddle. He'd dry quick in this weather.

Kip said, "Good thing you didn't lose your britches, what with Rose waitin' for you back at camp."

"Don't think she's waitin' for me."

"You okay?"

"Okay." Del kicked his horse into a trot. He didn't even know what he was feeling anymore.

"Your face says 'no'."

"You mean my pasty white face?"

"Yeah, that one."

"I'm okay. I…" He left the words dangling in the night air. What was there to say?

Kip said, "Your frettin' brings to mind somethin' my pappy used to tell me. He'd say, if you see ten troubles comin' down the road, nine will likely be off in the ditch before they ever get to you, and the tenth won't be anywhere near as bad as you thought."

Del nodded. "Your pappy sounds like a smart man. Let's go. Foreman wants us to search for strays."

****

Tyson had sent his two men to create their diversion in the dimming daylight. The cattle would likely stampede at their shots. As he thought about how he'd grab Lawson in all that chaos, he came up with a better idea. He didn't need to run Lawson down at all— he'd grab the kid. That would make Lawson come after him, and Tyson could take him at his leisure. The boy was the best bait he could have. He told Donovan to watch the draw for the return of the two shooters. Even as he said it, he knew they wouldn't be coming back.

Tyson stayed to the arroyos as he rode toward the drover's camp. Wasn't far. From a low, barren rise he surveyed the layout. Just like he planned, the cowpunchers had all left to run down the stampede. A cook stood near the chuck wagon preparing something. He ladled some to a boy, who ate vigorously. A young woman sat by a low campfire. Pretty. She beckoned to the boy and patted a spot next to her on a large log. A brown dog lay nearby. Was she the one Lucas Skinner told him about back at the fort? Tending Lawson? Even better. He'd kidnap the boy and the woman—who knows how she could come in handy?

He tied his horse off on a low shrub and skulked to the rear of the chuck. He knocked the cook out with a pistol blow to the back of the head, but the boy saw him and screamed. "Help!"

Tyson rushed over, his Colt aimed their way. "Git over here, both of you. Now. And shuddup!"

The dog barked furiously while the woman hugged the boy to her. Tyson swatted the animal aside as it charged. The woman and boy stood paralyzed.

"I said move!" He cocked the weapon. He should kill the dog, but he'd never liked hurting animals. His mother shot the only dog he'd ever had, and he'd never forgiven her. But he'd gotten even. Yes, he did. His kick sent the growling dog away again. He motioned toward the remuda, forcing Rose and Rodrigo ahead of him. "You the one minded Lawson back at the fort?" Her shocked expression told him all he needed to know.

A lanky kid smiled as they approached. "Hullo,

Miss Rose. Who's that?"

Tyson held his gun out of sight behind the woman. "Throw your hogleg away real easy, son, or you're the last person this pretty lady ever sees. Toss it by the barrel. Far. That's right. I need another horse. Go on and grab me that one there. Move!" He kept the pistol pressed against the woman's back. When the horse was saddled, Tyson said, "Give me the reins." He eyed the wrangler. "What's your name, son?"

"Laramie."

"Well, Laramie, you'll live longer if you stay right where you are." He led the horse back to camp, the woman and boy in the lead. Looking back, he saw the wrangler standing with a bewildered stare.

At the chuck wagon, the woman bent over the unconscious old man. "Buck! Buck!" She patted his face and glared at Tyson. "Get some water!"

Tyson said, "I put him down; I ain't gonna help him back up. Get away from there, you're goin' with me. The boy, too." He flashed a yellow-tooth smile.

"Stop!"

Tyson whirled to see Laramie aiming a shaking gun at him. He quick-drew and whizzed a couple bullets past the horsekeeper, who lit out back to the remuda. Tyson muttered, "Shoudda killed him. Gettin' soft."

As Rose worked on the dazed cook, she reached for his gun. Her body shielded the movement. "We can't just leave him here, he'll die. Let me tend him then I'll go with you." A quick glance at Tyson.

"No, he ain't worth my time—"

Rose whirled and fired. Hard to miss a big target like that, but she did.

He didn't. A shot to the shoulder laid her out. Tyson kicked her gun away. He pointed his barrel at her chest. "You're the second person I shoudda killed in the last five minutes. I was gonna be real nice to you, you bein' a pretty lady and all, but you shouldn'ta shot at me. Can't think of anyone still alive who done that." He cocked his gun.

Rodrigo yelled. "No!" He ran and punched Tyson in the stomach.

Tyson clamped a meaty palm on the kid's head. Held him at arm's length while the boy swung at air. He eyed Rose, gasping on the ground. "I couldn't take you even if I wanted to, now. Think I'll leave you as is. Tell Lawson it was Tyson did this. Tell him I got the boy, too. He wants to see the kid again, come after me. He don't have to worry about findin' me, I'll find him." He holstered his gun, then threw Rodrigo up on his horse. He swung up behind the boy and tipped his hat to Rose. "Pleasure spendin' time with you, ma'am. Hope you enjoyed it as much as I did, but reckon you didn't. Don't bother gettin' up, I'll be leavin' now."

****

Locating strays took Del a couple of hours. Darkness didn't help. He and Kip rounded up nearly forty head standing blankly in a couple of washes, which made his job easier. The weight of the animals' hooves on the sandy bottom produced small pools of water they were drinking their share of. Del had his hands full forcing them out of the bottoms. When cattle wanted something, it was hard to change their minds. He and Kip drove them out, then ran them in with the rest of the herd, which had settled some by now. The smell of water so close still made them edgy.

179

Del couldn't hide a grin. His mood lifted. "Stubborn beasts. But that was some of the most fun I've had yet. Yahooin' them out of those draws. Got a bath, too. Who'da figured?" He tipped his hat to Kip. "Pleasure ridin' with you, Kip Holloway. Think that arm of yours is gonna heal or fall off?"

"I'm bettin' fall off."

"Let's get you back to camp before it does."

They drifted over trampled land in dim moonlight, skirting the herd. A strong wind passed over Del, cooling him all the while. As suddenly as the sadness overcame him in the water, a certain peace came over him now, bringing with it a touch of comfort he hadn't felt in a long time. The two friends jabbered on as they rode back. Cowboying was beginning to have a certain appeal Del wouldn't have figured on. Nearing camp, he could tell something was up even in the faint light of the campfire. Drovers scurried about, gobbling food off plates, Goodwin shouting orders. What had happened? He slowed.

"Lawson! About time you got back. Raider shot Miss Rose and took the boy. Headed south. Sending two men after them."

Del's heart raced. Blood pounded in his ears. "Where is she?"

"In the chuck, along with Buck. He got knocked on the head."

He raced to the wagon and pushed the canvas flap aside. His heart leaped when he saw her lying there in her own blood. Rose lay on her back, eyes fluttering, shirt reddened at the shoulder. "How is she?"

Buck held a wet cloth to his head. "Can't say, she hasn't said anything. Looks like she's hurt pretty good."

He pressed on her wound to staunch the bleeding while Rose's moans filled the air. "Got to get her to a doctor."

Del gritted his teeth. His gut told him the assailant was Tyson. He reached for Rose's hand. Her gaze turned his way, eyes distant. What was he going to do? Should he get Rose to a doctor or run down Tyson and the boy? Rose closed her eyes. The moans stopped.

Del put two fingers to her neck. He exhaled deeply and nodded. "Okay for now. How'd this happen, Buck?"

"'Twer the same fella accused us of rustling his cattle a few days back. You all was gone after the stampede. He busted in here, knocked me out." He rubbed a spot on his head. "Miss Rose must have come to see about me and snatched my pistol. Must have fired it, too, 'cause a bullet's missing. Don't know if she hit him, but he hit her. Guess he grabbed Rodrigo and skedaddled. I don't know no more, things is a little fuzzy. Not good that she just passed out, neither."

What to do wasn't a question any more. Damn! Rodrigo would have to fend for himself for a spell. He rushed to the remuda for a fresh horse.

Laramie hailed him. "Sorry I couldn't do nothin' to stop that assassin, Del. He made me dive for cover, and by the time I got squared up again, he was flyin' out of here with the boy."

Del put a hand up. "Which way?"

"Off to the north. Maybe he figures we won't try to follow him, with the cattle all scattered."

Del stared into the distance. The stampede must have been Tyson's handiwork. Tyson knew he'd trail him—he took Rodrigo to make sure. His insides churned like that night at the ranch. The Good Lord had just let him have a little bit of peace then snatched it away. He jammed his hat on harder. "Get me your fastest horse. Wait. Think Shade's ready yet?"

"Been treatin' him every day with potions Buck makes up. Worked, too. Rode him some. He's fit as a fiddle." Laramie led the black stallion out and handed the reins to Del.

Del eyed the light pink scar on Shade's side. "You sure he's okay?"

"Wouldn't give him to you if he wasn't. What're you gonna do?"

Del whispered in the big animal's ear. "Gonna saddle him. Get me another set of reins. Hurry." Del made sure the saddle strap lay clear of the horse's wound. He rode Shade back to camp. His gut gnawed at him. He'd have to leave Rodrigo be for now. Rose needed his help first. He was the reason she was here in the first place. She'd spent days tending him. He owed her, but there was more to it than that. He'd wanted to spend time with her. Maybe take her on a picnic or two. Thought about how she'd felt in his arms. Remembered their kiss.

"Lawson!"

Del brushed past Goodwin and climbed into the wagon. "Buck, get me a blanket and some food. Water, too."

Stoney met him as he climbed out carrying Rose. "You ain't takin' her anywhere. We can fix her up right here, ain't that right, Buck?"

"No, it ain't. I can't do for her. Not with that bullet still in her. She needs a real doc. And soon."

Del mounted up while the cook kept his arms wrapped around Rose. "Hand her up, Buck."

"Can't. Not strong enough."

Del stared at Stoney. He held the man's gaze hard.

The foreman kicked at the dirt. He rubbed the back of his neck then cradled Rose from Buck and lifted her to Del. "Damnation, you are cussed stubborn, Lawson. Closest place is Fort Sumner from here."

"Not goin' to Sumner, they don't have a doc anymore. Santa Rosa's too far. Headin' toward Puerto de Luna. Twenty miles at most."

Kip nodded. "Better idea."

The foreman wouldn't let it go. "Never heard if they have a doctor or not."

Kip said, "Maybe not, but might be a shaman 'round there, from what I hear."

Del ignored Goodwin's remark. Couldn't afford to let that sway him. He squinted at Laramie. "Hand me that extra set of reins." The wrangler tossed them up. Del wrapped the leather straps around Rose's body then secured them to his own. Buck stuffed supplies in Del's saddlebags. The cook handed him a couple jugs of water and crossed himself. "Kidnapper's name is Tyson—said he'd find you if you followed."

Del slung a canteen on the saddle horn. "Knew it was him."

"You're gonna, ain't you?"

"Run him down?"

"Yeah."

The old cook's eyes misted. He and Rodrigo had been inseparable.

Del said, "I'd trail Tyson to the ends of the earth if I had to. Gotta care for Rose first, though."

Buck nodded and wiped at an eye.

Del looked north. Hard riding lay ahead, along

with a reckoning. Del held an arm around Rose, the reins in his other hand. A nudge and Shade lit out with Del's precious cargo tight against his chest.

If Rose was to live, Rodrigo would have to wait.

Chapter Twenty-Three

Shade settled into a middling pace over the New Mexican prairie. Del wanted to ride faster but didn't want to risk Shade striding into a gopher hole in the dark. How to hold the reins, hug Rose, and put pressure on her wound? He stroked Shade's neck and told him he was going to drop the leathers to keep both arms around Rose. Other than his wife, this would be the most he'd ever trusted anyone or anything in his life. The cowhide straps fell loose and bounced along Shade's neck. Del pressed his other hand over Rose's bleeding shoulder, praying to the Good Lord to bring them safely through. He guided Shade with his knees.

Rose felt limp in his arms. This was the closest he'd ever been to her. Not how he imagined their next embrace. He didn't want to hug her too tight, but he needed to keep pressure on her wound. He also didn't want to push Shade too hard. The stallion would run until he dropped, so Del kept him reined in. The cool evening air helped but made for an uncomfortable chill. Rose felt cold in his grip. He should have grabbed his heavier coat for her, but he'd had no warning he'd need it. Little he could do to keep her any warmer. His mind raced as fast as his horse. Would Puerto de Luna have a doctor? Where was Rodrigo?

He didn't expect Indian trouble but kept an eye out, anyway. The moon gave faint light to the way ahead.

185

Attacking in the dead of night wasn't the Apache or Comanche custom, although he'd heard from childhood about raids during Comanche moons. Please. Not tonight. Tyson's wicked face flooded his thoughts. The killer had been tracking him, that much was plain. Deep down, Del had sensed for some time it was him Tyson was after. But why? His father's cryptic words just before he died kept rolling through his head. 'I got a good surprise for you and your ma, son. Real good.' That's all the man said before he passed out drunk. Never saw him again. The 'surprise' must have had something to do with Tyson. Otherwise, why would the killer be after him? He'd known for some time his father ran with a gang in this part of the Territory, but that was all. Probably Tyson's. His mother's face grew dark whenever Del mentioned his father's name.

A murmur from Rose. "Uhhnn…"

"Rest easy, Rose. No need for talk. You've been shot. We're riding for help." She nestled closer against his chest. Damn! Puerto had to have a doc. After more hard riding, he pulled up near a narrow stream bubbling out of the earth. In the darkness, Del spread his coat on the ground and wrapped it around her. She blinked then closed her eyes. Del retrieved a water jug from his saddlebag and knelt beside her. "Here, drink please." When she didn't respond, he dribbled some on her lips, which she mouthed. He undid her shirt to look at her shoulder. Moonlight revealed ugly, dark streaks on her skin. He whisked his bandana off and soaked it in the stream, gently cleaning around the wound. Dabbed her forehead with it. She stirred slightly. He leaned close. "Wish we had more time to rest, but we have to keep going. Need to get you to a doctor quick as we can." He whistled for Shade, and the stallion strode from the creek. Del rested a hand on his mane. "Wish I could give you more time, too, but can't." The horse's big eyes seemed to stare into his soul.

He struggled to mount up with Rose. A kick to the flanks and the big horse was off. Del had a general idea where Puerto de Luna was, but in the dark it was hard to know the fastest way to go. He'd follow the river. Then again, lamplight from the town might be easy to see against the black of night—if his direction wasn't off. The westerly wind made itself known as it buffeted him. He leaned forward as much as he could, hugging Rose close. Wasn't the best time for the elements to be fighting him. The land was mostly flat prairie that came and went as Del searched the skies for Polaris. His mother taught him about the constellations as a child. She said find the North Star, it was a constant that could guide him on land and in life.

For her years of service to the Abriendos, his mother had been deeded nearly four hundred acres at the eastern edge of the hundred-twenty-thousand-acre Spanish land grant. For years, she served as household help at the big ranch house of el patrón, where Rodrigo and Del's son first became fast friends. In turn, she'd given Del two hundred acres to start his spread. The place his family lay buried now. Several evenings after that awful night he'd ridden in a daze to his mother's place—farm house and barn also burned to the ground. Saw the bloody dirt. The dog, lifeless nearby. No mother. He'd ridden on in shock, Rodrigo hugging him from behind. Never got to say goodbye to any of his family. Had been drifting ever since. He wasn't going to lose Rose if he could help it. At least tonight's sky was clear, but no storm could compete with the one he was living. In the midst of his worry, he thanked the Lord for bringing him this far. It had been a long time since he'd thanked the Lord for anything. His faith had all but gone up in ashes along with his ranch.

His hand over Rose's wound felt wet. Fresh blood, when he'd thought the bleeding had stopped. The ride's jarring was getting to be too much for her. Should he stop so she could rest or keep going? He'd push on—didn't know how much time she had. More pressure would likely slow the bleeding but would hurt her more. Had to be done, though. He pressed harder and kept riding.

"Ohh!" A moan escaped her lips. She squirmed in his grip, an arm thrashing. "No!"

He wanted to be anywhere but here, hurting her, but he couldn't stop now. "I have to, Rose, I'm sorry…"

Her whimpers stopped, and she went limp. His hand flew to her neck. No pulse. Wait. There. Weak. He smoothed a hand over Shade's neck. "Got to get help quick. Pick a way that's as gentle and quick as there is." He knew Shade didn't understand, but he felt better saying it. His arm cramped around Rose, but he couldn't afford to stretch it. Time dragged. Gradually, the dark countryside and the long night gave way to dim light. He scanned the distant landscape to orient himself.

He'd grown up southwest of here but had ridden this range occasionally, buying and selling cattle for him and his mother. Low heights lay to the north dead ahead. He nudged Shade left a touch. With daylight breaking, he spotted flecks of foam on the horse's shoulders and flanks. Rose's head still sagged to the right in his arms. In the pale light, her cotton shirt looked more red than white. He checked her pulse again. She'd made it this far, wouldn't be much longer, he hoped.

The small town's buildings gradually dotted the river basin ahead. When he pulled up at the mercantile on the near-empty main street, he eased Rose down and carried her into the store. "I need a doctor here! Where's the doc?"

An old man shuffled from canned food shelves in back. "Just openin' up. Who you got there, young fella?" He adjusted his thick eyeglasses.

"She's hurt—I rode a long way to get here. Where's the doctor?"

The storekeeper rubbed at a wild, white beard. "Don't got one, sonny."

No! Not after riding all this way. "You *have* to have a doctor—or someone!"

"Nope, got hisself shot foolin' with another man's wife. Onliest thing we got is Laila."

"Where is she?"

"Interesting lady, Laila. Pecos Indian shaman. That's a medicine woman. Stayed around here when her people up and left for Jemez. North and west of here. That was what, purt near ten years ago now. Don't hardly seem that long. She's a healer, but a scary one for sure." He chuckled as if there was something funny about that.

Del dropped a hand to his holster. "Last time— where is she?"

The man threw his hands in the air. "Just gettin' to that, young fella." He eyed Rose. "She don't look so good."

Del drew the gun. "Where?"

"A ways down the main road to the west." He limped outside and pointed. "You take the trail there for a few hours, past that pointy rise in the distance, then she's got a little hut—she calls it a tipi—up in the hills to the west. Near a small stream. Can't miss it."

"I need a wagon. My horse is done in."

With his arms still high, the shopkeeper said, "Two buildings down. The livery."

Del waved his pistol that direction. "You're comin' with me." Inside the stable, a gruff-looking sort was bent over, mucking a stall. "Hitch me a horse and wagon. Now!" He didn't have time for an argument, so he fired a shot through the roof.

The stabler hurried to the last stall and retrieved an old mare.

"Rub my horse down. Water and feed him." When the stable horse was harnessed, Del placed Rose in the wagon bed and told the merchant to get up front and drive. He sat and pressed against the wound. No response. "Go!"

The old wagon rattled west out of the livery.

Every few minutes Del asked, "How much longer?"

The old man always said, "Won't be long now."

Far too long later, the driver pulled up at a clearing by a small stream gurgling out of the low rises. "There's her place."

Del stared at a tall wikiup in a well-maintained camp. "What's her name again?"

"Laila."

The sun broke over the horizon as an old woman

emerged from bushes to one side of the tipi. She wore a beautiful tan buckskin dress decorated with turquoise and multi-colored beads. Her soft gray hair was pulled back in a pony tail. She was short, with penetrating brown eyes. She nodded at Del. "Saw you coming. Heard you before that." Without looking at Rose, she turned toward the tipi. "Gunshot. Bring her in."

How did the woman know?

"There."

Del laid Rose down on a circular, woven ceremonial rug. The early morning chill hadn't lifted yet, and he spread a thick, woolen blanket on top of her.

The woman knelt and moved a wet cloth over Rose's lips. She chanted a soft rhythm and spread her arms high and wide. Del hovered while she retrieved a jar of dark liquid.

"Hold her." Laila drew the blanket back and cut Rose's shirt off to reveal a bloody undergarment. The woman gazed upward as her fingers felt around Rose's reddened bullet hole. She cleaned the area with a soft cloth, then worked a foul-smelling poultice into the wound and placed a small piece of clean cloth over it. "Roll her to stomach." Her fingers played over the back of Rose's shoulder.

Del rubbed his forehead. Rose's face was ghastly pale. "What are you doing? Help her!"

The shaman rose and walked outside, where she thrust a knife blade into the small fire burning there. Inside, she sank to her knees and whispered to Rose. With no hesitation, she placed a finger on Rose's back and worked the knife in.

A muffled outcry.

Del breathed a sigh of relief to hear anything from

her.

Laila cut the new incision larger and deeper. Blood ran from the wound but not as much as Del thought there'd be. The woman stopped and wiped her brow. "Clean it."

Del wiped the area clear of blood with the cloth she'd given him. Laila dug into the cut again then probed with delicate fingers and drew out a mashed bullet. "A bone may be broken." Laila rose, her face a mask. Outside, she doused the bloody blade with water then thrust it in the fire. She seared Rose's back with the orange-hot blade then singed the wound in front. Rose screamed and fell senseless. A bitter, burning smell filled the air as pale smoke rose upward in the small enclosure. She poured rank liquid freely over Rose's shoulder, stuffed a small piece of leather into the back cut then placed a strip of leather on the rug underneath her. She turned Rose and fastened a thin piece of foul-smelling tan cloth to the entry wound. "Now, we wait." She knelt with her legs drawn up underneath and rocked back and forth.

Del's throat seized. "How long…do we wait?"

The woman gazed upward, singing softly.

His head spun. Rose's life hung in the balance, and he was powerless to do anything about it. There wasn't any air in the tipi. He burst outside and gulped breaths.

The storekeeper limped over. "Heard what Laila said. Guess we oughta head back to town. Nothing more we can do here." He clutched his dirty cowboy hat in both hands. His face held a pleading look.

Del stared at the ground. Rose lay so still inside. What if he left and she died? He couldn't stand the thought.

The shaman came outside. She seemed to flow over the ground as she walked.

"You may go."

Del raised a hand. "Now wait a minute. I'm staying right here."

She shook her head, arms folded across her chest.

"I'll stay."

The old man broke in. "That weren't a request. From the sound of it, that were an order. Laila don't ask, she tells. You'd be wise to leave your pride here and ride back to town with me."

The woman held Del's gaze hard. He sensed she was using a power of some sort on him. He tried to look away, then whacked his hat against dirty, dusty pants.

Laila was a statue.

He started to say something when she looked toward town.

Dammit! The storekeeper pulled him away by the arm. Del put up a weak resistance. All the air had gone out of him.

"She ain't gonna brook no backtalk. Let's vamoose. Your woman will be well taken care of."

His woman? He wrestled with that thought as he climbed aboard the creaky wagon. Could she ever be his woman? Would she? When the old man snapped the reins, the aged gray horse worked up to a walk. Del stared back at the medicine woman. Squatting motionless, she gazed skyward in the distance, an arm raised high.

He shook his head and tried to push the question away that filled his head.

Had he seen Rose for the last time?

Chapter Twenty-Four

Maybelle gazed at her reflection in the hotel room's wavy mirror. And cried. She'd been such a fool to ride out to Wilkins' ranch in the dark. A fool! There weren't many times she'd done something reckless, but her folly last night was among the worst. She was tired of living life's hard lessons over and over. How was she ever going to bring Wilkins under her sway looking like this? Rouge would hide some of the bruising, but not the cut or the swelling on her cheek. And the banker kept asking to see her. Just then came a soft tapping on her bedroom door.

"Oh, Miss Perkins. It's the desk clerk. Downstairs. You have a visitor, ma'am. Mr. Graham Bunch. Shall I send him up?"

"It's *Mrs.* Perkins. Give me ten minutes, then do so. Bring tea." Not much time to make herself more presentable. Maybe if she wore a striking dress he wouldn't notice her damaged face as much. After a quick change into a beautiful emerald brocade with gathered waist and high lace collar, another knock sounded. "Come in."

Graham Bunch stood in the drab doorway, hat brim held in both hands like a chipmunk. "Oh, my. I mean…you look…fine—better than the clerk described. Be back to…" He stopped his rambling and stood awkwardly. "Was this the credenza the clerk said

194

you fell against?"

"Why, yes it is. So very clumsy of me in the dark." Maybelle reclined in the room's red velvet upholstered chair as if she were holding court. She hoped she looked at ease, but the banker's reaction set her nerves on edge. Even if she didn't look her best, she could still appear to be in charge. As if nothing had happened. As if she hadn't been so foolish. "Please come in, Graham. I'm sure I look a fright." She waited for his response.

He stepped forward with a quick denial. "Not at all...Maybelle. You'll mend fast under the doctor's care, I'm sure. Not that you don't look fine right now, I mean...uh..." He stammered, a flush running up his neck.

Maybelle couldn't tell if the man was intimidated or shocked. Perhaps a bit of both. He was acting so skittish. Was he avoiding looking at her? "Won't you sit, Graham? Join me for a cup of tea? I've just ordered some; I'm sure it will be here momentarily."

The man rotated his black bowler in his hand. "Why, thank you, don't mind if I do. Right nice." He backed toward a wooden straight chair opposite her and sat. "I'm so sorry about your fall, Maybelle. It must have been frightening."

She nodded. It hadn't been frightening—it had been infuriating. "Yes, there I was, on the ground—I mean the floor, here, of course—and no one to look after me. I felt quite alone, to tell the truth." She fanned herself and glanced sideways at him.

Bunch said, "I wish I had been here to help you. Or that you had called on me afterwards."

"That is so kind of you, Graham. I'll be sure to send for you if I need any assistance while I'm on the mend."

"I'd do anything for you—I mean, to help you…in any way I could. Ask and I am at your beck and call." He made a slight bow.

She smiled inwardly. Even as awful as she looked, it felt like she still held his puppet strings. Maybe there was a silver lining in her injury after all. She smiled, her confidence buoyed again. The banker's sympathy was another card she could play when the right time came.

She fanned herself again. "Dear me, I'm at loose ends, and I feel a bit out of sorts."

Bunch brightened. "I know just the thing. When you are up to it, we'll go for a buggy ride."

She leaned forward slightly. "Could we? That would be quite lovely."

"It'll be the first thing we do when you're ready."

"Promise?"

"Of course."

A week later, she summoned the banker to her hotel room. The swelling was not as noticeable, and the cut appeared fainter under her blush. She stood to greet him and offered her hand.

He clasped it between both of his. "Your dress is just delightful. Like you are." This time he maintained eye contact with her.

It was the red burgundy silk, another of the ones she purchased in Denver. She flounced the hoop skirt, then let her fingers play on his shoulder. "Graham…I think I'd like to take you up on your offer today."

"My offer?"

"Yes, for the buggy ride. I feel like I'm ready."

His face reflected his excitement. "Wonderful. And

I have just the idea. It will be a surprise."

"My, aren't you the mysterious one."

"Let me escort you downstairs, and I'll have the carriage brought around."

Maybelle thought she knew what the banker had in mind. She'd planted the seed several times and suspected it had finally taken root.

Bunch helped her into the buggy, and they headed west out of Sinola on a slightly-rutted dirt road. The sky was a striking turquoise blue with billowing white clouds for company. Rolling brown landscape had finally given way to a light green spring hue. In the distance, broad sandstone formations rose north and south of the road and broke up the horizon. They travelled alongside a running streambed that cleaved gray rock walls. The water's constant murmuring gave her a certain reassurance. She was getting closer to her quarry, the murdering scoundrel who had her family killed. When she saw him through the window that night, Wilkins looked formidable. Now, she needed to be that as well—and more.

She vaguely heard Bunch chattering on about something as they rode. An absent nod when he looked her way. She said, "Yes, certainly."

He wore a puzzled look but prattled on.

They were on the same route she'd taken that careless night. "Where in the world are we off to, Graham? I'm all atwitter."

"You'll see, it will only be another little bit before we're there."

"Is it a place we've been?"

"No." He chuckled.

"Have we spoken about it before?"

"Yes!" Big smile.

"Is it…oh, I don't know. This is all very exciting; you must tell me!"

His eyes sparkled. "I can't keep a secret from you. We're going to visit Elijah Wilkins!"

"Oh my, you do know how to turn a girl's head. I'm thrilled." As if she hadn't known. "How much farther, dear Graham?" Was she laying it on too thick? Probably not. The banker didn't seem that perceptive.

"It's just past here. I hope he's home." They rode along, talking about nothing, until they reached a gradual bend in the bumpy road. "He doesn't go out much, being blind and all."

Blind! She thought back to his staring at the ceiling as she watched from the window that night. Of course. And she'd worried so much about her looks. She recognized the low white stucco ranch house when it came into view in the distance. Was he there?

A vaquero rode out of brush to the right of the road. He trotted his horse even with the buggy. "You come to see el jefe, señor?"

"Why yes, Andres, is he home?"

"I weel tell heem you are here." He galloped away.

When they pulled up to the front circle of the large, rambling house, a small man dressed in spotless white appeared on the steps. His outfit matched the color of the stucco. Bunch helped Maybelle down. The servant bowed slightly, then motioned toward the open, front double doors. A large man stood just inside, smoking a cigar. Maybelle blanched. Him.

Graham walked ahead. "Mr. Wilkins—Elijah— may I present Mrs. Maybelle Perkins."

Wilkins held a hand out, which Maybelle grasped.

The man brushed a kiss across the top of her hand. "I am honored to have you in my home, Mrs. Perkins."

"Please call me Maybelle, Mr. Wilkins." Her heart pounded loudly. She wanted to wipe her hand clean and strangle him, yet race away at the same time. A flush warmed her neck.

"And I am Elijah, your servant, ma'am." He touched a finger to his brow and motioned down the wide, main hallway. The man didn't use a guide pole, nor did he run a hand along the walls as he walked. He moved as if he could see everything. A wide door lay open on the right.

Maybelle sucked in her breath. The large room reeked of wealth. Outside the window that night, she'd focused on Wilkins, not his surroundings. Now she got a closer look at western elegance. She'd never seen crystal glasses or many-colored stuffed leather chairs. Oil lamp wall sconces gave the room a warm glow that reflected off polished wooden floors. A large portrait of a beautiful woman hung above the broad, tooled pine mantel.

Wilkins moved directly toward a chair, then turned and extended a hand. "Maybelle, would you sit here, to my right?"

He didn't grant Bunch a special place.

"My pleasure, Elijah." She let his name roll off her tongue. She'd been almost physically sick thinking about meeting the murderer but was getting more comfortable with the role she was playing. Graham had been easy prey. Wilkins, the murderer, would no doubt be tougher. The coward as much as fired the shots that killed her family. She settled back against the plush chair pillow, her face still flushed.

"Are you a little warm, Maybelle? Would you care for a drink to cool off?"

How did the blind man know that? Even though it was only midday, she wanted to drink a whole bottle. "Don't mind if I do…Elijah. Perhaps a nice…" she searched for the name of a proper drink—think!

"I have an excellent port, would that do?"

"Very nicely, thank you." At least she'd had one of those before. She glanced at Graham. He stared at Wilkins.

The rancher wore a smug smile. "And you, Graham, what would you like?"

"Uh, a whiskey, please."

Wilkins waved a hand in the air, and the small butler delivered the drinks. He poured a brandy for the rancher. "Graham has mentioned you to me, Maybelle. Says you are his best customer—next to me of course. What brings you to our fair territory?"

"Oh, dear me. Well, I've always wanted to come west. This country has its own beauty, different from the East, but striking all the same. I'm looking to make some investments here. I have been searching for a large parcel of land to start a cattle ranch on. It just so happens there's a grand tract not far from here that might do. Graham is helping me investigate it."

The rancher's eyebrows arched toward Bunch.

The banker raised his glass.

Maybelle slowly drew off her white cotton gloves. The lady in the Denver store said they were the latest. "I am trying to locate the owners now to negotiate the purchase. A place called the Abriendo Grant. Perhaps you've heard of it?" She let her last words rise in what she hoped sounded like innocence. She'd learned in

Denver that was the spread Wilkins was trying to steal. The assassin had the entire Abriendo family killed—all except for the boy, Rodrigo, who had been staying with her grandson at Del's that night. No doubt Wilkins planned to buy the Spanish grant with the gold coins stolen from the Abriendos when he had them murdered. Except he didn't have the coins.

Maybelle didn't know who shot her and gutted her place that night, but whoever it was, he worked for Wilkins. After her barn burned to the ground and the fire unearthed the gold coins, she realized what the night riders were after. She didn't know Ansel had stolen the loot, much less buried it there. Now, to think she might be able to hijack the Abriendo right out from under Wilkins' very nose and use those same coins to do it. And maybe steal the rest of the man's money in the process, with Graham's help. It would be sweet revenge—but bitter, nonetheless. No doubt Wilkins wouldn't react well to her scheme. Her heart fluttered as she waited for his response.

The rancher said a little too quickly, "What interests you about that land?"

"The Abriendo seems like a perfect location, don't you think?" She took a long sip of her drink to draw him in further. Placed the crystal glass back on the table. Centered it with a nudge. "Has wonderful grazing, good water, and plenty of wide open space." Had she said too much? "At least…that's what I'm told." Fanned herself. "Room to roam thousands of head. Cattle, that is." She knew it well. She and Del had worked there for years. "Around one hundred twenty thousand acres or so, isn't it?" Now, she was out and out mocking him. She drew a deep breath. "I heard they carved off a small piece which they gave to their household help. Imagine such a thing." Her heart leaped as she spoke those words. That gift turned out to be her ranch. And Del's. She took another long sip and twirled the small crystal's stem. The thick, dark port tasted like syrup, but the smooth drink didn't blunt her pain.

With a little maneuvering, Wilkins placed the brandy exactly in the middle of his table as well. He steepled his fingers and regarded her with a slight look of disfavor. "I've heard of the Abriendo, of course, but it would take a substantial amount of money to buy that land, even if an owner could be found. From what I understand, though, the family met with untimely...fates."

The bastard. Maybelle forced a lighthearted air. "Be that as it may, if no owner can be found—and from what I've been told it's likely there won't be—I suppose I'll buy it from the Territory. But I might consider...a partner..." She almost purred as she said the word. Another large sip calmed her some. She wanted to scratch his eyes out, but he was already blind. That urge fought with a desire to run away from all this as fast as her legs would carry her. Leave these horrid memories behind. Wilkins couldn't see her face or gestures, but the manservant could, so she'd be careful to hide her rage.

The rancher rubbed at his clean double chin. "Pardon me, Maybelle, but it sounds like you are already decided on this."

"Well, I suppose I am, Elijah. It would be so exciting, wouldn't it? A cattle ranch here in the great American West. But then, you know all about that. It just sounds so...romantic." Graham said Wilkins was a widower. She was looking for an opening. "I'm hoping to present an offer to territorial officials soon. We could be neighbors. Wouldn't that be delightful?" She cursed him under her breath.

Wilkins' jaw muscles clenched. Her false smile was now reflected on the blind man's face as well. "Quite. You mentioned the possibility of...a partner? Would you...consider me?"

"Oh, Elijah, I couldn't ask you, couldn't impose that way. You're just being chivalrous, I'm sure." She wanted to dangle him over the depths of Hell. For an eternity. She downed the rest of her drink. The warmth soothed this time.

"No, not at all. I would be interested. What did you have in mind?"

"Really. I can't imagine such an established, important person as yourself considering throwing in— partnering, that is—with a woman new to the West's ways. But that is so very gracious of you to offer." His face flushed. Apparently, he didn't like being on the dangling end of anything. Wonderful.

He squinted. "Very kind of you to say, but I *would* consider such a business proposition. Under the right terms, naturally."

The murderer had taken the lure. Now to find out how far he was willing to go. "Well, I haven't given it a lot of thought, of course, but perhaps we could work something out." She waved a casual hand in the air. "I did have a few free moments in Denver recently and inquired as to what the land might be worth. It seems— this is just a woman's uneducated guess, mind you—the price might be as high as fifty thousand dollars. Perhaps more." An enormous sum, just about double what she had. Could she entice the monster to part with the other half? Or maybe even all of it? She glanced at Graham, who sat with a small grin.

Wilkins drummed his fingers on the arm chair. "About what I figured as well." As soon as he said that, he frowned. "I mean, that sounds—" He stopped and motioned for a second brandy.

There it was. The opening she needed to knife him with. "Oh, I didn't know you'd been looking into it, too." She drew the 'too' out in a syrupy voice. Confirmation that she was on the right trail. That was all she wanted to know, and he'd just removed any doubt.

She put a hand up. Another drink would do nicely right about now.

Chapter Twenty-Five

Tyson's horse raced from the cattle camp with him and the boy. He weaved his way north in the dim moonlight. His plan had worked. Sort of. He had the kid but not Lawson. Yet. He tried to sort things out as he rode. Wilkins wanted the boy dead. Was there a way for Tyson to cash in on that? Trade him for some of the gold? All of it?

He was alone for the first time in a while. He'd ditched the remnants of his gang back at the Pecos. Gave a fleeting thought to whether any were still alive and grunted. Didn't care much, either way. He had the boy and would soon have Lawson. Things were coming together nicely for the first time since he couldn't remember when.

"What's your name, son?...I said, what's your name?" The boy shook in his arms. He backed off—didn't matter what the kid's name was, anyway. Tyson hadn't considered where he'd go. Never had thought very far ahead. He'd leave some sort of trail for Lawson. But he'd string him along before he waylaid him.

Weren't many towns of any size in this part of the Territory. Santa Rosa wasn't far, and he was well known there. Wouldn't take Lawson long to find out where he'd been. He wondered about the woman, though. She ought not to have drawn on him. Pretty little thing. He'd have taken her instead of the kid but wasn't sure Lawson would have come after her. And there was the problem of her gunshot wound. He smiled at his handiwork. The boy was the best bet. Tyson had pursued Lawson for the past year, but now he'd turned the tables and lured Lawson into trailing him.

Faint light ahead from the small village of Santa Rosa fought the gathering dusk. The long, dry ride with the boy parched Tyson's throat. He tied off at the hitching post in front of the town's only saloon. The place had a homey feel to it, or what passed for a homey feel to him, which meant no one had been shot yet. Grabbing the boy by the collar, he headed for the establishment's swinging doors. Inside, he sized the place up and made his way toward a table where two men sat drinking. The kid trudged behind.

Tyson leaned toward them. "Clear out, you're leavin'." One man objected and started to get up. He'd barely cleared his chair when Tyson jammed his gun under the man's chin. The other customer rushed from the saloon, followed closely by his pal. Tyson eyed the bartender. "Nice to see a friendly face. We're gettin' to be regular pals, ain't we?"

The bartender nodded ever so slightly.

"I said, we're good friends, right?"

"Uh, sure."

"More like it. Grab me a bottle straightaway."

The boy stood gaping.

"Siddown." Tyson motioned the man over.

The barkeep made his way to their table. He wiped a sweaty hand on his dirty brown apron and stared at Rodrigo. "This your son? Favors you."

"You know he don't favor me none. He's brown as

a berry. Look at me. Would you say I'm brown as a berry?"

"Uh…no, I wouldn't say so…wouldn't say nothin' of the sort…"

"Why'd you go and say somethin' dumb like that? Tryin' to irritate me? Gimme that bottle." Tyson snatched it and stared at the man. He thrust an empty hand out. "Didn't bring me a glass either, did you? Do I have to do all your thinkin'? And get somethin' for the boy to drink, he ain't much of a talker. Rustle us up some food, too. Was a dry trail here from…" He left the sentence unfinished.

When he'd downed most of the whisky bottle and finished off his plate, Tyson called the bartender back over. "Steak was right tough. Not gonna pay for a stringy steak. Fortunately for you, the boy here didn't let that bother him." He glanced at the young'un who seemed shrunken into the wooden chair next to him, then back at the barkeep. "Siddown."

The bartender held a hand out. "I cain't really do that. Got a full house tonight, need to be—"

"I'll say it once more. Sit." He dropped a hand off the tabletop. "That's better." He leaned forward. "Listen careful. Del Lawson's gonna—" Tyson paused. "You know him on sight, right?"

A nod. "Can't hardly miss him, 'specially with that crease in his hair you gave him." The man forced a short chuckle, his smiling gaze halted by Rodrigo's haunted eyes.

"Never mind that. Lawson's been followin' me for a while." Tyson glanced sideways at the bartender and shook his head. "Don't rightly know why, but he'll likely be by here in a few days." He drew his six-shooter and angled it on the table. "Don't tell him me and the boy been through…got it?"

The man nodded quickly.

Tyson rubbed at his chin and finished the bottle with a couple of swigs. Another plan formed in his mind. Sure, why not? "Hold on, I gotta better idea. Tell him we was here and left—headed for Texas. Dusty little town of Lost Creek. He'll know it—we both been there." A slight slur in his voice as he grabbed a nearly-full bottle from the gents at the next table and tossed another slug of whiskey down. They made no move to retrieve it.

The bartender said, "Sure. You can count on me." He leaned close. "Where you really goin', Pete?"

Tyson arched an eyebrow. "Ain't none of your business, now is it?" His new plan made more sense. He'd waylay Lawson as he made his way out of town toward Texas. Then he'd take the boy and Lawson south to Wilkins' spread. Make a deal with the rancher for the boy. Beat the secret of the gold out of Lawson. "Go fetch me another—" The saloon doors squeaked back and forth and conversation died away. Tyson's attention turned to a dusty cowboy who'd just jangled in. He had the look of a man who could handle almost anything, guns included. He stared Tyson's way as he strode to the bar.

"Who's tendin' here?"

The bartender raised a hand. "Be there in a minute."

The stranger motioned him over. "Whiskey. Pronto." He never took his eyes off Tyson. The wrangler's gaze settled on Rodrigo, who stopped eating and sat shaking.

Tyson glanced at Rodrigo, then the newcomer. He rose from the table. "What're you lookin' at, duster? Ain't nothin' over here of your concern. You'd best be starin' at your whiskey glass here on out."

"Didn't mean to rile you, mister. I know the boy, and I guess I know who you are, too. You're the one rode into camp aways back after rustling some of our cattle. Took the foreman by surprise, but then he set you straight. Sounded like you and Del Lawson had already crossed paths before that." He went back to his drink.

Tyson glanced around the room at the word 'rustle.' No one returned his stare. His hand eased to his holster. "Who're you?"

Without looking up, the cowhand said, "Nobody—just driftin'. Was on that drive 'til I got tired of takin' orders from a coupla dandies."

Tyson told Rodrigo to stay put. He started toward the bar. "I said, what's your name?" His hand rested on the gun stock.

The drifter gazed at Tyson. "Don't do nothin' to shorten your time on God's green earth, mister. I'm faster'n you any day of the week. That includes today." He stretched his arms apart on the bar rail. "Just came in for a drink. Your business is your business. Ain't mine."

Tyson squinted at the man. "Name's Tyson, Pete Tyson. Heard you say somethin' about Del Lawson—"

"Huh. Never met a more raggedy-ass cowpoke in all my life. He chafed me, shore did. The reason I left the drive."

"Why don't you tell me about it while I buy you a drink, mister—"

The cowhand glanced at Rodrigo, then back to Tyson. "Potter, Jake Potter."

****

Morning found Tyson coming down the hotel stairs, the boy in tow.

The desk clerk forced a smile. "Top of the mornin' to you, Mister Tyson. Sleep well?"

Tyson took a seat at a dining room table. "Fetch me some eggs, grits, and flap jacks. Keep the coffee comin'. Rustle up somethin' of the like for my little pal here."

The clerk disappeared.

Tyson grunted at Rodrigo. "If you could talk, you coudda told him all about me snatching you—but you can't, can you?" He chuckled at the pained expression on the boy's face.

Potter came in from the dusty street. He doffed his stained Stetson toward Tyson. "Mind if I sit?"

"Suit yourself."

He glanced at Rodrigo. "How'd you come by the boy? He sticks pretty close to Lawson."

"That's what I'm countin' on. Unless I miss my guess, he should be comin' this way—be here in a day or so."

"You *want* him to find you?"

Tyson took a long sip of coffee. He put the cup on the table and held Potter's gaze hard. "You ask a lot of questions for a stranger. Any reason?"

"I'd look forward to seein' someone take him down is all. Just wondered if you needed any help doin' it?"

Tyson put both hands flat on the table and leaned forward. "Do I look like I need any help?"

Potter leaned back and raised a hand. "Nope."

They sat in silence until the waiter brought the food. Tyson slathered his pancakes with butter and took a bite. After a long swallow of coffee, he stared at Potter. "If'n I did—and I'm not sayin' I do—you volunteering?"

"Just tell me what you want me to do. I got no problem backin' that pretend cowboy down."

Rodrigo ate without looking up from his plate, his eyes darting back and forth between the two.

Tyson finished his meal. He pushed back and wiped a dirty hand over his mouth. "I may have just the job for you."

Chapter Twenty-Six

Rose woke to a pungent smell in the small enclosure. It wasn't entirely dark, but the dim light made it hard to see. Was it a tipi? An Indian woman hovered over a little pot nearby. Whatever the odor was, it came from that bowl. Rose's eyes watered, and her skin tingled where it was bare. But her breathing came easy, and her head was clear. She placed a hand to her shoulder and pressed. She winced but didn't cry out. A few tentative stretches hurt, but they reassured her she could stand the pain. She glanced at the old woman.

Without looking up, the shaman said, "Worst is over. Bone not broken." She dropped bits of something into the pot and stirred.

"What is that?"

"Nothing."

"My name is Rose. Thank you for caring for me."

A nod.

A 'thank you' seemed too little. "May I...pay you something?"

The woman sat expressionless.

Had Rose offended her? "You are..."

"I am called Laila."

The name she'd dimly heard when Del brought her in. Where was he? And where was she?

"Three days now. You are strong."

212

She'd been here three days? She ought to have an appetite but didn't. A quick scan of the interior revealed woven ornaments strung halfway up the hide sides. Bright colors in the pale light. A circular object with a star-shape woven inside caught her eye. It seemed to give off its own faint glow.

"Shaman circle. Heals."

A fleeting vision of Laila pressing it on her chest and chanting came and went. She pushed herself to a sitting position. "May I have something to eat?"

"Venison is outside."

She struggled to a sore stand on wobbly legs and pushed the buckskin flap aside. An afternoon sun hung low in the sky. A cache of meat hung in a gnarled mesquite tree. She put a hand to the trunk and stood on tiptoes to reach a haunch. The cooked venison peeled off easily and she brought a piece of thigh back in. "Aren't you worried animals will get that meat?" She nibbled at the food.

"No one bothers Laila. Drink." She handed Rose a small clay cup of dark liquid.

"Is this the medicine you've been giving me?"

A nod.

As foul as it smelled, Rose expected to have to choke it down, but the brew swallowed smoothly. It warmed her throat and filled her stomach. "That was…very good. What do you call it?"

"Nothing."

Nothing. Like her life was turning out. Injured and stranded here with no way to leave and no money to leave with. She didn't usually feel sorry for herself, but the emotion surged now. Where was Del? She knew why he left, why he had to leave, but still, it hurt.

Laila interrupted her thoughts. "Help is coming."

"Someone's on the way? How do you...know?"

"Soon."

If only that were true. She let hope flicker in her soul for a moment. Probably not Del—she was sure he was chasing her shooter and Rodrigo. Who else knew she was here? And where was here? She sat up on the soft, decorative woven rug, feeling thankful, yet uneasy. For now, the potion was doing its job, calming her, easing her discomfort. Eating more of the venison revealed how famished she was after all. The meat was tender and delicious. Smoked somehow. She washed it down with a cup of clear, cold spring water. "You seem to have some kind of magic."

Laila shook her head. "The men think so, so I let them. What I know I learned from my ancestors. Not magic." For the first time, the woman wore a small smile. "You are healer, too."

The shaman was full of surprises. Rose nodded. A full stomach and her eyelids soon drooped.

A hand to her shoulder woke her. "Wha—"

"It's me, Rose. Kip. Kip Holloway."

"Kip?" She propped herself on an arm. "What are you doing? How did you know where I was?"

"Your sweetheart told me before he rode off with you."

"Del? He did? He's not my...um..."

"Your smiling eyes say different. His do, too." Kip's laugh filled the wigwam.

"They do?" A blush warmed her face, and she put a hand to her cheek. She remembered little of the ride here besides the searing pain in her shoulder and Del holding her. "Where are we?"

"Outside the little town of Puerto de Luna a good way. Laila's a well-known Pecos Indian healer along this trail. Del hurried away with you before I had a chance to tell him about her. She's gotten you back on your feet sooner than you should be. We'll head out in the morning, okay?"

"Head out where?"

"Back to the cattle drive."

"Del's not there, is he? Rodrigo?"

Kip shook his head.

"Then I'm not going back, either. My guess is he's tracking that outlaw. The one who took Rodrigo."

"I'm sure he is. Figured you might say that, so I already told Stoney we wouldn't be back for a while."

"You did? I'm sure that made him mad."

"You'da thought so, but he just nodded and waved me away. Took it pretty well, all things considered, said he's never dealt with anything like you and the boy on a drive. He also said something surprising. Said they'd try to sell the rest of the beeves at Fort Union and Trinidad instead of goin' all the way north to Denver. Sounded like they might be on the return trip sooner than later."

They walked out of the tipi together. "Uh huh. So Del is after…"

"Tyson, Pete Tyson. Laila said Del headed back toward Santa Rosa so that's where we go. Unless…"

"What?"

"It ain't likely, but it's possible Tyson's lookin' for you. Probably would've taken you back at camp if he hadn't shot you. Could be he's doublin' back this way."

"How would he know where I am? I don't even know."

215

"Del said this is Tyson's homeland. He probably knows there's only a few places Del could've taken you for doctorin' hereabouts, this bein' the closest one to our camp. Could be that Tyson's watchin' us right now."

Rose shuddered. The thought of that monster having her in his sights again gave her the shakes. She forced the image back. "I don't think Tyson would head this way with Rodrigo. Tyson's evil, but I doubt he's smart enough to have thought this all through. Del said Tyson murdered his father, who rode in Tyson's gang. It was Tyson who raided Del's ranch house and murdered his family. But Del heard Tyson utter another man's name that night before he passed out. Del didn't remember who, but he said it sounded like someone else ordered his family killed and his ranch burned."

"Could be, I suppose. Right now, what matters is getting you safely to wherever we're goin'."

"Santa Rosa is the only way we know Del went, so that's where we'll ride. And safe isn't the most important part of this right now. Finding Del and Rodrigo is."

"You're the boss." Kip gazed east. "If I know Del, he'll go after Tyson in a straight line."

"How far is it?" She flexed her shoulder.

"A few hours. We can rest up here tonight and still be there late morning." Kip hesitated. "We don't have to ride real hard, just keep a good pace."

Rose shook her head. "Let's don't wait, let's leave now. And don't ride slow 'cause of me." She hoped she'd be able to keep up. She thanked Laila, who gave her a small bottle of the dark liquid, and mounted up with Kip's help on the other horse he brought. "Let's go, slowpoke, time's a wastin'." A kick to the horse's flanks and she lit out.

Kip shook his head as he watched her leave. He was almost jealous Del had somebody like Rose so set on finding him. But Del would do the same for him. He spurred away hard.

Rose struggled with the need to hurry, protect her shoulder, and keep an eye out for Tyson.

Kip pulled up miles later for dinner. There'd be no cook fire tonight. He tugged some of Buck's provisions out of his saddlebag. He laid out fry bread and beef jerky, followed by coffee beans and water, but without a fire the latter two didn't mix well.

Rose smoothed a small spot on the cool ground and wrapped the beautiful blanket Laila gave her around herself. She glanced his way as silver stars pierced the clear night sky. "We're going to find him, aren't we? Please, Lord." She hoped he would say 'yes.'

"Been trailin' long enough to have notions about things. Don't know for sure how these worries are gonna turn out, but I have the feeling we're on the right track."

That was good enough for Rose.

They rode at first light, her thoughts circling back to the cattle drive. Was Daisy all right? The dog would stay in camp with Buck after Rose left, wouldn't she? Why did Tyson take Rodrigo and leave her? How scared the child must be, away from Del. And her. Where was Del? Nothing was right. Everything had spun out of control—a feeling she hated. She let herself think a thought that she'd stuffed away time and again. She had no family left back east. Her whole world now was—Del. And Rodrigo. Kip's suggestion that she ride back to camp held no appeal. No reason to do that anymore.

She spurred her mount, her life little more than a question mark.

Chapter Twenty-Seven

Del searched the roughed-up ground in front of him as he rode Shade. Tracking Tyson was near impossible on this cattle-scrambled earth. Where would the man go? Tyson must know the land as well as Del did. Did the killer have a hideaway? If so, why hole up somewhere where Del couldn't find him? Unless he planned to waylay him on the trail. He knew Tyson was drawing him in, but he'd take his chances. He had to, to rescue Rodrigo.

What kind of track would Tyson leave? Del wasn't sure. The only thing he could do was head for one of the few villages that dotted the expansive Territory. He'd start with Santa Rosa, the nearest place of any size. The surrounding landscape reminded him of his devastated ranch. He'd never been back there, had never considered going.

The simmering sun retreated behind the western heights. Del scanned the summits. Winter snow still blanketed the tops and usually didn't disappear until July. More this year than normal. Snow-fed streams that used to meander through the valley were near-rivers. Cottony clouds dotted the blue sky and the sharp aroma of blossoming sage filled his senses. Shade was holding up well—the horse had better stamina than Del, who felt every bit of his twenty-nine years. He wished he hadn't taken Potter's blows in front of Rose. Or

Rodrigo.

The miles piled up as the sun went down. Closer now to Santa Rosa—and his ranch, but he didn't want to think about that. Del recognized the low bluffs in the distance ahead, broad and sturdy like a signpost. His son was seven when he got his suspenders caught on a tree there, and he thought a bear had him. Del smiled, remembering how Johnny's legs flailed as he tried to escape, then teared at the thought of his son moldering in the ground. He couldn't let such a thing happen to Rodrigo. A little thicket in the heights ahead would be bed tonight. As good a place as any. Short, green cedars clung to rocky earth at the base of low bluffs. Gray granite had yielded some time back to rounded, reddish-orange sandstone as he rode toward the Pecos. He dithered between camping on flatter, open land or slightly rising pine and aspen terrain. He dismounted and smoothed Shade's muzzle. "Let's get you watered and oated up, big fella." Del let the reins drop, and Shade ambled to the small stream that gushed down the hillside. After fetching the grains, Del gave a low whistle, and the horse returned to the modest campfire.

Del warmed his hands over the rising flames, fueled by scattered deadwood scavenged nearby. He'd pulled a long-dead tree trunk to the fire as a seat. If Tyson was laying for him, this would be a good spot for an ambush. Most likely, Tyson wouldn't strike until night fell. The small fire would give him away if Tyson was near, but maybe that would be a good thing. Lure the assassin. He wouldn't get much sleep tonight, although Shade made a good lookout.

Beans again. Flames warmed the clumpy pintos in his blackened coffee mug. He considered. If an attack was coming, let it happen now—right here. He mashed some coffee beans and brewed the pieces in his hot cup. Wasn't the best he'd had, but not the worst, either. Didn't matter, he wasn't looking for fine dining out here on the plains.

The moon snuck up into the dark sky while he wasn't watching. It cast pale light on the little camp. He couldn't make out Shade anymore but knew the horse was nearby. He undid his bedroll near the fire and placed an army blanket on top with a saddle for a pillow. He hoped the empty, lumpy roll would throw a murderer off for a moment. That's all the time he would need. He gathered handfuls of brown needles nearby and made his bed farther up into the pines. Good field of vision.

He was drifting off when he was roused by Shade's shrill neigh. Turning on his side, he heard a *whuff! whuff!* coming from the dense trees above him. He'd only heard that sound a few times before, but enough to know it was a bear. Shade clattered away into the darkness. Del glanced toward the fire, now not much more than an orange glow. He sprang from his makeshift bed and grabbed a medium-sized branch laying by the fire ring. Light from the embers revealed a young black bear. It charged but halted when another growl split the night air. A different pair of eyes glowed in the darkness. Now he had two terrors to fend off. Not good odds.

As the animal rumbled toward Del, a wolf dashed between them. It stood with front legs splayed and teeth bared. The wolf's hackles rose as it tensed in the weak firelight. The bear stood on hind legs and roared, louder than anything Del had heard in his life. A slight wind carried the animal's rotten breath with it. The creature thumped to the ground and scuffed a paw through the earth, bellowing. The wolf stood its ground with fierce growls that set the hairs on Del's neck on edge. He stood transfixed.

The bear shifted to the right, mirrored nimbly by the wolf. A move left brought the wolf that way with louder snarls. The bear raked the ground again with more *huffs*. It shook its black head and loosed another bellow. Louder, longer growls in return halted the beast in its tracks. More swipes with its thick paw. The bear hesitated, then lumbered into the trees but not before a nip to its backside by the wolf sent it loping away.

Del's heart thumped. Had he really just seen that? From the black of night, a bear charges him and a wolf appears out of nowhere and chases it off. He kept a tight grip on the wooden club in his hand, senses as alive as they'd ever been. The wolf never looked back as it disappeared into the trees.

Del sat by the fire. More like fell down. He stared motionless into the embers, eyes still saucers. Daybreak found him curled against the chill. A nicker and he forced his eyes open. Shade stood nearby, bobbing his head as if to say 'get up!' Del unlimbered, his body still sore from the beating he'd taken from Potter. The fire pit was out, and he wasn't sure he wanted to go to the trouble of setting it again just for a warm breakfast. Shade came first, anyway. He undid the leather straps on his saddlebag and drew the bag of oats out. Usually he spread them on the ground, but with this gravel he held handfuls up to the horse's mouth. He and Shade were becoming a team—at least he felt that way.

Rooting around in the saddlebag, he pulled out

hardtack biscuits and several pieces of beef jerky. He swung up in the saddle—he'd eat while he rode. Needed to be on his way again.

There! What?

In the distance, a wolf loped along with him. Might be the same one from last night. What was the animal doing? He squinted. Was it the wolf from his ranch? Looked like it could be. But what was it doing out here, following him?

Del swung Shade closer. The wolf angled away and kept the same distance between them. Wasn't much Del could make of his travel companion, so he'd let things play out as they would. Trotting easily on a ridgeline, the wolf didn't look like it could have scared a bear away, but Del knew from experience that looks weren't everything. Shade glanced the animal's way often. Somehow, being trailed by the wolf didn't worry Del. If it was the same one that used to roam his ranch, he didn't have anything to fret about. If it wasn't, well, that was another matter.

The wolf sat on its haunches on the crest of a hill, as if waiting for him. Del squinted. It was the one from his ranch. He'd found the wolf injured as a yearling and dropped venison in the hills from time to time. Didn't take long for the animal to heal, but it still roamed close to the ranch after that.

Del fingered the bullet around his neck. He didn't know where the wolf was going, but he knew where he was headed. Santa Rosa. Had to see if Rodrigo—and Tyson—were there. The animal would surely be gone before then, wouldn't follow him into town. Soon, Del peered down on the outskirts of the small village. It sat nestled in the low Pecos River basin, green ribbons to either side of the river. The wolf was still his companion. As he angled down, it moved ahead of him, trotting farther to the west with a long howl. He reined Shade in and reminded himself he was here to rescue Rodrigo. He glanced at the wolf. The animal stared back.

Del couldn't tear himself away. He laid the reins on the right side of Shade's neck, whispering, "Let's go, boy." Shade shifted back up the slope, and the wolf started away at an easy trot again. Del didn't know what to think. What was he doing following a wolf? As he rode, the landscape became more and more familiar. The land where he grew up. Where he'd been household help in hacienda Abriendo. Where he and his mother worked for years. Where his son and Rodrigo had become fast friends. Where his mother's ranch was…where his spread was—where his family used to live…

None of this made any sense.

He rode a long time in a daze of swirling memories. It looked like the wolf was leading him home. But why return to the site of his greatest sorrow? There was only hurt there. The animal slowed. His old ranch was just beyond those heights ahead in a little valley. He stopped Shade, and his head sank to his chest. When his heartbeat slowed again, he smoothed a hand over his beard. An urge to turn back raced through him.

He took a deep breath. "Go on now, go." Shade crested the low rise, and Del laid eyes on the blackened devastation below. His soul stiffened. More than a year hadn't softened the wretched scene. He nudged Shade down toward the ruined farmhouse. Visions of his wife and son played in his head. Her tending her vegetable garden, long brown hair in a bun, always in a spotless white apron, so proud of her tomatoes. Jimmy and his curly sandy hair running himself ragged playing 'catch me' with his dog in the dirt yard.

Del pulled up short of the scorched earth with its burnt offerings. He eased off Shade and eyed the desolate wreckage. Charred wooden shards lay scattered. Iron bars that were once straight lay twisted and mangled. A melted barn door lock here, a shattered window there. Just like his dreams. As a vision of that night flooded his mind, Del glanced away. The wolf sat on the same ridge it always had. Before he knew it, Del sank to his knees. He placed his hands flat on the ground before him. Tears made dark wet spots in the brown earth. He glanced toward the crude grave markers he'd first made for his wife and son when he could barely stand, or think, much less honor them properly.

He moved on wooden legs to their makeshift memorials and stared at the simple carved pieces of wood. They carried no words. He knew then why he was here—what he had to do. In the ruins, he uncovered some tools that hadn't completely burned up. A singed ax, a metal adze for finishing. He already had a Bowie knife. Years ago, he'd planted several live oaks nearby. He'd dug the graves near them. They stood in a semi-circle around the gravesites. A glen, of sorts, to protect his family.

The inscriptions came harder. What to say about his loving wife and full-of-life son? He'd never imagined he'd ever be without them, much less so soon. He'd given up trying to figure out God's plan in all this.

The only good thing about the past year was that time had worn down the harshest edges of his sorrow and the deep ache wasn't as unrelenting anymore. Acceptance was coming his way, grudging as it was. Simple memorials came to mind.

Kate Lawson
She Loved Life
We Loved Her
1842-1870

~

Sonny Lawson
The Best Son
A Man Could Have
1862-1870

Over the next few hours, Del squared off a couple of wooden barn slats that hadn't burned to pieces. Between the adze and his knife, he fashioned proper inscriptions on them. The words that stared back at him still didn't seem real. He smoothed the rough, weathered wood with the adze. Iron nails he'd found scattered in the barn dirt secured the pieces together. Every whack of his ax drove wooden headstone posts deeper into the still-soft ground. When he was confident the markers wouldn't get blown or washed away over time, he laid the ax down. He paused and removed his stained hat, staring with blurry eyes at the two impossible placards. It was little enough to say to honor his family, but they were good words. Honest words.

Clasping his hands in prayer, he asked the Lord to keep his family safe in His warm embrace and comfort them, comfort him until they were together again. He thought of his mother, shot that same night. She had such a hard life; it wasn't right. He prayed for her soul as well, then raised his hat to the heavens. "Thank you." He should have done this…when it first happened. "Thank you for bringing me back here, Lord."

A swipe at his eyes and he gazed in the distance. The wolf sat motionless on top of the rim. Del eyed the sky. Dark storm clouds gathered, and the wind picked up. This wasn't the breeze that gently rushed to either side of him as it passed. This wind swept the ground clean as it went about its work. A harbinger of rain, probably hail. Del stared at the heavy gray swirls blowing up in the sky. A thunderclap split the air and rain plunged from the sky in sheets, driven almost horizontally by the roaring wind. In no time, Del was drenched, but he stood like a statue, hat in hand. No hail.

The storm didn't last long—the most violent ones never do. As the rain pattered to a halt, the sun squeezed through patchy clouds and picked spots to bathe. A glint from the remains of the leveled barn caught his eye. Del walked toward it, the gleam growing brighter, pulling him almost like a beacon. He looked down at something shiny lying among the ruins that the windswept rain had uncovered. What was it? He reached and retrieved a gold locket in the shape of a heart on a thin gold chain.

Kate's.

His throat seized, and his eyes filled. She'd been so proud of the piece, always wore it around her neck. The biggest purchase he'd ever made. He could see her clearly again for the first time since… He held it in the palm of his hand for a moment, then pried the precious treasure open, remembering what was inside. A small, delicate painting of the two of them—newlyweds. Cost nearly every cent he had. They were so young. She smiled out at him. He smiled back as he drank in the picture. How he loved her. He couldn't believe this had come through the inferno undamaged. Their wedding seemed so long ago. Like another lifetime.

No.

He closed the locket and draped it on her marker. Their marriage was this lifetime. Time to start living again. His return had served as a powerful reminder of that. The emerging sun dried his clothes and warmed his soul. He gazed around at what once was—and could be again. The markers were proper monuments. He placed his hand on each for a moment, then swung up on Shade.

The wolf was gone.

Chapter Twenty-Eight

Maybelle rode lost in thought on the buggy ride back to town from Wilkins' ranch. She'd used the killer's greed to draw Wilkins in. That had gone very well. Now, she needed to turn her attention to ruining Bunch's relationship with the rancher. "Graham, that was a lovely visit. He's a most gracious man, don't you think? I can see why you like working for him…being his banker, I mean."

Bunch snapped the reins, and the buggy lurched even though the horse was already trotting at a good clip. His face reflected his displeasure. "I *don't* work for him. I've always looked at it as more of a partnership, and I'm sure he does, too. I advise him on quite a few things. He's constantly telling me how much he appreciates it." The banker almost said it with a 'humph!' at the end.

"Oh, I didn't mean to belittle your rapport with him. I hope you didn't take it that way, not at all. But I must confess I was a bit taken aback by how he tended to overlook you during our visit. Perhaps he was just out of sorts. I'm sure it was nothing intentional, certainly." She hoped her seed of doubt had found a good place to root. "No doubt he relies on you for all manner of things. As I do. Why, what would I do without your guidance as I establish myself in this new land?" Her deceits were tripping off her tongue almost

229

effortlessly now. "I think my face is healing well."

Evidently, Graham's burn hadn't settled yet. He rode silently.

"Graham?"

"Yes, of course. Um…your face looks fine. Good, in fact. An excellent recovery so far."

So far? What did he mean by that? Except for the puffiness, she thought she was masking the cut rather well. She fanned her spreading flush in the cooling air, even though the setting sun had already taken the edge off the afternoon heat. Maybe she'd dug at his ego a little too deeply. She'd back off. After all, she'd just prepared the earth. She couldn't expect to see the crop yet. When Graham pulled up at her hotel, she leaned toward him and rested a hand on his arm. "I meant to mention, I'd like to discuss some financial matters with you. I value your opinion and would appreciate your thoughts on the Abriendo land. Dinner, perhaps?"

"Certainly, Maybelle, that would be very nice. Just so happens I do have some opinions on the matter. I'd look forward to sharing them with you."

"Seven, then?"

****

Maybelle took her time. It was almost half past seven when she promenaded down the stairs. Her late arrival didn't seem to bother Graham, though. He rose from his chair. She'd taken care to look her best. A light red rouge highlighted her cheeks. Hair swept up. The emerald green dress was one he'd seen before, but his eyes shined as he regarded her.

"Don't look now, but all the men in here are staring at you. And wondering how I got so lucky."

Maybelle offered her hand, when a sudden

melancholy swept over her. She hoped the banker couldn't detect the distress she felt. Is this what she was turning in to? A scheming woman full of vengeance? She thought back to…before. Ansel wasn't much, but she had the ranch, some land, a couple of cows, a small garden. Del and his family were near. Life was good—simple, but good. She had everything she needed. And now, here she was in a strange town, dining with a man she didn't really like. Plotting against the richest rancher in the Territory. A bitter taste fouled her mouth.

"Maybelle?"

"Yes…Graham. Um…what a kind thing to say." She glanced around the room. "I do like this hotel. It's so nice to dine with you tonight…and spend time together." She stuffed the harsh memories away and fanned herself. Her focus switched to raising the banker's temperature. He pulled her chair out, and Maybelle sat, drawing off her white gloves. "I do hope they have good pork here; it's my favorite. I like it even better than beef. But I suppose I should keep that a secret if I'm to have a cattle ranch." Her smile widened as the sadness faded.

The banker leaned forward. "Yes, quite. Would you like to discuss the Abriendo before we order?"

Maybelle waved a hand. "I'm sure we'll have time enough for that. Wasn't Elijah a gracious host? Something no doubt you've seen many times before. Just delightful, he was."

Graham responded with a clipped 'yes.'

"I must say, I was a little surprised he didn't offer us any biscuits or cookies. But then, I have an appetite now as a result, so all was not lost."

"He is a widower, after all. Perhaps the niceties of

231

entertaining have escaped him over the years. Would you like me to order for us?"

Maybelle harkened back to a previous dinner with him, and the same question. This time she'd speak up. "What a kind offer." The waiter approached. She said, "Why don't I peruse the menu for a moment? You're familiar with the dishes, Graham, so why not order for yourself? I'll just be another minute." She reached for the menu the waiter offered to the banker. "Thank you." Her eyes scanned the page. No pork. She looked at the waiter. "The T Bone steak, is it tender?" She'd draw this out.

"Yes'm."

"I'll have that well done, please." She handed the menu back. "I'll have a whiskey also—your best, thank you." Might as well discard some of her airs—no more wine.

Graham's eyes gave away his surprise. "A whiskey, Maybelle?"

The edges of her mouth turned up. "Would you like one, too?"

"Why…yes, I would, don't mind if I do."

When the waiter brought the drinks, Maybelle raised her glass. "Here's to a new partnership, and I'm not talking about the one I just made with Wilkins."

The banker beamed.

She took a gulp and paused to let the drink settle. Warmed her from the inside out. She leaned forward. "Now, about that land. What do you think of me buying it?"

Graham set his glass down. "I've always been partial to that grant. The Abriendos were wonderful people. Well known. People that rich always are. They didn't bank with me—they didn't bank with anyone, unfortunately. Turns out they should have. There's a rumor their wealth was stolen from them. That a large quantity of gold disappeared when they were killed. Talk is it was coins." Silence lingered between them.

Maybelle felt the blood drain from her face. She downed the rest of her glass. "I...don't know that I've ever heard about that." Her mind flew. "So, they were killed? The whole family?"

Bunch nodded. "Father—the padron—wife and two daughters, all shot down a little more than a year ago. Made big news around here, as you can imagine."

Cotton filled her mouth. "Yes...I suppose so. Something as horrible as that would." She motioned to the waiter. "Another whiskey, please." A furtive glance at the banker. "Graham?"

"Certainly. The evening has become even more interesting than I thought it might." He held up two fingers.

Maybelle's heart quickened. Surely Graham could hear it pounding. Had he put two and two together? That it was the Abriendo coins she deposited with him? Was he on to her? He must be. Money was his life, and he probably knew where all of it was around here. She kicked herself. She thought she'd been so smart. She sat mute, unable to maneuver the conversation anywhere safe.

Graham leaned in. "Turns out there was one survivor, though, a young boy. He had the good fortune to be visiting an anglo friend on a nearby ranch at the time. Name of Rodrigo. Now the only living heir, assuming he's still alive."

Maybelle blanched at the name. Rodrigo had been

visiting Del's family when the murders happened. She said a little too quickly, "Any reason he wouldn't be? Have you heard anything about him?"

"You seem interested in what happened to him." The waiter brought two drinks on a tray and placed them on the table.

Maybelle wanted to throw hers back but left the drink sitting there. It felt like she was the one being dangled now. A sudden vision of Del reflected back at her in the bar glass. Another flush. "Yes, well...of course I'm...interested in the boy. If he's...still alive, then he could...claim against the land, couldn't he?"

The banker left his drink alone, too. "Yes, he could, but no one knows where he is, or even if he is still alive. An uncertainty like that would muddle your plans to buy the grant unless you found out one way or the other. And Territorial officials don't like uncertainty."

Her clever plan was unraveling. Damn! She should have changed *all* the coins to currency in Denver. She would have, but a banker there warned her if too much new gold hit the markets all at once, officials would investigate. She didn't need that, so she kept the rest in coinage. She hadn't considered how much a slew of gold coins would stand out, especially to a local banker in a small town. Stupid! Now she really needed to draw Graham into her web, or hightail it. Every instinct she had told her to flee, to take the money, and disappear. Start a new life somewhere more civilized. Leave Wilkins and his henchman be. Bitter judgment already awaited them in eternity.

Her head said run, but her heart said otherwise.

She knew she'd waded into dangerous waters, but

she'd been in rushing currents before and was a strong swimmer. Graham was the immediate question mark. He was close to Wilkins, but how close? Could she entice him to turn on the killer? Persuade him away? It would likely take money—something she had plenty of. Buying him off would probably work—money already had a hold on the banker.

She didn't really care about the land, anyway. All she wanted was to ruin Wilkins. Use Graham to steal the man's money if she could. Break him. Fling his wealth in the Pecos for all she cared. All money had done was get her husband killed, her ranch and Del's destroyed, and his family murdered. Damn money anyway!

With a deep breath to slow her thumping heart, she took a large swig and motioned for him to do the same. Now was not the time to be timid. "Graham, I'm going to take you into my confidence. Can I trust you with something?" She leaned back, twirling her glass in her hand, her heart still rapid-firing.

"What is it, Maybelle?"

"I asked you a question, Graham. I need an answer."

"Depends on what you have in mind."

"Not good enough, forget I mentioned anything." She downed the last of her whiskey and started to rise.

The banker put a hand up. "Wait a minute. Please. Will you sit back down and tell me what you're thinking?" He finished his drink and called for two more.

"Are you worthy of my trust? Last time I'll ask." She ran a hand over her wounded cheek. Still tender. As she sat, she felt as vulnerable as she ever had in her life.

"You're familiar with the Code?"

"Of the West? Of course, everyone is."

"It speaks to the honor in a man. Takes the place of law around here, so I'm told. I'm calling on your character right now, Graham."

"All right, fair enough. Yes, I will hold what you tell me in confidence."

The bartender brought another two glasses, and Maybelle took a big sip. The raw whiskey went down smoother now. She stared at the banker. "I need your help in destroying Elijah Wilkins." There it was, an audacious declaration out in the open between them. She was surprised when it elicited no visible reaction. She cleared her throat. "My real name is Maybelle Lawson, not Perkins."

"I already know that. Go on. What's your plan?"

The slightest of winds could have bowled Maybelle over. She sat back in her chair. "What? How...how did you know?"

"Wasn't hard, figured it when you first brought the coins in. Wanted to see what you were up to."

She beheld the man. "Graham Bunch! I ought to slap you silly. Letting me go on and on, flirting with you, making a fool of myself. Why I never!" As mad as she sounded, a small smile played around the corners of her mouth, followed by a burst of laughter, the first time she'd laughed since she came to town. The banker smiled and laughed, too. The whiskey was doing its job when a worrisome thought struck her. "You're very...close...to Wilkins—have you told him about me?" She held her breath.

"Thought about it, but was just intrigued enough to want to see this play out some more."

"You wicked man, you've been fooling me while I thought I was deceiving you."

"About the size of it." Another smile. "What do you have in mind?"

Maybelle considered. There was no reason to hold anything back at this point. "I was going to use you to help me steal Wilkins' money. The things he values most. Ruin him."

The banker covered Maybelle's hand with his. "I know what Wilkins and Tyson did to you and your boy's family. No need to go into that. Wilkins gets plenty talkative when he drinks too much, which I always make sure he does when I'm around. He's nothing more than a lowdown skunk." He sipped his drink.

"Graham, you devil. You've been toying with not only me, but Wilkins, too. You are a mysterious sort. I wouldn't have thought it."

"No, I suppose not. Here I am, the small-town beguiled banker, mooning over the beautiful new woman in town. Turns out a lot of that is true, though. You are a magnificent woman, Maybelle. And sometime you must tell me the real story behind how you cut your cheek."

Maybelle blushed. She took another sip as she regarded the man. How unexpected. But how relieved she felt, with him now in on her ruse. She raised an eyebrow. "Partners, then?"

"Partners."

Glasses clinked in the night.

Chapter Twenty-Nine

As he rode from the destruction that was his ranch, Del glanced back, his spirit calmer. A detour took him by his mother's old place, lying in ruins as well. He'd figured she was dead, what with all that blood, but he hadn't been in any shape to stay and find out. And Rose. Would he ever see her again? Or Rodrigo? He'd finally done right by his wife and son, but now those he was closest to were in parts unknown.

He'd scout Santa Rosa to see if Tyson lay in wait for him there. If Tyson had hurt the boy... A morning's ride brought him to a low bluff overlooking the small town. He dismounted and smoothed a hand along the big horse's neck. "How'd you like to be mine here on out?" Shade's ears perked forward, but his head stayed buried in the oat sack Del held open. "I'll take that as a 'yes'. When you're done, we got some business to do in that town." He shook his head. Here he was, having a conversation with his horse. He'd been around too many animals and not enough people.

Del waited until the setting sun dimmed the landscape. He eased Shade down the gentle slope and halted a distance away from town. The saloon wasn't hard to pick out with its lights and noise. The livery was this side of it, downwind and far enough away so cowboys in the bar smelled the perfumed saloon girls instead of horse dung. No lights on in the slanted-roof structure, but that's where he'd start. He walked Shade there and stood in the open door, surveying.

"Can I help you, mister?"

Del whirled. A bent, aged man shuffled up behind him.

"Scared you, I did?"

"Good way to get plugged, old man. Sneakin' up on folks is an invitation to see the pearly gates real quick."

The man held his arms high as he came. "No need to shoot. I ain't sported nothin' dangerous since my wife died."

Del had to laugh at that. "Just wanted to stable my horse, see if you had any room. Any new horses here lately?"

"Had one a few days back, but not for long. Bartender said you might be comin' by, if you're who I think you are, Del Lawson."

"How'd you know my name?"

"Bartender said as much. Said to be on the lookout for you. You can talk him up at the saloon. Somethin' I'd do if I was you. Want me to keep your horse handy? Nice lookin' animal, that one."

"Thanks. If you'd rub him down and feed him, I'd appreciate that. Did the stranger have a boy with him?"

"Yup. Didn't look like the young'un was enjoying the company, neither. Didn't say anything, didn't have to—face said it all." The stabler pointed. "Saloon's that way."

Del walked toward the noisy bar. He slowed at the entrance while two drunk patrons barged past him into the street. He studied the place. The usual crowd of poker players, boozers, saloon gals, dogs on the floor.

He remembered the bartender and walked over. "Beer, please."

Recognition registered in the man's eyes. "Be right there." He finished pouring a drink and started toward Del.

A cowboy leaned on the bar and held a mug out. "Hey you, come back and gimme another."

"In a minute."

The drunk grabbed him by the shirt and pulled.

The bartender knocked the man out with a thick piece of wood from underneath the counter.

He walked over to Del. "Know who you are. Seen you in here before. Know who you're after, too. Tyson lit out a few days ago. Want that beer now?"

He thought about downing a glass—or two. "No…thanks, just water. Did he say where he was goin'?"

The bartender poured from a pitcher. "Yeah, mentioned a little town by the name of Lost Creek, in Texas. Said you'd know it."

Del hadn't figured on riding to Texas. So the butcher wanted to drag this out. "Did he take the boy with him?"

"Yup. Not sure why he has him in the first place, but I can guess. I recall you was in here before with the kid a while back. Don't know as you would remember though, 'cause you wasn't makin' much sense. Your head was plenty messed up. I'm guessing by Tyson, the way you two seem to follow each other around."

"Doesn't matter. If he comes back, tell him I'm headed to Lost Creek." Saying the town's name made Del consider. First, he'd have to cross the Pecos. At night. Then a trek across Comanche territory, which almost guaranteed he wouldn't live to see the sun rise. He guessed Tyson was waiting for him, not in Lost Creek, but somewhere outside town that direction. Del drained his water and walked out. At the stable, he rubbed a hand over Shade's muzzle. Just then, the stabler came up beside Del.

"Sure a pretty horse. How'd he get that gouge in his side?"

"Got hurt doin' his job, goin' about his business, just like you oughta be doin'. Don't know why, but sometimes people get hurt doin' right."

"Never gave it much thought. You sound like you might know about that."

Del paused. "Thanks for caring for him. How much do I owe you?"

"Not a penny."

"It takes money to keep this place open, doesn't it?"

"Don't worry about me, I'll just charge the next fella double. Maybe somebody who cleaned up at a crooked poker game that night. That'll make up."

Del swung up on Shade.

The old man said, "Why not rest up here for a bit? With them clouds, gonna be blacker'n the devil tonight."

"I've lost enough time already, thanks."

"Wasn't concerned about you, was thinkin' of the horse."

Del couldn't even draw sympathy out of a stable hand. He shook his head.

The man reached out with a bag of oats. "Here. Take care of that horse, and he'll take care of you."

Del wondered when the last time was that someone

looked after him? Well, Rose did back at the fort. He tipped his hat to the stabler, and his thoughts returned to her. She'd recovered, hadn't she? He didn't want to leave her at Laila's, but had to. Shade snorted, and Del patted the horse's neck. "Let's go, boy." He trotted out of the small town into the darkness. The pitch-black night wouldn't be to Del's advantage if Tyson was waiting in ambush. Still, he hoped he was. He'd start east, the direction Tyson wanted him to go. Make it simple to find him.

Wouldn't be hard for Tyson to figure the route Del would take out of town. Easy for a bushwhacker to lay up nearby and take him any time. Del pursed his lips. If he was going to get ambushed, he'd make Tyson earn it. As Shade trotted to the edge of town, Del pulled the horse up. Why give Tyson the advantage in the dark? No, he wouldn't do that. Let the chill night air work its frosty edges into the killer's cold heart. He turned back for the stable. Night sounds rose from the surrounding landscape. The occasional coyote clamored from nearby hills, yipping to others of its kind. For once, he'd made a good decision. Maybe he'd understand all this better when it was behind him, but he didn't know what that meant anymore. Didn't seem like his problems were headed that direction anytime soon. Melancholy weighed on him.

Del eased off Shade at the livery. He'd been pretty short with the stabler on the way out. Time for a different tack. He walked Shade into the dim surroundings smelling of muck and dirty straw.

The old man didn't look up from the harness he was laboring over. "I work better at night—don't know why, just always have. You can put him up in that third stall there."

Del eyed the man. "Thought you might ask why I'm back already."

"Nope, not my business, like you said earlier."

Del pursed his lips. Why did he go out of his way to put people off? "I, uh, didn't mean it like that. Sorry." He scuffed at the dusty ground. "Mind if I ask a question?"

"Not as long as you don't mind if I don't answer it."

"Fair enough."

"What's on your mind?"

"That man with the boy, did—"

"The one with the eyepatch? Smelled worse than this place? Yellow teeth?"

Del nodded.

"Talkin' about Pete Tyson."

"You know him?"

"Everybody knows him, he's been a predator in these parts a long time. Worse than a mountain lion."

"How was the boy?"

"Quiet, but has smart eyes. When I locked on his I saw lots of pain. Wanted to help the youngster, but that crusty bandit told me to stay away."

"He's not a bandit; he's a killer."

The stabler's eyes widened as he hammered a piece of iron. "Always suspected it. They was gone the next morning, and he stiffed me for the tab. Done it before, shoudda been smarter this time."

"Which way'd they go?"

"Headed south and west."

"Not east?" He should have asked him earlier, instead of the bartender.

"Why would he go east? Ain't nothin' but prairie dogs and Indians itchin' for a tussle out that way."

So Tyson didn't go to Lost Creek. Of course not. Del would have been furious if he hadn't figured that out. "Any idea where Tyson might go?"

"Onliest thing I can think of is the Wilkins spread. Biggest rancher hereabouts, has thousands of acres down the way. Elijah's even meaner than Tyson. Has to be to keep him in line. Heard tell he's blind but sees everything."

Blind. "So Tyson works for this Wilkins?"

"Folks say he does Wilkins' dirty work. They say he does some on the side for himself, too."

Del considered that. "I know why I'm after him but not why he's after me."

"If you ain't met him, and you ain't pissed him off, then you must have somethin' he wants."

"I couldn't have anything he wants. I don't have anything anybody wants."

"Better think again. You must have somethin'. Rumor has it Tyson was involved in some murders a year or so ago. Folks say lots of gold got stole about that time, too."

Ire rose in Del's throat. "He's the one killed my family."

"Sorry to hear that, young fella."

"The gold, was that the Abriendo's?"

"Don't know for sure but it's likely, 'cause there's only one person around here with that kind of money." He held a hand up. "Don Abriendo. Also heard they was gold coins. A couple would do me just fine right about now."

Del didn't know much about the Abriendos, even

after working there for years, but that had to be who the stabler was talking about. It was only luck Rodrigo happened to be at Del's place that night. He and his wife had been keeping the boy since the Abriendo murders.

The gold coins must have gone missing if Tyson was looking for them. Maybe he thought Del knew where they were.

It was starting to make sense.

Chapter Thirty

Tyson forced the boy onto his horse and trotted out of Santa Rosa. He'd left the drifter, Potter, there to waylay Lawson outside of town. Tyson would enjoy prying Lawson's secret out before he killed him.

Ambushing Lawson would give him time to make a deal with Wilkins. By the time Potter brought Lawson to the ranch, Tyson would have either traded the boy for gold, or done Wilkins in. Maybe both. Kill Wilkins and the gold was as good as his. He was tired of being the rancher's errand boy. Besides, from what he'd seen, Wilkins' men didn't seem to have any love for him, especially the Abriendo vaqueros. Likely, they wouldn't be any trouble if he made a move. How many ranch hands were there now? Twelve, maybe fifteen, last he knew.

He loosened his hold on the boy. Even if the kid jumped off the horse, there was no place for him to go. He'd been getting on Tyson's nerves ever since he kidnapped him. Hadn't said a word as they rode barren stretches of the Territory. What was he thinking? Did he know anything? He'd tried to force him to talk, with no success.

Tyson percolated. Wilkins wanted the boy dead so there'd be no Abriendos left. Then he could buy the huge spread that rumor said held gold deposits in its hills. And what about Lawson? What if he didn't know where the coins were? The way Ansel clammed up facing death, Tyson wasn't sure he told anyone where he hid them. Would be just like him to take the secret to his grave. Had to admire him, though. Didn't go begging, like lots of others Tyson killed.

He looked forward to coming face to face with Lawson—hurting him even if the dirt farmer didn't know anything. Maybe Lawson would take after his father and go silently to his death. Stubbornness likely ran in the family.

Tyson pulled up in the small village of Puerto de Luna and dismounted. The boy reached toward the reins.

"Get down."

He swung his little legs to the side and dropped to the ground. Stared off into space.

They were in front of what passed for a saloon in this tired little settlement. Always Tyson's first stop. "Inside."

A few slouchers leaned on a makeshift weathered door lying atop two chairs and masquerading as top of a bar. A man stood to one side, talking with customers. He looked Tyson's way. "What'll you have, mister?"

"Whiskey." Tyson pointed to a table with two chairs. "Bring the bottle over there."

"What'll the young'un have?"

"Nothin'."

"How about a nice sasparilly, son?"

"I said, nothing." Tyson took a seat, the boy sagging into the chair next to him.

The man brought a whiskey bottle and glass and set a sasparilla in front of Rodrigo.

"He don't get nothin'." He dropped a hand under

the table. "Understand?"

The man turned away and walked toward the bar. Without glancing back, he said, "Shoot me in the back and you'll take five slugs before I hit the floor. Understand?" He joined his customers again. In a whisper, he said, "Dunno what's goin' on with that snake and the boy. The kid flat out don't look like he's here of his own accord, and that don't set right. Reminds me of my son, wherever he is." He took a drink. "I gotta idea." He laid out his plan and glanced back at the unlikely duo.

Tyson fumed all the while. He hadn't been defied often, but this was one time he wouldn't be able to settle things with a gun. And in a dumpy, sleepy place like this. He itched his bad eye under the patch and considered. No advantage to him getting caught up with this tinhorn bartender and his yokel friends. He poured a shot and stared at Rodrigo. The boy reached for the glass in front of him but not before Tyson swatted it away.

The bartender's eyes locked on Tyson's at the sound of breaking glass. He brought another and set it down in front of the boy. He stared at Tyson. The outlaw reached his gun hand down to his holster.

The bartender shook his head. "Wouldn't do that, mister. Good way to get dead quick. Over what?" A smile broke out on his face, and he turned back to the bar. He poured another whiskey, came back and set it in front of Tyson. "This one's on the house—we like to keep things friendly around here."

Tyson nodded. It had been a while since anyone bought him a drink. Maybe this wasn't such a backwater after all. He threw his whiskey back and decided he was going to kill Wilkins. He'd have to find a way to keep the rancher's wranglers out of play. Maybe he'd bust into their bunkhouse and cow them. He knew some, and those he didn't would know him by reputation. He'd dangle gold in front of them to seal the deal.

The barkeep brought another drink over. "This here's from that gentleman with the whiskers at the end of the bar—ain't really a bar as you can see, just an old door. Why don't you come join us?"

Tyson squinted. There was the boy to consider, but Tyson pointed a dirty, meaty hand at him. "Stay right there, or I'll whip ya." He knocked the drink back, ambled toward the group and nodded at 'whiskers.' "You all got any food? Been a while since I et."

The bearded man shook his head. "Nah, this is where we do our drinkin', not eatin'." Laughter. "Looks like you had a dusty ride, but then everyone has a dusty ride gettin' here!" He guffawed along with the others, all grimy themselves. "Pull up that rickety chair there."

Tyson relaxed some. "Don't mind if I do."

"My name's The Turk. That's 'cause…well…I guess I don't rightly know why!" More laughter. Glasses refilled all around. The Turk introduced the men one by one. He turned to Tyson. "What do you go by, mister?"

"Name's Tyson, Pete Tyson." It had been so long since he'd said his first name that it sounded strange hanging in the smoky air. These men seemed like a decent bunch, not like the dregs he'd been traveling with the last few years.

The Turk stood. "Here's to Pete Tyson." They guzzled their drinks. The Turk wiped a dirty hand over his mouth. "Have a seat, Pete. What brings you to our fine town?"

One of the others stood and held his glass high. "Here's to our fair town." They pushed chairs back on the wooden plank floor and worked to a stand. The Turk poured and glasses clinked on their way to empty again.

"Ah'm...prospecting."

"For what?"

"Gold." Wasn't exactly true, but close enough.

The Turk waved a hand in the air. "Aw, pshaw. Ain't been any gold to speak of here for some time, neighbor. Why I remember a time when there was so much around they was thinkin' about lining the street outside with it."

Another man lifted his drink. "Here's to gold and lots of it." Another liberal top-off followed by quick swigs and drained glasses.

Tyson belched. "Never can tell when you're gonna run across gold. I'm gettin' closer. Can feel it."

Whiskers leaned in. "What's the boy's part in all this?"

Tyson leered. "He likes my company."

The Turk motioned to Rodrigo. "Come on over, son, and set with your—"

Tyson banged his glass down. "Bound to be some gold around here. I get a certain itch when I'm near it, and I got that now."

The Turk eyed the small circle of men. "I got a certain itch too, but there ain't no women folk here to scratch it!" Laughter erupted. The Turk grabbed another bottle from under the door. "Somethin' to be said for cheap whiskey. Who'll have another?" Everyone held glasses out his way as he slopped liquor into each. "Last one finishes, buys!" Five glasses hit the bar, followed by Tyson's.

"You boys can shurr throw 'em back all right. I ain't had as mush practice lately, been ridin' the range. Guess I'll buy the next round."

"Sounds like you got more trail dust to drown, cowboy." The Turk poured another for Tyson and himself. "Let's you and me get to the bottom of this bottle, whaddya say? That'd make for a surefire good night, right?"

"Goodnight. That'sh the name of the trail hereabouts. Loving, too, but he din't fare so good."

The Turk nodded. "Ran into the Comansh by the Pecos, not far from here. T'weren't a good end. Gangrene and all." He wiped at his mouth while the others stared at Tyson. "Speakin' of the end, let's finish this, huh?" He raised the bottle high.

Tyson nodded. "Purt good st…shtuff, tashtes bettur ahl the time."

The Turk snuck a look at the boy, who'd drawn a worn out chair up next to them. "Mark of a good whiskey, right boys?" They all raised empty glasses. "So tell me about this gold."

"Can't. Ish somethin' ah been trailin' fur a time now. I get my handsh on that cow…coward Lawshon, he'll remember me more'n he already duz. Remember what I did—took from him. Remember me for sh…shurr…"

"Don't know no Lawson." The Turk caught the boy's stare, and he put a finger to his lips. A smile at Tyson. "One more, huh? You're holdin' your own real good tonight, Pete. You're all right, ain't he, boys?"

They all nodded. "Can't let you drink us under the table, though."

"I drunk better'n you all (hiccup) under." He rubber-necked around the room. A sneer curled his mouth. "Thish is the biggesht crap hole I seen in a long time. You boysh look like you belong here, too." He raised his empty glass. "Gimmee 'nother and we'll shee who's shtill shtandin'." He slammed a fist on the door, breaking out a worn, wooden panel. "I gotta pee...but firsht lemme have 'nother." He turned to The Turk. "What, you quit...tin'?"

The Turk shook his head. "Nope, you're a hard man to keep up with." He reached under the door and retrieved two large, dirty glasses. "This oughta finish us off." He poured a small amount in his and the rest of the bottle in Tyson's glass. "Cheers." They lifted mugs and swigged.

Tyson slammed his glass down and busted another panel. "Thish ain't any kinda bar like I ever seen, but beatin' it up ish fun." He struggled to a stand and hitched his pants up with a belch. The foul stench filled the air. Spittle ran down his beard. His eyes drooped. "Whish...way?"

"You mean to the outhouse?"

"Yeah. Whaddya think I men. You ain't too smart...Turd." A wobble.

"Ain't got one."

Tyson reached to put a hand on the back of a chair, but The Turk pulled it away before he could steady himself. Nothing broke Tyson's fall as he hit the warped floor face first. A couple of broken teeth flew away like chiclets. Blood pooled around his mouth as he lay senseless. A dark puddle stained his pants.

The Turk kicked Tyson in the ribs. No response. "Rotten-ass bastard. Got a ten dollar Stetson on a five cent head. Jimmy and Sam, get this piece of crap the hell out of here. Load him on my wagon and trundle 'im down to the Pecos. Work 'im over some more and tie 'im up. Leave 'im for the mountain lions. Better yet, maybe the Indians'll get 'im. Well done, boys." He kicked Tyson again between the legs. "Gold, my ass." He turned to the boy. "Nothin' for you to be scared about anymore, son. What's your name?"

Rodrigo stared wide-eyed at men the likes of which he'd never seen before. His heart pounded in his chest as he looked at the man who'd taken Tyson down. Was the same in store for him?

The Turk sat and put an arm around him. "That man'll never hurt you again. What's your name?"

"R-R-Rod...Rodrigo." The word stuck in his throat. He had to force it out.

"Rodrigo—that's a good name. How'd you come to be with that piece of trash?" He poured the rest of his whiskey on the heap on the floor.

Rodrigo wanted to spit on Tyson, but his mouth was too dry. "It...he kidnapped me." He watched them carry the killer out the swinging doors and hoped he'd never see him again.

He gazed at the ragged men and his eyes grew moist. Where was Del?

Chapter Thirty-One

Kip kept the horses he and Rose rode to a measured trot. Laila's tipi lay long behind them as the sun approached the western heights. "How you feelin', Rose? We won't be goin' too much farther today."

"My shoulder aches, but it feels better than I thought it would this soon. Laila is a miracle worker."

Kip nodded. "She has that reputation. Be beddin' down short of Santa Rosa tonight. Pillows, sheets, and a hot meal will have to wait 'til tomorrow."

"Sheets and pillows sound awfully good. Seems like a long time since I've had either. A hot meal will be nice, too. I've had enough of broths, even if Laila's helped me heal."

Kip squinted. "See that low rise in the distance ahead? Small group of pines on it? Looks like a good place to hole up tonight, dry and out of the wind. Might be a stream at the base." Kip searched the darkening sky. A storm was blowing up out of the west. Dark clouds gathered as if armies joining forces. Kip raised his collar. "Sorry, but can you ride any faster? The sooner we get to that little shelter the better."

Rose glanced behind as a gray sheet of rain gained on them. She kicked her mount, and a stab of pain stole her breath. Even without spurs, her horse seemed to know she was in a hurry. They reached cover as the squall caught them. She dismounted, and her world

254

turned a blinding white. "Kip! Kip!"

"Here! Just behind you. Keep moving forward. Should be a low rock formation dead ahead."

Hail surged from the heavens and drove her to the ground as hard missiles pounded her back. The horses found what protection they could. Rose rounded into a ball in the flattened grass and mud, shivering, losing consciousness. Kip wedged his arms beneath her and lifted, folding her shaking body to his. He squeezed them both against the leeward face of the low rocks. A tall, wide pine canopied the worst of the hail, now turning back into a gray downpour. Kip retrieved his bedroll and an extra blanket and bundled Rose in them. The rain slowed to an annoying drizzle, and the sun dodged clouds to make a welcome appearance.

Late afternoon rays warmed Rose as Kip built a sputtering fire. Her shivering quieted, and feeling returned to her face. "Thank you for taking care of me."

Kip grinned as he fed scattered wet kindling into the laboring fire. "Didn't have a choice. Del would skin me if I didn't."

"You like him, don't you?"

A nod. "There's somethin' about him. I don't make friends easy and Del don't seem to either, but we took to each other right off. He's about as levelheaded as they come."

"Yes, he is, and so are you."

"Don't know about that, but I never had a good friend. Don't know if it was me or them. Del strikes me the same way." Kip gathered some larger pieces, and the fire popped as it went to work on damp wood. "And I know how much he cottons to you. Hard to miss the glint in his eye when he's with you."

Her heart jumped. "Does he say that?"

"Doesn't have to. Easy to see."

"Tell me about him, Kip. Tell me about Del. You're like two peas in a pod. I don't know much of anything, except for the misery he's carrying."

"He doesn't share much about that but it's festering inside. Has he told you he's been wandering for a while, drifting with Rodrigo? That he's homeless? Still, he's the kind of fella men like spendin' time with. I'd trust Del with my life. Reckon I actually did."

"Why does Rodrigo stay with him?"

"Not sure the boy has anywhere else to go. Plus, he depends on Del, even though he doesn't say anything. Don't know what he saw that night, but it must have been terrible bad to shut his mouth like it did."

Rose wondered. "Del doesn't say much, either."

"That's just him. Don't think he ever misses a chance to be quiet. He seems to be opening up some with you around, but I know there's a part of him he keeps tucked away that's blacker than night." Kip shrugged. "Got to come out sometime, though. And when it does, it usually turns up in some pretty bad ways."

She thought back to the fight Del had with the cowhand that Stoney Goodwin dismissed. Did Del overreact? Should he have let things go? She'd been called worse than a whore before. Had lived with worse. She brushed that memory away. Maybe if they'd had more time together, she would have told Del how she felt by now. It wouldn't do, though, to say anything to Kip first. "Yes, sadness and anger have a way of surfacing…" She put a hand to one eye, tears welling.

Kip glanced away.

"Smoke from the fire."

"Uh huh. Got something on your mind?" He stirred the embers with a stick. The fire flared and lit the dimming day for a second.

"No…it's just that…" The confused words dangled in the air, the same way they swirled in her head. "I'm sorry, I'm going to bed now. I'm exhausted." Kip gathered pine needles for her bed, and Rose pulled Laila's thick, woven blanket over her. A generous gift she couldn't repay. She stared at the clearing sky and wished the same for her heart.

Morning brought a dreary hangover from the storm. Gun barrel-gray cloudbanks hid the sun.

"Sorry the fire's out, Rose. Was too sleepy to keep feedin' it last night. Could use some warmin' this morning, though."

"Don't build one on my account. That was the best sleep I've had in a while. Besides, we won't be here long, will we?"

"No, breakfast will be quick. There's only the rest of the coffee and some biscuits to eat. It's cold, but I'm gettin' to where I kinda like coffee that way now. But then I ain't had a choice lately." He laughed. "Buck slipped me a can of peaches, too."

After they'd eaten, Kip filled their canteens in the nearby creek. The horses looked like they had survived the storm well with plenty of forage. Kip fed them grains for stamina, although the trek today wouldn't be as long. "Should be easier ridin' today. We'll take our time gettin' to Santa Rosa, likely pull in early afternoon."

"Don't slow on my account, Kip. I'd like to get there sooner rather than later. Do you think Del's there?" She hesitated. "And Tyson?" Her stomach jumped at the name.

"Don't know. If they ain't there now, they probably been there. Not many places Tyson could go with a kid around here."

"I've been wondering about that. Why would Tyson kidnap Rodrigo?"

Kip said, "Maybe to lure Del for some reason. Trap him."

"That's what I thought, too, but why?"

"Only reason I can think is Del has something or knows something that Tyson wants."

Rose shook her head. "Unless you know something I don't, Del doesn't have anything. Everything he owns is on him or his horse, so it must be that Tyson thinks he knows something. But what could tie Del and Tyson together? Do they have anything in common?"

"That they do. Del told me one night he knew it was him Tyson was after."

"Why?"

Kip squinted. "His dad was an outlaw. Del thinks he probably ran with Tyson's gang until he got killed. Del's not sure how that happened, but he figures Tyson killed him or had him killed."

"Tyson killed his father, too? He murdered his family and almost got him?"

"Meanest bastard I ever heard of—and I seen plenty."

"Del's in trouble, isn't he?" Rose's bottom lip trembled.

"Del will be fine. Just about the smartest man I know. He won't slip and let that motherless skunk dry gulch him. If I was Tyson, I'd be worried about Del finding *him*."

They mounted up for Santa Rosa. Rose stared blankly into the distance as their horses strode onto the muddy basin.

Nothing was right anymore.

Chapter Thirty-Two

Maybelle left the dinner with Graham early. She'd had too much to drink and didn't want things leading anywhere she hadn't planned on. And right now, Wilkins was her target. But Graham was growing on her. Was it the whiskey or the man? She wondered. After agreeing to a partnership, she felt something when their eyes met.

When she first came to town, she'd had vague ideas how to take Wilkins down. All very delicious ways, all brilliant if she could pull them off, but doubts still unsettled her. Maybe if she had some experience being a siren she'd feel more confident. As she walked into the hotel dining room for breakfast, Graham rose from his chair.

"I hope I haven't kept you waiting long."

He bowed. "Not at all. I was catching up on the latest news. This paper's only a week old. May have given me an idea. Sounds like Wilkins is poised to put his money with yours and buy the Abriendo. Wouldn't you agree?"

"That's what he says. Wait a minute, Graham. If you knew the money—the gold—I brought with me was the stolen coins from the Abriendos, wouldn't Wilkins know that, too?"

"He would if someone told him you brought coins here."

"You mean you didn't? Why wouldn't you? You don't owe me anything."

"Like I said last night, I wanted to see what you had in mind. And...I don't mind saying, you interest me. I mean, uh, there is something..." His words died off, and he raised a hand for the desk clerk. "We'd like to order now."

Maybelle breathed a sigh of relief. She saw Graham's nervousness and smiled inwardly. Even with her bruised face, she could still have an effect on a man. She leaned forward. "What are you thinking, Graham?"

"Just that you no doubt shocked Wilkins when you mentioned you were going to buy the Abriendo. Nice touch, but if I know him, he's not about to let you do that. He's probably trying to reach Territory officials now. Why don't we pay a visit to the telegraph office after breakfast and see if he's sent anything? We just had a line strung from Santa Rosa last year."

After they ordered, Maybelle said, "We can't stop him from sending a telegraph to buy the land, can we?"

"No, and we don't want to. We just have to make sure it ends up where we want."

"What do you mean?"

"I dropped by there last night after you left and gave the telegraph man a new address for Territorial officials. In case Wilkins wanted to send one early this morning. I told the clerk the Territory office just moved."

"Why would that help?"

"That's where Wilkins needs to send a wire guaranteeing the money to buy the Abriendo. Meaning that sum is as good as there already."

"So?"

"The new address happens to be a bank account under the name of Territorial Real Estate Trust."

"Sounds official. What is it?"

The cook brought their food and left. Graham said, "Why don't we eat first?"

"Graham Bunch, how dare you leave me hanging?"

"Um…this bacon is some of the best I've had today. How's yours?"

"I'm going to throw this biscuit at you if you don't tell me right now."

"Hold on," he said, his mouth still stuffed.

Maybelle could tell he was chewing slowly just to annoy her. Her first reaction was anger, then the humor of his tease hit her. She smiled and dug into her pancakes. This back and forth was as much fun as she'd had in a long time. No pretend to it, no more scheming. Just playful banter. "Graham, my goodness you are a devil, but I must say you are an entertaining—and surprising—one." She continued eating, a bit taken aback at her interest in him.

Graham laughed. "And you are the most intriguing woman I've ever met, madam." He raised his coffee cup. "To you. And our partnership." He wiped at his mouth. "So…that real estate address may not be what it appears to be. I set that up myself some time ago."

"Why would you do that?"

"I've known for some time that Wilkins wanted that land. I figured having an official-sounding account might come in handy sometime. I'm sure you've noticed that Wilkins treats me as one of his servants."

"I hadn't really—"

"Well, of course you had. You're a smart woman, not much escapes you. I handle Wilkins' money, and

I've been kowtowin' to him for too long. When you came to town, I got an idea how we might relieve him of some of it."

A sudden thought struck Maybelle. "Oh, my word. You might have the same thing in mind for me. You are indeed a plotter. I should watch myself around you." It was a dangerous game they were playing, but she was intrigued.

"No need to worry about your money. I've had a letter of surety regarding your coins and currency posted at the Denver bank I work with. Your assets are safe. Plus, you're too…remarkable…to steal from."

Warmth moved up her neck. Maybe she didn't want to hide it. "Sos's if I understand this, when Wilkins transfers money to Territory officials, he'll actually be giving it to you."

Graham beamed.

"I love it, absolutely love it."

"But that's not all. I'm going out to his ranch today to settle the terms of a new loan he wants in order to buy the whole spread. That would take you out entirely, which no doubt will appeal to him. If all goes according to plan, that loan will also be part of the money he deposits to my account."

Maybelle leaned closer. "So after he's sent all his money and the bank's as well, what then?"

"Well, not only will he not get the Abriendo, but he'll owe the bank a substantial amount he won't be able to pay. He'll be wiped out." Graham took a last drink of coffee and dabbed a napkin at his mouth. "Here's the best part. I—the bank—will foreclose and take his ranch. I leave for his place after breakfast."

Maybelle stared at her dining companion.

"Exquisite. I could kiss you, Graham."
"Only if I can kiss you first."
Maybelle blushed.

Chapter Thirty-Three

Del decided not to stay the night in Santa Rosa. Even though he'd been in the saddle days on end, he needed to run Tyson down. Images of that unholy night at his ranch pierced him like knives every time he thought of the killer. A picture of Rodrigo riding alone with Tyson flashed through his head. He had to find the boy. He didn't want to lose the time he gained by not riding to Lost Creek. No, he'd start out again tonight. He wolfed a couple of stale biscuits he washed down with a cup of coffee at the hotel. Would have to do. At the stable, he took extra time to feed Shade. He stroked the horse's neck and drew him close. "Hate to run you again so soon, but gotta get Rodrigo." Shade's big, brown eyes never left Del's.

The stabler said, "Don't know why you're leavin' tonight. Plenty of time to get an early start in the morning. You don't even know where Tyson is, do you?"

Del waved a hand. "No, but odds are he's on his way to Wilkins' place. You said that's who he works for."

"Well, at least let me get your horse some more oats before you go." He took hold of Shade's reins and led him to the grain bin. "Why don't you sit while I feed him? Fourth stall there has clean straw. I know, that's where I bed down."

Del nodded. He opened the stall door and rested on the soft pile. Almost as good as a pillow. He figured a two-day ride ought to get him to Wilkins' ranch, but then he didn't exactly know where it was. Shade gobbled while Del sat alone with his thoughts. He hoped Rose was healing well by now. Please. Maybe she was already on her way back to the drive or even on the way north. His heart clutched at the thought. She'd catch a coach from Denver and be gone. Home. Another person he'd likely never see again.

He leaned into the straw. Where was his home these days? He glanced toward Shade. His feeding was taking longer than it should. The stabler kept giving the horse small handfuls. Del cradled his head on his arms. The next thing he knew, he woke to find he'd slid to the bottom of the stack of straw. Dark surrounded him as he surveyed his surroundings. Damn! Might as well stay the night now, grab a few more winks and be off early. Shade nickered in the stall next to him. The stabler snored somewhere in the dark.

A shake to his shoulder. "Time to get up, young fella. The day's slippin' away."

"Whattimeisit?"

"Thought you was gonna sleep the day away. It's near nine in the morning. You and your horse was plenty tuckered. Should be ready to take whatever the trail throws at you now, though."

"Any place I can get somethin' to eat? Had enough cold jerky."

"I'll rustle up some grits and coffee, see what else the hotel has. You go on and get your gear together and your horse saddled up." The old man returned a while later. "Snuck a couple of biscuits off'n the table, too, when the cook weren't lookin'. Taste pretty good." He gave Del the coffee, grits, and a biscuit and a half.

"Thanks. What do I owe you?"

"Nothin'. You're the best entertainment I've had in months—you ridin' in here all in a lather, chasin' after a fella, then curlin' up and droppin' off in nothin' flat." He chuckled.

Del shook his head. "Thanks for your hospitality, but time I was ridin'."

"Goin' to Wilkins' spread?"

Del hesitated. Probably wouldn't hurt to tell him. May be a good thing in case someone was looking for him besides Tyson. He wasn't sure who that could be, but why not? Might even be a good idea if Tyson came back through—the two of them had to face off sometime. "Yup. Don't know any other place Tyson'd go. See if I can run him down."

"Whatcha gonna do when you get there?"

"Don't know. I'll figure it out—always do." He smoothed a hand over Shade's muzzle and the horse bobbed his head.

"Well, now, Wilkins' place is gonna take some findin', even as big as that spread is. I hear tell you gotta follow the Pecos down toward Fort Sumner then turn west, hard. More than a day's ride to the mountains ahead. South of the Abriendo grant. Ever heard of it?"

Del nodded. A place he knew well. "Thanks again."

The old man waved goodbye and pitched another fork of dirty straw.

Shade settled into an easy stride south. Del kept an eye out left and right as they rode. Wouldn't do to let Tyson take him unawares. The sun climbed high and shone warm on his face. A gentle west wind wound its way around him. Silence laid claim to a deserted landscape. An almost eerie quiet. Light green rolling hills spread to the horizon, dotted with small green shrubs that had survived everything nature had thrown at them. The wind picked up and a glance west revealed a terrifying sight. In the distance, a billowing, brown sandstorm towered in the desert sky. He'd seen enough of them growing up. Fierce winds always propelled them, some even blotting the sun.

He kicked Shade into a gallop and gauged the size and speed of the dark, swelling cloud when he heard someone riding behind him. He stole a look back just as a bullet flew over his head. He spurred Shade forward and hugged the horse's mane. "Hiyahh!" To his right, the sandstorm gained strength. No way he could outrun it. Riding directly into it was the only tactic that might shake the lone shooter, whoever it was. Another bullet cut the air around him. Couldn't stop. He glanced back again. Tyson? Del wasn't sure, but he was still in the gunman's range. Had to be a rifle he was firing. If it was Tyson, what had he done with Rodrigo? The first grains of wind-whipped sand stung his face. Needed to reach cover, even if it was only made up of swirling earth.

A roar deafened Del as a deadly wall of sand and dust engulfed him. He cinched a bandana over his mouth and snugged his hat hard. Swirling chaos blotted his sight and stole his breath. Short, staccato breaths were all he could manage, then one deep breath as the storm struck full force. A shocking cold numbed him. He closed his eyes tighter. Nothing to be seen, anyway. Sand plugged his ears. He pulled Shade down next to a small rock. Grit filled his nose and forced itself into his mouth. Grating sand felt like it was scouring a layer off his exposed skin. The roar filled his senses.

Where was the shooter? Had to be Tyson. At least the storm kept the assassin from finishing him off. Shade's breathing became labored and jolted Del back to the storm. He curled himself over the horse's head to shield him from the biting sand. Del fumbled for his Colt but hesitated to draw it away from the protection of the leather holster. No. He needed it. He yanked the gun free and quickly stuffed it under his shirt. May not keep much grit away but better than getting clogged in his holster.

Tears ran off his cheeks and were whisked away by the sandy assault. How much longer before the storm passed? Minutes became hours as he and Shade lay huddled with sand mounding around them. At least there weren't any more shots. Maybe the intruder's gun fouled. Maybe he'd lost sight of Del. He hadn't been lucky too often in life, but this was one of those times. The blizzard of dust was keeping him alive. So far.

Time stood still as he lay bent over his horse. Breathing and keeping Shade's mouth clear became his only focus. Wouldn't do any good to worry over when this frenzy would let up. Storms like this had a life of their own and didn't give in easily. Del couldn't tell if it was day or night any more. Usually these squalls hit earlier in the afternoon than this ornery one did. He tried counting time by the number of his breaths, but quickly gave that up.

His thoughts turned to Rose. He should have told her how he felt, although he hoped that kiss said more than his words could have. But women liked to hear the words, too. His wife had made that clear. If he ever saw Rose again, he'd tell her. If he lived through this, he'd court her. Ride to Denver if he had to, then figure his way east from there. But there was Rodrigo to think of, too. The boy needed him. He needed the boy. He wouldn't have thought that before the drive. But it was time for Rodrigo to talk again, get back to living, if only Del could figure a way to help him do that. If he even lived to see them again.

Harsh blasts of sand within the roiling storm pelted them. It was getting harder to move as the constant battering took its toll. Short, quick breaths dizzied him. Sand mounded higher around them. How much longer could they last? Despite the screaming gusts, he drifted off into a hazy dream world.

A change in the wind's shriek brought him out of his stupor. He sensed, rather than felt, the storm lessening. It was, wasn't it? Please, Lord. He dug sand off his body and Shade's. His eyes were slits. Sand clogged both ears. The wind was weakening for sure. He checked Shade. The horse's mouth and nostrils were covered in sand. He quickly cleared them, but Shade's tongue hung loose. Del couldn't tell if he was still breathing. He had to be, he couldn't lose his best horse. The sand came in erratic rushes now. Dear Lord, please. He poured a little water over the horse's face. Breathe! He opened Shade's mouth wide and cleared his throat of more grit. There. An ear twitch, then snorts again and again. The horse opened his grit-filled eyes so wide they looked like they'd pop out of his head. Just about the best thing Del had ever seen. He poured the rest of the water over both their heads. It took several minutes for them to breathe normally again.

The devilish storm continued to move off east. Dell raised a hand to the heavens in silent thanks. As he surveyed the surroundings, he spied two sandy lumps nearby. A horse and rider, the horse buried and the rider nearly. Must be the shooter. Finally, he'd come face to face with Tyson. He struggled on unsteady legs to the smaller lump. He rolled the man to his back and wiped sand away from his face. What?

Potter!

What was this jackass doing here, shooting at him? He checked for a pulse. Weak. The man had caused Del nothing but trouble. And there was what he said about Rose. Let the sand have him.

Del gazed at Shade, who had worked to a wobbly stand, still snorting. He wanted to ride away and leave, but it was like an invisible hand turned him around. Damn! He knelt by the gunman and cleaned debris from his mouth. He wasn't going to do more than that. Soon Potter gurgled, sending a sandy, wet stream down his bearded chin. He opened crusted eyes and stared at Del. Recognition set in along with hacking coughs. Potter reached for his gun but came up empty. He struggled to all fours but couldn't stand.

"I oughta kill you, Potter, for all the trouble you've been." Del leaned close. "You're about the sorriest excuse for a man I've ever seen." He tried to spit on the ground. "There's nobody would miss you, either. Is there? You got no friends, and right now you're just a twitch away from going to Hell. You know that's where you're gonna wind up, and I'm itchin' to give you an early start." He cleaned more grit from his Colt and aimed the barrel at the man's forehead. Would it even fire? His outstretched arm wavered, and he reached his

271

other hand to grasp the gun stock as well. Shoot him. He thumbed the hammer back…Pull the trigger, dammit! Pull it!

Del's gun dropped toward the clean-swept ground. His shoulders slumped and he squinted at the bully. "Damn you! Drop your belt and empty those cartridges into your hand…Now throw 'em away. Give me your hat and boots. Dump half your water." He tried to whistle for Shade, but nothing came out of his parched mouth. He left Potter standing with the start of a sneer as he rode away.

The rogue hollered after him. "I'll see you again, sodbuster. Don't you doubt it!"

Del's insides roiled. Every instinct he had screamed in him to turn back and settle up with Potter—something he wanted almost as much as he wanted to kill Tyson. He pulled Shade up short, then paused. No, the man wasn't even worth a bullet. Let the elements be his judge. He nudged Shade's hindquarters lightly, and Potter was soon a speck. Baffling how a billowing storm probably saved his life. He headed southwest again for Wilkins' ranch. Tyson and Rodrigo were likely somewhere ahead. At least he only had one killer after him now.

He hoped.

Chapter Thirty-Four

Tyson's head spun as he stumbled to a stooped stand. The sun was just past high. His ribs protested while he rubbed a hand over the crusted blood on his face. His crotch ached. He didn't know how he got here, dazed and bloody at the edge of the rushing Pecos. Last he knew, he was in that dingy little town's makeshift saloon. Only remembered snatches of the beating. His lips were swollen and his good eye half shut. He brushed dirt from his shirt and felt a piece of paper sticking out of his pants where his gun belt should have been. He unfolded it and squinted.

'I ever see you again, I'll kill you.'

A face flashed before him. What was the man's name? Tu…something. No one had ever beat him like that. Not since his mother. He surveyed his blurry surroundings as sun bathed the afternoon. No gun, no horse, no food, no water. No kid. Just as well. He'd always fared better on his own, anyway. He told himself he didn't really need the boy. He'd still find Lawson. He just didn't know exactly how right now.

He stumbled to the water's edge and dipped a hand in the cold current. His hat would have made a better cup, but it was gone, too. Cold water shocked him as he splashed his face and jerked back, drawing a moan. He leaned on all fours until he caught his breath. What now? No boots, damn cold toes. A hardscrabble gravel trail led away from the river. He'd start there. Set one foot in front of the other. Need to avoid that bastard…whatever his name was. After an endless trek, he was relieved when a few scattered buildings came into view. Better find cover and wait until the sun went down.

A small wash to his left looked like it would serve the purpose. Sunken a few feet with a sandy bottom, it was topped with a few scraggly mesquite shrubs to keep him company. He crawled in and sank to the bed. He awoke to spy a coyote peering at him from the edge of the cut. A hand wave shooed it off. It didn't trot far, as if it could tell Tyson was more meal than threat.

Tyson drifted between sleep and wakefulness. Gave him time to think about his circumstances—his life. Damn his mother. All the times she lay passed out on the small kitchen floor. If only things had been different… He could have been courting that woman back at the cattle camp instead of shooting her. Maybe he would have even had his own drive, or herd, or ranch. A small place he could raise a family. A wife and a son. Maybe two or three. But those weren't even wishes any more. These days he took more pleasure in wrecking other men's plans. Spreading his pain around so it didn't all fall on him.

Waiting was one of the few things he was good at. Gave him time to do some figuring. The sun was a bright orange globe sinking behind the western heights, taking its striking colors with it. Dark blue clouds eased in as dusk claimed the sky. Another hour or so and he'd be on his way into town. Yips and howls caused him to scan his surroundings. Hills to the north no doubt held critters he didn't want to come across in the dark. He didn't care about coyotes, he could handle them—maybe—and bears wouldn't bother him, but wolves…wolves were different. They hunted in packs. The howling seemed to be edging nearer. They'd surely find him hiding here. He'd leave for town earlier than planned. As he tried to get up, his whole body rebelled. Legs wobbled, sharp pains shot through his ribs, and his head throbbed. Maybe the wolves smelled his blood and were following the scent right to him. Fear forced his legs forward. The squishy bottom grabbed at his feet like quicksand as he dragged himself out of the shallow cut.

Wolves were on his trail. He didn't need to see them to know they were there. Run! He couldn't. Is this how his life would end? So different than what he'd always imagined—a standoff on a dusty street, followed by a fiery shootout where he killed most of them. But not all. There were too many, and his gun only held six shots. Bullets riddled him, but he didn't feel them. Strange. He sank to his knees, the sky a brilliant blue canopy. He'd finally find peace in death. The pain, the anger, would be gone.

He shook his head to clear it. Were the wolves still after him? There weren't any wolves. Yes, there were. The small town lay in growing darkness ahead. A stumbling gait drew him closer. He drove one leg in front of the other. Shallow breathing took its toll. He gasped for breath as he reached the outskirts. He lunged ahead and looked back. No wolves, no howls. Had he imagined it all? It seemed real. His pain was real, though—he didn't know much of anything else. He lumbered into the dark of a weathered wooden overhang. Stooped to catch his breath as much as he could, bloody feet throbbing. He watched the sun's shadows move through town, revealing hiding places, shifty paths, and cover tailor-made for ambushes.

He needed a horse. And a gun. Water. He lurched toward the open door of the small saloon, where he'd gotten the crap kicked out of him. The urge to look and see if—the Turk, that was it—was inside was almost overpowering. But certain-death didn't appeal to him, and he shrank back into the darkness. No sign of the boy. A couple of drunks stumbled from the bar. He couldn't take two, but he might be able to handle one.

Later, another drunk staggered out into the empty street. He wasn't sure how he'd take the man down, but knew he had to. He wobbled after him to a hitching post several small buildings away. As the drunk freed the horse, Tyson yelled. "Hey! You left money on the table back there." He walked as if he were drunk, too, but it was no act. Wouldn't be hard to fool this alky. "Here it is." He clutched an empty fist toward the man, who turned to face him.

"Wh…what? Money?"

"Yup. Yours."

The drunk leaned forward, and Tyson swung with all the strength he could muster. His fist snapped the man's head sideways and dropped him like a rag. Tyson clutched his side and toppled as well. There was no air in this street. Get up! He crawled to the drunk, lifted the six shooter from the man's holster, stuffed it in his pants, and struggled to a bent stand. Pulled the drunk's too-small boots off and stuffed his feet in them. Checked the horse's saddle strap and grabbed the horn. Lifting a foot into the stirrup, he gave a short jump and grabbed at his ribs. When he was finally mounted up, he walked the horse out of town. Wouldn't do to gallop—would attract too much attention, even at this hour, and his body could hardly take the trotting. The bouncing sent waves of pain through him, somewhat eased by the thought that he was after Lawson again. He spied a canteen hanging off the saddle and emptied what little was in it. The drunk carried a fine rifle and blanket. Nice of him to leave them for him, and in such good condition, too. He'd head back to Santa Rosa to see if Lawson had been through yet. If not, he'd stay until the sodbuster showed. Would give him time to heal up, too.

Fifteen miles at the most. Maybe twenty. Thirty? He could take anything for that distance—or so he thought. Pain clouded his vision, and wolves sounded in the distance again. Real and unreal blurred together as he struggled to stay in the saddle. Those trees were moving. The wolves nipped at the horse's heels. He wrestled the pistol from his waist and fired blindly into the night until the hammer clicked empty. He toppled to the ground. The wolves...the wolves. When he woke, his horse stood motionless nearby.

He rode into Santa Rosa hugging the horse's neck. The street was empty this late at night. Faint light from the saloon told him the bartender was still there. He pushed at the swinging doors and fell to his knees. Then blackness.

When he opened his eyes, morning light streamed through a filmy window. He lay on a ragged bed in a small, dusty room and rolled to his side. His ribs told him to stop. As he inched off the cot, the barman walked in.

"I seen you in better shape'n this. Who'd you run

afoul of?"

Tyson's mouth was leather. "No...body you'd know. Get me something to eat, willya? And something to wash it down with."

"Sure. That'll be one dollar. Cash on the barrelhead." He held his hand out.

"Whaddya mean? I never pay you."

"And you never remember my name. Today, you pay. Them days is over."

Tyson felt a familiar rage welling inside him. He could squash the man like a bug, but he was in no shape to do so. "Fish a silver out of my vest. My ribs is busted up."

He rifled through Tyson's pockets. "Nothin', Pete. Guess you go hungry. I'll ladle some water for you, though." He turned to leave.

"Wait! I got...stuff...in my saddlebags that'll do." Tyson didn't know what was in them, but it was his best bet. "Go bring 'em in."

"Not much in a saddlebag I'd want, but I'll fetch 'em." The bartender came back with the bags over a shoulder and flopped them on the room's small table.

"Open 'em up, uh...there's valuables in there."

"Like what?"

"Look and see." Tyson hoped there was something.

The bartender pulled out crumpled dirty clothes and a mostly-full whiskey bottle. A couple of tough hardtack biscuits, some jerky, and matches. Sorry coffee beans rounded out the contents.

Tyson grimaced. "See? You can have all that stuff, includin' the bottle. I'll throw in the clothes, too."

The man took a sip. "That's a first-rate whiskey."

"Told you. You can cut this good stuff with the

rotgut you been servin'. Start pourin' this early, then when your customers are drunk, slip your rat poison in. I'll just have one last drink. Gimme that bottle." The bartender kept it out of reach. "I swear, when I'm healed up, I'm comin' for you."

"You don't scare me no more. Lawson's lookin' for you and said he's gonna find you. When he does, that'll be the end. Can't come none too soon, neither."

Tyson squinted. "He been through recent?"

"Yup. Reckon you're gonna run into him sooner than you want."

"Where is he?"

"Don't rightly know, sometimes my memory fails me."

"I'll kill you for that."

"No, you won't. You'll be lucky to still be alive in a few days. Got a hunch you're gonna cross paths with Lawson before you even know he's anywhere around."

An unfamiliar feeling ran through Tyson. He'd always been the hunter. It had been a long time since he felt hunted. He had a choice to make. He could stay in Santa Rosa and see if Lawson showed again, or he could ride to Wilkins' ranch. With no money and no food, the decision was easy. At least Wilkins might let him stay and feed him.

Maybe.

He'd lay up there to heal. The ride from Santa Rosa would take more than a day. With his injuries, probably closer to two. Things weren't going well. He didn't have the boy or Lawson, had gotten beat silly, was riding a stolen mare, and had no place to go. He'd hang if they found him. His dreams of the gold were drifting away with the wind. He better light out of town quick, so his horse wouldn't stick out so. He watered the animal at the town trough, then was off. His head pounded. Riding didn't jog his teeth—one in front was already knocked out, but his crotch was on fire where he got kicked. He kept a tight hold on the reins so the mare didn't ride off at a gallop. The route west stretched over mostly scrub terrain scoured by the wind. The land didn't hold much of interest, but it was a desolate tract he had to cross. No wonder the Comanches hadn't pushed this far west.

Wilkins' place was a green oasis in a desert. It boasted forested hills with water and grasslands, like the Abriendo. Tyson had always liked riding there from Wilkins', never cared much whether the Don's vaqueros saw him or not. Searched the slopes for the rumored gold ore the hills supposedly held. Never told Wilkins what he was doing and never found anything. Just like the gold coins he'd stolen from Don Abriendo's house, then lost to that damn thief, Ansel. Where were they? Get rid of Wilkins and he'd take over. Have the ranch hands hunt for the ore. Pay 'em in gold coin he'd recover from Del Lawson when he found him. The idea amused him. He always did like making others do his bidding.

The setting sun brought relief from the day's heat. Even though the heart of summer still lay ahead, land hereabouts near-broiled during the day. Tyson pulled the mare up next to a trickling stream he'd had his eye on for miles. He labored off the horse and hobbled it. No sense letting the animal think it could do what it wanted.

He lay down on a patch of rocky ground that sparse pine needles didn't soften. Tomorrow would bring him that much closer to rest, a square meal, and a soft bed. From the saddlebags, he pulled out hard jerky and even harder biscuits. They'd have to do. The horse could find its own forage.

In the morning, he struggled up into the saddle, his good eye still puffy. Couldn't afford to lose that one, too. The last leg south into Wilkins' place didn't wear him out like he thought it would. The sun was heartless, but he was just ornery enough not to let it get to him. In fact, the closer he got to the ranch the better he felt. The ass-kicking he got in that no-account village was behind him. Almost like it never happened, but his missing tooth was a constant reminder.

He crested a familiar hill and spied the large hacienda. Wilkins said he'd kill him if he came again without the boy, so he had to lay out his proposed trade quick. An outrider joined him on the way in. The little man in white on the porch disappeared into the house. Tyson slid off the horse and paused to let the pain settle. He knew his reception wouldn't be good, but it didn't matter. He'd strike a deal with Wilkins—the gold coins for the boy, even though he didn't have either yet—rest up, then be on his way again after Lawson.

When he saw el patrón standing in the doorway, an odd thought struck him. They only had one good eye between them. The man's scowl wasn't a good omen— all the more reason to be on his way again quick. He stuck a hand out as he approached. "Good to see you, Elijah. You're looking well."

"Can't say the same for you. How'd you get so beat up?" He turned back to the house without shaking Tyson's hand.

The man was blind. "How'd you know?"

"My butler. Those bruises and that missing tooth don't help your looks any. I suppose you want to come in." He walked down the main hallway to the library. He called back, "You're probably hungry, too, from the looks of you."

"Why, thank you kindly. I'd appreciate a warm meal. Been awful cold out on that prairie at night."

Wilkins raised a hand, and a servant disappeared. He soon reappeared with a tray of meats and breads. "Drink?"

"Thank you, don't mind if I do." He forced himself to act nice. He'd just as soon kick the rancher's ass like he'd gotten kicked around. He grabbed several pieces of beef and wolfed them down.

"There are plates, you know."

"Sorry. Pretty hungry." He didn't need a stinking plate. And bring out the whiskey, not this wine crap. "Sometimes I forget my manners. My momma taught me better." The hell she did. The only time she paid attention to him growing up was when she slapped him around. He picked up a plate and loaded it with more pork, grits, and biscuits. Washed it down with the red wine. Wasn't so bad, he'd have another glass. Or two.

"Thought I told you not to come back without the Abriendo kid and Lawson. I know you don't have them."

"No, I don't." First time he'd ever been honest with Wilkins. He was willing to see where it would lead.

"I just said that. Where are they?"

For one of the few times in his life, Tyson had thought this out. If he confessed, there was no reason for Wilkins to let him live. If he pretended to have the boy, he might live to see another sunrise. Lying always came easiest, anyway. "Lawson's dead. I ambushed him back in a cave on the trail. I got the kid stashed all comfy. Just me bein' nice, I guess."

Disbelief showed on Wilkins' face. "Why did you kill Lawson?"

"Had to. Only had one horse after his died. Nothin' else to do but shoot him. Besides, didn't need him no more."

"Then he must have told you where my gold was."

Tyson nodded. "Took a while to pry it out of him, though." From the scowl on Wilkins' face, Tyson figured lying was the only thing keeping him alive.

"Tell me!"

"Why don't we have a nice dinner and talk about it. Better yet, I can show you. We'll have to ride for it, anyway."

"I said, tell me."

"Don't think I'm gonna. I figure you like me about as much as I like you. If I tell you where the gold is, you got reason to like me even less. So why don't we pretend we're partners now? At least until we get to the coins. In the meantime, I'll let you know when I feel up to travellin' again." Tyson motioned to the servant. "Get me a bottle of whiskey." He paused. No reason to be rude about it, now that he was in charge. "Please. And I'd like to sit in that chair, Elijah. Thank you. Why don't we light up a couple cigars?" He hadn't realized he held so many aces. Hollow ones, but Wilkins didn't know that. "Oh, and if you're thinkin' of killin' me, I'd think again. You won't never find the boy if you do. And if you don't find the boy, you won't get the Abriendo. Looks like you're stuck with me." He blew a smoky O that drifted the sullen rancher's way.

Wilkins drummed fingers on the arm of his chair. "Just what kind of partnership did you have in mind?"

"The kind where you get the kid and I get the gold coins."

"I'll give you ten percent."

"You ain't in a position to give somethin' you ain't got. Half."

"You've developed a brain somewhere, Tyson. Quite a surprise, I must say. Never thought you had it in you." He paused for a long sip of brandy. "Half it is."

Tyson grinned. "Here's to a short, but profitable partnership." Half, hell. He'd take it all. As he raised his glass, though, he wondered. Wilkins wasn't usually one to give in so easily. What was the rancher up to? No doubt still planning his demise. Tyson needed to string this sham out as long as possible, then when he was healed, he'd kill Wilkins and take over the ranch. That's what he'd do. It dawned on him that he didn't really need to find the gold coins after all. This ranch was as valuable as gold. Thousands of cattle strewn over a wide range. Countless head from the Abriendo herd. Most of the Don's vaqueros came over, too. When he took the ranch over, he'd make it right with Wilkins' hands. Besides, he couldn't kill them all. Shrewd.

An air of ill will filled the room as the two men lifted their glasses.

Chapter Thirty-Five

Kip pointed in the distance. "There. Santa Rosa." A few low-lying buildings lay ahead in a little basin hard by the Pecos. The river gorge laid claim to some of the few trees and stunted mesquite shrubs for miles around. "Sometimes we stop there on our way north to provision up and...uh, let loose."

Rose couldn't help a small smile. "I know what you all do, no need to explain. Let's hurry before the sun disappears."

Several horses waited at the rail in front of the town's only hotel when they pulled up. Kip dismounted and disappeared inside. Rose wondered what kind of reception a dusty, black cowboy was going to get. She stretched her shoulder back and forth. The pain was still tolerable, even after all the riding they'd done since Laila's. The woman was undeniably a healer. An aroma of cooked beef drifted out of the hotel as she dismounted. Hunger gnawed at her insides. She didn't care what they had to eat; she was having it. When she entered the building, Kip came out of the kitchen with a smile.

He motioned to a table. "Ma'am, please have a seat. Your feast is on its way. Plus...a surprise." He took his hat off and bowed low, then cackled with laughter. His cheerfulness was infectious. A cook came out to the small dining room carrying a savory platter of cooked meats. Sliced beef, surrounded by medallions of pork.

"Sorry, Kip, but I'm starving." Rose forked some meat and pinto beans onto her plate and asked the cook for a glass of wine. After a large glass of water and her first few mouthfuls of food, she downed half the wine and took a deep breath. "So what's the surprise?"

Kip's smile widened. "Thought you'd never ask." He called for the cook. The aproned man came out, a young boy behind him. Rose glanced at the youth, then froze. "Rodrigo!" She jumped from the table and wrapped her arms around him. "How did you get here? How did you get away from Tyson? How—"

Kip interrupted. "Good grief, Rose. Give the boy a chance." He chuckled at the surprise on her face.

Her eyes grew wide. "Rodrigo, can you talk?"

Rodrigo's bottom lip trembled. He nodded.

"You can talk?"

"Yes…ma'am." His eyes filled.

Rose hugged him to her again. She felt him snuggle into her embrace. Her head spun. "I have so many questions. Tell us everything. Sit right here by me. Have something to eat. You're so thin."

Rodrigo recounted how he'd seen her shot at camp and didn't know if she was dead or alive. The hard ride with Tyson, wanting to run away, but he couldn't. The awful closeness of Tyson with his bad breath and foul odor. The stop here in Santa Rosa and Tyson's attempt to send Del to Lost Creek. The ride to the other little town and how the man beat Tyson and took him away. How he rode Tyson's horse here. How he waited for Del or her to show up, hoping he hadn't missed them both already.

Rose sat transfixed as Rodrigo talked. He'd been through so much at such a young age. "Why…are you talking…now?"

"I am not so afraid anymore. Ever since that night at Mr. Del's ranch, I did not know what to say, so I said nothing. Mr. Del always seemed to know what I was thinking so I did not have to talk. And when they took that man Tyson away, well, it was him who scared me most. It was just me and Mr. Del for a long time. He took care of me when he was not even taking care of himself." Tears flowed down his cheeks.

Rose wiped at his nose and hugged him again. "You don't have to worry; you have people who care about you. I'll be with you—" She stopped. What was she saying? That she'd stay with Rodrigo? The thought startled her. She let the idea swirl in her head. She realized she couldn't leave Rodrigo to fend for himself again. Couldn't stand the notion. After dinner, she took him by the hand to the registration desk. "Do you have a room for me and the boy?"

"Yes'm. Got a small one top floor. Only four bits. Okay? There's an outhouse back yonder, and breakfast is at seven. No drinkin', fightin', or—" The clerk blushed. "Uh, you know…"

Rose squeezed Rodrigo's hand. "That'll be just fine." She turned to Kip. "Aren't you going to check in, too?"

He put a hand up. "Don't worry about me. I'll find a soft spot to bed down. Always do. See you in the morning." He tipped his hat and headed for the saloon, whistling a familiar tune.

On the way up the stairs, Rose stared at Rodrigo as if she still couldn't believe he was here. And all right.

Del will be so happy. Her heart thumped. Where was Del? Was he okay? How would she ever find him again?

Morning brought a knock at the door. Rose opened it to find Kip there with the biggest grin she'd ever seen. "What's got you so happy?"

"I just found out where my best friend is. Yours, too."

"You mean Del?"

Kip nodded.

"Where is he?"

"See, I was on my way to the livery last night after a spell at the saloon when who should I meet up with but the stabler."

Rose squinted. "So? Tell me!"

"So the man asked me where I was comin' from. When I told him, he said he'd put up another fella from a cattle drive recent. When I described Del, he said, 'Yep, that's him.' Said he stayed the night then left."

Her heart thumped. "Del was here? How long ago?"

"A couple days."

"Where did he go?"

"Said he was heading to a ranch owned by a man named Wilkins. Ever hear of it?"

"No, where is it?"

"Not exactly sure, but the old man gave me rough directions. Southwest of here a ways. Why don't we have some breakfast and talk this out? Come on Rodrigo, you can have anything you want this morning." Kip wrapped an arm around the boy, and they headed downstairs. "Let's give Miss Rose a chance to freshen up, okay?"

Rose almost beat them down the stairs. "I splashed my face and have what I need. Let's go."

"No breakfast?"

"Grab some biscuits and water."

"Ain't there anything else you want to take?"

"What else do I have any more except what I have on?" She wore the plain blue cotton shirt and baggy cloth pants she had on back at camp. Pant legs rolled up to her ankles. "Don't get too close, I haven't bathed in a while."

"That makes two of us."

She pursed her lips. "Should we leave Rodrigo in someone's care? It's liable to be rough."

Rodrigo raised his voice. "I am not staying here. I will go after Mr. Del with you or without you. If you try to leave me, I will follow." The boy jammed both hands in his pants and thrust his chin out.

Rose knelt in front of him. "If you go, you have to promise to obey me—to listen to what I say. Do what I tell you. Can you do that?"

Rodrigo nodded. "Yes ma'am, I will."

Kip said, "Then let's eat a proper meal before we set out. I ain't hittin' the trail with my stomach pressin' up against my backbone. No tellin' what we'll find out there. Or won't find. I'll be back in a minute." Kip walked to the stable, where he hailed the owner. "How far to the Wilkins place?"

The owner blanched. "Wilkins? Why do you ask?"

"Guess I'm just a curious sort. How far?"

"Not sure what your business is, but it's a good day and a half distant. Head west for most of a day and toward sunset angle south. It'll be just short of the low range ahead. There's a hardscrabble trail on the

289

outskirts of town that'll get you started."

Kip said, "Any water?"

"Nope, not unless you reach a little town called Sinola, but that's off to the south of where you'll be. Elsewise, nothing to drink unless you get a gully washer, then you can swim there." The man laughed at his little joke.

"What can you tell me about Wilkins?"

"He's a bad'un. Biggest, richest rancher hereabouts. They say he's buried more than a few people who got in his way. Mean. Maybe you oughta think twice about going there. I hear he don't take kindly to strangers."

"Thanks all the same." In the mercantile, Kip took his time picking out foodstuffs and blankets. Cartridges and matches. Extra water skins. Just about all they'd need. He hoped the coffee and vittles would do for Rose, too.

He loaded everything in his saddlebags and laid the gear pouch crosswise on his horse. No need for Rose or Rodrigo to carry it. Back at the hotel, Rose had ordered him a fine breakfast. Coffee, biscuits with marmalade jam, two eggs, bacon. She startled him by asking if he would pray first.

"Um…I'm not much at prayer-makin', ma'am. Wouldn't know where to start or how to end."

"Why don't you just say what you're thankful for?"

Kip hesitated. "Reckon I can do that. Do it a lot anyway." He bowed his head. Rose and Rodrigo did the same. "Lord…you know I ain't much. You know all the bad things I done, but you're still there for me. For all of us. I feel you with me. I do. Happens at the strangest times. Like when I'm ridin' the range on one of your strong horses, gazing at the beauty you've created for us. Thank you…" He paused. A sniff and a swipe at his nose. "Thank you for bringing Rose, Rodrigo, and me safe so far. If you would, keep Del safe, too." He paused. "I guess that's it, Lord. Amen."

Silence filled the room. Rose eyed the black man across from her. "That was about the nicest prayer I think I've heard, Kip Holloway. Thank you." She brought a hanky to her nose. "Let's eat." After several mouthfuls, she said, "What are we going to do now?"

Kip said, "The way I figure it, Del must still think Tyson has Rodrigo. Things might be different if he knew better. Then again, maybe not. I'm sure he has it in mind to kill Tyson, whether the man has Rodrigo or not. Settle a score. Best we find him before that happens. Wilkins' place is a day and a half away. Not sure we should head there direct, though. Man at the stable mentioned a little town of Sinola, not that far from Wilkins' ranch. I think we ought to ride that direction and scout around, see if Del's there. Not much we can do if he isn't. Can't just be bargin' into Wilkins' place askin', 'Is Del here'?"

Rose wore a small frown. "No, I suppose not."

After breakfast, she got a horse for Rodrigo and set out southwest. The day dawned with pinkish strips of thin clouds the sun soon chased away. Kip eyed the light blue sky. The day would be a scorcher, aided by a westerly breeze that already blew hot. Rodrigo led. The boy knew the country better than either of them.

Kip trotted next to Rose on the gently-rolling, shrub-pocked landscape. "Rodrigo's a natural rider. Makes sense. Del said he was raised on a large cattle ranch west of here. Already rides better than some of the hands on our cattle drive."

"Better than Del?"

"Not hardly. You should see Del on a horse—not many like him. But maybe I should talk to Stoney about bringing Rodrigo on." He smiled sideways at Rose.

She shook her head. "I know you're kidding, but please don't say that. I may have…" Her words disappeared into the crisp morning air.

"What?"

Rose put a finger to her mouth and nodded at Rodrigo. In a whisper, she said, "Don't mind me, I was just thinking…out loud. He's been through so much…I don't know how he handles it and still manages to smile. He's a good boy." Her voice caught.

"Sounds like Del's not the only one you've taken a shine to. He'd be lucky to have you and Del in his life here on out."

"Kip Holloway, don't you go spreading any such notion around. I'm still heading north, to Denver. Then…" Her words drifted away on the morning breeze.

"If we was playin' poker, I'd say that's a sure enough bluff and call you." Kip guffawed and rode up next to Rodrigo.

Rose's mind wandered. What *were* her intentions? She hadn't thought further ahead than finding Del. And Rodrigo. What then? Had she been foolhardy to leave the drive to chase after them? Being rash was not something she was accustomed to. How did she come to be here, on a stark New Mexico plain, searching for a man she'd only known a little while? She wouldn't have thought it. Finding Rodrigo here was strange enough. What had happened to Del?

The three zigzagged over the arid land on their search for Sinola. They sweltered in the saddle as the day wore on.

Rose said, "Maybe we should have gotten better directions back in Santa Rosa."

Kip glanced sideways at her. "You mean maybe I should have gotten better directions."

"I'm sorry, Kip, I didn't mean you. We all want the same thing. To find Del and keep him from getting hurt. Reunite him with Rodrigo."

The boy hadn't said much on the ride. The farther west they went, though, the more he stood in the saddle, scanning the austere land before him.

Kip said, "You see somethin', pard?"

Rodrigo pointed in the distance. "Those mountains. They are the ones south of our land, the Abriendo. I could see them from my bed. They always made me feel happy."

Kip eyed the distant heights. "That's good. Keep heading us the right way." He turned to Rose. "But we still don't know where Sinola is."

Rose said, "Since we know those mountains are south of Rodrigo's land, Sinola must be pretty much dead ahead."

They rode in silence as heat rose and turned the land hotter than the sun that baked it. Barren terrain shimmered in the distance. Rose wiped a bandana across her neck and patted her brow. Rodrigo and Kip pulled their hats low. The horses trudged ahead at a slow walk.

Kip said, "We better water the horses; they're lookin' puny."

The small caravan halted with no cover. Kip took the last of the three water bags, held it to each horse's mouth, and squeezed. After he pulled it away, he offered it to Rose, who shook her head. Rodrigo did likewise. There wasn't much sloshing as he placed it back on his saddle horn. He swung up just as his mount staggered a few steps and went down in a heap, a deep rumble in her throat. The horse labored for breath.

Kip sprang clear. He knelt by the animal and stroked her neck. The horse stared unfocused, snorting for breath. Kip put a hand to his forehead, looked skyward and yelled into the empty air. They'd been a team a long time. He quick-drew, put a bullet through her head, and slumped.

Rose jumped at the sound and stared wide-eyed. "Couldn't you…" She stopped. There wasn't anything else to be done. Her shoulders sagged.

Kip took his time getting up. "I'll ride with Rodrigo. That'll be less weight than riding with you, Rose."

She nodded while her heart raced. They'd better find Sinola fast, though the horses couldn't manage more than a walk. Sinola…Del hadn't ever mentioned the town. A town they needed to reach soon…

Chapter Thirty-Six

Maybelle sat by the hotel's front window, watching for Graham to return from Wilkins' ranch. Her fingers tapped the rocker's arms. A cup of tea rested on the low mahogany table next to her. Every now and then, she popped up and paced the small sitting room. What if his plan didn't work? What if Wilkins was on to them? Like Graham had been on to her? Her pacing increased until the desk clerk asked, "Mrs. Perkins, is there anything you need? Anything I can do for you?"

"No, thank you, sir." What she needed was Graham to show up with a smile on his face. Another hour passed. The longer it went, the more likely something was wrong. Fretting was getting to be her constant companion. Toward early afternoon, she felt a hand rest on her shoulder. "Oh, Graham! You're back. Tell me everything." She couldn't detect anything from his face.

"Looks like you slept here all night." A small smile crinkled the corners of his eyes. "I thought you'd be pacing, waiting for me to return. Here I come back and find you dead to the world."

"I was, I...never mind. Tell me good news. Please."

"He's a cagey one, all right. He took the loan out, but he's not quite ready to hand over his money. Wants to see you again first."

Maybelle's stomach did a little flip flop. "See me?

Whatever for? Did he say?"

"No, but I imagine he wants to pretend to get the terms of the partnership in place. Wouldn't be surprised if he wants to negotiate a different split."

"What?"

"Don't worry, that would be a good sign, really. My guess is he's still planning to buy the Abriendo without you, but he doesn't want to tip his hand. So he'll continue to meet to lead you on."

Maybelle wasn't convinced. Something didn't feel right about what Graham was saying. If Wilkins was intent on buying the Abriendo by himself, why have more meetings with her? Was Graham holding something back? Playing both of them? Was her gold safe with him? Had she developed feelings for another thief? She turned to him with the most pleasant smile she could muster. "Fine. Did you set a time for our meeting?"

"I did. With your permission, I said we would be out again tomorrow afternoon."

"You'll accompany me?"

"Of course—we're partners."

Maybelle wondered.

****

Morning came on a gray wind. The kind of day that made Maybelle question if fall wasn't around the corner. It was far too early for the days to start getting cooler, but this one was making a good stab at it. She'd take an extra shawl with her to Wilkins' place. She didn't fear the man like she did that night—that reckless night—when she first saw him. Anger had replaced that fear. She looked forward to this meeting. If he turned the tables on her, she could always shoot him. She didn't really want to kill him—she just wanted his soul. She'd pay almost any price to get it, too—he had already cost her so much.

She planned her conversation as they rode. Graham sat mostly silent this trip, which was curious, not his normal manner. Perhaps he was thinking the meeting through, too. Or maybe he'd already planned it with Wilkins, and she was riding into a trap. She'd put her small derringer in the red brocade bag that hung off her arm. It held two bullets, all she would need if the worst happened. If her gold was already gone, if Graham had stolen it like he planned to steal Wilkins' money, then she had little left to lose.

Graham spoke up as they neared. "I would suggest you go along with what Wilkins says, whatever he offers. That will reassure him that he's in control. He'll make the terms sound good, but I'd recommend asking for them in writing."

Maybelle nodded. That sounded like good advice, but a piece of paper could disappear in so many different ways. They rounded the last bend, and the same vaquero appeared out of nowhere.

"Thees way, señora, señor." He escorted them to the main house. Maybelle couldn't put her finger on why, but things all of a sudden felt different. Her hands perspired lightly. She wiped them discreetly on her red dress. She put her hair up for this visit. She didn't know why, the man couldn't see. Could he?

The same little man in white took the horse's reins and swept an arm toward the rambling ranch house. She'd never heard him utter a word. Hard to believe a blind man would prefer mute help. Wilkins stood in the open entryway, an engaging smile on his round face.

Maybelle took a deep breath and stepped into the unknown.

In the library, the rancher indicated the same seat for her. The large overstuffed chair felt like it was going to swallow her this time. Wilkins was in a jovial mood, as if she were entertaining him.

"Thank you for accepting my invitation, Maybelle." He called for drinks as they sat. "I thought we could spend some time discussing the details of our venture." He chuckled and took a sip of brandy.

Strange that he would find something like that amusing. She'd watch her drinking this time. A sip of port flared at first, then a warm sensation filled her.

Wilkins lit a cigar. "Why don't we get down to business? You don't mind, do you? For starters, I thought I would put a little less in to buy the Abriendo. Say, forty percent. After all, you'll be relying on my experience in running a large cattle operation after the sale. Fair, don't you think?"

Maybelle didn't know what to say to that.

Before she could object, Wilkins said, "So it's settled then. If we're lucky, Territory officials will speed our purchase. They're usually very easy to work with, especially when bribed sufficiently." He blew a smoky 'O' toward Graham with a wide grin. He took another sip with a look of satisfaction. Like he held all the cards. Graham nodded for her to agree.

Maybelle's alarms were clanging, but Graham kept nodding. "I suppose…that would do. Should we get it appraised first, as there's no owner and no asking price?"

Wilkins frowned. "Don't see why. When the land office sees our money, I don't think they'll have any trouble producing a deed. Fifty thousand dollars ought to do it. Includes a 'fee' for their services."

Graham spoke up. "It would be nice to handle this with no surprises. Have you talked with the territorial real estate officials yet, Elijah?"

"Let's just say they're aware of what Maybelle and I are planning and have no objections." Another contented-looking puff.

Maybelle couldn't make sense of that. What had Wilkins been doing behind her back? He'd already approached the proper land agents? Or maybe Graham did it on his behalf. She couldn't be sure of much of anything right now. "Do we have an accurate map of the land?"

"Why, yes. I took the liberty of having one drawn up." Wilkins strode directly to a large table behind him. Placed a hand on a sizeable chart. "Look how far the Abriendo stretches from east to west and north to south."

It was as if he could see, which made her even more nervous. "I suppose you've also had papers drawn up?"

"Not at all. Didn't think we'd need them. I know you're not familiar with how things are done in the West, but out here a handshake has the same weight as a signature. The Code, and all. You're familiar with the Code of the West?"

"I've heard of it." Little good the Code did for her and her family. They were murdered anyway and no justice—so far. She dithered about whether to go through with this. No contract, nothing written. There was only one thing to do—figure a way to get his money before he stole hers. Graham was the only one who could make that happen, but was he friend or foe? She was in so deep she might as well go all the way. She offered her hand.

Wilkins grasped it with a big smile. "There, that's done. Now, let's relax and enjoy our time together. Can the two of you stay for dinner?"

Why not? "Yes, certainly, we'd like that, wouldn't we, Graham?" The man hadn't said a peep since sitting down. Hadn't touched his whiskey. His face revealed nothing. What would she do if the only person she trusted had turned against her? Had her heart betrayed her again?

"Kind of you, Elijah." Graham rose from his chair. "Long ride here, think I'll freshen up before dinner."

Wilkins waved a hand, and the small servant swept an arm toward the hallway.

When Graham was gone, Wilkins leaned close to Maybelle. "I don't get a good feeling from our friend Bunch these days. Do you?"

The man was fishing, but she'd become uncertain how she felt about Graham, too. She chose her words carefully. "He is someone I've come to regard…as a friend. I look forward…to working with him—and you—for years to come." If the banker's plan was indeed on the up and up, that last part would come true.

If not…

The dinner was superb. A rib roast with mashed potatoes, green beans, and fresh bread. Rich gravy. For an unexpected treat, the white-coated servant brought out fresh raspberries on a silver tray. Made all the better with a drink she'd heard of before, but never had—champagne. The little man filled their crystal glasses.

"I thought we would celebrate. I've been keeping

this champagne for a fitting occasion and I can't think of a better one than this." Wilkins gazed her way. "Can you?"

She raised her glass toward him and sipped. So good, even if the company wasn't. If this was her last supper, it was a fitting end to a delicious meal. Not that Wilkins would kill her—at least she didn't think so. Between him and Graham, had she already lost her money? She didn't care about the gold coins, but it was the only leverage she had to get at what he cared about most—his land, his money, his ranch. That's what she wanted to take. Everything he valued.

Wilkins beamed as he finished his drink. From the end of the long table, he said, "Won't you stay overnight, Maybelle? We've had such a nice time; I hate to see it end." He raised his glass in her direction and took another long swallow. "Ah, that is good."

What was she to do? She couldn't stay here in the lion's den; she already felt like easy prey. Her tone turned coquettish. "Oh my, Elijah. What would people say? A widow staying the night in a handsome bachelor's home? I can just hear the clucking now. As much as I would like to, I must not take you up on your kind invitation." What she'd like to take him up on was a high ladder and pitch him off.

"Ah, more's the pity. Another time, perhaps?"

"Why, certainly. This has been such a pleasant evening. Thank you for your gracious hospitality."

"My pleasure."

Maybelle tried to smile. The syrupy conversation was sickening.

Wilkins rose. "One last business item, if you will. Please make sure your portion of the fifty thousand is deposited with the territorial real estate fund, with proper annotation as to its purpose, of course. If you could do that tomorrow, that would be most appreciated. My forty percent is already there." Fake smile.

Maybelle tried to hide her surprise. Wilkins had been so confident she would agree that he'd already put his money in?

Graham spoke up. "I already took care of that, Elijah. Saw to it myself, today."

Maybelle's heart stopped. What had the banker done? Already moved her money without her knowledge? He'd tricked her. The money was gone. Gone. She'd been a fool to come here with such a fortune. She should have stayed away and searched for her son and Rodrigo instead. Left Wilkins alone. She rued the day she got off the stage and met Bunch. The hurt she felt when she looked at him was a familiar one. How could he do that to her?

The banker bowed to their host. "I hope our visit hasn't been too taxing, Elijah. Good evening." He took Maybelle by the arm and led her out to their buggy. She walked in a daze, then pulled her arm from his grasp. When they were riding away, she started to cry.

"Won't you let me explain, Maybelle?"

She turned away, sniffling. She wanted nothing to do with the man and hated that he witnessed her weakness.

"Maybelle. Look at me!"

She turned further away. They rode the rest of the way to town in silence. At the hotel, she sprang from the buggy and slammed the front door behind her. She raced up the stairs to her room. Turned the key and locked the door. Plugged her ears until the knocking stopped.

The next morning, the desk clerk tapped lightly. "Mrs. Perkins, would you like me to bring you some breakfast? Change your…uh, chamber pot?"

"No!…Yes. Please come in. I will dine downstairs while you…attend me." She walked to the dining room. There sat the schemer Bunch. Maybelle started to turn away, then stopped. She may not have anything anymore, but she still had her pride. Neither Wilkins nor Bunch could steal that from her. She thought about screaming at the banker, then bit her lip. What good would it do? She had decided to leave for Denver and sweep the town's dust from her clothes as she did. Her time here with Wilkins and especially Bunch, had been just another painful lesson. She was tired of drinking out of life's short straw. She took a table a discreet distance away and motioned to the clerk. In a soft voice she said, "What time does the coach leave?"

The man leaned close. "High noon ma'am, if it's on time. What with them raids of late, though, may be later."

She thanked him and noticed Bunch trying to make eye contact. She angled her chair so her back was to him. When the waiter came, she asked for the cheapest thing on the menu.

"That would be biscuits and gravy, ma'am."

"Then that's what I'll have." She'd been smart enough to keep a few gold coins and some currency, but that was all. Deep breaths returned her heartbeat to normal. She brushed a hand through her hair. Bunch cleared his throat behind her.

"Mrs. Perkins?"

Silence.

"Ma'am?"

She leaned away from him.

He moved around so he faced her. "Well, goddamn it, Maybelle, you're going to listen to me!"

She started to get up.

"Sit down. I mean it! You are the most stubborn woman I ever met. Hear me out, willya?"

She turned on him. "Why should I? Haven't you done enough to me?"

"Yes, I have. I have made you the wealthiest woman in this part of the Territory, maybe the whole Territory."

Maybelle blinked rapidly, her tongue tied. "Wh…what do you mean? You sold me down the river with Wilkins. That's what you said last night."

"Last night was for Wilkins' benefit, so he'd think he was still deceiving you. Did you actually think I would betray your trust?" She saw the hurt in his eyes. "All the money—yours and his—is in that real estate account just like I told you, and you are the only signatory. All you have to do now is transfer everything to some other bank in Denver, your choice. He'll never find it. Wilkins' loan money is in there as well. He's ruined—you've done it." A little shake of the head and he turned to go.

Maybelle stared in disbelief. How had she misjudged the man so? She wasn't even getting mad at the right people anymore. "Graham, wait!" She rushed from the table after his retreating form. "Talk to me, please. I'm so sorry for doubting you. I'd give anything to make it right."

Graham turned toward her. He leaned in.

"Anything?"

She hesitated. "Y-yes."

"Then give me a big kiss right out in the middle of main street."

Maybelle blushed. "Oh, Graham. I couldn't kiss you in front of everyone."

"You said anything. Main street it is." He took her by the hand and led her out of the hotel. In the street, he caught her by the waist and drew her to him. "Our first kiss."

She lifted her chin. "I hope it won't be our last." They both giggled when their lips met.

Graham grinned. "Let's try that again, shall we?" This time their kiss lingered, their bodies pressed close. Applause rang out as people cheered from the sidewalks. Maybelle regarded her banker. There would be no more doubting him, wondering.

He said, "Better that time, for sure."

She grabbed him in another embrace. "This time I'm kissing you."

Chapter Thirty-Seven

Del closed in on Wilkins' spread, Santa Rosa far behind. He knew the rough location of the ranch, having grown up in the same general area. He'd never met the man, but everyone knew about him. A rotten sort who gave big ranching a bad name. The farther west Del rode, the more familiar the territory became. Off to his right was the peak with the clipped gray granite top, the only height visible for miles around. Barren desert flew by as Shade settled into his familiar rhythmic cadence.

Del's route to Wilkins' ranch would take him south of the Abriendo, as well as his mother's old place. He hadn't been by there since that night. A vision of her blood blackening the ground flared in his head. Her life had seeped so deep into the soil it looked like it would never fade. Neither would his memory of her.

The ride gave him time to take stock. What was he going to do when he got there? Someone that rich would have plenty of vaqueros working for him. He had to figure a way to slip by them and plant the dynamite he stuffed into his saddlebags in Santa Rosa. To do that, he'd need a distraction. Maybe he'd light a couple sticks near the bunkhouse to set the ranch hands to scrambling. Then sneak up to the house and set off several more. Even if the blasts didn't kill Wilkins, the smoke and chaos would give Del enough of an advantage to finish him.

He imagined the scene as he rode. Wilkins on the floor, blindly staring up at him, pleading for his life. The acrid smell of gunpowder stinging Del's nose. The air filled with hazy smoke and broken bits of things Wilkins treasured lying in ruins around the man. The rancher offering him all his wealth to live. Del drawing his gun...

An image of Tyson replaced Wilkins. Del would kill him, just as sure as Tyson killed his family. There couldn't be any forgiving for that. But something nagged at him about the butcher. Maybe Del wouldn't drag it out, maybe he'd shoot him on first sight and be done with it. Torturing Tyson wouldn't bring any of his family back. He knew what his father would do if he were still alive, but he wondered about his mother. What would his wife say? He saw her flinty stare now. Get down in a cesspool with someone and you get as filthy as them. He wouldn't go that low but he'd kill Tyson all the same. The sooner the better. He wanted all this behind him. Find Rodrigo. Tell Rose how much he loved her.

The blazing sun had done its worst. He'd been riding west for almost a day, and from what he'd heard, Wilkins' ranch was still miles ahead. Del cursed himself for not packing more water before leaving Santa Rosa. He should have brought another water jug. Shade had just finished the last small swig. Del shook his head. He knew better, knew the desert, but still had made a greenhorn mistake. Worst of all, Shade was the one suffering most. The horse had to have some water. If only there was a creek bed near. They could drink up and get back to—

A wheeze from Shade and he slowed. Del pulled the horse up and dismounted. Horses don't labor for nothing. He shouldn't have pushed Shade this hard, considering what the horse had been through. Another mistake. He ran a hand over the big colt's neck and stared into his eyes. The alarm they reflected told him Shade was done in. The horse couldn't afford a third mistake. Del had a choice to make, and he had to make the right one. Which way to go?

Del eyed the western horizon. Shade couldn't go any farther. If he kept on toward Wilkins', he'd be lucky to get there. Even if he did, he'd be thirst-crazed and in no shape to do Wilkins in, anyway.

Del didn't know exactly where they were on the faceless plain. "Well, boy, we been in tougher scrapes than this." He gazed south at the flat expanse that spread to the horizon. Sinola was somewhere that direction. He hoped it was closer than Wilkins' place, but it was still his only choice. He scanned the landscape for some cover. Partly-treed low hills rose south in the distance. He gripped Shade's reins and started that direction. "Remember the stampede the rustler started—Tyson started—that we got caught in? You held your ground until that steer gored you. Probably saved my life. No doubt about it, you did save my life. Such as it is." Shade plodded slowly. Maybe they hadn't been in tougher scrapes. This one would take all the good fortune he had, if he had any left. Del would try for those distant piñon pines, lay up, and let Shade rest. The sun was still a flaming, golden disk in the afternoon sky, which meant more searing hours before it cooled.

Reaching shelter wasn't going to happen soon at

the rate Shade walked. The horse should be lathering in this heat but wasn't. Del wanted to hurry, but he needed to conserve energy. Horse and man slogged over soil that wasn't much more than sand and pebbles.

The hills danced in the distance as the sun refused to relent. Del's feet baked with every step. He could only imagine how Shade was holding up. "Come on, boy. We can do this. Just over there." Del had stopped sweating, too. He wanted to shed his clothes but knew he shouldn't. His wide-brimmed hat provided faint protection, but he imagined fitting his whole body underneath. Bringing Shade under, too. A horse and rider were always at risk in this desert. If the horse didn't survive, the man didn't.

The trees still shimmered in the distance.

By the time they neared the small copse, Shade barely moved. Del unsaddled him and pulled Shade down under scant cover on a bed of small needles scattered over rough ground. How had these few trees survived with no water? There had to be some. He scoured the piney rise.

There.

He hurried over to a trickle gurgling from a rock outcropping. An underground spring. He knelt, the rocky ground bloodying his knees, and patted drops on his stinging, swollen lips. A scoop of his hat captured more. He rushed to dribble some on Shade's mouth. The horse lay listlessly. Del poured hatful after hatful over the horse's head and neck. Shade finally responded, and Del helped him struggle over to the spring. He bathed the horse's body again and again and paused to drink his fill. Shade would be all right but couldn't travel. He'd have to leave the horse with what little was left in the oat bag and come back after he got to Sinola, wherever that was.

The wait until the blistering sun brought cooling dusk seemed to take forever. Del hesitated to leave. There were no guarantees Shade would still be alive or even here when he got back. But he had to reach Sinola. Both their lives depended on it. An image of Rose drifted through his mind. Would he ever see her again? No sense hoping for things that likely weren't going to happen. Life ripped those fictions away long ago. He grabbed a piece of deadwood for a walking stick.

A trek at night held its own dangers. Scudding clouds made it hard to keep a straight path. Critter sounds filled the air. Del picked a dim spot in the distance ahead. When he got there, he picked another. And another. Even as the heat of the day cooled to crisp air, thirst made him drink more than he wanted. He discarded the last of the two small jugs he'd filled at the copse. Sinola better be near. At least darkness would make it easier to see any town lights. His eyes seemed fixed in a perpetual squint, protecting from the sun during the day, searching for light at night.

How long had he been walking? More like lurching. He resisted running his tongue over swollen lips. Time stood still, like the scattered stars above. His left leg gave way. The one Potter kicked in camp. His staff came in handy now. He leaned on it as he pushed on. How much farther? He was slowing. Stopping more. Willing himself forward. Don't go down to a knee.

A flicker ahead. Were his eyes deceiving him? Was it a faint light? He tilted harder on his stick and moved faster. Every now and then the light appeared, then disappeared. His leg started to buckle again, but he refused to fall. He jammed the stick down his left pant leg for more support. Quickened his pace. There. If it wasn't Sinola, it didn't matter. It was some place. First thing he'd need was a horse to go back for Shade.

He stumbled down the small main street to what passed for a stable. The sign said he'd found Sinola. The doors were closed but Del inched them apart. A woman's voice came from inside.

"Who's there? Whaddya want? We're closed."

Del fell down in the opening and rolled to his back. Forced air into his lungs. "Need…a horse." He blinked his eyes open. A light came toward him out of the darkness. A woman swayed an oil lamp over him.

"Don't that beat all."

He lay in what looked like a barn. The large woman knelt by his side. Del croaked. "Wh…who are you?"

She smiled. "A better question is, who are you?"

He tried to get up.

She put a hand on his chest. "Just rest easy there, cowboy. You been out a while. Where in the world did you come from?"

Del struggled to form a word. His mouth was leather. He slowed his words. "I n-need a horse. Got to get my horse. He's out there in a…bad way."

"You're the one in a bad way. You need to be restin' up, not ridin' out. Here, drink this." She handed him a ladle full of water.

"Do you have…one?"

"Yeah, but there's no way to find your horse tonight. Daybreak will come soon enough."

"Get me some feed, water and jerky, please. I'm

leavin' tonight." Del drained the rest of the ladle.

"If you're so all-fired set on goin', I'll up and go with ya. You'll be lucky to even sit a horse, much less ride."

"Thanks. My name's Del. Del Lawson."

"I'm Sonny. Don't ask me why. Horses are over yonder. Fill your water jug there." She piled water skins and provisions in their saddlebags, boosted Del up on his horse, grabbed hold of his reins and they were off into the night. "Which way?"

Del took his time. He had to get this right. He searched the stars for Polaris. Clouds had cleared somewhat, and he picked out a dim sandstone formation in the distance. Yes, that was one he passed. "That way."

Sonny shook her head. "I know cowboys love their horses, but I ain't never seen one act as dadgum foolish as you."

"That horse saved my life. I owe him. Simple as that. A man doesn't have many good friends. Lucky to have one or two. I got one, make that two—and Shade."

They trailed north following dark markers Del pointed out. He couldn't be sure they were the right ones, the same ones. If they weren't—he didn't want to think on it.

"Tell me your story, Del. We got time."

Del tried to piece the last few days together. He told Sonny about leaving Rose and—

She interrupted. "That your woman?"

"If she'll have me. If I ever see her again." He told her about the search to find Tyson. Riding through Santa Rosa, the trickery about Lost Creek, Potter's ambush south of town amid the sandstorm. Riding for

Wilkins' ranch and Shade being played out. The desperate walk to find Sinola in the dark.

"You've had quite the adventure, Del Lawson."

"Feels more like a nightmare. Need to find Shade quick." He sent up another silent prayer. By the time Del thought he might be near Shade's shelter, clouds had snatched most of the pale moonlight away again. Sonny kept a steady pace up the same ravine. "Like as not, you followed one shallow valley, not crossing from one to another."

"Think you're right. Can't remember climbin' over any rises. Just hope this is the right basin." Soon, dim morning light peeked above the distant horizon.

"Anything look familiar?"

"No. Was just a little bunch of pines on a low rise. Was lucky I saw it, my eyes ain't been workin' too well the past couple days."

"That's one thing I'm still good at. Seein'."

They passed several small copses but no Shade. The ride was taking forever. Del wondered if they had somehow missed the shelter or if Shade was gone. Another one ahead. A faint whinny as they neared. Shade! In the breaking light, the horse rested on his haunches. Shade wobbled to a stand as Del rushed to him and wrapped his arms carefully around the animal's neck. He checked the horse over. No other obvious wounds. At least there had been water here. Shade had his fill of grain, and Del eyed the horse's saddle. He'd leave it, no sense weighing Shade down with anything extra. He gazed at the vast, unbroken vista that surrounded them. Didn't care if he ever came this way again.

"Let's get you to Sinola, boy!" He eased Shade

313

along with Sonny's horse and it took a while, but Shade started limbering up again. Del allowed a small smile. It was slow going but didn't matter how long the trip back took any more.

Chapter Thirty-Eight

Their two horses were past done in as Rose, Kip, and Rodrigo cast eyes on Sinola in the early afternoon distance. They'd been closer than they thought when they bedded down for the night. When she reached town, Rose led her tuckered horse past a few sparse, modest buildings on the main street. She staggered to the livery where she rested her hands on her knees. Rodrigo plopped onto a dirty bed of straw, and Kip crumpled where he stood.

The stabler took stock of the horses. "From the looks of it, you all rode a fair piece to get here. My name's Sonny. Don't ask. If you wander back down the street, you'll come to the only hotel in town. Tell the clerk Sonny sent you. On second thought, maybe you better not!" She cackled to the rafters as she tugged the horses to the water trough. "They'll be fine, just need some pamperin'."

The three travelers walked into the hotel lobby. The clerk eyed their dusty clothes and wearied bodies. "Can't have you bringing in half the dirt in the Territory. There's a pump outside you can put your heads under."

Rose quarreled with the clerk until a female voice came from the dining room. "Don't be silly, Charles. The woman can clean up in my room. You can find a room for the other two, can't you...Charles?" Maybelle

Lawson waved a dollar bill in front of the man.

"Why, ordinarily…uh, it's a bit…unusual ma'am, him bein' uh…"

Graham spoke up. "You mean him being a black man and all?"

"Uh…we don't…there's places down in the barn, uh…"

Maybelle rose. "Don't you go pulling that on me, Charles. I won't stand for it. Find him and the boy a room—now." Two dollar bills disappeared into the clerk's hand.

"Yes'm."

Kip removed his hat. "May I be so bold as to ask your name, ma'am, so I can thank you properly?"

She'd drop the pretense of 'Perkins'. Didn't need it anymore. "Maybelle Lawson. And yours?"

Rose turned toward the woman. "Did you say Lawson?"

"Yes, why?"

"Do you have a son named Del?"

Maybelle raised a hand to her mouth. "Oh, my Lord. You know my son?"

Rose's heart thumped. "I can't believe it. You're Del's mother! He thinks you're dead!"

"Dead? All this time he's believed me dead?" Grief welled in her throat.

Rose nodded in disbelief. "He said you were shot, saw all your blood but not you. But how…what are you doing here?"

Maybelle said, "Please. In all this excitement, I forgot my manners. This is my…banker, Graham Bunch."

Rose extended her hand. "Nice to meet you, sir.

My name is Rose Lyle. This is Del's best friend, Kip Holloway, and this is Rodrigo. Please excuse our appearance, we've been riding a long time to get here."

Maybelle blanched. "This is Rodrigo? Why, you've grown so tall I didn't even recognize you. You and my grandson used to play for hours..." Her voice faded. "I'm so glad to see you again." She gave the boy a big hug and wiped at her eyes. "Do any of you know where Del is?"

Rose said, "We heard he's on his way to the Wilkins ranch."

"Wilkins? Why?"

"Del said Wilkins had a man named Tyson kill your husband, and Del's wife, and their son. And shoot you. Almost got Del and Rodrigo, too. No doubt he's on his way to kill Wilkins."

Maybelle brushed a hand over her wounded cheek. "We have to stop him. I couldn't take losing him again. Wilkins will have him killed, either by his ranch hands or Tyson."

Kip said, "Tyson? Rodrigo says he's likely dead."

Rose wilted. "Do you mind if we sit? We're exhausted and so dirty."

Maybelle motioned to the clerk. "Please bring us something to eat and drink."

Graham took her by the arm. "Perhaps we all better sit down and talk this through." As they sat across from each other in the hotel lobby, Maybelle queried Rose. "Please tell me all about Del—and you."

Rose studied the woman as they talked. An agreeable blend of courage and concern. She wondered if her face still reflected the surprise she felt. Rodrigo sat next to Rose in a chair she'd drawn near. Before she knew it, he'd snaked his little hand into hers. The talk shifted from Del to how they all came to be there.

Maybelle described the way she and Graham ruined Wilkins, even though he didn't realize it yet. Her eyes crinkled whenever she looked Graham's way. "Cleaning him out was more gratifying than killing him."

Rose knew all about that. Her father had been cleaned out more than once at cards, until it finally caught up with him. She told Maybelle about Del coming to the fort, tending his wounds, joining the drive, and her injuries. Mostly, she talked about the good man her son was, which brought tears to Maybelle's eyes. Stopping Del had to be next, though. Rose asked, "Can we get to him before he reaches Wilkins?"

Graham pursed his lips. "Not sure how we'd do that—we don't know where he is. And from what you say, it sounds like he left Santa Rosa for Wilkins' place a day or so before you did. So he should already be there. Which may not be—" The banker stopped.

Rose stared into the distance. Was Del even still alive? She should have made him stay with her at Laila's, but she'd been in no shape to do that.

Graham leaned forward. "Why don't I ride out there tomorrow and see? Wilkins won't think anything of me visiting. I'll tell him we want to talk more about the partnership."

Maybelle said, "I don't think we ought to wait. If he's there, he's in trouble."

Rose leaned forward with both hands on the table. "I'm not for waiting, either. We need to find Del now."

Kip said, "Well, that leaves me and Rodrigo. Guess

he'll have to stay here and take care of me." He grinned as the boy's face lit up.

Graham turned to Rose. "I understand you want to hurry, but it's already too late to make the trip today. Besides, we don't have a plan. Why don't we get some rest then ride out in the morning?"

Rose shared a room with Maybelle for the night, and Kip shared another with Rodrigo.

At daybreak, Maybelle and Rose joined Graham in the dining room. He said, "I've just gotten a message from Wilkins' man."

Maybelle's heart pounded. "What's it say?" She never wanted to see Wilkins again but knew she had to. "Tell me, Graham. I'm a nervous wreck."

"Says he's looking forward to our visit, and I have a suspicion why. My guess is he wants to change something—like the split—again."

"What would make him think I'd agree to anything like that?"

"I know him. My guess is he figures since you went along with forty-sixty, you'll agree to even less. If he proposes something like that and you refuse, he'll probably call the deal off, then try to buy the land before you can."

"Are you suggesting I go along with whatever he says?"

"Might be a good idea to put up a little fight, then appear to give in. He'd believe that more than no objection at all. Besides, we already have his money, so the split doesn't mean anything at this point. Our real purpose is to find Del, but we'll pretend it's just a friendly visit."

Maybelle pondered that. Sound advice. "So are you

saying we should treat it more as a social occasion?"

"That's right. We're there to enjoy ourselves."

Maybelle frowned. "I'll think on it. In the meantime, shouldn't we be getting out to his ranch?"

Graham said, "I'd recommend we wait until later in the day. That way we'll be there toward dinner time, which would fit with a social outing."

Waiting didn't feel right to Maybelle. She needed to see if Del was there.

Rose shook her head. "No. Let's leave now."

Kip came down the stairs, followed by Rodrigo. "Any news about Del?"

Rose gave Rodrigo a little hug and shook her head. "No, but I'm so worried. His chances of taking Wilkins down alone aren't good. Not at all."

Kip nodded. "Right about that. Breakfast can wait."

Graham started to interrupt just as Rose glanced out the hotel window. A bedraggled man lurched past. She leaned forward for a closer look and screamed. "Del! Del!"

****

Del thought he heard someone calling his name. He looked toward the hotel to see a woman hurrying toward him. Rose? Was it really her? Kip and Rodrigo, too? What? He ran his tongue over blistered, chapped lips, his ears pounding. He forced words from his parched throat. "R-Rose. It's you…"

Before he could finish, she embraced him in a tender hug and kissed his cheek. "You're alive! I was afraid I would never see you again." She hugged him again.

Del put a finger to his raw lips then placed it

against hers. He glanced at Kip with a painful smile. "You, too?" Del wrapped an arm around Rodrigo's shoulders and drew him close. How did the boy get away from Tyson? He wiped a hand over dry eyes. A sound behind him caused him to turn. A woman lay faint in the dust of the street. A man knelt by her side. "Who is that?"

Rose smiled. "Why don't you go see?"

Del walked on peg legs and stared at…his mother! He tried to kneel beside her, but it felt more like a collapse. He traced a rough hand lightly over her face and eyed the pink scar on her cheek. "I don't understand." The man pressed a white hanky to her forehead. His mother stirred, opened her eyes at him and nearly swooned again.

Del's world spun. Rose and Rodrigo stood to either side of him.

Rose smiled. "Aren't you going to say 'hello'?"

His mother was regaining her senses. He wanted to hug her, but part of him still couldn't believe she was alive. All this time she'd been dead to him. He'd grieved her loss through the bottom of a bottle, and now here she was. Del stood unsteadily and took hold of her hands. He gently pulled her to a stand and hugged her tight. She cried softly against him, then big sobs shook her body. How did all this come about?

Del turned to Rose. He realized how grimy he was—face burnt, lips cracked, clothes stinking of dried sweat. "I want to hold you, but I'm pretty dirty—"

Rose pulled him close. "You don't get off that easy, Del Lawson." She kissed his cheek, and he felt a rush of warmth down to his toes.

He smiled at Rodrigo. "How'd Rodrigo get here?"

Rose said, "Why don't you ask him yourself?"

"What?"

Rodrigo tugged on Del's pant leg. "I got away from the bad man. I think he is dead."

Del's mind reeled. He stared at them, mouth agape.

Rose took his hand. "You look terrible. How do you feel?"

"Just like I look, I guess."

Maybelle put her arm in his. "You're so thin, let's get you something to eat."

When he woke up in the stable this morning, he would never have believed his mother would soon be holding his arm. Nor Rose kissing him. "I was on my way to get a bath, wash my clothes."

Rose said, "That smel…sounds, like a good idea." Her eyes crinkled. "I'll order you breakfast."

Del bathed, shaved, donned his damp clothes, and joined them back at the hotel. He feasted on steaming ham steak, runny eggs, chewy biscuits, and coffee that at least smelled drinkable. "This was almost worth crossing that infernal land for." He grinned at Rose as warm food filled his stomach. Her sandy hair and pretty face were backlit by sunlight coming through the window. That beautiful image fought with Del's need to finish what he came for.

Graham said, "Do we still need to go to Wilkins' place? Everyone is here safe and he's already been ruined."

Del squinted at him. "Not gonna spend the rest of my life lookin' over my shoulder. Need to put an end to Wilkins and Tyson. Time to finish it. But no reason for anyone else to go. I'll be back tomorrow."

Rose said, "But Rodrigo thinks Tyson's dead."

"Tyson's not dead. I can feel it in my bones."

Maybelle said, "I'm not letting you go there by yourself." When Del started to object, she put a hand up. "I'm going with you, and that's that."

"Me, too." Kip brushed a napkin across his mouth.

Graham said, "Might be a good idea if your mother and I got to the ranch house first."

Del wondered about him. Was he more than a banker to his mother? "Good idea. Distract Wilkins. Kip and I can create a diversion to occupy his ranch hands then hit the main house." He kissed Maybelle on her wounded cheek and turned to Rose.

She said, "Don't bother. I know what you're going to ask. Rodrigo and I will stay here until you return."

Del said, "Thank you—I need to know you two are safe." He drew an arm around her. "Besides, you're on your last legs, what with that wound and your ride here."

Graham asked, "What's the plan if things don't go right?"

Del grimaced. "Isn't any." His throat tightened. This had to work.

As the sun shone high in the sky, Del walked with Rose to the livery and waited until they were alone. "I've never been too good with words, but I promised myself if I lived through that miserable trek here, I'd tell you I love you." Del's heart thumped as her greenish eyes held him captive. "You don't have to say anything, but—"

She stopped him with a kiss. "Time I said what I feel. I love you, too, Del Lawson. I must not have been sending a strong enough signal if you haven't figured that out."

"My pa always said I wasn't too smart." He grinned and kissed her back. The thought of spending the rest of his life with this woman—even if he might not live out the day—amazed him.

When all was ready, his mother and Graham pulled away west in a buggy. Del drew a hand over Shade's muzzle. "Can't take you with me yet, but rest up and we'll ride these plains from sunup to sundown." He led another horse out of the small corral. A quick check of his equipment—water, rifle, pistol, dynamite, matches. Didn't need food—this would be over today.

Kip met him there. "You had enough kissin' yet?"

Del laughed. Leave it to his friend to lighten the mood.

They mounted up. Kip said, "What kind of diversion did you have in mind?"

"He has cattle, right?"

"Lots, from what I hear."

"Let's start with them." The rest of the ride passed with Del lost in thought. Kip left the drive to help Rose and him. Rodrigo was safe. He trailed behind a mother he thought dead for the last year. Now they were chancing everything to try to take down a killer. Was Wilkins worth the risk of losing all that? Their plan had to work, or the rancher would win again.

Del followed the buggy at a distance. Wilkins' spread was somewhere this side of the Manzana mountains ahead. After crossing several basins, the jumbled landscape rose slightly ahead. The small troupe followed a faint trail that wound upward. A sixth sense told Del to slow as he neared the top of the rise. He eased to a stop near the buggy on a shrubby ridgeline that gave way to a shallow valley below. Thousands of head roamed the grassy flatland. Intense sunlight reflected off a large, white hacienda in the distance.

Maybelle said, "We'll ride on ahead. Once we're inside, will you wait a while before starting anything?"

Del nodded. A lump rose in his throat as he watched his mother buggy away. She and Graham pulled up in front of the ranch house and were ushered inside by a little man. A helpless feeling came over him. He could take care of himself but was powerless to protect her. Again. There was Rose and Rodrigo to think about, too. At least they were safe—weren't they?

****

In the library, Maybelle used what wiles she had left on Wilkins. "Elijah, I swear, I am so jealous. We women have to primp and fuss more as we get older to try not to look like old ladies. And then there's you. I'll bet your looks have improved with age, and my guess is you don't even pay attention to it. It's not fair." She put on a pout for a moment. Was she overdoing it? Not according to the smug expression on her host's face.

"I have been fortunate, Maybelle. Not much worries me. Drink?"

That was no doubt true. Wilkins likely hadn't spent one iota of time thinking about the murders he'd ordered. "Yes, I believe I'll have a whiskey. That's what most men drink out here, isn't it?"

Wilkins raised an eyebrow. He motioned to the servant with a smirk.

Maybelle made small talk while sipping. A sound made her look behind her. A scruffy-looking cowboy stood in the library entrance.

Wilkins said, "Mrs. Perkins, Mr. Bunch, I'd like you to meet Mr. Jake Potter."

The rancher's introduction didn't fool Maybelle. The man was a hired gun if ever she'd seen one. Scruffy clothes, big iron on his hip, dirty black beard, mean-looking glint.

Wilkins said, "Did you require something, Mr. Potter?" The rancher looked like he was chewing something sour as he spoke.

"Tyson wants to know—"

Maybelle's eyes flashed. Tyson!

"Forget it, not important." Potter took a step back and disappeared toward the rear of the house.

Over a dinner of fine beef and brandy, she tried to forget about Tyson, but her heart raced throughout the meal. Maybelle broached the subject of their partnership. "Things seem to be moving smoothly, Elijah. You did say you already deposited your part of the purchase price—am I correct about that? Forty percent, isn't it?"

Wilkins leaned back in his chair and stared upward. "I'm glad you brought that up, my dear. I've been thinking on it, and I believe a thirty-seventy split would be more in order. My thirty, of course. Nothing against you, understand. It's just that you have so much to learn about ranching. My time and experience have to be worth more than ten percent, wouldn't you agree?"

Maybelle felt a sudden chill, as if the shootist was still standing behind her. "I thought we already decided on the split, Elijah. Did something change?"

"Not at all, not at all." He gave a small wave of the hand. "But enough business talk for tonight. Why don't we revisit this in the morning?"

A flush ran up her neck. "But we won't be here in the morning."

"Surely you'd indulge a blind man and take me up on my offer to stay the night? I have so few visitors."

Wasn't hard to figure why. She'd never met a more cutthroat person. She glanced at Graham for help. The thought of staying under Wilkins' roof—with that gunman Potter and perhaps Tyson, too—unnerved her. The banker gave a little shrug and looked back at their host.

Maybelle tried to think of another excuse, but her mind was a wall. She said, "Thank you for your kind hospitality Elijah, but we don't plan on staying."

Wilkins leaned forward, a fake smile on his pasty face. His tone turned ominous. "I must insist. It'll be dark soon—too dark to make a safe trip to town. Potter told me he spotted wolves on his way in. I wouldn't want anything to happen to my new partner, now would I?"

Maybelle blanched. What did he mean by that? The dining room's walls seemed to close in.

Wilkins lifted his brandy. "I'll ride into town with you in the morning and send new instructions to my bank in Denver."

She snuck a furtive glance out the window. Her mouth betrayed her. "Then I suppose…we'll stay…"

He took a long sip. "That's good, fine."

As Maybelle settled in her room, she locked the door then jammed a chair under the knob. What did Wilkins have up his sleeve? Outside, fading dusk lit the harsh landscape. She closed the flimsy cotton curtain that didn't quite cover the window. A sense of dread blanketed her as she stared at the bed, her family's killer on the loose so near.

It would be a sleepless night.

Chapter Thirty-Nine

"Del! Hey!" Kip smacked him on the arm as they sat their horses, scanning Wilkins' spread below.

Del snapped back. He wished he had Shade right about now. The big black could outrun anything on the range. "Let's go."

They spurred their mounts down the rise and tethered them to low bushes in a dry arroyo shy of the big house. Moonlight would be their friend soon, but for now they kept low as they crept to the square bunkhouse. Del pressed up against a slat-wood side. The wranglers must be playing cards, it was noisy enough inside. There were several different voices, Del couldn't be sure how many.

He whispered, "They're hard at it, let's check the main house." They ran in a crouch and flattened against rough stucco. Del eased upward and snuck a peek through a closed window. His mother sat in a large chair next to a larger man. Must be Wilkins. The strain on her face was like a beacon. Graham sat to one side and another man stood behind her—Potter! How was that sidewinder still alive, and what was he doing here?

He thought for a moment, then motioned to Kip. They drew toward the back of the house. Kitchen help was outside preparing the evening meal, surrounded by a roaring brick oven and boiling pots cooking something savory. Flour flew freely in smoky air as tortillas appeared out of the jumble.

Del cupped a hand to his mouth. "Potter's inside. Don't know how, or why, but that can't be good. Hate to, but I think we need to wait until it's darker." Silver moonlight dappled the land by the time Del and Kip eased the corral gate open. Several horses bolted through the opening and disappeared onto the open range.

Del and Kip skulked to the ranch's well. They placed a stick of dynamite in the worn, wooden bucket and retreated back to the shadows of the main house. Del fought the urge to bust in. After what seemed an eternity, muffled conversation inside died down, and the library's oil lamps went out.

The heavy front door lumbered open, and Del saw the butler. The little man motioned to a vaquero who led the buggy away toward the barn. Del's heart pounded. For some reason, his mother was staying the night. That wasn't the plan. "We need to get in there soon, or my mother doesn't stand a chance." He turned to Kip. "I'll wait for you to ride out a ways. When the well explodes, light your dynamite off. That'll scatter the herd, and the wranglers won't know which way to go."

Kip said, "Sounds good. Hope this works—for all our sakes."

"Just don't go gettin' yourself killed, okay?"

Kip wore a small grin. "I'll try to remember that."

They shared a long handshake. Del hoped it wasn't for the last time as he watched his friend hurry toward the arroyo.

Del waited, then lit the dynamite in the well's bucket. The deafening explosion blew the well's stones apart and filled the air with debris. Kip's booms soon echoed back from the dark valley. The thunder of running cattle sounded on the grassy flat. Wranglers burst from the bunkhouse, yelling and cursing. Del rushed for the front door, pistol drawn. In the foyer, he heard voices down the dark hallway. Shouts, followed by curses. A woman screamed and a door slammed. Had to be his mother. Where was she? He needed to get her out of the house safely, even if it meant letting Wilkins go.

Del crouched his way down the dim hall toward the back of the house. A shot rang out from in front of him. A bullet whizzed over his head, and he flattened against the wall. Running footsteps echoed ahead and faded into the bedlam outside. He came to the first bedroom door and twisted the knob. A glance inside showed no one. Across the darkened hall, he opened another closed door into a large bedroom. Even in the dim light, the furnishings looked luxurious. Must be Wilkins'—also empty.

As he neared the kitchen, shouting came from outside. A deep male voice yelled at someone to get moving. Del came to a third bedroom door and tried the knob. Locked. He knocked softly, hoping his mother was inside. "It's Del."

"Del!" A key jangled in the metal lock. The door inched open and Del peered in.

"It's me, Ma."

His mother rushed from behind the door and trembled in his embrace. He said, "It's all right, let's get out of here." Del sensed someone else and turned to see Graham by the room's small window.

The banker said, "Looks like Wilkins is out back.

Maybe we can slip down the hallway and out the front door."

"Mother, do you still carry that derringer Pa gave you?"

"Yes, but it's been years. I don't even know if it works."

"Hope we won't need to find out. Loaded?"

"Yes."

"Both of you stay behind me." Halfway to the front door, a shadow appeared in the hall ahead.

"Got you now, Lawson." In the dim light, it looked like the man had a gun trained on them.

Who was it? Del squinted into the darkness. Tyson! Finally, face to face with his family's killer.

"Hands up! Guess I'm about the last person you expected to see here, huh? Turns out I don't need you anymore. This ranch is worth more than those coins I was after. Someday I'll find 'em, but you won't be around to see it, 'cause you'll be six feet under. Just like your pa." A short chuckle. "And your—"

A shot rang out from behind Del. Tyson staggered, put a hand to his head, and stumbled back into the library before Del could get a shot off. Faint moonlight through the open front door backlit an empty hallway.

Maybelle kept her derringer pointed dead ahead. "I'd recognize that voice, that man, anywhere—even if it *was* dark that night."

Del backed the three of them away, his Colt still at the ready. "You two get back in that bedroom, lock the door, and jam the chair up under the knob. I'll leave Tyson 'til later. I'm goin' after Wilkins." He hurried out the back where Wilkins shouted orders to ranch hands who weren't there. Potter stood next to the

331

rancher in the moonlight. Del drew down on him. As Potter cleared leather, Del's bullet tore into Potter's gun hand and the six shooter flew away.

"Kick it over here."

Just then, Wilkins wheeled and pulled a gun from inside his dinner jacket.

Potter yelled at Del. "Watch out!"

A bullet kicked dirt up at Del's feet. Wilkins may be blind, but he could tell where Del was. His next shot took a chunk from Del's calf. Before Del could return fire, another bullet had already hit the rancher.

The large man grabbed at his belly and tumbled to earth like a rolling log. Del rose and stood over him.

A shot rang out from somewhere inside the house.

Wilkins stared at the starry sky. "This wasn't supposed to happen. I can't be...killed, I'm Elijah Wilkins, I'm..." The man curled into a groaning ball.

Del eyed Potter, who'd managed to retrieve his gun and fire the killing shot. His gun barrel pointed at Del looked like a cannon this close. Potter slowly holstered it then wrapped a bandana around his bloody hand. Del couldn't make sense of it. As Potter started to turn away, Del asked, "Why'd you shoot him and not me?"

The man's face was stone. "I owed you."

"For what?"

"For not killing me back there in the storm. I always pay my debts, even to somebody I don't cotton to. Makes us square." He called back over his shoulder, "Tyson's still inside. He's your problem." The man disappeared into the darkness.

Del shook his head. He limped to the house and found Maybelle's door standing open, the lock shot off and the room empty. His heart caught, and he peered down the hall. A light from the library shone dimly ahead.

A voice called out. "Come join the party, Lawson. Most everybody's already here, we're just waitin' on you."

He wavered. If he went in, Tyson would no doubt shoot him. But if he didn't, Tyson would likely shoot his mother.

"Come in with your holster empty and your pistol held high, stock up."

Del heard the cock of a gun.

"Got my six shooter pressed up against your mother's head. She is your mother, isn't she? That's what Wilkins said. How is the old crook, anyway? Heard some shootin' out back. Sounds like you mighta took care of some business for me." Tyson's laughter echoed in the hallway. "Get in here, Lawson. Now!"

No way around it. Del walked in with his hands in the air, fingers wrapped around his gun barrel.

Tyson held a pistol on Maybelle with a bloody hand to the side of his jaw. "Put your shooter on that table there. Looks like a nice piece—nicer'n mine. Should fit fine in my holster." When Del hesitated, the killer fired, a bullet skimming Del's ear. "Next one is through your heart. Looks like you already got shot, though."

Del placed his gun on the table next to him.

Tyson chuckled. "That's better. I said I don't need those coins anymore, but I still want 'em. Tell me and you live. No need you and your ma dyin' over 'em like your pappy did."

A hot flush ran up Del's neck. So Tyson *had* killed his father. He'd always known it in his heart.

The assassin pointed his gun at Del's chest. "Where are they?"

Del squinted. Was the man wobbling some? "Don't care if you believe me, but I don't know anything about them."

Tyson aimed his gun at Maybelle. Her derringer lay nearby on a table. "Tell me, or I'll shoot your mother. Kill her this time."

Del didn't doubt it. Tyson held all the cards. No sense in trying a bluff. "Never did know. Guess my pa took that secret to the grave when you killed him. Just shoot me—not her—and be done with it."

Tyson took his bloody hand away from his cheek and stared at Del. "I reckon I believe you." He swung his Colt Del's way.

A noise caused Del to glance toward the hall. Kip! His friend stood in the open doorway with a gun aimed at Tyson. "Drop it, you motherless dog."

Tyson hesitated, then slowly lowered his Colt.

Kip strode in and Tyson's gun flashed upward again, just as a bullet smashed into him.

Maybelle's shot struck home, ripping high into Tyson's chest. The killer swung his gun toward Maybelle and a shot from Del tore through Tyson's neck. The man didn't even grab at his wounds. He tottered, knocked over an oil lamp and tumbled into one of Wilkins' large, leather chairs. He wheezed his last with a small grin as fire snaked its way across the carpet.

Del closed Tyson's unseeing eyes, then hugged his mother like it was the last time he'd do so. Mixed emotions swirled inside him. His family's killers had finally reaped what they'd sown, but Del still wasn't at peace. He traced a hand over the mangled bullet around his neck while fire ran up the heavy drapes.

Kip yelled, "Let's get out of here."

Del led them out of the smoky, fiery room as Rose rushed in the front door with Rodrigo.

She wrapped an arm around Del and helped him to the front veranda. "Don't be mad; we couldn't wait any longer. Sit, please." She ripped a piece of cotton from her hem and tied it around his calf. Rodrigo leaned against him.

Del wasn't sure how he felt. How he *should* feel.

Wilkins' wranglers and the Abriendo vaqueros rode up. A voice from the rear of the house shouted. "Wilkins is back here. They killed him."

One of the cowhands said, "Is Tyson dead, too?"

Del nodded.

"Shoudda happened a long time ago, but Wilkins was our boss and you killed him. Y'all throw your hands up."

With one hand held out toward them, Del said, "Hold on. Tyson killed my father, almost got my mother and me, killed my wife and son. Shot Rose here and left the boy an orphan. On Wilkins' orders." He struggled to a stand. "All for gold Tyson stole from this boy's family. Gold that none of you would have ever seen any of. You owe Wilkins the same loyalty he showed you. None." Del stared at them. "Please don't shoot any of us."

The riders looked at each other as if searching for someone to tell them what to do. The small servant stood framed in the large doorway. He spoke Spanish to the vaqueros, who holstered their weapons.

Del rubbed a hand over the back of his neck and

eyed Wilkins' men. "Ease your guns down, will you, boys? No reason for any more killing today. For what? Wilkins? Hell! The man was nothin' but low-down scum, and you all know it."

As if by signal, the cowhands lowered their pistols. One said, "What do we do now?"

Graham spoke up. "I'll make sure you all get six months' pay. The cattle are yours and the vaqueros' now. Why don't you herd them over to the Goodnight trail and on to market in Denver? They'll bring a pretty penny. I'll make out a bill of lading. Come see me in the morning."

Vaqueros and cowhands wheeled away for the range.

Simple relief coursed through Del. It was over. He turned to his mother. "How did you shoot Tyson? You'd already fired once in the hallway."

She said, "I was just lucky he never took my gun. Your father, bless his wayward soul, gave me a two-shot derringer. Probably robbed some fancy stage coach lady of it. When Tyson looked at Kip, I grabbed it and fired. Knew it wouldn't kill him, but figured you or Kip would get him."

Del shook his head. "I almost forgot. Where's this gold—these coins that so many died for? Anyone know?"

Maybelle said, "Reckon I do. I have them, but they're really Rodrigo's. His family's, but that's only him now. Graham here used them to ruin Wilkins—which is all I ever wanted."

Graham interrupted. "All *we* ever wanted."

She smiled at him. "I've been thinking. Why don't we put Wilkins' money back in the bank? It's nothing but blood money anyway."

Graham took her by the hand. "I was hoping you'd say that. It'll be there for his son if he ever comes back."

She turned to Del. "I'm planning on rebuilding my ranch. Would the three of you like to come stay with me when it's finished, or are you going to rebuild, too?"

"Don't know, kind of depends." Del smiled at Rose.

She grinned back.

Maybelle wound her arm around Graham's as flames spread throughout the ranch house and lit the night.

Kip mounted up. "I'm headin' back to the drive. Say my goodbyes."

Del reached a hand up. "Say goodbye for me, too, willya? Why don't you come on back when you're done? Been thinkin' about goin' into cattlin' and I'll need a partner."

"Somebody to keep you out of trouble is more like it. Sounds like somethin' I could handle, seein' as how I already have experience doin' that."

Rose said, "Would you please bring Daisy back with you?"

"Happy to." Kip tipped his hat and swung away.

Del hugged Rose and his mother. He said, "There's somethin' I have to do." I'll meet you all back in town in a day or so." As he rode away, he had unexpected company. Rodrigo trailed behind over shadowy, trampled ground. Del slowed to let him catch up. "Would it do any good to tell you to go back?"

"No. sir."

"Then come on." His horse's measured gait would

bring Del to his destination by morning.

Daylight. He and Rodrigo rode down the slight slope overlooking Del's destroyed ranch. He walked the mare to the black debris that was his family's home and dismounted. Ran a hand over the markers on the two gravesites. Removed his hat, grasped Rodrigo's hand, and prayed over his family. He took the mangled bullet from around his neck, paused, and handed it to Rodrigo. The boy closed his fist over it. With a nod from Del, Rodrigo heaved it into the destruction that was Del's life. Del rested a hand on the boy's shoulder and gazed at the familiar hillside.

A wolf stood, then disappeared over the ridge.

A word about the author...

Mike Torreano has a military background and is a student of the American West. He fell in love with Zane Grey's novels in the fifth grade when his teacher made her students read a book a week.

His published works include "The Trade," in an anthology titled *Remnants and Resolutions*, and two traditional western mysteries, *The Reckoning* and *The Renewal*, both published by The Wild Rose Press.

He's a member of Western Writers of America, Rocky Mountain Fiction Writers, Pikes Peak Writers, and The Historical Novel Society.

He brings his readers back in time with him as he recreates western life in mid-to-late nineteenth-century America.

He lives in Colorado Springs with his wife, Anne.

A Score To Settle is Mike's third western, all set in The Old West. Find *The Reckoning* and *The Renewal* on Amazon or thewildrosepress.com or wherever books are sold online.

Visit his website at:
www.miketorreano.com.

CPSIA information can be obtained
at www.ICGtesting.com
Printed in the USA
LVHW081117201020
669268LV00015B/824